AF427522

THE VIPER & THE ROSE

J.D. SEMMES

For those of you who just want to sit back and relax after a long day
and be transported to a magical realm full of powerful,
possessive, incredibly gorgeous Fae, with a significant age gap...
this one is for you!

CHAPTER 1

CALISTA

Six Weeks Prior

"Hey, get your nasty shoes off my coffee table! You little heathen!" I chastise my youngest sister Hazel, causing the three of us to burst out laughing.

Hazel, Everleigh, and I have been sitting around my apartment all evening watching scary movies. It is one of our favorite past times and we try to have a horror movie night at least once a month if not more.

Weird enough, I find them relaxing in a way. I can easily fall asleep while listening to the chainsaw and screams from all Leatherface's victims in The Texas Chainsaw Massacre. Aunt Ellie says it's because my mom loved scary movies. She would even sit alone in the dark and watch them when she was pregnant with me.

"Don't be such a prude, Calista. Let's do something adventurous tonight!" Hazel offers after removing her nasty shoes from the table.

"What? Don't you think staying in on a Saturday night and watching scary movies is adventurous enough for us?" Everleigh our middle sister teases, eyeing Hazel over the rim of her wine glass as she takes a sip.

"Maybe I can convince the captain to let you come out to our next crime scene. That should get your adrenaline flowing. Eve and I get enough 'adventure' at work."

"It's not the same...let's do something we have always talked about doing." Hazel says, raising an eyebrow in challenge. Hoping that will motivate us to accept whatever crazy idea she is about to suggest. "Let's finally figure out who murdered our mothers..."

Eve and I just stare at her in utter silence.

Hazel, Everleigh and I are not blood related, but they are my sisters non the less. The three of us were thrown together under horrendous circumstances when I was only four years old, and not only have we been inseparable since, but they are also my greatest blessing.

Up until I was sixteen, my sisters and I were led to believe that our mothers were driving home together in the rain after an evening at the cinema in our hometown of Houston, Mississippi, when their car hydroplaned off the rain-slick road, and into a large tree. All three had reportedly died on impact.

But the truth was much more gruesome.

As it turned out, our mothers were butchered in their beds on the same night, not even hours apart.

After the truth about our mothers' deaths was revealed: Eve, Hazel, and myself made a pact; one day we would uncover the person that is responsible for our mothers' murders.

Hence how we all ended up in law enforcement in one way or another. We now work together, performing our different roles, at the Washington DC Metropolitan Police Department (DCMPD).

"W-We..." Eve stutters, trying to complete her train of thought.

I step in trying to help Eve out; even though I'm just as flabbergasted as she is right now.

"Hazel, we have no clue where to even begin. Not to mention we know absolutely nothing about our fathers so it's not like we can go to them for any help" I remind her flatly.

Which our fathers probably wouldn't know anything about our mothers to begin with; seeing as all three seemed to be very short flings or one-night stands.

"What we do know is that our mothers were suspicious that their coven's High Priestess was working with the Dark Fae King...but to accomplish what?" I sigh, "And we also know our mothers tried to summon a High Entity of Light to help give them the powers they would need if they were to stop the High Priestess."

"What if they actually got through to the Entity and they just didn't know it?", Hazel urges, sitting on the edge of her seat, looking at us with pure excitement. "Maybe the High Priestess figured out they were turning against her and killed them herself?"

"Whoa...pump the brakes. I think you have had enough drinks for tonight, Hazel. You can't just go around casually throwing around accusations of murder. Maybe we should call it a night. We have all been busting our incredibly toned asses off at work and could use the extra sleep.", Eve interjects playfully...always the peacekeeper.

"Oh, you just want to leave now so you can go hook up with your secret 'lover boy'. We are going to find out one of these days who it is, you know!?" Hazel shoots back.

"Hey, let's take a breath and calm our tits." Wow, who would have ever thought I would be the voice of reason when it comes to the three of us and our bickering? "Haze, it seems like you have already set up a plan for us so let's hear it... Where do you suggest we start? But let's avoid pinning the High Priestess with murder charges until we have some solid evidence."

We never had any substantial clues to point us in any particular direction. The Chickasaw County Sheriff's Department in Houston, Mississippi seemed indifferent to finding the real killer and the case went cold.

The investigating detectives chocked up the murders to 'crimes of opportunity' committed by a drifter passing through town. They stated in the local paper that someone driving through our small town might have spotted the three friends leaving the cinema and decided to make them their next targets...like a Ted Bundy wannabe.

Our Aunt Eleanor calls 'horse shit' and I could not agree more.

What I do know, with one hundred percent surety regarding this case is that the Sheriff's Department dropped the ball. Hell, they didn't even try to catch it in the first place.

They basically turned a cheek to save themselves the extra work of figuring out what really happened that night.

"Alright so hear me out..." Hazel begins, "I think we need to try to summon an Entity of Light just like our mothers did. If we contact an Entity maybe they can help us figure out what happened to our mothers. Like I said, maybe their summoning ritual *did* work even though they thought it had failed, and the Entity witnessed something the night of their murders, anything, to point us in the right direction. Or maybe the Entity itself killed them..." Hazel finally comes up for a breath of air before continuing. "Look I know it sounds crazy...like what are the odds of the Entity of Light we summon knowing the same Entity that responded to our mothers all those years ago? Or even crazier, the Entity being the *exact one* our mothers summoned. Anyway it goes, I think this is our first step...Are you in?" The pure thrill that is radiating off Hazel is intoxicating.

Almost making me forget the bat shit crazy plan she just pitched to us.

Again, Eve and I just stare at Hazel in stunned silence. It is obvious that Hazel has put a lot of thought into this, and it seems really important to her that we give it a try.

Why after all these years she has decided now is the time to investigate solving our mothers' murders? I have no clue...

After several more seconds have passed, and Hazel is just sitting there looking at the two of us with such hope and desperation in her eyes I finally cave and give in.

"Okay...so how do we go about summoning an Entity of Light? And if it is possible that an Entity of Light murdered our mothers, are you sure we should? I mean we would literally be 'following in our mothers' footsteps' if we perform the summoning ritual...the 'footsteps' that possibly got them killed!" I point out, slightly hoping to scare Hazel out of this insane plan.

"You cannot possibly be entertaining this plan?" Eve cuts in, whipping her head around to look at me. She sounds like she is about to pop her top. "Not only are we ill-prepared to face any consequences that come from performing such a ritual, if it even works, but we have no idea how to summon an Entity of Light! Our mothers were practicing witches and failed! We use our powers here and there for menial tasks, and I think it is going to require way more power than I use when I warm up my nightly baths. We are going to get ourselves in a shit load of trouble or worse, *killed*!", Eve's voice has risen into a yell by the time she's through with her lecturing.

"Oh My Goddess Eve!" Hazel declares, rolling her eyes dramatically.

Hazel has always loved to 'stick it to the man' and say Goddess instead of God. She says it is to empower her fellow women by reminding them that women are just as 'bad ass' as any man.

"Everything will be fine, worst-case scenario is it doesn't work, and we have to start back at square one." Hazel ensures us with confidence. "I have it all planned out...I will get the ritual from Aunt Ellie that our mothers used to summon the Entity of Light." She points to me, "Cali, you do all the research we need about the ritual itself and read up on our mothers' case file again. I know we have looked a thousand times but what will one more hurt?" Then turning to Everleigh, "Eve, you get the ingredients we need for the ritual. Specifically, 'bone' chalk, it is made from ground up human bones."

Finished delegating our duties out to us, Hazel sits back and just grins from ear to ear. I don't know whether to be excited with her or terrified. Probably the latter.

Eve begins shouting at Hazel hysterically, "Bone chalk! Made from *human bones*!? That is *ALL* you need for me to get!? Should I just borrow one of the bodies from the morgue!? Just to be sure we have everything we need!?"

Eve is the calmest and levelheaded out of the three of us, so seeing her reeling out of control is a rare sight.

"And how do you plan on getting the ritual from Aunt El? Do you really think she will just hand it over to you? She knows how dangerous it is...besides she may not even know or have it." I chime in, ever the voice of reason tonight.

"Don't worry, let me handle Aunt Ellie. I have my ways at being super persuasive..." Hazel assures with a wink.

"Alright then..." I say, running my hands through my hair. "I guess we are doing this. Just be safe, we can't get our mothers back and I don't want to lose either one of you as well."

The tension in the room finally begins to calm.

"We have a plan, and we know our roles...Hazel when you get the ritual we will meet back up and plan on how to perform the summoning. Then we can set the date and time to go through with it. Sound good to everyone?"

They both nod in agreement, as we all settle back down on the couch underneath our comfy throws to finish the movie. I highly doubt any of us are paying attention to the movie any more though... we are all most likely lost to our own thoughts now.

I just pray this isn't a huge mistake that leads to us following in our mothers' footsteps all the way into our very own graves...

CHAPTER 2

CALISTA

Two Weeks Later

I guess this is happening...smack dab in the middle of my living room of all places. We played a very professional game of rock, paper, scissors to decide the lucky winner of who gets the pleasure of having the 'creepy, demon-looking' summoning circle under their living room rug.

I had never wanted to lose anything more in my life...but damn when you're good you're good, what can I say?

Hazel was able to find the exact spell our mothers had used to summon the Entity of Light all those years ago. Apparently, she owes Aunt Ellie a 'huge' favor for handing it over, and she had to promise her we weren't going to *use* the spell.

She lied and told her we just thought it might help with the investigation...yea right.

Eve had gotten all the ingredients needed for the ritual. Where she was able to find the creepy 'bone chalk'? I didn't ask.

I on the other hand couldn't find anything new in our mothers' case files, which I wasn't really expecting too at this point. But maybe if we pull this off, we may get our hands on some critical information needed to get our wheels spinning in the right direction.

"Alright one containment circle filled with runes for protection complete", Hazel states turning to us with a huge smile on her face and bone chalk in hand.

"You better make sure you drew those correctly because I don't want anything coming through and deciding to stay. I like my privacy, and if I have to live my life with Casper the friendly ghost following my every move, I-will-shoot-something...and it will probably be you, Haze."

"Harr, harr, very funny!" she deadpans.

Eve is still struggling to get on board with this plan of Hazel's. She looks like she has already seen a ghost, and we haven't even started yet. Her face is pale, eyes wide with fear, and she keeps biting on her bottom lip.

I approach her and take her by the hand, leading her into the kitchen on the other side of the room. We have a second to chat while Hazel double checks that she has copied everything correctly.

"Look you don't have to do this" I whisper to Eve. "You can just hang back in the hall or downstairs and we can get you when it's over. Most likely nothing is going to happen, but I understand the hesitation and uncertainty you are feeling."

And believe me, I do.

While Eve leans over the kitchen island with her face buried in her hands, I retrieve us two shot glasses and a bottle of tequila. Filling the glass to the rim I gently slide a shot over to Eve, hoping that maybe a shot will help take the edge off her nerves.

"No, I'll be fine...I just can't stop thinking about what we are going to do if it actually works? Are we going to hunt their killer down and 'un-alive' them? Because I don't think we are going to be able to plant evidence on this twenty-four-year-old murder to get the killer arrested like we normally would. And we can't go to the police and tell them we summoned an 'Entity' who told us who was responsible....so what next?" I can hear how stressed and worried she is. She keeps looking off to the side or down at the floor; anywhere to keep her from having to look at me.

"Stop! Don't even start thinking about the next step...just be in the here and now. I know we are trained to think ahead but right now we just need to be present, and then we will go from there...Okay?" I place my hands on her shoulders and give her an encouraging nod.

"Okay" Eve finally concedes, staring at me with those brilliant blue eyes of hers as she raises the shot glass to her lips and downs the tequila in one gulp. I quickly follow suit before we link hands and walk back over to the new chalk art on my floor.

The three of us stand around the circle staring back and forth at one another. Unsure of how to begin.

Finally, Hazel starts us off by pulling a small knife out of her laptop bag. Both mine and Eve's eyes bulge out from our skulls. We know we have to offer the 'Entity of Light' a 'part of ourselves' for the summoning to work, and for them to provide us with the information we need. But in this moment, everything is just becoming so real.

"Alright, let's begin." Hazel inhales a deep breath. "We first need to make a small slice on our palms to dribble enough blood into the middle of the circle. After that we need to connect our hands and repeat the spell three times; once for each of us. Whatever you do, *don't* break the circle...we keep our hands together until the end. Got it?" Hazel finishes, her gaze and tone suddenly very serious.

"Got it!" Eve and I respond together and nod.

The blade slices along my palm leaving a trail of blood in its wake. It isn't the worst pain I have ever felt but it definitely hurts! Enough to still make my face scrunch up and release a hiss from the pain.

As I watch my blood hit the circle drop by drop, I literally feel as though I am giving a part of myself away, a part I can never get back. It feels personal and weird, but I guess that is the whole point of the offering.

After everyone has sliced their palms, we finally clasp our hands together around the circle.

We all take a deep breath and exhale slowly, before beginning the chanting of the spell.

It is in a weird language...it sounds like a mix between Latin and Faerie. I only know a few simple Latin words from some spells we learnt when we were younger, but I cannot speak any Faerie. I can only recognize it when I hear it.

It takes less than two minutes to complete the chant. I'm not sure if something was supposed to happen right away or if it takes a while to work, but there is now a stillness in the air. The room is so silent you could hear a pin drop.

Our gazes keep traveling around the room as we anxiously wait and search for any sign that something might be happening. We stand in the middle of my living room, the kitchen is directly behind me, Hazel has her back towards my bedroom hallway, and Eve stands directly in front of my living room couch.

Right as we decide to give up, a strong gust of wind burst through my apartment. The apartment windows are closed, so that couldn't have come from a natural breeze...could the ritual have actually worked? Are we in the presence of something supernatural?

Right as my thoughts begin to swim away with me, the candles around our circle and the ones we placed on the kitchen counter extinguish.

Panic immediately starts creeping in, but within the time it takes us to finish gasping from fright, they flare back to life...as if nothing at all had happened and it was all in our imagination.

That's when we hear him...

CHAPTER 3

CALISTA

I can feel it within the power that flows through my blood. A familiar power that twins my own, calling out from across the veil. A strong powerful pull I cannot ignore. This can only mean one thing...the time has finally come. The plan I set into motion twenty-nine years ago is at long last coming to fruition. The patience I have endured the last 130 years is going to be well worth the look on the king's face, as he falls from his throne and realizes I am the one responsible for his downfall. Whoever is reaching out from the other side of the veil better be prepared for what they are getting themselves into...because I am certain that if I can feel the strength and immensity of their power calling from another realm—then so can the king...

"Well, well, what do we have here?", a tall shadowy figure begins to emerge out from the pitch-black corner over by my front door. But before I can fully comprehend what's happening and the fact that the ritual worked, the Entity reappears in the middle of the circle.

"For what reason would divine creatures such as yourselves have for summoning someone of such high-power?" He inquires of us, all the while slowly taking us in from head to toe. It appears his eyes are searching for something specific to latch onto as they rake along our bodies. The intensity of the look sends chills down my spine.

The Entity before us radiates power and has a deep sultry voice that demands authority. He is hands down one of the most beautiful men I have ever seen. His hair is a dark chocolate brown; so dark it almost appears to be black, his eyes are a captivating mix of green and brown, I would call them Hazel but that doesn't seem to do them justice. The deep green of his eyes puts me in mind of the color of fresh moss on a beautiful spring morning. The green is then perfectly encapsulated within a light caramel border. Within the green of his eyes there are golden flakes that seem to glimmer with his every movement.

His skin is very fair and shines as if it is reflecting the light of the moon.

And he is wearing a fitted dark black suit that shows off his muscular physique; with a black undershirt and deep red tie to pull it all together.

The three of us just stand there staring at the male who has appeared before us. Our eyes are widened in shock that the summoning ritual worked. We look back and forth between one another, silently asking who is going to be brave and speak up first.

My mind is racing...how are we supposed to address such a powerful Entity? I highly doubted the ritual would be a success, so I never researched anything about 'how to show respect to a High Entity of Light?'

I clear my throat preparing to address the Entity.

"Hi-Hello...um...Mr. Entity of Light...sir..." I look over at my sisters, my eyes pleading for one of them to step in and put an end to my humiliation. However, my pleas go unanswered...*chickens*.

"Thank you for answering our summons. I hope it wasn't too much of an inconvenience. We were hoping that maybe you would be able to provide us with some answers that could help point us in the right direction to uncover who killed our mothers..."

I feel so small under the intensity of his stare.

He takes his sweet time to respond, causing me to break out into a sweat as my nervousness increases. It's like he can literally see the small bead of sweat currently trailing down along my spine, and he's waiting for it to make its descent all the way to my ass before he decides to finally speak again.

"Is that all..." He drones out with a huge arrogant smirk on his perfect face. "Just summon me here to solve a murder? Well, that shouldn't be hard at all..." His voice is dripping with sarcasm.

"Our mothers were all murdered on the same night twenty-four years ago." Hazel cuts in, and his gaze now falls upon her. "The police in charge of the investigation couldn't have cared less about finding who was responsible. We made a promise twelve years ago that one day we would figure out who is to blame for their murder. There were zero clues to point us in the right direction, well, except for the one that led us here..." she looks back at Eve and I while taking in a shaky breath.

However, before Hazel can continue the Entity *laughs*.

How dare he laugh at us for wanting to find our mothers' killer.

Anger begins to *boil* up inside of me at the audacity of this Entity. Yes, he is more powerful than I could ever wish to be, but if he wants to start a fight, I will go down swinging.

I begin unconsciously clenching and unclenching my jaw when his laughter finally stops and he speaks up...

"So, you lovely creatures summoned me here wasting my time and patience; all because you want me to help solve a murder? A murder that happened *twenty-four* years ago?!" he shakes his head back and forth while grinning from ear to ear like a mad man. "Wow you really must be desperate if you risked angering such a powerful being with this ludicrous request."

His words finally cause me to snap and begin to yell out, "How Dare Y—"

"Wait, what do you mean by a *clue* having already led you here?" he asks cutting off my outburst.

Maybe I'm imagining things but judging from the Entity's tone and sudden interest in what Hazel just said, it seems to me like he is now suddenly intrigued by this situation.

Hazel begins to explain to the Entity how we ended up here tonight, standing around this summoning circle talking to him.

"Five years before our mothers were murdered, they did one thing together that always stood out to us...they performed this very same ritual to summon upon an Entity of Light. They had suspected that the High Priestess of their coven had struck a deal with the Dark Fae King, and nothing good was going to come from it. Our mothers planned to ask the Entity for more power to go up against their High Priestess, and the Dark Fae King, if it came down to it." Hazel's gaze drops down to the floor as she releases a sigh of defeat. "However, the ritual was unsuccessful...or at least they thought it was..."

The Entity is staring at Hazel with such intensity; like he is locked in on every single word she is saying. I wonder why he is suddenly taking interest in our story?

"And now we are here. In front of you." I state dryly, splaying my arms out to the sides while still clasping on to my sisters' hands. "We summoned you here tonight in hopes that maybe you know the Entity who answered our mothers' summons, or maybe by some miracle *you* are the Entity that answered them." I swear I see something resembling shock or surprise flash through the Entity's eyes, but then again, it was gone so fast that I can't be sure. "Or maybe they were right all along, and no Entity answered their summons that night..."

After I finish speaking, I find myself having a stare down with the Entity, an Entity that could smite me for any reason at any second and the universe wouldn't bat an eye. Though apparently my sense of self-preservation has jumped out of the living room window, because I continue standing here, trying to exude strength and confidence.

Fake it till you make it...

Luckily, Eve finally steps in, saving me before I can do or say anything stupid. "This ritual to summon a High Entity of Light like yourself was our only lead. We considered the High Priestess herself as a suspect, but there was no incriminating evidence found at the scenes of the crimes." Eve hesitates as if she's taking the time to consider her next words carefully. "However, we believe that the summoning ritual *did* work for our mothers. And that for some reason the Entity of Light just did not want to reveal itself to them or grant them their request." Eve turns to look at me and Hazel for a nod of approval before she continues. Then slowly she turns and looks the Entity dead in the eyes and states the accusation that has been sitting restlessly in our minds, "We believe the Entity may have killed them."

The gold in the Entity's eyes seems to flare to life like embers from a fire as his eyes fixate on the three of us.

His anger resulting from our accusation emanates off him like solid waves of heat, as if a fire burns beneath his skin.

I can relate.

I quickly interject before this whole situation takes a turn for the worse, "We don't have any reasons as to why the Entity would have killed our mothers, but like we said this ritual was our only lead. It is the only thing we know for certain that they did together to try to stop their High Priestess... Heck, maybe the High Priestess somehow caught onto them and had the Dark Fae King send his 'flying monkeys' after them."

Hazel quietly snickers and Eve shoots me a 'what the fuck is wrong with you' look if I had ever seen one.

No, I don't really think our mothers were killed by 'flying monkeys' because they don't exist...at least I hope not anyway. I was just throwing stuff out there and happened to watch too much *Wizard of Oz* as a child.

"Flying Monkeys?" The Entity questions with his face scrunched up looking completely confused.

"Sorry, I was being sarcastic. Don't you and the other high-power entities get to watch classical movie masterpieces?" I try my best to hold it together but there is no way to look at his face and not laugh out loud. It can't be helped. His look of pure confusion is priceless.

Doing my best to kill my laughter I quickly explain to the Entity what the hell I was talking about. "They are characters from a movie, *The Wizard of Oz*, the bad witch has "flying monkeys" that go out and do all her evil deeds for her... On second thought, don't watch it, those monkeys gave me nightmares for weeks after I first saw it."

I shake my head and release a quick shiver. The images from my childhood nightmares that those damn monkeys caused me had started to flood back into my mind.

Silence, complete silence, as we all just stand there looking at one another. The Entity seems different now somehow.

His body is all tensed up like something we said is bothering him. Maybe he does know something after all?

Or he's imagining the flying monkeys...poor guy.

"I'll help" he agrees, sending a rush of relief through my system.

Unfortunately, my relief is short lived...

"But on one condition...the three of you will help me destroy the Dark Fae King." He smiles as he takes in the look of absolute shock and terror that is plastered on our faces.

I am speechless, and it seems like the other girls are as well.

As he finally realizes we have no clue how to respond to what he just threw at us, he speaks up again. "Do we have a deal? Or have you been a complete waste of my time?"

When we still don't answer he continues, "You willingly offered up a *part of yourself* when you called upon me...and the part I want is your *powers*. I will help you find whoever is responsible for your mothers' murders, and in return, you will use your powers to help me defeat the king."

He wants our powers!? Is he mad!? Why would he want *our powers* when he is a powerful Entity of Light!? I'm pretty sure an Entity of Light trumps any Fae King that's out there. He should be able to take care of whatever situation he has going on with the Dark Fae King without even lifting his pinky.

But no, instead he wants three *basic* witches?

Yes, our powers came naturally and are unique, but we are by no means powerful enough to defeat the Dark Fae King. Out of all the Light Entities out there we summon the suicidal one...great just our luck.

"Hold up!" I blurt out, as I finally manage to find my voice. "Let me get this right...you will help us *try* to solve our mothers' murders, which puts your existence at minimal-to-zero risk, if we in turn allow ourselves to be *eviscerated* by the Dark Fae King!? How is that fair!?"

I release my sisters' hands and start pacing back and forth and pulling at my hair as I will myself to calm down. I was slightly hoping that breaking the circle would cause him to disappear, but nope he is still here in the middle of my living room.

"No!...NO!" I come to a stop directly in front of the entity, throwing caution to the wind. "I will not risk mine or my sisters' lives over this. We have lived our lives not knowing the truth of our mothers' deaths this long, we can get the answers we want in the afterlife when we see them again." And just to make sure I'm clear I add, "When we are nice and old and have lived nice long lives...not anytime soon by the hand of the Dark Fae King."

However, the entity quickly retorts not willing to accept 'no' as an answer.

"Oh, but you will accept my deal, you fiery little creature..." The Entity walks right up to the very edge of the circle; as close as he can get to me, but I don't back down. "You did so when you performed the ritual. You promised me a part of yourself, and I chose your powers. We can do this the easy way or the hard way...that will be your choice to decide on; our deal is not." We continue our stare off with one another; neither of us backing down. I refuse to let him see any fear...all he will get from me is my anger.

"Fine, we accept!" Hazel spits out.

"NO!", Eve and I both shout in unison looking at Hazel like she has lost her damn mind. I'm pretty sure she has but it is too late, the words are already out of her mouth.

What on earth is she thinking?! Does she suddenly have these 'Wonder Woman' type powers we are unaware of?!

"Fabulous!" The Entity purrs. His satisfaction is evident all over his *perfect* face. A face I so desperately want to ram my fist into repeatedly. I just can't decide if I want to do it before or after I ram my fist into Hazel's face for getting us into this mess.

This death sentence!

"I can already tell it is going to be a pleasure working along-side you divine creatures.", he says as one side of his mouth curves up into a sinister smile. "Now, I must be going, but next time we meet I expect more information on your mothers' murders. How were they murdered? Were they together or found separately? And most simply, their names."

Before the Entity disappears back to where it came from my senses finally come back to me. "Wait, when should we summon you again? And more simply, what is *your* name?" I spitefully ask. "Oh, and how the hell are we going to take out the Dark Fae King?! That seems like important information we need to have!"

"Oh, don't you worry yourselves...I'll find you." He winks at us wickedly sending another unpleasant shiver down my spine. "I will inform you of your role in destroying the king the next time we meet. And you can call me Cerberus; *rightful* Unseelie King of the Fae Realm."

And in the blink of an eye, he's gone...

CHAPTER 4
CALISTA

Present Day

Another day, another dead body here in the fast-paced gruesome world that has become my life. I can't complain too much given that, by the age of twenty-eight, I was able to rise in the ranks to become lead detective in the homicide division of the DC Metropolitan Police Department. Sometimes I feel like my success is unfair given the fact that I have 'abilities' that provide me with a very sharp edge out in the field. My abilities basically allow the murder victims to *speak* to me. I'm not talking about sitting down and having a conversation with the deceased, but I can see glimpses through their eyes in the seconds just prior to their death. This allows me to gather specific details about their killers.

"This is our third body in two weeks. Is there a serial killer convention in town or something?" I joke with my partner Sebastian, or Seb as I call him.

Seb and I have been partners for five years, since the first day I started my career as a detective for the DCMPD. He is now an honorary member of my small family here in DC; that being my sisters and me.

Everyone at work teases us about our relationship, saying that we should just go ahead and 'get together', but that is *not* happening. Not that Seb isn't attractive, because he is! He stands at 6'4, blonde hair, blue eyes, and a super ripped body...your typical pretty boy. He is the type of handsome that every woman wants to take home to mommy. I just never saw him that way, I had that instant 'friend zone' feeling as soon as we met.

Not to mention my relationships never work out. I attribute the failures to the fact that I gave my heart away over ten years ago. The saddest part is that the man I fell in love with was a figment of my imagination concocted in my dreams when I was a teenager. I used to dream almost every night, of this enchanting world cocooned in darkness and starlight. Everything within my dream world felt so *real*, and it was there in those magical lands that I met and fell head over heels for the most beautiful man I had ever seen.

But I am too busy and too broke to tackle the 'I fell in love with my literal *dream* guy, and now all my relationships in the real world are doomed to fail' issue with a therapist.

"Ha, you ain't kidding. If we don't nail this sucker soon you know the department is going to call in the 'big guns'", Seb responds from behind his desk.

The 'big guns' as we refer to them, are the FBI. It always seems like when they get involved with our cases chaos always ensues. They cause us more roadblocks when trying to help them to solve the case than a literal land slide would. They make it especially tricky for my sisters and me to use our 'abilities' to solve the case. There is just so much red tape to get through that sometimes the risk of being caught isn't worth it.

"Well then, I guess you should stop swiping 'left' on that dating app of yours and come on. Let's get over there before someone contaminates the scene." I tease at Seb.

"You're just mad I haven't swiped 'right' on your profile...*yet*" Seb retaliates shooting me a wink, and we both erupt with laughter.

You see so much death and evil doing this job, so making each other smile or laugh to lighten the mood just comes with the territory.

Arriving at the scene inside of a small herb and spice shop, we are informed by our forensic team that it appears to be the same M.O. as the last two murders. The victim is female; however, she seems to be in her fifties where the last two females were in their late twenties. The manner of death is still the same though. Her eyes were removed, and her throat was slit. The former happening first; telling me the murderer is trying to get information from his victims. What information they are looking for has yet to be figured out since we cannot seem to find a link between the first two victims.

"Any luck finding anything that will give us a lead?" Seb questions the forensics team.

"Zelch, zero, nada…whoever is doing this is covering all their tracks. I am starting to suspect that there may be more than one killer involved though." Josh, one of the forensics guys, speaks up to inform us.

I stick him with a questioning look as I approach him, "Explain" I demand.

Josh looks away with a blush creeping up his neck before he finally regains his train of thought. I swear it's like some of these men have never spoken with a member of the opposite sex before, seeing as how they act so bashful around me and the other women back at the precinct.

"If you look at her wrists and ankles you can see that she was not restrained by ropes or chains…it doesn't look like she was restrained by *anything* during the act. Not even a zip-tie. And personally, if I was getting my eyes gouged out, I wouldn't be sitting still patiently waiting for the psycho to finish, I would be fighting to get away. But here there is no sign of struggle against any form of restraints. So, I imagine we are looking for two or more good size men; at least one to hold the victim without leaving any defensive marks on her skin, and the other to gouge the eyes out."

Both Seb and I take a position on opposite sides of the victim while Josh explains his reasoning, bending down to assess the victim ourselves for any signs of restraint.

And Josh is right, there aren't any.

Another ability of mine is I can tell by looking at the victim's body if their death was perpetrated by a supernatural being. Their body gives off a blue hue that only I can see that acts as a 'fingerprint' and lets me know if we are looking for something supernatural. If their body doesn't exhibit a blue hue, then I know their killer is nothing more than a basic human scumbag. But our last two victims, including our current, have all given off the notorious blue hue. Which supports what Josh discovered; a supernatural being could possess the powers to hold a person in place without ever having to lay a finger on them.

Although the Mortal and Fae Realms came to an agreement thousands of years ago to live peaceful, separate lives, separated by a thin veil; every now and then something supernatural has been found to cross over from the Fae Realm.

"Wouldn't there be handprints from the person doing the re-straining? Bruising? Like you said the person isn't just going to sit still while having their eyes gouged out, so there should be signs of a struggle between the victim and the one restraining her." Seb asks looking back to Josh.

"Correct" Josh responds, "Whoever is doing the restraining must be strong and doesn't need to use much effort or force to keep the victims in place. Keeping any handprints from appearing on the victim's skin. Like I said I think we are looking for two or more men; large/strong men. And I'd bet my next paycheck that if we go back and look at the previous two victims, we will find the same thing… nothing; no signs of restraint at all."

"And you are positive there were no traces of a paralytic or tranquilizer in the first two victims?" I ask flatly.

"Double and triple checked, but nothing was found." Josh assures us, looking as confused as I am.

"Damn it!", I exclaim. "Seb, head over to the morgue and take a look, if they do not have the bodies anymore go through all the pictures taken to see if you can find any sign of restraint or lack thereof."

"On it boss", Seb says sarcastically with a two-finger salute, and grabs Josh for a ride before heading over to the morgue.

I'll look around the shop for any other clues to help us link this victim to the suspect or previous victims, and then I'll meet him back at the precinct.

I received a text from Seb before I even made it back to the office. As Josh pointed out to us there were no signs of restraint on the previous two victims either.

This case has already thrown us a curve ball, so now we must pitch or get off the plate. Meaning the FBI will be stepping in soon if we don't come up with any evidence leading us to the killer/killers.

Instead of heading to my desk when I get back to the precinct, I decided to swing by the forensics lab down in the basement. Everleigh is there and I'm sure she is working on finding any evidence from the items brought in from the two previous victims.

Luckily for me, my two 'sisters from another mistress' have also taken the same route in life. They have joined me on the force at the DCMPD but are assigned to other teams. Everleigh works in forensics and Hazel is our little IT geek.

Not only do they know about my 'abilities', but they possess abilities of their own that bring something different to the team. Put us three together on a homicide investigation and we are unstoppable. We haven't failed to solve a case yet.

Eve can sense power like I can but in a different way; she can gather clues from nature when she is near a being with supernatural power. She may feel a rumbling of the earth, a strong breeze blowing in the direction towards the power, or flames from a simple candle nearby may flare up to alert her.

Her abilities deal with the earth and nature, so it only makes sense that those forces help her be more aware of her surroundings. She can use her abilities to call upon wind, water, air, fire, and the earth itself when needed.

Eve is only a year younger than me and fits the definition of a blonde 'bombshell' to the tee; with her long blonde hair, bright-blue eyes, heart shaped face, and a cute petite nose to top it all off.

She looks so peaceful when she is lost in her work, I almost hate to disturb her with bad news.

"Hey Eve! Working hard or hardly working?" She looks up from what she's doing when she hears my voice.

"Oh no, what's wrong?" She questions me.

"Who said there is anything wrong? I mean other than the string of murders and having an official 'serial case' on our hands?"

"Your face, if you scowl any harder you will have a literal unibrow. Let's hear it." She stares at me with bored curiosity as I instinctively reach up to inspect my brow.

I explain to her our most recent discovery about there being no physical signs of restraints having been used on our victims.

"How did we miss that?" She says in surprised disbelief.

"Well, here is the cherry on top…their eyes were not 'gouged out' they were *burned out*, like from the inside out."

Looking at her face that has now scrunched up with concern I want to tease, "Now who has the unibrow?", but I refrain.

Taking pause, I glance around the room to make sure we are still alone before I continue quietly.

"Look, you know I told you girls that it was something supernatural and very powerful. I still can't get a glimpse of the killer or hear anything spoken between them and the victim before they slit their throats. Whatever it is, it is *strong*, strong enough to block me out of the victim's mind. We need to figure out a connection between our three victims fast…before we end up face to face with this supernatural being."

I always want to have a leg up on our suspects, but even more so when I know they are of the supernatural variety. We have seen everything from Fae disguised as huge wolf-like creatures leaving victims mauled in the middle of the city streets, witches from both realms using black magic, vampires draining their victims dry in unconventional ways (two fang marks on the body make it too obvious), and worst of all...the crimes of creatures called Volge. I have only laid eyes on one crime scene where it was rumored to be a Volge attack, and the victim's body was just a husk of the person it belonged to. The Volge can drain their victim's body of its organs and muscles, leaving a skin covered skeleton, by simply touching the victim's skin. Talk about terrifying.

Every time I try to look through the victim's eyes (figuratively speaking since theirs were burned from their sockets) to get a glimpse of the killer or any identifying factors that could help, all I see is a figure cloaked in shadows. I can vaguely make out an outline of a large male figure judging by the height and width, but the inside of the outline is filled with pure darkness. Shadows swirl all around the figure, acting as a shield of sorts.

This makes me wonder if this supernatural killer is searching for someone with abilities like mine in particular? Someone who can see through the eyes of the dead. And the killer/killers are using their power to make sure this person doesn't see them coming.

The only issue with that theory is I am the only one I know of with that ability, and that leaves me with a very bad feeling that *I* am exactly who they are looking for... But as to why I have no clue. And why they think these victims may be me or maybe know how to find me, I have no idea. I had never seen any of these women until I was staring down at their lifeless corps.

Eve begins to pace back and forth, tugging on her hair at the roots. "Ahhhh" she quietly cries out with frustration. "I don't know what to tell you. Whatever this thing is they are good and know how to cover their tracks. I'm doing the best I can; maybe we will have better luck finding something to help us ID them from the victim you saw today?"

"Well, that brings me to why I actually stopped by..." I say as I slam down a small worn-out brown leather book on the table in front of us. Eve stops her pacing to look between me and the small brown book. I can tell by the look on her face she has no idea where I am going with this.

"Open it" I tell her.

Raising her brow in question she does as I ask. Seconds later she frowns up at me unimpressed.

"It's just a list of names with herbs and spices listed next to them…", she gasps as she finally puts together what she is looking at.

"See I found this laid open on the counter from today's victim, and for some reason it caught my eye. When I started to look through the names I found three that were very interesting. The two previous victim's names Jessa Walkens and Valerie Elkins are written in here." I flip through the pages and point to each victim's name.

"But even more interesting and *shocking!*", I say as I stare up at her. "Is that I also found *your name* listed in here as well," I jab my finger down sternly on her name, "mind explaining that?"

Eve just stares silently at her name as her jaw hangs towards the floor. Finally, she looks at me, blinking rapidly a few times then asks, "Is your most recent victim Tilly Townsen?"

"Why yes, it is Everleigh, but please do continue…"

"She is the owner of the local spice shop…where she not only sells spices and herbs, but also other 'hard to find' ingredients for spells, rituals, and what have you." She looks up to see me staring at her intensely then continues, "She is a local witch, but she is super nice and doesn't bother anyone. And she certainly does not condone practicing 'blood or black magic', so I don't know why she would be targeted and killed by anyone."

Everleigh slumps into her chair and places her face in her hands. I can tell she is upset with this new information. I'm not sure how close she was with Ms. Townsen, but it seems they were at least acquaintances.

"Well, since you and her are both witches" I whisper, "then it is probably safe to assume that our previous two victims were also witches since their names are also in her book."

We both stare at each other with a look of unease.

"Which means not only do we have a serial killer on our hands, but most likely a serial 'witch' killer." I conclude, praying I'm wrong this time.

If I'm right about this then our predicament just became even more dire.

"Do you think the killer looked at the names in this book? If so, why didn't they just take the book? Why did they just leave it behind? Oh gosh, my name! Since my name is in there, I could be on the killer's radar now!" Eve begins shaking as her thoughts continue spiraling out of control.

I'm honestly surprised that this realization took her as long as it did.

"Whoa there, sis" I say calmly while rubbing her shoulders to try and help soothe her racing mind. "You know Hazel and I are not going to let anything happen to you...but just in case carry around a large water bottle with you wherever you go, and you can just drown the fucker where he stands before he even lays a hand on you.", I say jokingly, and laughter from the both of us fills the air as we picture that mental image.

After regaining her composure Eve informs me that she will investigate our suspicions that the names listed in Tilly's 'little brown book' were her 'witch' customers. The herbs listed next to them were most likely what they liked her to keep in stock for them or what they most recently purchased from her.

As I'm turning to leave and head back to my office I stop dead in my tracks. Looking back at Eve, I ask her...

"Why is your name in that book next to 'Calcite chalk'?"

"That is the 'bone' chalk we needed to use for the containment circle and protection ruins last month when we did the summoning ritual. We couldn't just use children's sidewalk chalk.", She laughs uneasily shaking her head.

I leave and head back to work, feeling even more uneasy than I did before speaking with Eve.

CHAPTER 5

CALISTA

It has been four weeks since we did that ridiculous summoning ritual. Four weeks since we last saw that Dark Fae bastard that let us believe he was an Entity of Light.

I have been praying every day since that he has forgotten about us. That way we don't have to worry about that insane deal Hazel got us into.

When he left us with that *small* detail that he was the *'rightful'* Dark Fae King, all three of us were on the verge of having a brain aneurysm.

He just dropped a bomb on us and then disappeared.

I took my foot and immediately broke the chalk circle, so it wasn't functional anymore.

We also had to digest the possibility that our mothers had also summoned a Dark Fae; given we performed the exact same ritual they had when they were attempting to summon an Entity of Light.

It was nice to have work to take my mind off that *huge* mistake we had made. But since my conversation with Eve earlier today and putting together that this serial killer seems to be targeting witches; I can't help but consider the timing of everything.

What are the chances that witches start showing up dead one week after we accidentally summoned a Dark Fae into our realm?

The victims' deaths appear to be from a supernatural being. One that can manage to burn the eyes right out from the victim's skull without having to use any kind of restraints to hold the victim in place. The victims having their throat slit seems to me like a diversion to throw off the investigation. It leads detectives away from suspecting anything supernatural...because why would a supernatural being kill in such a mundane human way?

With all this running through my mind I pull out my phone to send a group text to Eve and Hazel:

Me:

> *Hey, come over around 7 tonight for take-out? We also need to discuss something important about the current murder cases.*

Hazel:

> *Yay! Murder talk and take-out... wouldn't miss it for the world!*

Eve:

> *Sounds good*
> *See you then!*

The rest of the workday seems to fly by with everyone in such a frenzy over our captain officially announcing we have a 'serial killer' case on our hands.

With all this shit piling up on my plate it's going to be spilling over the sides in no time.

All I know; is that if we somehow live through this shitshow we are currently starring in, I am going on a nice long vacation.

The girls and I ordered Japanese take-out for dinner. The mood in the room was very apprehensive throughout the entire meal. Eve had caught Hazel up on everything we put together earlier today right after I left the lab.

She had Hazel look into the previous two victims; to see if they may have also been witches, or women who dabbled in witchcraft for the *thrill* of it from time to time.

Hazel is our 'wild child' at the young age of twenty-six. She has that whole 'innocent' librarian appearance wearing her nerdy black framed glasses, with her short dark brown curly hair, stunning chocolate brown eyes, and adorable spattering of freckles across her cheeks and nose.

But one shouldn't let her geeky demeanor fool them…she would be the first of us to jump up on the bar at the local pub and start dancing to some Def Leppard or AC/DC.

I had politely and patiently waited for everyone to finish eating before getting down to business. I didn't want to sour the taste of everyone's food with my gut-wrenching suspicions.

However, now that the three of us have finished eating and are cozied up with our favorite fuzzy throws on my living room floor; sitting around the coffee table and sipping on the Italian Moscato wine we love so much, it's time to get down to business.

"Alright, now for why I asked you two over tonight… The conversation I had with Eve earlier today got me to thinking about the timing of everything that's taken place over these past four weeks."

I ensure I have their full attention before sharing my suspicions. Stating them aloud makes them seem too real, so I don't want to repeat them.

"Here me out, what if this string of murders has something to do with us performing that stupid summoning ritual last month?... We did the ritual four weeks ago and the first victim was found dead one week later... AND we accidentally summoned the freaking 'rightful king' of the Dark Fae! This can't all be a coincidence, right?"

Both Eve and Hazel look at me with wide eyes, their jaws dropped and faces pale. It was as if I had just informed them of something incredibly shocking; like I was abducted and probed by aliens or some other crazy shit. I was unsure if they were still engaged in the conversation. Their eyes were glazing over as though their minds had wandered off.

Hazel rises to her knees as she alarmingly informs us, "Jessa Walkens and Valerie Elkins, the first two victims...they definitely played around with witchcraft."

Getting Hazel to take things seriously is always tough, but I can tell she is truly scared. I'm scared too. Her findings, along with my suspicions and the timing, make more sense now. "I can't confirm if they were actively practicing witchcraft, but their hard drives show they had an interest. If I had more time, I could check on security footage, but Eve just told me today."

I gently reach over and place my hand on her arm, hoping to provide a small comfort before her fear takes over and runs away with her attention. She did great; especially seeing as she only had a few hours to investigate. Hazel was the last to join us at the DCMPD, but oh how much easier our jobs became once she did.

Hoping to get the look of failure off Hazel's sweet baby-doll face, I hurriedly step in to inform my sisters of the security information my team has already discovered. "Neither woman had any type of security cameras other than a ring doorbell on Ms. Elkins front door, but it didn't show anyone coming within twenty yards of her door before the murder. Her neighbors ring doorbell didn't show anything suspicious either. Also, in all three cases there was no sign of forced entry. When you consider that along with the way they were murdered, it screams 'supernatural' killer. Or kill-*ers*. Plus, they each had a blue aura surrounding them. Unfortunately, I can't tell my team that so now they are looking for a human suspect.

"And today after Ms. Townsen's murder, we now have three female victims, with a witchcraft background, and the names of the first two victims are listed as customers in Ms. Townsen's 'logbook' we found... So, both female victims have met Ms. Townsen before through her shop, but there is no evidence to give us reason to believe that the two female victims knew one another." As I'm about to finish up everything we know so far, I remember one very important piece of information.

Done providing comfort, I turn to scowl at Hazel as I aggravatedly point out, "And now *Eve's* name is also in Ms. Townsen's 'logbook' since she had to go get that stupid 'bone' chalk for the ritual! Now there is a chance that the killer saw her name and could target her at some point!"

Hazel looks at me like I just slapped her in the face.

"How was I supposed to know there would be a serial killer on the loose who apparently is hunting down people who practice witchcraft!?" Hazel shouts back at me.

As I'm about to respond to Hazel, Eve interrupts. "Enough arguing, girls. It won't help us. Yes, I might be on the killer's radar now, but all we can do until this psycho is caught is stay alert. Hopefully, my powers can detect anything supernatural and stall them so I can escape. If they are as strong as we think, especially if there are multiple killers, I doubt I can defeat them alone."

Eve must be delusional if she thinks we are going to let her risk her life 'hoping' that her powers are enough to save her. The first two victims were found dead in their homes, but the third, Ms. Townsen, was found in her place of business. That goes to show these killers are ballsy, so they could make a move against her anytime and anywhere.

Though I highly doubt the killer/killers are going to show up at the DCMDP while she is at work, there is still the matter of keeping her safe outside of work.

"Look, until we catch this ass-wipe, you are staying with one of us outside of work. Hopefully it's true in this case and there *is* strength in numbers.", I tell Eve assertively, so she knows this discussion is not up for debate. But she is not having any of it...

"I'm not going to change up my whole routine because I *might* have a killer coming for me at some point in the future!", she firmly states as she grabs the bottle of wine on the table to pour herself another glass.

Thankfully Hazel takes my side and comes to my aid.

"No, Cali is right Eve, we need to stick together now more than ever. Please, it will help us all breathe easier knowing you are not alone." Hazel pleads to Eve, turning on her puppy dog stare. I'm glad Eve is on the other end of that stare and not me because I always give in to the puppy dog eyes.

After another ten minutes of working out the logistics of Eve's current situation she finally caves and agrees to stay with Hazel until everything is settled. Or at least until we are certain that she is no longer a possible target.

This discussion has already gotten us riled up and we haven't even started dissecting my theory...that these murders have something to do with the ritual we performed four weeks ago.

It's going to be a long night...

"Alright, now back to my main concern for calling this meeting tonight...do we think these murders are linked to the summoning ritual? The timing just seems too convenient to me. We perform this ritual that summons a Dark Fae, into the middle of my freaking living room, and then one-week later bodies start dropping... Something isn't sitting right with me." I say, trying to bring us back to the more important topic of tonight.

Did we cause this to happen? Is the victim's blood on our hands? I shudder at the possibility...

"Shit...", Hazel's says before shoving her face into a pillow.

"I think you're right Cali. Ever since you mentioned it, I keep thinking to myself 'what are the odds?'", Eve says, confirming my fears.

Somehow hearing them back up my theory makes me feel worse. I guess I was hoping they would reassure me that it was nonsense, and that it was all in my head.

Hazel suddenly jumps up from her spot on the floor and begins to pace back and forth. Her face looks pained from all this information bouncing around in her head.

I know if the ritual does turn out to be connected to these murders in any way, she will never forgive herself. I'll make sure to remind her that even though Eve and I had our reservations about performing the ritual, in the end we both decided to go through with it too.

The blame cannot singularly be put on her; we were right there with her. If we go down, we go down together.

"We need to talk to...what was his name again? The Dark Fae we summoned. Maybe he can give us some answers to if these events are related." Hazel suggests, rubbing her temples as she continues to pace.

"Are you insane?!" Eve shouts. "Do the ritual again?! When we already think that is what got us into this mess in the first place?!.... NO, no, no, no!"

I hate that as much as every fiber in my body is telling me to leave it be; I know Hazel is right. We need to get the confirmation straight from the horse's mouth.

"She's right Eve", I cringe from the evil look Eve shoots at me. "Trust me I want to do this even less than you, but he might have information we need."

"We need to call Aunt Ellie, like now! He wanted answers about our mothers' deaths before the next time we met. He might just up and disappear again if we summon him without the information, he told us to find out." Before either of us can object, Hazel already has her phone out calling Aunt Ellie.

Why don't we already have this information? I think to myself as we wait for Aunt Ellie to pick up the phone. I'm a freaking homicide detective, and I have never investigated *how* exactly our mothers were murdered.

I guess maybe a part of me didn't want to know the details, like knowing those would make it too real, that our mothers really were murdered...

I remember when Aunt Ellie sat us down after I had turned sixteen and my powers started to cause issues (I accidentally killed my school's janitor); she had finally told us the truth about how our mothers died and the fact that they were natural born witches. She suspected, after watching my powers awaken, that their magic got passed down to each of us girls.

After having been told it was a car accident our whole lives, we finally found out that they had *actually* been murdered. Both my sisters and I had begged to know more. Why were they killed? How were they killed? Who had done it?

Aunt Ellie, however, insisted that she would tell us more when we were adults, that the details of their murders were too heavy to put on us at such a young age.

Even when looking into their case files after I began working for the DCMPD; there had not been details released on how our mothers had been found dead, just that they were 'brutally mutilated'.

Knowing that vague detail seemed worse than having known what exactly had happened. Having worked in law enforcement I have seen some sick shit, even before I broke into the homicide department, so the images that my imagination ran away with were probably *way worse* than what really happened.

No matter where I searched, I could never find 'details' about our mothers' murders, so I was left with that awful description and my own imagination. The lack of information in the Chickasaw County Sherif's Office case report was super odd. It's almost like they intentionally didn't record the information. Why would they do that? I have no idea...unless the information was so incriminating that they didn't want to cause the public to panic, or the person/persons responsible threatened them to not release that information.

Now here we are, fully grown adults, calling our aunt to ask for the information about our mother's murders. She has no reason to keep the details from us anymore, especially if we tell her why we need the information. I would prefer we keep her out of this mess but if she doesn't cooperate, we may not have any other option.

CHAPTER 6

CALISTA

"Hey sweet girl!", Aunt Ellie says to Hazel when she answers the call.

She always sounds so happy-go-lucky, which always makes me smile no matter what mood I'm in. I wish I could have that attitude towards life, but when you have seen all the bad that is out there in the world it's hard not to go into dark places at times. My mind can be the scariest place some days; especially after something horrific has happened.

"Hey, Aunt Ellie!", Hazel answers back enthusiastically. "I have you on speaker, Eve and Cali are here too! Say 'Hi'"

"Hey Aunt Ellie", we both yell towards the phone in Hazel's outreached hand.

The happiness in Aunt Ellie's voice skyrockets once she knows all three of her girls are on the phone with her.

The night of our mothers' murders the three of us were placed in the care of Aunt Ellie (Eleanor Wilks) our mothers' best friend. Turns out not only were the four of them the closest of friends, but apparently so close that all three of our mothers listed Aunt Ellie as our godmother in case something should ever happen to one of them.

"Hey, my sweet girls! To what do I owe this welcomed surprise?" Are you all still coming for Thanksgiving? I am making your favorite Cali...banana pudding."

"Mmm. That sounds amazing Aunt El! You always make sure I've gained at least five pounds before I leave the dinner table." Like I care though, her banana pudding is life changing. Once you've had a taste of hers, others will just be sad disappointments from there on out.

"Well, I need to make sure my girls are eating good now that you are taking care of yourselves. Y'all are so busy these days I worry you forget to stop and eat."

"Believe me Aunt Ellie...*we eat*! That is the one thing we *never* forget to do." Hazel responds and we bust out laughing in agreement. "In fact, we just finished eating dinner."

"But we would much rather have your home cooking every day." Eve adds. "And we will definitely be home for Thanksgiving; we have already asked off work."

"Oh, that's fantastic! It has been way too long since you girls visited". I could hear the sadness in her voice, which sends a wave of guilt crashing into me.

We literally visited her two months ago, where we grew up in Winchester, Virginia but it would be nice if we lived a little closer and could visit each other more often. Aunt Ellie moved us in to live with her parents in Winchester immediately after we were put in her custody. We grew up with Aunt Ellie and her family; we had grandparents, aunts, uncles, cousins and couldn't be happier; or none the wiser of the life that was taken away from us at such a young age.

All our cousins are married with children now, so we are the "old maids" and get hit with questions left and right about when we are finally going to find a man and settle down.

I will stick with my usual response, that 'I don't need a man to be happy or fulfilled in life'. That always gets me at least three eye rolls.

"So, we actually have something important to talk to you about Ellie." Hazel admits, finally getting to the reason for why we really called her. "I know this is hard to talk about, but we have to know more about the night of our mothers' murders..." Hazel pauses, looking toward us, her lips begin silently pleading for us to help her out.

When we don't say anything, she gives us a frustrated look and shakes her head in disappointment before she finally continues. "We need to know if you have any idea who is responsible *or* at least how they were killed. Basically, anything you know that might help us in finally finding their killer."

Silence stretches on for what feels like an eternity before I finally cave in and speak up. "Please Aunt El, you told us you would tell us when we were adults...well we are now, and we *really* need any information you can give us. Even the smallest detail you can remember might help. We can handle it, we promise."

After what feels like another lifetime of waiting, Aunt Ellie finally speaks up. Her voice is soft and shaky as she admits to us, "I guess I knew this day would come, but honestly I prayed it wouldn't." She releases a heavy sigh before asking, "Is everything okay? Why do you suddenly want to know?"

"I finally convinced Eve and Cali into the three of us working together to solve their murder. We promised each other when we were kids that we would solve it one day; and I just feel like it's finally time we stop dragging our feet and we get to work on it." Hazel explains. Making sure to leave out the bit about her getting us entangled in a deal with a very powerful Dark Fae.

"Well, I don't know what more you can do...the case is so cold, and the police just wrote it off as a random killer that passed through town and killed three women. They could not have cared less about your mothers' murders. It was almost like their job was to *not* solve the case." Aunt Ellie confesses with a shaky breath and asks, "Are you sure you really want to know?"

"Yes, please, any information you can remember... Please Aunt El." I beg her. Trying with all my might to keep the desperation out of my voice. I want her to believe we are just looking into this to satisfy our own curiosity; not that this information could be the difference between life and death for us.

Hazel, Eve, and I stare back and forth at one another; nodding in silent agreement that we are ready to learn the truth... no matter how tough it may be to hear.

"Okay girls...you deserve to know. I will tell you all I can but don't get your hopes up because I don't know much" Aunt Ellie begins after releasing another shaky breath. "You already know that your mothers and I were the best of friends. We met through our coven; I was not a *natural* witch like your mothers. They were born with their powers, but I had to use ingredients and incantations to perform even the simplest tasks...like bringing a pot of water to a boil on the stove. But they never judged me or acted like they were any better than me; they accepted me...lack of magic and all. I loved them for it. I never had close friends until I met your mothers.

"Your mothers had suspicions about the High Priestess. Cali, your mother, overheard the priestess conversing with a male one evening, although no male was present in the room. Additionally, she had a fresh cut on her palm, indicative of using her blood for an incantation. Following further observation, your mothers were nearly certain that the priestess was collaborating with the Dark Fae King. Although they could not confirm their beliefs, they remained confident in their suspicions.

"Our High Priestess had begun to look younger over the last year. They suspected she was bargaining for 'eternal youth' with the Dark Fae King, but what he was getting from this bargain they weren't sure. We all began looking for anything out of the ordinary happening, not just in our town, but on the local news. Hazel, your mother, brought to our attention that women were being reported 'missing' quite often in several of our surrounding counties. It could have been nothing, but your mothers always questioned if maybe the priestess had a hand in helping the Dark Fae King steal women away into the Fae Realm, which was and still is, highly illegal.

"They performed the summoning ritual that one night, but nothing seemed to answer so they figured it was a bust. After that we decided to just slowly separate ourselves from the coven. We didn't just up and leave. We were afraid that would raise too many suspicions within the coven. The High Priestess did scold your mother once Cali, when she caught her eavesdropping outside her office, and after that your mother was sure she had become suspicious of her. We came to gatherings less often, and then finally we just stopped all together."

"Do you think the High Priestess had anything to do with the murders then?" Eve asks, finally joining the conversation.

"We had been out of the coven for nearly five years before your mothers were murdered, so I don't think so. Plus, the way they were found...I don't believe the priestess to be capable of such evil." Aunt Ellie goes silent as if she's hoping we have heard enough and will finally change the subject. But now I'm even more curious.

We are ready to finally find out what happened to our mothers, and we need to hear every pain wrenching detail.

Realizing her silence is fruitless, Aunt Ellie continues to expose the information we are so desperate to know. "All three of your mothers were found in their own homes, in their own beds... *brutally* murdered. Their eyes were missing, and their throats were slit.", she sobs the last part into the phone.

Between her sobs and how fast she blurted out that last part, I was barely able to make out what exactly she had said. Then again, maybe I'm just having trouble focusing because I am going into shock.

Pushing through her tears she sorrowfully continues to describe how our mothers were murdered. "But their eyes weren't just 'missing', the empty spaces where their eyes should have been looked as if they had been scorched...like their eyeballs had been burned right out of the sockets."

She seems to be regaining her composure, but the words she speaks next not only fill me with fear but also with sadness. Aunt Ellie takes in a deep breath before she blamefully states, "I believe that performing that ritual is what got your mothers killed. I was supposed to help them with the ritual that night, but I had to cancel because something important came up. But I truly believe that if I had been there that night, I would be dead now too. I think that something evil came through during the ritual, but as to why it didn't just kill them right then and there, I have no clue."

I look to my sisters with tear filled eyes, both of their faces mirror mine as tears roll down their cheeks.

She blames herself for not being there that night they did the ritual, but like she said, if she had been she may have been killed too. I think the universe was looking out for Eve, Hazel, and I; making sure we had someone we already knew who could step in and raise us...together.

She also shares in my worst fear...I think we may have unknowingly unleashed something evil into this realm. Just like our mothers may have all those years ago.

The three of us are dead silent. I am just staring at my feet. I can't even bring myself to try and lift my head; it feels too heavy. I'm not sure how my sisters are taking this information because right now I'm trapped inside my own head. They could be screaming at me for all I know, but I can't hear anything other than the voice in my head repeatedly chanting, "*Oh Shit. Oh Shit. Oh Shit. Oh Shit...*"

"Girls!?.... Girls!?... Answer me damn it!" Aunt Ellie yells out, raising her voice.

"We fucked up Ellie", Hazel admits, finally breaking out of whatever daze she has been in. "We fucked up *really bad...*"

"SHIT!" Eve shouts at the top of her lungs. It's the loudest I have ever heard her yell. The anger inside Eve's eyes as she looks dead at Hazel could make even Freddy Kruger soil himself.

But before Eve gets the chance to say or do something she would regret, Hazel breaks down into tears. She starts apologizing to us and begging for our forgiveness in between her sobs.

"Girls! What are you talking about!? What is happening? You are scaring the shit out of me! Will one of you please calm down and tell me what the hell is going on?" The panic in Aunt Ellie's voice is at a level ten...the highest the scale goes. "If you don't explain right now, I am getting in the car and coming up there *tonight!*"

Pulling myself together, wiping away my tears and fighting off my own thoughts, I'm finally able to formulate sentences again. "El, we performed the ritual...the same one that our mothers did...the same one you gave Hazel a few weeks ago..." I stop speaking, needing to take a deep breath to remain calm, but to also give Aunt Ellie time to process what I just confessed.

I figure the three of us are in for one hell of a tongue lashing.

"What?!" Her voice is so deceivingly soft and quiet, that it seems almost worse than getting yelled at. "Did something happen? Are you hurt? Are you in trouble? A—"

"We are fine Aunt El, promise. But we might have released something bad into our realm..." I confess, point blank.

"Go on....", Again her voice is filled with a false sense of understanding that sends goose bumps down my spine.

"The ritual worked...El. But the ritual did not summon an Entity of Light...it summoned a Dark Fae King." I quickly add, "Well the *'rightful'* Dark Fae King...we don't have the complete story yet. He agreed to help us solve our mothers' case. Bu—"

"What did you do!?...what did you agree to? A Fae isn't going to help a human out of the kindness of their dark soulless heart! Damn it girls! Wh—"

"He wants us to kill the *current* Dark Fae King." Hazel reveals, trying to stop Aunt Ellie from spiraling. Although, I'm not sure if that bit of information is what I would have chosen to help ease her mind.

"We know it was stupid; we aren't *that* powerful! We basically made a deal that he is to help us solve our mothers' murders, and then we are his sheep to herd to the slaughter." Eve deadpans. She's not even trying to sugar coat it for Aunt Ellie whatsoever.

Hazel and I both give her a stern look that says 'Really? Not helping! Did you have to put it like that?'

I was worried that Aunt Ellie might have passed out when she didn't immediately start freaking out...there was just empty silence over the line.

"Look Aunt El, we can discuss this more later, but right now we have a bigger problem. One-week after we summoned this Dark Fae, female witches started turning up murdered..." I inform her as I take the cellphone from Hazel's hand.

I can't believe I am about to say this next part...

Even my own mind is still reeling as I continue to process it. "Just like how you described our mothers were found..." Uneasy silence is still all that greets me on the other end of the line. "We were worried that these murders had something to do with the ritual we performed...and well now I think you pretty much confirmed it for us." I lay my head in my hands shaking it back and forth, silently hoping Eve or Hazel will step in and take over this conversation.

I still need to digest the fact that these women are turning up dead, murdered in the same manner that our mothers were. And even though it was several years prior to their death, our mothers performed the same exact ritual we did.

Did our mothers accidentally summon a Dark Fae too? Did this Fae just sit around and wait for five years until it finally decided it felt like killing them one random night?!

I need a drink...a *very* stiff drink.

"I'm coming up, I'm going to pack, and I'll head that way. Can I stay with one of you or should I get a hotel?" Aunt Ellie finally speaks up. Clearly panicking but I can't blame her. We did drop a huge bomb on her...and put ourselves in the direct line of the shrapnel.

"No!" Eve cuts in. "We don't need you putting yourself in danger. If you are here, we will be too concerned for your safety and won't be able to focus on our jobs...to find this 'supernatural' killer and stop them."

"Does this mean that whatever is killing these witches also killed our mothers? So, if we catch them, do we also catch our mothers' killer?" Hazel turns and asks Eve and me.

"It doesn't mean this is necessarily what or who killed our mothers, but I think we can now agree that something supernatural did kill our mothers... And it most likely came from the Dark Fae Realm." I answer. "Aunt El we need to go. Stay home. We will be careful, if we do need you, I promise we will let you know. But please stay away for your safety and our sanity. Thank you for giving us this information; it was more important than we even imagined it would be. Now we know these murders may be connected to our mothers. We love you and we will call you as soon as we have any more information." I spew out in a rush, trying to conclude this phone call as soon as possible. Now that we have the information we need, we need to get a move on.

Both Eve and Hazel quickly send their love to Aunt Ellie before I end the call.

We have work to do, and we need to get started now.

CHAPTER 7

CALISTA

"Do either of you remember his name?" I ask reluctantly. Finally submitting to the fact that we need to summon the Dark Fae again to figure out how to put a stop to these murders. Murders that *we* may have set into motion in the first place.

"Maybe we just perform the entire ritual again and he will answer us?" Hazel calmly suggests.

The fact that any of us are capable of remaining calm is a feat in and of itself. We have just learned how and why our mothers may have been killed, and that the blood of the three recent victims may be on our hands. I feel like our 'calm' behavior is just from us being in a state of shock, and that none of us are even slightly *okay* after learning this new information.

"Cerberus" Eve whispers. "His name is Cerberus, like the three-headed dog that guards the underworld for Hades."

Hazel and I share a look of confusion. I guess we're both surprised that out of the three of us Eve is the one to remember his name. Seeing as she was so adamantly against all this in the first place.

"Alright then, Eve, thanks for that *neat* little factoid." I reply, trying not to sound too sarcastic. "Do you think we can just offer up a drop of blood into the summoning circle again and say his name to bring him here? We should at least try that before we perform the entire ritual again...besides knowing our luck we will probably call forth *another* Dark Fae. And I for one have had enough Dark Fae interaction with our current one to last me a lifetime."

"Agreed, let's try the simple option first. Eve, can you grab the bone chalk from the trinket box on Cali's dresser? And Cali can you find us a sharp enough knife to make the cuts?"

I raise an eyebrow and stare her down with a questioning look. "Sure...but Hazel, how do you know where I keep the bone chalk?"

"I'm nosy" she retorts slyly, smiling from ear to ear and her chin held high like she is so proud of herself. "If you don't want me to find something then hide it better." She giggles. *Giggles*!

"I shouldn't have to hide *my* stuff in *my* apartment!", I snidely shoot back at her, rolling my eyes. But instead of wasting my time and breath lecturing Hazel about personal boundaries, I walk off to find my pocketknife.

I should probably save myself some time looking for it and just ask her where it's at; since she probably already knows...nosy little heathen!

Eve and Hazel have already reconnected the containment circle on my floor by the time I return to the living room.

Before Eve and I realize what's happening, Hazel steps up to the circle with a small drop of blood trinkling towards the edge of her palm.

I hadn't even realized that Hazel had sliced her palm until she was already about to let her blood drip into the center of the circle.

Hazel catches the look of surprise on our faces and grins, shrugging her shoulders. "What? I wanted to go first...plus I got us into this mess." Wincing, she turns to Eve and asks, "What did you say his name was again? I know it's the name of Hades' three-headed dog..."

Eve answers her while dramatically rolling her eyes, "Cerberus".

"Cerberus, right! Thank you". Hazel turns her attention back to the circle and states his name.

Her blood hasn't even touched the ground when his low gravelly voice invades our ears. Like the first time we met; we hear him before we see him.

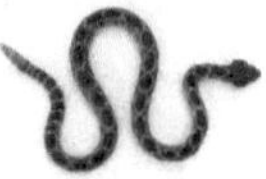

"Insistent little creatures are you not?" Cerberus states as he slowly emerges from the shadows by the front door inside my apartment.

He just stands there grinning, casually leaning up against the corner of my entry way closet, picking an invisible piece of lint off his immaculate black suit, complimented with a red tie, like he doesn't have a stress in the world.

How long has he been inside my apartment with us? He appeared before Hazel's blood hit the ground, so I know our summoning attempt didn't have anything to do with his appearance.

"Wh—, H—How long have you been there?" I ask him, stammering around my words. "You spoke before her blood hit the ground so how did you know we wanted to see you?"

"You needn't use blood to request an audience with me, just simply state my name." He pushes himself off my wall and begins slowly walking towards us. The way he walks almost seems predatory; like he is the feared hunter, and we are his prey.

"Oh great!" I respond sarcastically. "You're like Beetlejuice...God help us."

The girls quietly chuckle at my joke, which I'm sure went way over this guy's head.

"I do not know who this Beetlejuice creature is that you compare me too, but I can assure you that your so called 'God' will not be coming to your aid anytime soon, little witch."

"Never mind!" I give up, rolling my eyes and throwing my hands into the air. It's a shame that my quick wit keeps getting wasted on this uncultured Fae. "We called you here to discuss something urgent and educating you on famous 'pop culture' here in the Mortal Realm will take time we can't afford to waste. We need to get some answers that may help us stop this 'witch' serial killer we have on our hands." I turn and walk away from the Fae; giving him my back in hopes that he gets the false impression that he doesn't scare me.

I walk over to my living room window, leaning my forehead on the nice cool glass and taking a nice deep breath to refocus myself.

As I turn around to rejoin the group, Hazel jumps in and gets straight to the point...subtlety is not her strong suit. Why sugar coat it when you can go straight for the throat, I guess?

"Three women, all of whom have some connection to witchcraft, started showing up dead one week after we first spoke with you..." Cerberus doesn't have a chance to devour Hazel with his intimidating gaze, because she has walked herself right up into his face. It all happened so fast that neither Eve nor I could stop her.

She is either very brave or highly stupid...there has always been a fine line between the two when it comes to Hazel.

"Are you responsible for their deaths, or did you instruct one of your Dark Fae minions to do it for you? Or are you claiming innocence?" Cerberus's gaze narrows at Hazel following her accusations. I swear if looks could kill, she would be dead.

"How dare you insinuate that I have anything to do with this...I have no reason to want any witches' dead, however, you three are starting to change my feelings on that." he growls.

I swear the temperature in the room has gotten at least ten degrees hotter; you can literally feel the heat radiating off him. As if in sync, the hair on the back of my neck begins to rise right along with Cerberus's temper.

"Then please!" Eve begs in her sweet voice, bravely angling her body in between Hazel's and Cerberus's. "Please help us figure out who is doing this so we can stop them."

Cerberus releases a low, menacing laugh, that's accompanied by a devilish grin. "You dare accuse me of having something to do with these murders and then turn around and ask me for help in catching who the real murderer is?" He hangs his head toward the ground, shaking it back and forth in disbelief, before finally looking back up at us. One quick glimpse of the anger I saw there in his eyes has my feet wanting to run out of this room on their own accord.

He continues, letting each and every one of his words drip with disdain, "Let us not forget that you three have already made a deal with me in regard to helping solve your mothers' murders. I think I have been more than generous agreeing to help with that hopeless cause. Figure this one out on your own!"

Before he's able to up and disappear; leaving us with even more questions now than when he first arrived, I cry out, "Look can we just start over? Everyone, just take a breath and calm down."

I look around at each of them pleadingly, including Cerberus. "Sorry about the accusation. There are a lot of insane thoughts going through our minds right now, so we aren't exactly in the best head space. We just discovered how our mothers were killed...and it just so happens that they were killed in the *exact* same way as these other three women."

Something like interest flashes in his eyes, but it is there and gone so fast I can't be sure. My instincts tell me the only way to know for sure is to stay quiet and see if he takes the bait. I give the girls a subtle look that tells them to keep quiet and be patient.

Finally, after some very uncomfortable stares and what feels like hours, his curiosity finally wins out and he asks, "And how was it that your mothers were murdered? I did already make a deal with you to help solve their case, and I am a man of my word. So let me hear it."

I explain to Cerberus how our mothers were found brutally murdered in their beds; eyes scorched from their sockets and throats slit. I also make sure to quickly remind him that this is also the condition our current murder victims are being found in.

As I described how they had been murdered there was a tick in his jaw as if he was clenching his teeth together. I also could have sworn I saw pain in his eyes, followed by anger, but before I could blink, he was back to his usual 'devil-may-care' act.

I basically tell him everything Aunt Ellie had just informed us of earlier tonight. That we aren't sure if their High Priestess or the Dark Fae King had a hand in their murders. And most importantly for damage control, as to why we suspected that performing the ritual to summon him last month is somehow linked to our current murder investigations.

Cerberus listens silently while I explain everything. His temper has subsided to the point where it seems unlikely he will harm us tonight, though the outcome isn't certain as the night is still young.

"Do you know who answered our mothers when they performed the ritual thirty years ago?" I ask. "Or maybe no one answered them, and the ritual was a bust like they thought?"

He seems to study me and consider my questions before answering with a shake of his head, "No, I am not sure who answered them...if anyone even did answer them that is."

"We just thought that maybe something came through during the summoning that wasn't supposed to, in both their case and ours. And maybe you had a way to find out if we let anything out when we summoned you that is now running around killing witches..." We are both locked in a stare down with one another waiting for the other to speak up.

He is unnervingly quiet and gives off a sense of concern. It looks as though he is confounded by his feelings, like he has never experienced the feeling of worry before.

Is it even possible for Fae to show empathy towards a human? Especially a Dark Fae?

"I can assure you that only I came through when you performed your summoning incantation. And I would be willing to bet my rightful crown that whatever answered your mothers summoning back then did not cause them harm." He rakes his long fingers through his brownish-black hair; looking so disgruntled, before quickly adding, "If anything even answered their summons that is..."

A sense of relief floods my system; it feels like I can finally take a full refreshing breath of air. I can see it in my sister's body language the way their shoulders and spine relax that they are also feeling the same sense of relief.

It's as if the guilt we were feeling over these current murders is slowly rolling off our shoulders.

"Oh thank-" Hazel's starts, but her praise is cut short.

Instantly causing me to think that our feelings of relief were premature.

"The summoning you girls did may, however, be inadvertently responsible for the current murders you speak of." Cerberus states nonchalantly; like he didn't just tell us that our actions may be responsible for three women's murders.

"WHAT!?" all three of us scream out in question to Cerberus.

So much for that short-lived feeling of relief; now all I can feel is an overwhelming sense of guilt and dread.

What did he mean when he said that us performing the summoning ritual could be why these women are now being murdered? If he is so sure he is the only one that answered our call, then what could be the issue?

"I think it's time we all sit down and have a chat, little witches." Cerberus admits, not bothering to disguise the grimace on his face.

CHAPTER 8

KILLIAN

Four Weeks Prior

My father, King Erebus, has been quite the source of entertainment for the last two nights. He has completely lost his shit.

Apparently, he *felt* a power calling over through the veil that separates us from the Mortal Realm. A power he thought had been 'disposed' of twenty-four years ago. What the hell he was referring to I hadn't the slightest clue, but if it was causing him distress, I was in full support of it.

Ever since, he has been biting his advisors' heads off day and night. I can't be positive if he has even slept more than a couple hours...if at all. I have never seen him this distressed in my one-hundred and sixty-two years of life.

Whatever this is it must be an astronomical threat to himself or his precious crown, because I know he couldn't give less of a shit about our kingdom.

The Unseelie Kingdom used to be full of magics and wonders of all sorts, but since father became king, the kingdom has become a disgrace.

It appears karma has finally come to collect its due.

The only reason I have stayed here, trapped, in the Umbra Court is because I can't stand the thought of leaving my two friends, who are more like my brothers, at my father's mercy without my protection. If I left and father retaliated, I am positive they would be the first two he would go after just to spite me.

Every time I sit upon my throne, next to my father, amongst our most trusted advisors and generals in the Umbra Court; I always find myself thinking of ways to put myself out of this misery. To save myself from spending one more pointless moment with these people.

Father is a Tyrant, and rules by striking terror and fear into all the Unseelie Kingdom. He feels that if everyone in our kingdom fears him, they will be too afraid to rise against him.

That is why these meetings are pointless...no matter the issue that is brought to hand, the court is going to do whatever my father orders.

His so called 'advisors' are spineless ass kissers.

They merely sit back and encourage anything my father wants to do, even if it is committing mass genocide. I guess they feel that allowing my father to kill an entire population of Fae would be better than him killing them. All because they upset him by doing their damn jobs...

Luckily, my two friends Dante and Callum are at all these meetings, so I don't have to suffer alone. We can grab some ale after and bitch about whatever the tyrant is up to now.

Lord Dante is son to the Duke of Verigast, or as I call him Barrin. Dante and I grew up chasing each other all over the Castle of Shadows, sword fighting in the Moonlight Courtyard, and pranking the castle staff.

Our fathers were close friends, so Dante and his father would often visit, at least once within two fortnights. Verigast is located just to the East of the Castle of Shadows, no more than a four-hour journey on horseback.

Callum is the General of my father's royal guard stationed inside the Castle of Shadows, however his father General Olethros is the

General to the Kings Army, so Callum is still stuck taking military orders from his father.

If I didn't have to listen to him bitch about that fact at least once every day I would think something was wrong.

Mine and Callum's relationship got off to a rocky start. We were both two strong alpha males who wanted the respect and approval of both our fathers, so we were always throwing fist and exchanging blows.

And as we grew older, and ladies came into the story, it was a whole other battlefield we were fighting on.

Dante is the one who was finally able to bring us together... slowly. He befriended Callum, and if either me or Callum wanted to hang out with Dante, we had to start being civilized to one another.

In the end it all came together because now we are three friends/brothers, and I truly believe that any of us would lay their lives down to save the others. That is true family, the family I got to choose... Family doesn't always end with blood, and it's a shame for anyone that thinks it does.

I informed Dante and Callum to be on high alert today at this meeting because I have no idea how my father will be behaving himself, and I want to get as much information as possible about what is going on.

The doors to the throne room burst open, revealing my father who looks like he is dying for any reason to draw blood during this meeting today.

His shimmering light-gray hair has two distinct black stripes running down on each side of his head. Today though, instead of it being polished and slicked back like normal, it is very disheveled. There is hair sticking out everywhere as if he cannot keep his hands from pulling at it, it is even sticking up from the center of his onyx spiked crown.

His entire persona seems to be in a state of disarray.

His attire consists of a midnight black cloak latched around his chest, a black dress shirt with the sleeves rolled up, not neatly I might add, and dark gray slacks with black knee-high boots.

It looks like he also missed some buttons on his shirt...He does not look put together like he normally does; like a king should look.

"Are you all in on it? Have you been in on it this entire time? Counting down the days until your King's demise?" My father yells at the top of his lungs, swinging his finger around accusingly at the members of his court.

All of this before he has even sat upon his throne.

"Your King who takes care of you and all of those you love and hold dear! Your King who has made our Unseelie Kingdom the strongest in the realm!"

No one dares open their mouth during my father's rampage. He is completely livid. And what is all this talk of the Umbra Court planning his demise? He sounds completely paranoid.

"Are you not *Grateful*?!...You cowards should be groveling at my feet, begging my forgiveness for failing at your roles...to protect your king at all costs!"

"Your Majesty, if I may", Rafel my father's closest advisor inquires with a shaky voice as he takes a step closer to the dais where my father remains standing.

My father stills him with a vicious stare, but then he surprisingly concedes and gives a slight nod signaling Rafel to continue.

"Firstly, please forgive us Your Majesty for this terrible oversight. You are the greatest king to have ever graced these lands Your Majesty, and you have nothing but our undying love and devotion." Rafel pauses to take a deep breath. I suppose he does need to come up for air after sticking his head so far up my father's ass. "Our contact in the Mortal Realm has just assured us that the three witches you believed to be the catalyst to the prophecy were taken care of as you discussed twenty-four years ago."

Rafel's body begins to tremble, revealing the fear he has been trying to hide from the king. "However, it appears that all three witches each gave birth to a female heir."

Rafel's body jumps and his face cringes as my father begins to slowly rise from his throne, having only sat down moments before. "The contact cannot be certain if the girls ever came into their own powers since they were taken away to another location after their mothers were disposed of." Rafel quickly finishes, hoping to spare himself from my father's wrath.

My father slowly begins to descend the steps from the dais one at a time, never removing his gazing eyes from Rafel, who is now kneeling on the floor, bowing before the king's wrath.

"What do you mean they had daughters?" My father asks slowly, dragging out every word, every syllable dripping with rage. "If that were true, they would have been killed alongside those wretched hags that birthed them! Has the Umbra Court begun to go soft and spare children now?! And if that is so, then line yourselves up so I can personally rip your soft hearts from your chest!" Father begins yelling before finishing his rant.

There is no way every member of the Umbra Court is making it out of this room in one piece today.

Especially if the shade of red my father's face has become is any indication of how much blood he desires to shed.

"NO! I—I mean n—no—Your Majesty. The Umbra Court is here to serve, and we will kill whomever you order, age makes no difference." Rafel says, slowly looking back up with his beady black eyes to meet my father's gaze. He rises with his chin held high as he continues to assure the King, "Whomever was responsible for taking care of this directive had to have been misinformed. If the assassins had known there were blood relatives living under the same roof as the witches, they would have disposed of every living creature within the home."

I finally speak up to draw my father's attention to myself, in hopes to keep Rafel's head securely attached atop his shoulders. "King Erebus, how confident are we with the informant? Maybe they lacked that information to provide before you sent out your men, or maybe they left it out intentionally, not wanting the children to be harmed." Father doesn't even turn around to look at me, as if I am not important enough to warrant a response from him.

When he doesn't immediately respond I take this opportunity to do a little damage control. "I find that the possibility of a human informant gaining a conscious over the wellbeing of the children to be much greater than that of our Fae warriors taking pity upon children...especially human children."

The King finally turns and gives me his attention, but with the promise of death I see reflecting at me through his eyes I am wondering if I should have just let him rip Rafel's head off.

"You do not know of what you speak, *boy*." the king growls out disrespectfully.

I narrow my eyes in defiance. My father always belittles me in front of our kingdom. I believe he's afraid of me, his own son. I can see why though; since he himself killed his own stepfather, the late King Darien, to steal the crown and throne for himself.

I think he hopes that if I believe the Fae within the kingdom see me as an imbecile, the less likely I am to shove my knife straight through his wretched black heart and take his crown for myself.

"Then no harm should come from you asking them to come join us at the Castle of Shadows to discuss how this situation has come back around to cause you distress." I retort back scornfully.

I must have a death wish today.

"Lady Hera, a High Priestess within the Mortal Realm, is the one who informed me of the prophecy in the first place...the prophecy that speaks of my downfall. She has earned my full trust over the years working to aid in my endeavors throughout her realm and is an invaluable ally. That is more than I can say of you...my *son*." the king scowls at me in disgust.

That's it, I have had it with this Dark Fae bastard. I am sick of holding my tongue within the court; it is high time someone knocks this tyrant down a peg or two.

I rise from my throne but just as I am about to speak Rafel cuts in, "Your Majesty, Lady Hera did inform me that although she is uncertain of where the women stand with powers, she does know that they reside in a location called Washington D.C. And she will be of any assistance that she can to help you make sure you finally bring this atrocious prophecy to an end."

"Very well then...General Olethros!" Callum's father quickly walks before the king to stand at attention. "Call upon your best three warrior assassins and give them their directives. They are not to come back from this "Washington D.C" location until the three witches have been *dealt* with. And just so there is no confusion this time...*dead*...I want them dead! If they fail, I will line the throne room with their heads. Is that understood General?"

"Yes Sir, Your Majesty."

"At ease General"

"I will gather my three best men and send them out before the moon reaches full height." Taking a step closer to my father he implores, "Your Majesty, if I may, I would also like to volunteer myself to go along with my men to help find and eliminate these witches with haste."

"General, you will stay within the castle; I require your services for other matters. Do you have any doubts about the capabilities of your warriors?" the king inquires sternly.

"As you wish, Your Majesty." General Olethros nods, accepting the king's orders. "I will go see upon my men now. And I assure you they will accomplish this task with honor, for you, their king." General Olethros bows to the king and then hastily leaves the room.

There is still one thing in all this that I am dying to know, "King Erebus...*father*" his eyes blaze with fury as I intentionally slight him. "What is this prophecy that brings you such anxiety and anguish?" I ask mockingly with false concern.

I honestly don't expect him to respond, especially after I openly disrespected him in front of the Umbra Court. Hell, if anything I expect him to order to have my head cut off in a public execution.

After a few moments all the members present in the throne room are looking to the king and waiting for him to answer my question. They must not be aware of the prophecy either, which seems odd. Usually if there is a prophecy, let alone one regarding the current reigning royalty, more than half the kingdom would know it by heart.

"Thou Who Usurps the Throne
Shall Die by Threefold
Born of Mortal Flesh and Magic Souls
When the Power of the Trio
Come To Claim Thy Throne"

"Killian, what the hell is going on with your father? He is acting even more psychotic than normal. I was amazed we all made it out of the throne room alive today...and with all our appendages still intact." Callum asks, while indulging himself on *my* lunch I had brought to my chambers. He and Dante have made themselves at home, sitting in the lounge chairs around my fireplace.

"Seems to me like there is finally a threat to the evil bastard and his claim on the throne." I reply, knocking Callum's hand away from my sweet strawberry tarts. This man can eat enough to feed a whole army and still not be satiated. If it wasn't for all his daily training sessions with his warriors keeping him fit, I'm not sure he would be able to fit himself through my chamber door.

"I think the time has finally come for me to destroy my father and give the Unseelie Kingdom the king they deserve." I claim, staring both my friends right in their eyes, gauging for any reaction they might have towards what I just suggested.

Unsurprisingly, both Callum and Dante give the most devious of smiles and nod to one another before turning their attention back on me.

Dante enthusiastically nods and replies, "Count us in brother."

Followed by Callum's, "It's about time we take that son-of-a-bitch down. What do you have in mind?"

I can't keep the smirk off my face...I have the best companions a man could ever hope for in life. They are willing to lay their lives down to help me take down my tyrant of a father, the king whom they pledged a life of servitude to.

We all could be sentenced to death for treason if anyone were to find out about this and inform the king.

"I think we should covertly *visit* Washington D.C after your father's men cross through the veil." I say looking at Callum, popping a delectable strawberry tart into my mouth. "Then we find ourselves three *little witches*...and figure out why they are such a threat to dear old King Erebus...long live the king!"

We all have a good laugh before getting down to business. Strategizing on how we are going to hunt down these witches and what we are going to do with them once we find them. Because if it is the last thing I do, I will find them... Failure is not an option.

CHAPTER 9

CALISTA

Present Day

What in the actual fuck *did he just say? There is no way in hell that anything that just came out of his mouth was truthful...or factual. And if for some reason what he said is true, then the Mortal Realm is fucked... well and truly fucked.*

I just cannot allow myself to believe what Cerberus just told us. My mind is doing a complete tailspin; everything feels like it's spinning out of control...then again, the spinning could be from my incessant pacing back and forth in my living room.

This crazy ass Dark Fae really expects the three of us to believe that we are *'destined'* to destroy the Dark Fae King of the Unseelie Kingdom, and in doing so, keep the Mortal Realm from his dark rule and return the Unseelie Kingdom to peace!? Ha-Ha, ha, ha, ha, ha! He's got a sense of humor I'll at least give him that. Everleigh and Hazel must be just as mind blown as I am right now. Hazel is over by the back window just leaning her face against the wall with her hands over her head, while Everleigh is sitting on my couch with her elbows on her knees and her face in her hands, just staring at the floor.

Apparently if we are to believe everything Cerberus just hit us with, then it would seem, that our mothers were most likely murdered by the Dark Fae King's 'Fae assassins' due to him thinking they were the ones prophesized to destroy him. However, unbeknownst to him they each had a daughter, and my sisters and I are the true ones the prophecy speaks of.

Cerberus also believes that when my sisters and I summoned him during the ritual that the Dark Fae King must have sensed our powers; alerting him to the fact that he assassinated the wrong targets years ago, and that the actual threat to his reign is still out there.

Since the style of the current murders match up precisely to our mothers' murders, we can assume the king has sent his assassins into our realm to find and *eliminate* the threat. How he was able to pinpoint where our powers were coming from is unclear though...

I suddenly stop my pacing and march right up to Cerberus, my chest almost brushing against his, because what have I got to lose at this point right? It's either he kills me now or I die soon enough at the hands of the Dark Fae King or his assassins.

"So, to quickly recap here, you used to be the Dark Fae Prince... next in line to become the Dark Fae King...*but*...your stepbrother murdered the king, your father, and then pinned it all on you so you would be banished from the kingdom, and he could steal the crown for himself?"

Both Hazel and Everleigh rejoin reality when I begin confronting Cerberus. Stepping up behind me on either side as if to back me up if needed. Sadly, I can't imagine that even the three of us together could stand a chance going up against this powerful being standing before us.

"Correct...but I was sentenced to be executed not banished. The two Fae who were ordered to carry out my execution were very close with my father and knew that I would never cause him harm. They gave their lives to help me escape from the kingdom." Cerberus states with a look of sorrow and guilt behind his cunning hazel eyes.

"And there is supposedly a *'prophecy'* that foretells of the *'current'* Dark Fae King's demise...and you think it is talking about the three of us?" I ask skeptically, tilting my head and motioning to me and my sisters.

He gives a tight nod. I can't spot a single 'tell' to confirm if he is feeding us lies.

"And as long as the Dark Fae King believes us to still be alive, he will continue to hunt us down until we are dead?" I ask before quickly adding, "Even though we most likely are—*NOT*—the correct ones the prophecy is speaking of."

"Oh, I assure you, *you* are. And yes, King Erebus will not rest until he knows the three of you are dead and no longer a threat to his reign."

"How are you so confident that it is the three of us?" Everleigh asks, speaking up from behind my shoulder.

Not sure if it's just because my mind is under a hell of a lot of stress right now, but Cerberus looks almost *remorseful* in response to Everleigh's question. Of course, that only lasted maybe two seconds and then he was back to his 'I'm a bad-ass Dark Fae' self.

"If your mother's deaths aren't substantiating enough for you, then know I *felt* you...your powers."

I'm sure we are all giving him a look of uncertainty, or at least I sure am. What is so special about our powers? Of course, he felt our powers...we were doing a summoning ritual using our powers, and he answered. I bet if he answered anyone else's summons, he would feel their powers as well, right?

"Your powers are stronger than you know. I am the rightful Dark Fae King of the Unseelie Kingdom, I am one of the strongest Fae in the realm. But when you finally accept your abilities and all their strengths, together, you three will be unstoppable in the Fae Realm." Cerberus encourages, as he continues looking back and forth between the three of us.

"Individually you are each powerful in your own ways...but together you will be a formidable force." Cerberus remarks as he turns to walk off.

"Wait you can't just leave! You haven't even told us how we are supposed to defeat this...King Erebus! Or what this so called 'prophecy' states?!" Hazel yells as she grabs hold of his arm to force his attention back to us.

"Now that we know the king has a hand in these murders that are occurring, we need to be extra cautious. We must keep our meetings brief, given the chance that he or his assassins can sense my power here amongst this realm...it could lead them right to you. Stay vigilant, stay together, and look inside yourselves to see your true potential." He says before turning and walking off into the shadows of my apartment, leaving us standing there speechless.

However, right before the shadows completely devour him, he remarks,

"Thou Who Usurps the Throne
Shall Die by Threefold
Born of Mortal Flesh and Magic Souls
When the Power of the Trio
Come To Claim Thy Throne"

Again, he disappears, leaving us here in my living room staring dumfounded into a void of shadows. *Asshole*.

CHAPTER 10

CALISTA

The workday couldn't be over soon enough. I just want to get home, put on my comfy clothes, and drown myself with wine and horror movies until I can no longer think about the absolute shit-show we are now starring in.

After the bomb that got dropped on us last night, the three of us decided to call it a night. We all needed some time to process the information.

I decided to follow Hazel home and crash on her couch; I was a little spooked to sleep in my apartment alone after Cerberus said his presence may draw the Fae assassins to us. We stopped by Everleigh's to grab a change of clothes since she was joining us. Eve got the guest room seeing as how she was going to be permanently staying with Hazel; at least until this assassin/witch serial killer mess is dealt with.

"Let me guess...you and the girls pulled an all-nighter at the club?" Seb taunts as he saunters into the office, looking immaculate and handsome like always. His sky-blue dress shirt makes his brilliant blue eyes stand out even more than usual.

My mind is wound so tight it's all I can do to lift my eyes up to meet his. "What are you on about?" I ask, while leaning back in my chair with my arms crossed over my chest.

"I was just taking a guess at why you have your 'mega bitch' face on this morning is all. She always seems to make an appearance after a long night of little sleep and loads of booze." he teases, looking down at me with that smug smile of his.

If I didn't consider him a member of the family, I probably would deck him in the face for saying that. But then again, if he was my brother, I would most definitely deck him right in his perfectly straight nose.

Leaning forward I splay my arms out across my desk and look up at him with the sweetest *fake* smile I can manage. "Gee thanks Seb, you know just what to say to make a woman smile...No good morning beautiful!? Did I tell you how *awesome* of a partner you are? I only hope to be as *amazing* as you are one day."

Seb bursts out laughing and doesn't stop until he is finally seated down at his desk. Which annoyingly is directly across from mine.

Around lunchtime, the captain convenes a meeting to collect updates on our ongoing case and formulate a new strategy to apprehend the serial killer before he strikes again.

"Detective Adams", Captain Abrahm shouts. I swear the man needs hearing aids. "Where are we with our serial killer case?"

"CSI are still searching for anything solid to send us in the right direction." I respond, standing up to address my colleagues. "So far, we have confirmed that the first two victims did know the third, Ms. Townsen, the shop owner. It has not yet been confirmed if the first two victims knew one another, but their names were listed in Ms. Townsen's logbook that we found on her desk in the shop. They appear to have been customers of hers. We are currently unsure of any other links connecting the three women. I advised Lieutenant Daniels that it may be wise to contact all the names disclosed on that list to at least advise them to be aware of the situation. It seems highly unlikely that it is just a coincidence that two of our victims were on that list. I am awaiting permission to follow through on that as we speak, Sir."

"Permission granted Detective, take your team and get to work contacting those individuals. Do your best to not stir up panic...the last thing we need is the whole city up our ass, calling in at every little creak they hear inside their home. Then interview the first two victim's friends and family to see if they know of any connection between the two of them." He commands, dismissing my team and I to get to work.

"Yes Sir", I reply. Then I slowly turn and head for the exit. Little does the captain know, but my sisters and I have already taken care of the latter. The only link between the first two victims was they may have been fooling around with witchcraft, but I wasn't quite ready to reveal that just yet.

After speaking to Jessa Walken's mother and sister, I am now even more positive that Hazel's investigation into their backgrounds is correct. Both the mother and sister confirmed they had no knowledge of anyone named Valerie Elkins, and they knew most, if not all, of Jessa's friends. Neither of them recognized a photo of Valerie either.

The same was confirmed when I asked them about Ms. Townsen and showed them a photo of her. As we suspected, there was no personal relationship between these two either...just a shop owner and their customer.

So, unless they are extremely good at lying under pressure, I think we can check off that the first two victims had no personal relationship with one another or to Ms. Townsen. However, we will still go and speak to someone from Jessa's circle of friends and to Valerie's family and friends just to be sure.

"Want to grab lunch before we head over to speak with Mr. Elkins?" I ask Seb. Mr. Elkins is Valerie's now widowed husband.

"Hell yes, I'm starving! Burgers or Tacos?"

"Definitely Tacos!", easiest question I've gotten all day.

"So, Eve is staying at Hazel's now?" Seb asks, looking over at me from the driver's seat. Sporting his favorite pair of Aviator sunglasses. I always tease that they give me "Terminator" vibes when he wears them. However, I think all that does is encourage him to wear them whenever he gets the chance.

I glare over at him suspiciously before asking, "How did you know that? She just started staying there last night..."

Seb startles.

I just startled Sebastian. I don't think that's ever happened before. Now my curiosity is really peaked.

I can see him racking his brain for a quick retort to my question. There is no way in hell Seb is my sister's 'mystery man' we keep hounding her about...at least I hope not. The vibe in this car just got super awkward.

"You told me this morning remember? I'm pretty sure 'mega-bitch' was still in charge of your mind and body, so I understand if you forgot." He laughs, pushing me lightly on my arm.

I'm finally able to let out a 'silent' sigh of relief. My mind was all over the place this morning, so I probably did mention it to him and just forgot.

"Oh, sorry, my mind just isn't completely with it today." I say, smiling over at him. "But yeah, her and Hazel are going to be giving the whole 'roommate' thing a try...it's only temporary...she can move back once we catch this bastard." I turn and face out the window as the reality of what we are up against comes crashing back down on me. Just thinking about it makes my guts churn. Which is pissing me off because nothing comes between me and some delicious tacos.

"Maybe she should go stay with your Aunt Eleanor if you all are worried about her name being on that list."

"We tried to talk her into that already, but she refuses to leave me and Hazel" I explain to him, turning even more to face out the window so he can't see how concerned I really am for her safety now that we know what's really going on.

"Well, you know you three are my girls so if she would feel safer crashing at my place, she can..." he suggests, acting a little too nonchalant about his offer. "Or if that is weird all of you are welcome to crash, one of you will have to take the couch but we can make it work." he smiles over at me, and it really does warm my heart for how much he genuinely cares about me and my sisters.

"Do I get to share that big king-size bed of yours with you?", I ask giving him a sly smirk. "I promise to be the little spoon." I tease, winking over at him.

Seb bursts out laughing and I follow right along. His laugh is so contagious. I really needed this today...this moment makes my current situation seem a little less hopeless.

"No, but to be real, I don't think Eve's 'mystery man' would approve of her crashing at her *sexy* friend's house." I make sure to wiggle my eyebrows over at him all 'suggestively'. Which seems to only encourage our laughter.

"Oh shit! Mystery Man, huh? I think I could take him", he replies, shooting me a wicked grin. I couldn't imagine not having Seb in our lives. It's like he's been with us forever; the way our relationships flow so naturally together.

We drive in silence the rest of the way to our favorite taco spot, the Tipsy Tacos food truck.

Arriving back at the office around four o'clock, I write up a quick report of our findings today and take them to Lieutenant Daniels. As expected, there is no evidence that connects the first two victims... other than they both dabbled in witchcraft in some way, shape, or form. Of course, I yet again leave that little tidbit of information out of the report. Feeling exhausted, I decide to call it a day and go home early. I could really use a nap in my own bed before meeting back up with the girls tonight.

I can vaguely make out the sound of chimes, but they sound distant. Feeling woozy in my head I try to focus on the chimes, pulling myself closer to the sound. Finally, my conscience breaks through the fog in my head, placing me right back in reality where my cell phone is now ringing next to my head on my nightstand.

I shake my head back and forth trying to fight off the last of my brain fog. I hate the feeling you get when you are woken up in the middle of a good sleep.

Eve is calling me...has been calling me...looks like I have four missed calls from her. Finally, feeling coherent enough I answer her call. "Hey!" I say trying to sound awake, but I know she can hear the raspy tone of my voice.

"Oh, thank gosh!" Eve shouts, sounding relieved that she finally got ahold of me. "I have been trying to get ahold of you! If you hadn't answered this time Hazel and I were going to burst up in your apartment to check on you."

"Sorry about that...I must have taken a seriously deep nap; I was exhausted from trying to sleep on Hazel's lumpy couch last night."

"Hey, my couch is super comfortable!" Hazel yells in the background. Like always, Eve has me on speaker phone. I'm glad they both are together and taking Cerberus's warning seriously...when here I am all alone in my apartment. It's like I'm sitting around just asking to be horribly murdered.

Looking at the clock I curse, "Fuck! It's seven-thirty already? Damn that must have been some good sleep I was getting. I think I could have slept through the night if you hadn't woken me."

"Well get your lazy ass up and meet us at All Souls...Hazel is insisting we change up our Friday night routine, and I quote 'get our drink on'." Eve mocks, trying to imitate Hazel's voice.

All Souls is a local bar we frequent. The bar tenders know us well, and the patrons are mostly a super chill crowd. With a nice long bar, large dance floor, and several pool tables, it's the perfect place to meet up and release our pent up stress and enjoy ourselves.

I erupt with laughter, "So, are we getting drunk and making bad decisions tonight? That sounds like the plot of every scary movie we watch...you sure you don't want to snuggle up and watch other people make those decisions?"

I can hear them both laughing and begging me to come out with them. Of course, I'm going to cave in and go. They know I can never resist a night out with them.

"Fine" I drawl, giving in to their incessant begging. "What time am I meeting you there?"

"Nine o'clock...if you aren't there by ten, I'm calling the police." Eve warns. And I know she is serious.

"Roger that sis, and maybe you should put baby sis on a leash to-night.", I tease. "She already sounds like she is five sheets to the wind."

"Hey!" I hear Hazel shout as I end the call.

CHAPTER 11

CALISTA

Shit! It's nine-thirty already.

I decided to take a nice hot bubble bath when I got off the phone with my sisters. I must have accidentally dozed off, because when I closed my eyes, the water was nice and steamy, but when I finally opened them, the water was cold. But shit, I need the rest, these past couple months have been exhausting.

I decided to go all out tonight, full makeup, sexy outfit, the works. Ninety percent of the week I am a minimalist when it comes to makeup. But I mean who do I have to impress? Other than hitting the bars or going out to eat with my sisters all I do is work, day in and day out. It's not like I care to impress any of the arrogant assholes I work with, and the victims sure as hell don't care what I look like... seeing as how they are already dead and all.

I have on my red satin halter that is connected at the back of my neck by an embroidered black snake, slithering up my spine. Black dressy short shorts that complement the snake on my blouse and shows some cheeks if I bend over enough. I finished off my outfit with black satin high heels that wrap around my ankle with opened slats down the top of my foot.

Lastly, I straightened my long chocolate brown hair and made a smokey eye with black mascara to enhance my long dark lashes, drawing attention to the golden flecks floating throughout my emerald-green eyes. I also applied a little red-rose color to my naturally full, round lips to pull it all together.

I usually don't say this about myself but standing in front of my full-length mirror tonight, I can honestly say...*Damn I'm sexy*.

Right as I'm putting my cell phone in my little black clutch, Eve calls. *Gosh she is persistent.* I better answer before she calls the police to come bust through my door.

"I'm literally heading out the door now" I say, as soon as I answer the call.

"Forget about that...we have a problem...possibly a *huge* one." Eve whispers, her voice quivering. "We are at All Souls...I'm in a bathroom stall right now."

Shit, this really can't be good if Eve is desperate enough to hide out in a bathroom stall. That girl hates public restrooms, and there must be an *emergency* to get her anywhere near one.

"The whole restaurant is shaking like we are in an earthquake. And before you ask, yes, I'm the only one noticing it." Eve pauses taking in a shaky breath. "There is something *wrong* in here...and very powerful. I've never experienced an intense feeling like this before. I almost fell off the stool, it disoriented me so much. Do you think the assassins could be here?"

Her voice is becoming frantic. I need to try and calm her down long enough for me to get there.

"Eve, I need you to relax and take a deep breath for me." I can hear her take a big inhale through her nose and release it through her mouth. Good. "Where is Hazel? Is she safe?"

"Yes, she is still sitting at the bar, trying to spot anything unusual."

Hazel is telekinetic (moves objects with her mind) and telepathic (can hear people's thoughts). When Hazel is around the supernatural her powers come to the surface; she usually ends up with a horrible headache and loud screaming thoughts coming from the supernatural being. Her ability is very helpful when we are in a roomful of people, and we sense a powerful presence; she can usually pinpoint which being the loud thoughts are coming from and then I can confirm by seeing the being's true self. Another 'fun' ability of mine. I can *see* and *sense* power in the living, or 'beings' disguising themselves as such. I can see their true faces and get a sense of how powerful the beings are.

My abilities made their debut on the day of my sixteenth birthday. If you really want your friends and family to think you are insane, try explaining to them that the reason you no longer wish to leave your house is because every time you do you see 'monsters' that have you screaming and crying in public.

Aunt Ellie explained that the 'facial apparitions' I saw were those of the Fae. She told us how some Fae are beautiful beyond words and how others are the things of nightmares. She also explained to us that one of the most important things to remember is that even those that are most fair can be the most lethal.

"She can't seem to pick up anything with her telepathy. She believes they somehow have their thoughts shielded." Eve is finally starting to sound like she is getting her nerves under control. "Can you please get down here and see if you can figure out who my powers are reacting to? It's so strong, I wouldn't be surprised if there is more than one being here tonight."

I'm trying hard to keep the thought of that possibility out of my head. I need my mind to be clear and focused when I arrive at All Souls. This way, if the Fae assassins are there, my sisters and I may stand a small chance at making it through tonight with our eyeballs safe in their sockets.

"I'm already on my way, go back to the bar with Hazel and act like everything's normal." I started out the door as soon as she said something wasn't right, so it won't take me too long to reach them.

They should be safe there...the serial-killer-assassins wouldn't be crazy enough to strike in public, would they? Nope, erasing that thought from my mind.

"Love you sis!" I tell Eve before ending our call. Then I take off walking as fast as I can in these stupid heels; of all the nights I decide to dress up...

Thankfully I have been doing extra cardio at the gym, otherwise I would be panting and struggling to catch my breath as I finally arrive at All Souls. I'm making a mental note to toss these damn heels in the trash tomorrow...or at least to the very back of my closet.

I pretty much ran the last block here. I started feeling a strange *'pull'*, that kept getting stronger the closer I got. My magic has never done that before, so I have no idea what it could be trying to tell me. And that scares me...

I pause before I round the corner to the entrance of the bar; just long enough to compose myself. I want to go in looking completely normal, so I don't raise any concern from the other bar patrons.

As soon as I walk into the bar, that *pull* that I have been feeling has my eyes shooting straight over to the end of the bar. There I see the most gorgeous man I have ever laid eyes on...and he is staring right back at me...

I am instantly overcome by this overwhelming sense of having met this man before; that I know him somehow. However, I know I would never have forgotten a face like his, it would be a crime to...his beauty is otherworldly.

He is wearing a plain black T-shirt, jeans, and black biker boots. His whole outfit makes his light blond hair, and stunning dark eyes stand out even more. The way both his T-shirt and jeans tightly cling around his defined muscles, I can tell he has a hard, ripped physique.

The way his T-shirt pulls tightly across his broad chest while the sleeves wrap tightly around his large muscular biceps has me licking my lips. Then those thick muscular thighs that look one wrong move away from ripping his jeans in two. Don't even get me on that sexy strong jawline...

Seconds later; the unexpected arousal that suddenly overtook my brain and body settles down, and my heart no longer feels like it's going to fly out of my chest and straight into this stranger's hands.

That's when I finally remember why I am here...my sisters need me. *Shit!*

Averting my eyes from the stranger down the bar, I look around finding my sisters sitting not eight stools away from him. I take the stool to Eve's left so I can keep the handsome stranger in my line of sight. When I chance a glance over her shoulder, I find he is still staring at me. I avert my eyes from his quickly, hoping he can't see the blush that's creeping up on my cheeks.

"Hey, are you all alright?" I ask my sisters as soon as my ass hits the stool.

Before Eve can get a word out Hazel lets out the most excited scream and shouts over to me, "Yesss! You made it! I told the bar tender we are dancing on his bar later tonight!" She slings her arms around my neck and plants a sloppy kiss on my cheek. I can't help but to smile and roll my eyes at my crazy little sister.

I'm now starting to wonder if this *being* inside the bar is blocking her telepathy ability, or if maybe she is just too drunk to use it.

"Hey, we are fine. Thanks for getting here so fast." Eve says, smiling over at me. "Obviously Hazel isn't too concerned about it at the moment." We both laugh, shaking our heads at our little sis.

"Of course, how are you feeling now? Still experiencing that earthquake?"

"It's calmed down a lot, there is still a constant rumble, but I'm trying to keep my magic in check."

"Do you have any clue as to who it could be? Or if it's *multiple* beings?" I ask as I casually look around trying to spot the culprit.

"No, it's like trying to use a compass in a room full of magnets... my magic is all over the place." Eve says. Concern is plastered all over her face.

"Well, I did notice the most gorgeous man in existence sitting at the end of the bar...don't look!" I quickly grab her hand as she begins instinctively turning around to look. I don't want her to give away that we are talking about him. "*Casually* turn around to get Hazel's attention for something and then sneak a peek." She nods and then does just that.

"Holy Hell!" Eve sounds astonished, looking at me with her mouth hanging open. "He is delicious...he could have me any way he wants me...upside down...sideways...Owe!" She looks at me with a silly frown after I finally reach over and slap her arm to shut her up. "What was that for?"

"Well first off I saw him first, so I call dibs, but more importantly, he is *not* human." I pause, chancing another glance his way, this time he doesn't see me do it. Lowering my voice I continue, "At first, I didn't notice it." Probably because I was too busy drooling. "There are black *shadows* emanating off him. They are faint but they are there. He must be super powerful because I can't even see his true face...or maybe that is his true face. He's literally drop dead gorgeous, so I'm guessing a High Dark Fae. And it makes sense because the High Fae truly do look like humans; extraordinarily beautiful humans, that is. What we see is their true face, so they have no need to disguise themselves."

I give Eve a casual smile so if anyone is paying attention to us it will look like we are just having a normal conversation. Not discussing the fact that the assassin sent here to kill us may be sitting at the other end of the bar.

"So, what should we do?" Eve asks, trying her best to seem calm, but we both know on the inside she is losing her shit.

What is he—Oh Shit!

"We shut up and play it cool, because he's coming this way." I inform her, smiling and laughing at her like she just said something funny.

I noticed him moving from the corner of my eye while Eve and I were talking. It looked like he was heading in our direction, but I wasn't sure. While laughing at Eve, I looked up to follow his movements...and his eyes were dead set on me. Confirming my suspicions that he was heading directly for *me*.

This gorgeous, but most likely, dangerous Dark Fae, gives me a sweet flirty smirk before coming to my other side and leaning his elbows down against the bar. My eyes go wide giving Eve my *'Oh shit! What do I do?!'* look. Before I plaster on my own flirty smile and turn around to face him.

Hazel has no idea of what's happening right behind her; the cute guy sitting beside her has her full attention, but maybe that's for the best since she is already drunk. I can only imagine what information she would let slip to our Dark Fae assassin friend here.

When my eyes lock onto his, both of our smiles instantly turn genuine. It's like the muscles in my cheeks have taken on a mind of their own. I can't help but smile at him...and it seems like I'm having that effect on him too. It feels like we have smiled at each other like this a hundred times before.

Shaking his head full of luscious blond hair; he breaks eye contact and stares down at the bar before returning his gaze back to mine. His dark eyes are even more stunning up close; they are such a deep blue that they could pass as grey. It's like staring out at the ocean in the middle of a storm.

"Can I buy you a drink?" he asks. His deep, dark, husky voice matches perfectly with the bad boy persona he is giving off. Not to mention just the sound of his voice is enough to make my toes curl.

I feel so giddy! Like a freaking schoolgirl who just got asked to prom by the most popular boy in school.

I don't know what is wrong with me tonight, but this man has some sort of effect on me. And I don't completely *dislike* it if I'm being honest with myself.

"Well, that depends..." I reply in a sultry voice, while grinning up at him.

"Oh yeah?" he says, smirking down at me "On what?"

This man is so tall that if I stood up next to him, he would still be towering over me. Even with me sitting on this bar stool I only come up to the upper part of his chest.

"You have a name stranger?"

His lips curve into a devilish grin; I'm sure with looks like his, he has never had a girl play hard to get with him before. I hope he likes a challenge...because he is going to get one.

"Killian" he answers, holding out his hand for me to shake.

Giving in to his devilish charm I place my hand in his before jerking it back immediately.

Ouch! His hand just shocked me! It felt more *weird* than *painful*, but I still wasn't ready for it. It was like an electric current shot between us, more of a vibrating sensation than pain.

"Whoa! Sorry about that I guess we have more of a connection than I thought." He lets out a low chuckle as we both shake out our hands.

He felt the shock too...I wonder if it has anything to do with him being a Fae and me a witch? Strange...does that mean he knows I have magic now? Shit!

Extending my hand back out towards him to try again, I smile and tell him my name, "Calista".

His grin returns as he reaches out and shakes my hand, "Pleasure to meet you, *Calista.*"

The sound of my name coming from his lips captures my breath. This man is so *dangerous*...assassin or not.

"So can I get you that drink?"

"Sure", I reply with a smile, "Rum and coke please".

The bartender returns shortly with our drinks. Killian ordered himself a whisky neat...*gag*...I hate that stuff.

Killian turns to me and points to where he just came from at the end of the bar, "Care to join me down there?"

I scrunch up my eyebrows, giving him a look that says, 'Why? Are you going to kidnap me?'

He must understand because he quickly explains, "It's much quieter on that end, we can actually hear ourselves think."

He makes a fair point, so I accept his invite and tell him to go save us a seat. I explain to him that I don't want to leave my friends without telling them where I am going first. Luckily, he doesn't seem to mind and goes back to the end of the bar to grab us both a stool and wait.

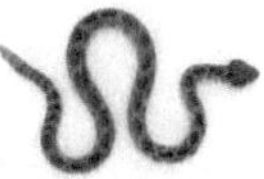

Both Eve and Hazel turn to face me so fast once Killian walks away that I wouldn't be surprised if they just gave themselves whiplash.

"What happened?" Hazel asks, her words only slightly slurring. Obviously, Eve has filled her in on what's going on.

"He got me a drink and asked me to join him down there." I gesture to where he is sitting at the bar.

"He's hot! Are you going to go?", Hazel asks, still too drunk to understand the seriousness of the situation we might be facing.

Laughing at my oblivious sister, I tell them both that I am going to go sit with Killian in hopes of getting some information from him. Maybe he is the one sent here to kill us, or maybe he is just a powerful Dark Fae who happens to be in the same bar as us tonight.

I doubt we will get lucky enough for it to be the latter, but here goes nothing.

As soon as I join Killian down the bar, I begin my questioning. I can't help it; it's like the detective in me instinctively takes over.

"Thank you for the drink. Are you new around here? Without meaning to sound like an alcoholic...I come here a lot, but this is my first time seeing you here."

He gives me a short laugh, if you can call it that, "Yeah, I just got into town a few days ago. I wasn't planning on staying long, but after taking in some of the *scenery* I'm thinking I should change my plans." He is staring right at me grinning from ear to ear. He must think he is so slick using that line with his handsome smile and that cute little dimple...

Shit! Focus Calista, focus.

I release a short laugh and roll my eyes, before locking eyes with him again. "Wow! Does that line work with all the ladies? Or just the extremely desperate ones?"

His facial expression becomes serious as he looks me dead in the eyes and says, "I've never said that to anyone before; surprised myself if I'm being honest. But as soon as I saw you walk through those doors, I *knew* I had to talk to you."

"Did you now?", I ask looking at him skeptically.

His stare keeps growing more intense by the second, "I feel like I know you somehow, but I know we haven't met. I would have remembered. With a beautiful name like *Ca-list-a,*" he lets my name roll off his tongue, enunciating every syllable, "and the exceptionally gorgeous woman it belongs too."

Damn, he's good!

There goes my stupid heart fluttering all over the place again. Maybe I'm not acting a fool over some man I just met, but instead, I'm just getting ready to fall over dead from an undiagnosed heart condition...yeah, I'll go with that.

I feign to be unaffected by his smooth talking, scrounging up another eye roll for him.

Noticing, he laughs and shakes his head. "No, I'm serious though...have we met before?"

Surprisingly I can hear the sincerity in his question, which brings me back to how I felt when I first locked eyes with him when I walked into the bar. I had felt like I knew him somehow, as well.

"That's strange...because when I first walked in and saw you, I could have sworn I knew you somehow too. I'm pretty good at remembering faces, it comes with my job. And though something about you seems strangely familiar, I am certain I have never seen you before tonight."

We both sit silently, staring intensely at one another; like one of us is a puzzle the other is trying to solve.

His entire body language and demeanor puts me in mind of the man I fell for in my dreams. From the moment my abilities started to appear at the age of sixteen right up until my eighteenth birthday, I dreamt of him almost every night. But when I turned eighteen my dreams just stopped...and I was left heartbroken, mourning over a man that only ever existed in my subconscious.

Killian finally breaks the trance we seemed to have fallen into. "So, you were checking me out when you first walked in?" he feigns surprise while flashing a wicked grin. He knows damn well that I saw him, we had locked eyes with each other for at least a solid thirty-seconds.

"Ha-ha, you think you're sooo funny. Sorry to tell you this but I was just trying to make sure you were breathing. It was hard to tell with your jaw hanging on the ground surrounded by a ginormous puddle of drool." I tease, grinning back at him.

We sit at the bar a while longer; teasing back and forth and throwing back a couple more drinks. The chemistry between us is insane; sometimes the looks he gives me sends a shiver shooting straight down my spine and into my toes.

Why does he have to be a powerful being; most likely a Dark Fae assassin here to kill me and my sisters?

Sounds about right though. A hot funny guy finally shows interest in me, and the feeling is mutual, however he most likely plans on killing me later.

It doesn't bode well for a healthy relationship.

"So, what is it you do for work? I know it involves you remembering a lot of faces." Killian asks, recalling the statement I made earlier about my job.

He's even a good listener?! Why do all bad things in life happen to me!? Great, now even my inner monologue is depressed he's off limits.

"I'm a homicide detective for the DC Metropolitan Police Department." I keep my eyes on him to study his reaction; if he is the one responsible for the murders maybe I can spot a tell. "What about you? Is it your work that brought you to town?" Now I got him.

"I'm freelance actually...I used to work for a tyrant, then I woke up one morning and finally decided it was time for a change."

"Oh? And what exactly is it you do now...being *freelance*?" I'm trying my best to give him an alluring stare, but damn, it's been *too* long since my last date with a man. I'm just hoping that I'm coming across like I think it's *super* attractive that he is his own boss and that I *genuinely* want to hear more.

"I'm afraid that's confidential...If I told you I'd have to kill you."

Cough, cough....

His reply catches me off guard and causes me to choke on my rum and coke. I'm glad it didn't shoot out from my nose, but so much for playing it cool.

The look he is giving me right now is so devious. I would bet money he is over there silently laughing to himself because of the irony of what he just said. He is going to try and kill me no matter what.

"That's too bad", I take a slow sip of my drink, never taking my eyes off his. "See there is a serial killer on the loose right now, and without your cooperation in answering my questions I may just have to put you down as a suspect..." I consider giving him a smile or a wink to play off what I just said as a joke, but the concern and seriousness I can see on his face makes me hesitate.

"Is that so?... What if I told you I was here looking into that same exact situation as well?" He asks, dead serious.

I'm sure you are since you are the one doing the killing!

"Then I would tell you that you are full of shit! I know every person involved with this case." I retort, sounding very accusative.

"Whoa" Killian concedes, holds up both hands in surrender. "Didn't mean to make myself a suspect, I was just pulling your chain."

Now every nerve in my body is on high alert...something just isn't sitting right with me. We both keep staring at each other like we are both waiting for the other shoe to drop.

Before I have the chance to make up an excuse to leave his company, Def Leppard's *Pour Some Sugar on Me* starts blaring from the speakers around the room. I silently send out a *Thank You* to Hazel. This gives me the perfect excuse to leave.

"Welp, that's my cue...thanks again for the drinks. I hope you have a great time in the city while you're here." I excuse myself, getting up about to walk back to where my sisters are seated.

"Wait!" Killian tries to insist, but then Hazel comes up beside me grabbing my arm and pulling me away.

"It's on! Come on! You promised me!" Hazel keeps screaming at me until I finally turn and follow her through the crowded bar.

"Can I see you again?" Killian shouts after me.

"Sorry!" I say pointing towards my ears as if I can't hear what he just said, even though I heard him just fine. He may be the most exquisite being I've ever seen, but I'm not going to schedule a time to meet up with him so he can kill me. I'm aroused, not stupid...

I reluctantly hop up on the bar with Hazel to perform my duty as big sister and look crazy right beside her, as we try our best to look sexy while dancing atop the bar. I notice Killian stop below where I'm currently swinging my arms in the air and swaying my hips to the beat.

Looking down at him, I can see he has a napkin in his hand that he is offering up to me. I take it and watch as he gives me a sly smile and walks out of the bar.

After the song goes off, the girls and I find our way back to our seats. I tell them everything that happened during my talk with Killian. Even the fact that both of us felt as if we had met before tonight.

We have another drink and then decide to call it a night. They keep insisting I stay with them at Hazel's, but I just want to sleep in my own bed. Hazel's couch makes me restless, and I really need the rest. After ten minutes of their incessant pleading and begging, they finally give up and agree to let me go home so I can sleep in my own bed. I promise them I will call them as soon as I get back to my apartment safe and sound.

When I finally arrive back home, I reach into my clutch to find my phone and call my sisters. However, my fingers find something else...the napkin Killian had handed me. I had just crinkled it up in my shorts pocket until I was able to toss it into my clutch.

I study the napkin as I walk to my bedroom, fully intending to fall asleep entirely clothed.

It is a regular napkin from the bar. On the backside, it appears that he has written something:

I think we can help each other. I'm staying at Hotel Hive.
I look forward to seeing you again.

   -Killian

CHAPTER 12

KILLIAN

"He's back!", Callum calls out to Dante as soon as he sees me walk through the front door. "We thought you would be back by now. Started to get worried about you." he says before looking at me concerningly. "Everything go, okay? You look like you saw a ghost..."

I didn't intend to show back up wearing all these emotions on my face, but these two are my best friends so if anyone is going to notice it would be them. I can only imagine the look I have on my face right now, because I feel like I did in fact see a ghost tonight. The ghost of someone I searched for across all Stellaris for years trying to find. Before finally accepting defeat.

I always wondered if maybe she was a figment of my imagination, that my mind configured knowing how badly I longed for companionship. It was just a twisted trick my mind played on me, allowing me to give my heart away to this imaginary being only for them to just disappear and take it with them.

I never in my most desperate of times had considered that maybe she didn't reside in the Fae Realm at all. That maybe the woman who stole my heart ten years ago came from a different realm. The

Mortal Realm...she was a *human?* That's an impossible thought, right? Humans cannot just come and go as they please into the Fae Realm, and even if they could it's against the Human-Fae agreement.

All I know is now I have more questions than ever before...

"Whoa shit, you're right he doesn't look so good. Dante to Killian... snap out of it!" Dante yells, snapping his fingers in front of my face, pulling me out of my entrapping thoughts. I hadn't even noticed him enter the room with us.

I walk over and take a seat on the couch opposite Callum. Dante follows, sitting in the chair across from us both. "Shit" I mutter, rubbing my hands back and forth across my face, trying to figure out what to say next. "I think I finally found her...she has been here in the Mortal Realm all along." I say looking between them both.

"Wh—" Callum starts but Dante interrupts.

"You mean *her?* Like the girl we searched all over Stellaris for because she was 'the one?'" Dante asks, doing the air quotes and all. I give him a subtle nod, because I'm still not sure if I'm correct or if it's just wishful thinking. But I would recognize that fair skin and adorable round nose anywhere, especially those mesmerizing green eyes. I still see them every night when I close my eyes.

"Shit!" Callum exclaims rising from his seat. "So, she is a human? She was here the entire time? No wonder we could never pick up a trail on her."

"I didn't find shit on your dad's men" I inform Callum, "On the way back here I was passing by this bar when this weird feeling came over me. I couldn't shake it; it was like *something* was telling me to go inside. Next thing I knew I was walking inside and ordering a drink. I sat there for about a half hour and was about to pay my tab and leave when I felt this *pull*...like there was a string inside of me and something was tugging on the other end. The pull of the string became so powerful I swear I could almost visualize it in my mind. That's when I looked up and saw *her* walk through the doors."

Callum goes over and grabs us all a beer while I continued walking them through my night and my encounter with Calista.

"What are you going to do if she doesn't show up here?" Callum asks.

"Oh, she will show. She wants to catch these guys as much as we do, and if she is anything like who she used to be, the uncertainty will eat away at her until she finds out what I know."

I rise from my seat and walk over to the kitchen where I rest my hands on the counter and hang my head. "She thinks I may be the killer." I turn and head for the hallway that connects to the bedroom I'm using during our stay. I need to lay down and think...and hopefully get some sleep. My brain is overloaded right now though, so I don't know if I will be lucky enough to accomplish that.

Before disappearing into the hallway, I turn back around to face my friends. I want to see their reactions to this next bit of information I need to share with them.

I casually disclose to them, "Oh, and I'm almost positive we found our three witches...it's her...and her two companions."

With that I leave them both slack jawed and staring blankly at one another while I head off to bed. We can discuss it more in the morning, but for right now my world has been turned upside down.

I could feel the power flowing from her when she sat next to me...I think she was trying to get a *read* on me, but I blocked her out. I also felt the essence of power coming from the two women she was drinking with at the bar; even as weak as it was.

Now I just wait for Calista to take the bait...because I know she won't be able to resist gaining pertinent information...or *me*.

CHAPTER 13

CALISTA

Killian is arrogant...I'll give him that. Thinking he can lure me in with his cryptic message so tactfully written on a bar napkin. Well, I have news for him, he is going to have to do more than that to get me alone with him.

He is now number one on my suspect list after the conversation last night at the bar and this message I've been staring at on my kitchen island all morning.

I really want to run a background check on him, but I know next to nothing about him. I never asked for his last name or where he is visiting from. The only real information I can work with now is that he is staying at Hotel Hive. That super swanky hotel right across the street from the campus of George Washington University.

Besides that, given that I am ninety-nine percent sure he is a Fae; he would only be in the system if he has had any prior convictions within the Mortal Realm.

I guess my next step is to take a nice hot shower to wash off my hangover from last night and then call Hotel Hive to inquire about Killian. Firstly, I want to confirm he is really staying there. Once I get confirmation on that, I will need any information he might have provided them. How long has he been there? Does he have a set departure date? What credit card does he have on file?... etc.

He said he's only been in town for a few days but if he is the person involved in these murders, he would have had to have been in town over the last four weeks.

So, I will start there and work my way back, tracing his financial records off the card he provided the hotel. Even if he has only been staying with them a few nights, he could be hopping from one hotel to the next. Trying to not grab anyone's unwanted attention or raise any suspicion.

After a nice long, gloriously relaxing shower, I made the mistake of calling Hotel Hive to ask about Killian...who is supposed to currently be staying there. Living the life of luxury while he hunts down me and my sisters to do God knows what to us.

Yes, that was my plan, but now I need another shower *and* a strong drink after speaking to the front desk supervisor at the hotel.

According to the hotel, their system shows Killian has been staying there for almost a month now. His first night stay was three days prior to the first murder. He also paid in cash, which they frown against, but he was very *persuasive*...go figure.

I guess I'm not the only one who can't help but fall prey to his charming smile.

Their system also shows that he currently has no departure date set, they have been allowing him to pay in advance by the week.

The supervisor tried to play it off like they absolutely do not condone this type of stay in their hotel, but when she checked to see who it was that originally checked him in... she was shocked to find it had apparently been her.

She swears she has no recollection of allowing this, and strangely I believe her. It would be hard to fake the level of shock and anger that was in her voice.

This encounter just further confirms my suspicions. I suspect Killian is a Dark Fae assassin, a powerful one. There is no telling what types of powers he possesses. He might have mind control abilities that influenced the supervisor's decisions.

I'm not one to believe in *coincidences*, so the timing of Killian's arrival and the first murder doesn't sit right with me. I want answers...no I *need* answers. And I'm going to get them straight from the killer's mouth.

I know I'm being careless by not informing my sisters of what I just discovered and what I am about to do, but I don't want to put them in any more danger than they already are. I'm going to Hotel Hive, and Killian and I are going to have a nice long chat...unless he kills me before I even open my mouth.

CHAPTER 14

CALISTA

Leave it to the Fae assassin to stay in the best suite this place has to offer, on the top floor no less.

I had a while to think about how I wanted this interaction to go on the drive over. I decided to go in as Detective Adams, not Calista, in hopes of keeping it professional. The detective in me will at least hear the man out; as opposed to plain ole Calista, who will just deck him in the face before the conversation even gets started.

I brought my badge, handcuffs, and gun just in case things go sideways and I end up needing them.

I really hope I won't need them.

Standing before the door to his suite, I take a moment to gather my senses before going to knock. I can't help but notice the strange pulling sensation I felt last night at the bar has come back. I started to feel it again when I entered the lobby, and the intensity of it seems to keep getting stronger the closer I get to the door.

I'm starting to think it's my instincts way of telling me I'm in the vicinity of danger.

I hastily use my fist to knock loudly against the door three times before I can second guess this reckless plan of mine. I am silently cursing myself for not telling my sisters where I've gone or what I'm up to. If I disappear, they will never know what happened to me, which seems cruel now that I think about it. I wish I had thought about it like that earlier, because unfortunately it's too late to turn back now.

The door begins to open, and before Killian's face even comes into view, my fear and anger start taking over. As soon as his face enters my field of vision, instinct takes over and my fist goes flying straight into his nose.

Shit!

So much for Detective Adams taking control; it looks like Calista is running the show today.

Killian jerks back in shock but quickly recovers. He just stands there looking at me with both surprise...and is that...*pride?*

I can see the blood pouring out from his nose, but instead of taking a swing or cursing at me, I swear this crazy man *smiles...*

If he is hoping a smile will put me at ease, he is sorely mistaken.

His reaction to getting punched in the face has me feeling even more unnerved. This seems to cloud my better judgement, putting me in fight or flight mode. And without further thinking I throw myself at him.

To his credit, he doesn't just stand there and take it... No, he fights back.

My fist and feet are flying everywhere, and despite how hard I'm trying, I cannot land another hit to this man. He is astonishingly fast...*inhumanly* fast.

No matter how hard I come at him all he does is dodge and block my attacks. He hasn't once tried to land a blow of his own, even though we both know that he is more than capable.

This shouldn't surprise me at all, but it does. Seeing as how harming/killing women seems to be his forte.

Then again, if we keep this up, I may pass out from exhaustion. Which then would give him the opportunity to burn my eyes from their sockets without having to restrain me....

Focus Calista!

The only things I have managed to harm in this fight are two glass vases and one table-side lamp. The hotel is not going to be happy about it.

Killian must decide to put an end to my embarrassment, because he finally takes hold of my arm and flips me over his shoulder, causing me to land flat on my back and knocking the air from my lungs. Before I can regain my breath or even register what is happening Killian drops down to the floor, straddling my body.

He takes both of my wrists and restrains them above my head using only one of his large hands. His other hand gently grabs my chin, making sure my gaze stays fixed on his.

Ever so slowly, he leans down until we are sharing the same breath. Our lips are a mere inch apart and our eyes locked, as he runs his thumb along my bottom lip and quietly whispers, *"What are you?"*

This question takes me by surprise because I have no idea what he is talking about. Unless he can somehow sense that I'm half witch by using his Fae abilities? He appears to be so deep in thought that I don't even think he meant to say it aloud for me to hear.

I feel the grip he has been using to restrain my arms loosen; and I take full advantage of it. I buck my hips up toward his groin, throwing him off balance. Using his moment of surprise; I wrap my leg around his waist and my arm around his shoulder and then flip him over onto his back. Reversing our positions.

His arms are extremely long, so I am basically lying fully on top of him trying to restrain his arms above his head. Our faces are so close I must physically hold my head back to keep our noses from touching.

Even though I'm currently holding the dominant position, I know he can throw me off with ease. Stretching my body out so far to restrain his arms is using all my upper body strength and keeping me off balance.

But he doesn't seem concerned at all that I swapped our positions, and our roles are now reversed. In fact, there is that sly smile again, and a look of *wonder* on his face.

"What in the hell are you smiling about pretty boy?" I scowl down at him. And I swear this man is insane because his smile widens at my words.

"There's my little *Viper*" Killian says calmly.

As soon as that name leaves his mouth my world stops spinning. All I can manage to do is stare back at him...speechless, as long repressed memories from a made-up world in my dreams come crashing back.

He called me his little Viper. He said it was fitting because I was smart, mysterious, and sometimes vicious. And he was my Rose, because like a rose he was beautiful to behold but could cause you pain if you weren't careful of the thorns.

How does he know that nickname? Can he dig into people's past dreams and memories? That is the only way he could know that name...

"Ho—", I go to ask him how he knows about the nickname, but I'm interrupted.

The door to the suite unexpectedly opens, and two extremely huge men enter the room. Before they have time to take in the scene before them, I am rolling off Killian and pulling my gun on them.

"Freeze!" I shout out in warning. "Put your hands above your heads and don't move...or I will put a bullet in your skulls."

Shockingly they both do as I say and slowly raise their hands above their heads. Like Killian, these men are stunning...*and* dangerous. The hair on my neck is sticking straight up; confirming the danger that just entered the room with us.

Both look strong, with corded forearm muscles and bulging biceps. They could probably bench press me with only one arm. The one on my right has midnight blue-black hair and mesmerizing dark blue eyes that draw you in. The one on my left has dark brown hair that complements the deepest green eyes I have ever seen. Their green eyes could captivate anyone, human or Fae.

As I sit there dumbfounded by their overwhelming presence and beauty, the one with midnight blue hair starts *laughing*! Laughing!?

This helps to wake me up from whatever stupor I let myself fall into.

"Did you just get your ass kicked by a human chick?", blue eyes teases Killian.

"Go to hell, Callum" Killian retorts, before slowly turning to face me and the gun I have pointed at his friends. "Guys this is Calista." Both guys wave awkwardly while keeping their hands in the air. "Calista this is Dante", the man with green eyes smiles at me and nods. "And this asshole" he says pointing at the one with blue eyes, "is Callum", this man also nods hello, still sporting a huge smile from laughing so hard.

"Now that we all know each other would you mind not pointing your gun at our heads?" the one called Callum asks me.

Killian turns to look me in my eyes. "You can trust them" he assures me.

"I don't even trust you and now I'm supposed to add two more strange men into the mix?" I respond, making sure they can hear the frustration in my voice.

Very slowly, Killian reaches over and places his hand on top of mine, applying the slightest pressure that has me lowering my gun. All the while looking me in the eyes, silently pleading for me to drop my weapon.

Reluctantly, throwing all my training and better judgement to the wind, I drop my gun and re-holster it.

Killian beats me to my feet but as soon as I'm up I begin putting space between myself and the three of them.

"Who and *what* are you? Tell me now! And don't bullshit me." I demand, studying each of them closely.

"Alright, we will tell you everything, but can we please sit down first?" Killian asks, and I finally notice the dried blood on his face from where I punched him.

"No! I have three dead bodies and a serial killer or *killers* to find. And here you three are...arriving in town right when the murders began. Curious, don't you think?" I keep backing away from them until my back eventually hits the kitchen island, forcing me to stop.

"We will explain everything...but I for one am going to sit my ass on the couch. You pack a punch to be so small." Killian says walking over and sitting on the white sectional that takes up most of the space in the living room area.

I can't help but smile and internally give myself a pat on the back for that compliment. Even if he didn't mean for it to be one.

"Are you or are you not the ones responsible for these murders?" I snap off at them, demanding they give me an answer.

"Calista, I know we just met but I swear we want the same thing. And *NO*, we have not killed anyone since we came to town. And yes, I lied about how long I've been in town, but only because I knew that if I gave you the real timeline you would suspect me even more." Killian says, maintaining his innocence. Dante hands him a tissue off the side table to clean the blood off his face; Killian graciously accepts.

And maybe I've officially lost my mind... but I think I believe him. I don't know what this pull is between him and I, but my gut is telling me he's innocent. And a huge part of detective work is trusting your gut.

I've just always struggled with giving people my trust. It seems like every time I do I end up disappointed again and again. Even in my job, I consider what my gut is telling me, but I usually don't act on it until I have factual evidence that coincides.

This situation is trickier. I have nothing to go on besides my gut feeling...and my gut is telling me to put my trust in not one but three strangers.

I slowly make my way into the living room and take a seat on the opposite end of the sectional. Deciding that I should at least hear them out and see what they know about my case since I'm already here.

The four of us sit on the couch studying one another, waiting for someone to speak up.

Killian's friend Dante breaks the silence. Without sugar coating anything he reveals, "We are Unseelie Fae...and we are here trying to find three witches that a prophecy in our realm speaks of." Killian and the other friend—Callum I think—look at Dante stunned. I guess they didn't expect him to spill the beans on their identity so soon.

Thankfully Dante is unfazed by their looks and continues, "King Erebus, does not want this prophecy to come to pass, so he sent three of his best assassins to find and kill the three witches."

Shit, well he just confirmed our worst fears.

I can feel the blood draining from my face. So much for not giving anything away. They would have to be idiots not to catch on.

Dante must be the first to notice my fear because he assures me, "*We* want to find the witches before the assassins find and eliminate them."

Why does everything keep coming back around to this ridiculous prophecy?! I've heard it several times the past couple days and I still believe it's just a bunch of hogwash; I can't make heads or tails of it, but I never was good at figuring out riddles. My philosophy is if you have something important to say then say it! Life's too short to be cryptic or beat around the bush. However, being straight forward would make life too simple, I guess.

"So there just happens to be *three* assassins and *three* of you?" I point out, eyeing them suspiciously. "And just what do you plan to do with these three witches, if or when you find them, before the assassins take them out?"

Killian gets up from the couch and moves to sit on the coffee table in front of me, leaning forward so we are eye to eye. He appears to believe that looking directly into his eyes will help convey the truth of what he is about to say.

Or maybe he just likes being close to me...

Nope, not going there... Snap out of it, Cali!

Killian gestures back to his friends, "We are a package deal, if you will. It's just a coincidence there are three of us... I don't trust anyone else to not report us to the king for treason." The sincerity of his words is evident. "We wish to keep the witches safe...and hope in return they will help us free the Unseelie Kingdom from King Erebus's tyrannical reign."

What. The. Actual. Fuck!?

Why are these powerful Fae men desperate for mine and my sisters help in defeating their king? Hate to break it to them, but I think they need to go back to their own realm and reevaluate this prophecy...because whatever 'witches' it's referring to isn't me and my sisters, that's for damn sure!

My mouth has dried up to the point where I literally can't pull my lips apart to respond.

When I continue to just stare at Killian, he begins to rant, "He is an unchecked tyrant that has tainted the reputation of the entire kingdom. He has made a mockery of our people, corrupting their ways of life and all we stand for."

By the time he is finished trash talking his king he is seething. I can see the true sorrow and anger in his eyes...he truly cares for his kingdom and the people within.

Though I might believe all he is telling me. I still can't reveal the truth about me and my sisters until I fill them in on everything I've learned.

Hell, maybe the three of us can use these guys to help kill the assassins and then just drop out of our part of the deal.

That sounds so wrong to say, especially with the way Killian is staring into my soul right now with his stormy grey eyes.

"If you are here to keep them safe then why not go ahead and take out the assassins?"

Callum slowly shakes his head before turning to face me. "Believe me we've tried. But we can't let them discover we followed them here, or the king will have our heads. Since we are having to lay low, by the time we finally pick up their trail it's too late, and someone else ends up dead. No matter how hard we try they are always one step ahead of us. Like we said...the king sent some of his best." Callum says solemnly, looking genuinely upset about their failed attempts.

"Well, this is all very interesting, but what does it have to do with me? Your message said that you thought we could help each other out...doesn't sound like you guys are any closer to catching these bastards then me and my team back at the precinct." I question, pushing back at Killian to see how he responds.

Dante and Callum shoot me a knowing smirk from behind Killian. That sight alone gets my guts churning and I feel like I'm going to be sick.

Shit! They know...

Killian's lips begin to curve up into his signature cocky grin before he confirms my worst fears. "Here is what I was thinking... just hear me out. We-," he points to him and his friends, "will find and kill the assassins the king sent over. And then *you* and your *two friends* will help us eliminate the king."

I'm trying my best not to give anything away, but by the grins these boys are giving me I know I'm not fooling anyone.

How did they figure it out? I have no clue, but I plan to find out.

I know I should be playing it cool and telling them they are crazy, but from the sound of blood rushing in my ears I know my face must be white as a ghost. Even so, I remain speechless...just staring back into Killian's eyes, drowning in them, and trying my best to come up for a precious breath of air.

Not waiting for me to pull myself together, Killian leans in close enough for me to see the shimmer in his eyes. He then reaches up running his fingers along my cheek as he pushes a strand of hair behind my ear and asks in a low, deep voice, "What do you say *little witch*? Do we have a deal?"

CHAPTER 15

CALISTA

I've been in interrogation rooms less tense than inside this hotel suite. With all six of us inside this one room together you can slice the tension with a knife.

After Killian called me out for being a witch; and suggested we all make a deal to help each other out, I immediately picked up my cell and called my sisters. Luckily, they were both together, so I didn't have to waste time chasing them down.

I told them I had enlightening information on the assassins and to meet me at Hotel Hive, giving them the number to Killian's suite.

My sisters immediately started asking me questions, but I told them it would be best if I just explained once they arrived. I also made them promise to remain calm once they arrived; needless to say, that did not go as well as I'd hoped.

In hindsight I'm so glad I sent them a text on their way over telling them to keep their powers in check no matter what, or it could have been a whole lot worse.

I didn't *lie*...I just 'withheld' some pertinent information. Like the fact that this new information came from three huge Fae men, and that they were about to show up to a hotel room to find me and said men waiting for them.

I never admitted to Killian whether his claim of me being a *"little witch"* was correct. I wanted my sisters to be here to decide together if we wanted to reveal that information to these strangers. I know I may be insane bringing them here with these powerful Dark Fae, and I normally wouldn't risk their safety, but for some reason my gut is telling me we can trust them. At least to some extent.

It should go without saying that my sisters lost their shit when they arrived and took in three huge Fae standing behind me. It took a few minutes of screaming and yelling back and forth at each other before they finally accepted my apologies for the ambush.

After calming down; as much as someone could in this situation, I finally coaxed them into sitting down so the men could reiterate to them exactly what they had told me.

And now here we are just sitting on opposite sides of the room, staring awkwardly at one another...

I asked the men if they would mind stepping out for a minute to let my sisters and I talk in private. I was taken aback by how easily they agreed to step out of the suite to give us space.

After we were sure they had left and weren't in the hallway trying to eavesdrop on us, my sisters quickly turned around and accused me of losing my damn mind.

It felt like it took hours to convince them that I think we can *trust* the men long enough to help us stop the assassins. I made sure to clarify that I am using the word 'trust' very loosely given our current circumstances. After they finally accepted that I hadn't completely lost my mind, they seemed to relax...*slightly*.

It wasn't like we were going to be stuck with these men forever, and once they held up their end of the deal...who's to say we must hold up our end?

Is that wrong to consider? Yes.

For me, trust is a fickle thing. It can be easily broken or changed by a person's actions or situation, and it is simply unreliable. I like stability and consistency; and trust is neither of those.

So yes, it is wrong to betray their trust, and it will feel even worse if they uphold their end of the deal. However, my main goal is to ensure my sisters, and I make it out of this shit show alive. And I will do whatever it takes to ensure that happens.

The girls and I finally came to an agreement that we would confide in these men and share with them our true identities, that we are indeed witches. However, whether we would uphold our end of the deal was to be determined.

We still needed answers...for starters why does everyone think the prophecy is talking about the three of us specifically? Do they plan on lending us some of their own powers to defeat the Dark Fae King? Because our powers are subpar at best...

About fifteen minutes later there is a knock on the door before the three men re-enter. They came back bearing coffee...like that will win us over.

"Oh, thank God!" Hazel exclaims, as she quickly walks over to grab herself and Eve a coffee from one of the guys.

"No problem, but you can just call me Dante" the Fae says, giving Hazel a sly wink before releasing the cup she was trying to accept from him.

Hazel, however, just scrunches up her face in disgust and walks back over to stand in between Eve and me.

Killian seems to make it his job to personally bring me my coffee; all while giving me one of those shy half smiles of his. I can't help but smile shyly back at him before quickly looking away and rejoining my sisters in the kitchen.

The fact that I seem to have the ability to make this six-foot-seven beast of a man act like a shy schoolboy awakens a swarm of butterflies in my stomach.

Thankfully, my sisters appear to be more at ease now. They seem to be making themselves at home, looking through the refrigerator and cabinets for cream and sugar.

I can't help but silently laugh at this entire situation. Not even thirty minutes ago I thought my sisters were going to give themselves a heart attack or brain aneurysm from how upset and scared they were. And now here in this very moment, their biggest concern seems to be 'who doesn't put cream and sugar in their coffee?!'.

"So, have you come to a decision?" Callum asks, after we all make our way back to the living room. Me and my sisters decided to sit on the opposite end of the sectional. This way we can still face them, but there is still plenty of room between them and us.

Eve studies Callum for a moment, narrowing her eyes as if trying to intimidate him. I take a slow sip of my coffee to keep from smirking at the thought of that ever happening. My sweet blue eyed, blonde hair sister going up against this six-five, two hundred plus pound man made of pure muscle. He wouldn't even need a weapon to win a fight...his body itself is a weapon.

She shakes her long blonde hair behind her back before she informs the men. "We will work with you to help bring down these assassin Fae sent by *your* king to hunt and kill *us*. But why in the world do you think the three of us can help you defeat the king?" Eve takes a pause, as she notices Callum now narrowing his gaze at her, but when he doesn't answer, she continues speaking. "The way you speak about your king makes him sound very powerful. So powerful that none of you have gone up against him, and you three are way more powerful than us. So how is it you expect the three of us to have any luck at taking him down?"

Hazel jumps in adding, "Yeah, the way we see it is we are either going to be killed by these assassins or the king himself. The only ones benefiting from this deal are you three."

All three of the men just stare back at us with confused looks marring their handsome faces.

Dante leans forward with a doubtful look on his face. "Surely you must be more powerful than you are telling us. Seeing as how the last we saw of the king he was scared shitless...of the three of you." Dante says accusingly; like we are intentionally playing down the strength of our powers.

This discussion seems like it is getting us nowhere. On my left I have a stare down going on between Hazel and Dante, and on my right, Eve and Callum. Killian and I just keep looking back and forth between the four of them, waiting to intercept whoever throws the first punch.

Thankfully before any blood gets shed, Killian finally speaks up, breaking the tension that's continuing to build up between these four.

"Why don't we start by you three showing us your abilities? That way we can see what all we are working with?" he optimistically suggests.

Boy are they in for a shock...

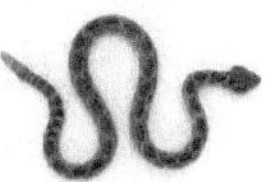

My sisters and I exchange knowing looks before erupting into laughter. These men are about to be extremely disappointed if they think they are about to witness some amazing feats of power. After we recompose ourselves, we nod silently in agreement that it is time to reveal our abilities. Our 'amazing, all-powerful' abilities that are supposed to defeat the Dark Fae King.

This is going to be so embarrassing...

Hazel steps up first; moving to sit on the coffee table so she can look the men directly in their eyes. She stares at Dante first but only for a couple seconds before a smile crosses her face. Next, she stares at Callum and lets out a huge laugh. When she stares at Killian though, all I can see is a look of uncertainty on her face.

Hazel shakes it off and focuses her attention back on the three guys in front of her. Then she reveals her ability...

Looking at Dante she states, "What the hell is she looking at?", which gets her a look of surprise on Dante's handsome face.

Turning to Callum she says, "Killian is going to get us killed thinking with his dick". Callum looks like he just got called out for stealing candy from a baby.

In a flash, Killian turns and puts Callum into a headlock. "Fuck you man", Killian scolds as he gives Callum a painful looking noogie.

Dante's hysterical laughter isn't helping matters. It's especially not helping Eve or I to keep a straight face. But finally Killian releases Callum, shoving him into the back of the couch.

I couldn't stop myself from looking over at Killian after Hazel revealed Callum's thought. I was dying to see his reaction. And I'm glad I did...was it just me or did Killian look like he was blushing?

When he finally releases Callum and looks back up, his eyes instantly lock onto mine. I just smile and bite my lower lip to keep from laughing. I had a feeling, but his actions were all the confirmation I needed. I think *I* may be the one distracting said 'dick'.

"We get it, you can hear people's thoughts" Killian says, trying to quickly change the focus of the conversation. "What did mine say?"

Hazel just stares at him before releasing a frustrated breath. She hesitantly admits to Killian, "I can't read yours...it's like you have a forcefield around your mind".

"What a shame" Killian says lazily, with his devilish grin. He seems to be more than happy with that outcome.

"Is there anything else?" Killian asks raising a brow.

Next thing I know a pillow is flying across the room and hitting Dante upside the head. Everyone burst out laughing...except Dante of course. Dante gives Hazel a look that promises payback, but instead of showing fear, Hazel just happily gives him her biggest *fake* smile.

"It's going to take a lot more than a pillow fight to kill the king... is that all you got, *little witch*?" Dante taunts Hazel, which succeeds at getting under her skin.

Hazel stares daggers at him before replying, "I'm not sure *macho man*, I've never had to use my abilities for anything more than getting things that are out of reach around the house. Killing a Fae King has never made it onto my priority to-do lists before now."

"Great so your powers are utterly useless to us...or not the powers so much as the *wielder* of those powers." As soon as those words leave Dante's mouth Hazel lunges at him.

Luckily, Callum intervenes, catching Hazel by her waist and pulling her back before the two of them can start going at it. At this very moment I'm not sure if they would start throwing punches or dry humping, because I am sensing some sexual tension brewing between these two. Even with Callum awkwardly sandwiched between them, they both continue standing there toe to toe, just staring at one another.

Realizing that neither one of them is going to back down first, I decide to cut in and hopefully embarrass them into submission. "Okay you two...either make out already or sit down because it's Eve's turn for 'show and tell'". Instantly my plan works and both Hazel and Dante return to their seats.

Trying a little too hard to *act* grossed out by my comment, if you ask me...

Eve rises and moves to the center of the living room. Without saying a word Eve removes the lid of her coffee cup and the coffee begins flowing out into the air. She makes it swirl around her head and makes circles in the air like smokers make rings of smoke. Once the coffee flows back inside the cup she brings it to a boil, rewarding herself with a freshly heated cup of coffee.

She explains to the guys that she can manipulate the elements. Admittedly, she has never pushed her powers to see how far they can go...because she has never had a reason to. She shows them another example by using the house plant on the kitchen island; making its vines grow and wrap around the bar stools sitting beneath the island. Eve also explains to them how the elements alert her when there are supernatural beings nearby.

The guys don't even comment on Eve's display of powers when she is finished, they just sit there nodding their heads in approval. Or at least I think it's approval. Either way, Eve just stands there. I guess she is waiting for the guys to speak up and provide her with feedback, or insults like they did with Hazel.

In attempts to avoid another conflict I hastily rise and announce, "My turn!". This grabs Eve's attention and before she has a chance to argue I am standing next to her urging her to go back to her seat.

I didn't want the guys to start running their mouths and pointing out how Eve's powers were 'useless' against the Fae King as well. I mean we did warn them...but still...seeing the look of disappointment on their faces still stings.

Killian's eyes seem to light up when it's time for my demonstration. I almost feel sorry for the poor fool because he is about to be severely disappointed.

"Well," I begin before pausing to clear my throat, "I can do most everything my sisters can—but I also have other abilities—one in particular I work hard to keep suppressed."

I have Killian's, Dante's, and Callum's full attention. They are locked in on me waiting to hear what I'm going to reveal next. Their anticipation is written all over their faces.

"I can burn beings alive from the inside out, just by simply touching them." I avert my gaze and look down at my feet, not wanting to face their judgement. However, all I hear is a long whistle and single hand clap. This has me quickly looking back up. Where I discover the whistle and clap were coming from Callum. He doesn't look disappointed at all...in fact he looks impressed. Dante's face on the other hand seems indifferent; he doesn't appear to be impressed or unimpressed. Then when I look over at Killian, I see he has a huge smile on his face.

I *hate* the fact that I am so happy to have his approval. And it doesn't matter how hard I try to fight against these feelings I'm experiencing towards him, something in my chest still begins to flutter.

"I can also *see* beings for what they truly are...but for you three I just feel immense power radiating off you." I step closer, intentionally locking eyes with Killian as I tell him, "I can see shadows rolling off you...they are very light, like a grey smoke, but I can still make them out if I really focus." His eyes open wide in surprise, I guess he wasn't expecting me to be powerful enough to see through his shields. And he does have a shield up...a very powerful one. That must be what is keeping me and the girls from being able to get a good read on him.

"Interesting" Killian murmurs, seeming somewhat bewildered.

"Very" Callum agrees.

Probing, Dante asks curiously, "And how is it you know you have the ability to roast said beings from the inside?"

Before they start throwing questions and accusations at me, I go ahead and quickly tell them about the regrettable *incident* I had with my high school janitor. This horrendous event haunts me every day of my life. I make sure to clarify that this experience was the one and only time I've ever displayed this specific ability.

For all I know it could have been a fluke, a one and done type of thing.

I was on my way back to class from the bathroom when I ran into Mr. Ned, the school janitor. No one else was around. The school hallways were completely empty since classes were in the middle of sessions, and there I stood face to face with the creepy Fae janitor. As if he had sensed that I could see his true self he began to advance on me with deliberate intent.

In a panic I told him to stay back while I retreated a few steps. He kept telling me to 'hold on' and that 'everything is fine I just want to help you with something', but in my panic when he got too close, I reached out and grabbed his wrist. Mr. Ned's eyes sprang open with fear as I continued to stare into them, while mentally willing him away. I was overcome with fear, but more so, I was angry...angry at this creature, this Fae, for showing such aggression. As his eyes continued to stare into mine, I began to feel this fire burning inside me. Yearning to be released. So, I opened the flood gates inside my mind and released it...

I had no idea what I was doing. I just felt like I was literally going to burn alive from the inside out if I did not somehow discharge this fire roaring up inside me. Demanding to be set free. Well as it turned out the fire within my mind and body left me and went into Mr. Ned...flaying him on the inside. I could see the red glow on his skin from my fire incinerating him from within. I could see him trying to scream but the pain he was in would not allow it. At last, he was able to utter 'Your foot', right before the whites of his eyes turned a fiery red like that of a heated branding iron and he dropped dead at my feet.

I ran...ran back to class as fast I could. I couldn't get help. I had some-how just roasted a man alive from the inside out like a microwaved Hot

Pocket. Warm to the touch on the outside, but a steaming hot, melted mess on the inside.

After I returned to my seat in class, I couldn't hear anything anyone was saying for the blood rushing in my ears. When my breathing settled and I could finally start to think in coherent sentences, I heard snickering from several of my classmates sitting around me. When I turned to ask them what was so funny I saw them looking down towards the bottom of my chair... or to be more specific at my right foot. There I stared horror stricken, for on my right foot was a long strip of toilet paper stuck to the bottom of my shoe. I had just killed a man or Fae-man, that was just trying to save me the embarrassment from my peers.

When I'm finished telling my story, everyone is looking at me with pity in their eyes.

Callum grabs my attention with his kind words, "Calista it was an accident, you never meant to kill anyone." But his words just bring more guilt to life inside of me. Maybe not intentionally, but some part of me knew, deep down, that the fire coming to life inside of me wanted to cause damage. And I wielded it, setting it free.

I can see Killian assessing us in his head as he rises. Standing before everyone he summarizes, "So, it looks like we have ourselves a witch that's telepathic/telekinetic, one that can manipulate the elements, and one that can do all that, plus is a pyrokinetic."

He grips his chin between his thumb and pointer finger, appearing to be deep in thought. After a moment I can see an idea taking shape in his head and he states, "I see your concerns because your powers are very mediocre." *Wow, harsh much Fae-hole?* "The King would destroy you in a matter of seconds if you tried to go up against him right now. However, I say we team up to divide and conquer. Each of you ladies will pair off with one of us, and we will work with you to help strengthen and awaken your powers to their full potential. Hopefully you three can rise to the challenge and become formidable adversaries to the Unseelie King."

I can't help but look skeptical as Killian discusses this plan of action.

Do these three truly believe that *they* can help us come into our powers? The chances of that being successful are highly unlikely, and even if it could possibly work...we have no clue as to how much time it could take. And seeing as how the king has already sent assassins to kill us; it doesn't seem like we have a lot of time to work with. Days? Maybe weeks if we are lucky?

Killian clears his throat intentionally to get my attention. He must have been able to tell from the voided look in my eyes that I was letting my mind wander off with me. "So, do we have a deal? We help you ladies eliminate the Fae assassins you have on your hands. While also helping you to build up your powers. Powers that you will then use to help us eliminate the Unseelie King." Killian extends his hand for me to shake on and seal the deal.

Before doing so though, I look over to my sisters to make sure they are okay with accepting this deal with our new Fae friends... *frenemies?* Whatever the hell they are to us now.

Giving me their nods of approval, I slide my hand into Killian's rough callused one, feeling the *pull* between us become so much stronger than before. Standing straighter with my chin held high I state in agreement, "We have a deal".

Now my sisters and I need to pray to every God that has ever existed, that we don't come to regret this deal we just made...

"Now we pair off" Dante announces, crossing his muscular arms across his chest and walking over to stand next to Killian. I swear he was looking right at Hazel when he said it.

Hazel must have noticed because she quickly adds in before we break off into pairs, "Fine but I am not pairing up with Da-"

CHAPTER 16

CALISTA

The pairs ended up being: Myself and Killian; go figure, Eve and Callum, and lastly, Hazel and Dante.

If stares could kill, we would all be dead right now from the death beams Hazel is shooting at everyone. She really didn't want to be paired up with Dante but in the end, it made the most logical sense for her to work with him.

Callum, being a war general, could help Eve work on homing in on the elements around her to assist her during an altercation. He will not only show her how to defend but also how to attack with each element. Having not been a stranger to actual battles, he will help run her through different types of scenarios she may find herself up against; especially when we finally face off against the king.

Dante, being the son to the Duke of Verigast, has been bred to not only wield a sword as a weapon but also his mind as one. Given how Hazel's abilities both involve the mind, it makes sense for her to work alongside Dante. He can train her on how she will be expected to portray herself in the Fae Realm; especially when trying to get close enough to the king to use her powers against him. As well as, how to use her mind and voice in conjunction to manipulate those around her. Basically, the power of persuasion, she will be able to use people's own thoughts to her benefit...saying what needs to be said to get the outcome she desires. He will also have her practice reading his thoughts from increasing distances while having a shield cast over his mind; so not only will she have to break through a mental shield, but she will also have to focus over long distances.

Killian is the strongest of the three Fae. He has been trained for battle, knows how to manipulate his words to accomplish what he needs, and he can use his mind to influence others. Among many other abilities he *assures* me he will divulge to me along the way.

Unsurprisingly, to me at least, he volunteered to work alongside me helping to strengthen my existing abilities and to uncover any dormant abilities that I may have. And by *volunteered*...I mean voluntold.

Killian *voluntold* everyone I would be working with him; literally calling out right off the bat, "Calista is *mine*". Possessive much? However, I guess Dante and Callum must have agreed that he was the best choice to pair me up with, because neither made the slightest argument when he called 'dibs' on me.

"Now that we have partners squared away, maybe we should discuss I don't know... *How* we plan on catching these assassins?" I say sarcastically, walking into the kitchen to help myself to a glass of water. I don't even bother asking if they have glasses, I just rinse out my empty coffee cup and fill that up with water.

I'm right in the middle of taking a nice long gulp of water when Dante offers up to the group, "We could use one of you witches as bait..."

Water erupts from my mouth and goes all over the kitchen floor, and my shirt. Dante just looks over at me with a wolfish grin; he knows damn well I would never allow me or my sisters to be used as *bait*! Everyone else looks unfazed by Dante's suggestion. Killian and Callum are too busy trying to bite back their smiles from seeing me spray water all over the place, like I'm their own personal indoor fountain.

Anger begins to stir inside me. I quickly sit down my cup and look back at Dante, he appears to be so smug and happy with himself thanks to the reaction he got from me. Fuming, I storm across the room heading straight for him. I can't even wait until I reach him before I start going off on him. "Excuse me, what did you just say? Because I know you didn't suggest that one of us act as bait!", I yell motioning to me and my sisters.

Dante closes the distance between us and looks down at me menacingly, "Oh, but that's exactly what I'm suggesting, *little witch*." I'm starting to understand why Hazel can't seem to stand this one.

The way he mockingly said those last two words has me seeing red, and I'm about two seconds from kneeing this cocky bastard in his groin when Eve suddenly steps into my field of vision, breaking us apart.

"Wait! Maybe he's on to something..."

I blink several times to make sure I'm not imagining things, and that I correctly heard what came out of Eve's mouth. I look at her feeling both shocked and pissed that she is even entertaining his ridiculous idea. She is the one who was dead set against performing the summoning ritual that brought these asshole assassins here in the first place, but now she is suddenly okay with offering one of us up as bait?! Her unexpected bravery is commendable...but *stupid*!

"The assassins saw Tilly's list back at the shop and *my* name is on there. I could—"

"No!", I cut her off before she has the chance to offer herself up like some self-sacrificing nun. We would be relying on these three Fae men we just met to keep her safe...*Dark Fae* men to be exact. And I am in no way ready to grant them that level of trust.

"Besides, we aren't completely sure if they are even using that list to go after anyone. There hasn't been another murder since the list was even discovered..." Hazel adds, backing me up. Hopefully that means that only one of us has lost our mind.

"Sedrik", Callum supplies looking up at us with thoughtful eyes. Dante and Killian both nod in agreement to their friend; like he just confirmed the answer to a silent question they had been asking themselves.

"Sedrik?" I repeat back to them. Placing both hands on my hips I stare them down with a look that says, *'this better be good'*.

"He's one of the assassins the king sent over, and he is a tracker; a damn good one too." Again, both Killian and Dante give exaggerated nods of agreement as Callum explains who this Sedrik guy is.

Killian runs a hand over his face releasing a hiss, "Shit, I forgot he was with them." He almost sounds regretful, like he was dreading the fact they would have to eliminate him. Judging by the vibes they are giving off, I think it's safe to assume that Sedrik is a friend of theirs.

Are they really going to sacrifice someone they care about for three random 'witches' they just met? Here is yet another reason I am not ready to put my full trust in them.

I turn to Killian confused, "Why does this information matter?"

Dante beats him to the answer, "He can track *power*, or more so the source producing the power. But he can only track power while it is being used or if it has been used recently enough that he can pick up the remnants of power."

"So, all I would have to do is use my powers while you all lie hidden and wait for them to come after me? Sounds easy enough, right? What could go wrong?" Eve asks nervously. Her attempt to keep her voice steady did not work, the shaking in her voice is obvious.

She looks over to me and Hazel for approval.

Well, she won't be getting it from me, that's for sure. Maybe I should call Aunt El and tell her what Eve is volunteering to do. She would be down here and dragging Eve back to Winchester before I could finish saying 'Super-cali-fragil—'...or whatever that dumb ass Mary Poppin's word is. Or better yet, I could just lock her up in a cell until her common sense comes back. I'll just tell the guys back at the precinct that she lost a bet.

Before I have a chance to follow through on one of my desperate ideas my cell phone rings. Removing my phone from my back pocket I see that Seb is calling me on a Saturday. That usually only happens when he wants to make plans to hang out or something bad has happened with work; and given our recent events I'm going to take a guess that it's the latter. I reluctantly step away from the group to answer the call, leaving them alone to plan out Eve's suicide mission.

"What's up Seb?" I unintentionally snap out at him. But I don't have time to feel bad about it because I need to get back in that room before they all agree on something ridiculous.

"Damn, what has your panties in a bunch this early on a Saturday?" He chuckles, I guess there is no hiding how frustrated I am at this early morning call.

"Why are you calling, Seb?"

"We need to make a house call", he replies seriously. Which tells me my earlier guess was correct, this has something to do with the serial killer case.

"A house call? Since when do we make house calls on Saturdays?" My annoyance level is now an eight out of ten.

"Since this woman *swears,* she is going to be our serial killer's next victim. Well killers, plural, since she thinks *three* men are stalking her."

My jaw drops to the floor. It takes me a couple of seconds before I can finally form a coherent sentence let alone think straight.

"Shit! Okay, text me the address and I will meet you there. And wait on me before going in; I want to hear every detail she has to give us."

"Got it boss. And sorry about interrupting your fun filled Saturday." Seb hangs up before I get a chance to tell him where to shove his sarcastic comment.

I quickly rejoin the group and rush straight up to Killian to confirm, "You said there are three assassins, correct?"

Eyeing me suspiciously he slowly nods, confirming my question.

"Well, then before you go offering up my sister like a sacrificial lamb...I might have a lead."

CHAPTER 17

CALISTA

Olivia Wells, possibly the next target of our Fae assassins, is quite the character. She has short pink spiky hair shaved on the sides, nose and eyebrow piercings, and a 'go screw yourself' attitude that I admire. However, her eccentric look and personality make her an easy target to pick out in a crowd.

She informed us that she first noticed her three stalkers last night during her shift tending bar at Lost and Found. I personally haven't been there, but I hear that atmosphere is very inviting. I guess me and the girls have gotten stuck in a rut of just going to All Souls, so we hardly ever go somewhere new these days.

She provided us with the profiles of the three men. The only detail that really stood out is one of the men had a large scar running down one side of their face. Apparently, they sat in a booth across from the bar for hours. They only ordered one drink each that she knows of, and she's not even sure if they drank them. The entire time they were there they couldn't seem to look away from her, even her coworkers pointed out her *admirers*. She said they thankfully left an hour before closing time, and she had one of her male coworkers take her back to her place after locking up.

This morning though, while drinking her coffee and looking out her living room window, she saw the same three men standing across the street from her apartment. She immediately called the cops, but they were gone by the time they arrived.

She had been notified by our department that her name was found on Tilly's list; and instructed that even though it was probably nothing to worry about she should still stay vigilant and aware of her surroundings until the person/persons responsible for the string of murders was detained.

Thankfully, she didn't hesitate to reach out. I'm glad they didn't attack her before she got in touch with us.

We encouraged her to go about her day as she normally would, with just a little extra caution and vigilance; like she had already been told. I called the station and assigned patrols to be stationed outside of her apartment and outside the bar where she works. Someone is to also always have eyes on her whenever she leaves the apartment.

I called Killian on the way back to my apartment and confirmed with him that the profiles Ms. Wells provided us did match those of the Fae assassins. Now that it was confirmed, it was time to go hunt us down some Fae bastards.

The game plan was simple. Tonight, Killian and his boys would case her apartment, keeping out of sight from my officers. While Seb and I go undercover acting as regular patrons at the bar Ms. Wells is working at. Hazel picked up burner phones for Killian and the guys so we could all easily keep in touch. If anyone gets eyes on the assassins, they are to contact the others for backup before moving in.

Olivia's shift at the bar tonight is from nine p.m. to two a.m. The plan is to meet Seb there at midnight, right about time for the nightlife to start picking up.

I still have an hour to kill before I need to head over, and what better way to do that than with a nice hot bubble bath...

Knock Knock

Who the hell is that?

I check my phone to see if I have any text messages or missed calls from anyone telling me they are coming over...but I find nothing.

I despise unannounced visits. You can never achieve *full* relaxation when you are laying around your house in nothing but your bra and panties, when in the back of your mind you are always wondering if someone is going to just pop over unannounced.

Or maybe that's just a 'me' problem...I seem to have a lot of those.

With Fae assassins running around I check to make sure my pistol is still sitting on the side table next to my door. I then slowly begin opening my door. When it's wide enough for me to stick my head out, I peek around to see who the hell decided to just show up at my place. Then I find myself speechless, staring up at the six-foot-seven gorgeous Fae pain in my ass...Killian.

"What the hell are you doing here? I didn't tell you where I lived..." Okay, maybe my greeting is slightly rude, but how the hell did he know where to find me?

"Hello to you too, little witch" he replies, pushing his way past me to step into my living room.

"Nice place yo—"

I throw my hand out signaling for him to stop moving before he has the chance to finish talking. The audacity of this man thinking he can just waltz into my home without being invited has my anger boiling.

"Excuse you?! You can't just let yourself in to someone else's home...and you were not invited so please get the fu—"

"I'm coming with you tonight", he informs, cutting me off. Clearly, he didn't get the memo that only I am allowed to cut people off mid conversation in my house.

What the hell is he thinking? We have a plan...a plan that he is already screwing up. He is supposed to be with his boys right now keeping an eye on Olivia's apartment. And he better not be playing the 'knight in shining armor' shit, because I am not a damsel in distress. I can take care of myself all on my own. I don't need a huge alpha-hole treating me like I'm some delicate little princess that will break at the slightest touch.

"Like hell you are!" I bark at him while closing the distance between us. I put on the 'mega bitch' face, as Seb calls it, before demanding that he get back to his post with Callum and Dante, and to get the hell out of my apartment.

My face must not be as intimidating as I thought because Killian just gives me a sly grin and walks out the door.

"Wait!" I shout, and he slowly turns back around with that grin still plastered on his beautiful face. "How did you find my place?" Because I know there is no way one of my sisters would have given him my address without checking with me first.

Completely ignoring my question, Killian just turns and looks at me, letting out a deep laugh while shaking his head. He steps forward until my chest is so close to his that I have to hold in my breath to keep my small breasts from touching him.

He slowly leans down with his eyes glued to my lips. My heart is beating faster than a hummingbird's. *Is he trying to kiss me?! Am I going to let him?*

This thought has me startling and stumbling back a step. When I regain my footing, I look up to see him smiling and shaking his head. "Bye Calista", he says in a low deep voice, and then he is suddenly swallowed up by shadows.

I gasp in shock, but I'm not sure if it is from the shadows or the way my heart leapt from hearing my name come from his lips in that deep sensual voice.

As fast as they came the shadows dissipate, having taken Killian along with them.

Was I really going to let that Fae-hole kiss me? Maybe I'm wrong, and Hazel is the only sane one left. Looks like I'm losing my mind along with Eve.

CHAPTER 18

CALISTA

Sebastian and I have been here at the bar almost two hours now and we still haven't seen anyone that fits Olivia's descriptions. On a positive note, Olivia has been working the bar all night and it doesn't seem like she is letting her current situation throw her off her game. She has been slinging drinks left and right with a huge smile on her face.

Texting with Callum, everything on their end seems to be going smooth as well. He said there has been zero suspicious activity in or around her apartment.

With only thirty minutes left until the end of Olivia's shift Seb and I decide to let loose a little and enjoy ourselves. Since this whole night is turning out to be a bust anyway.

Of course, my luck, as soon as Seb leaves my side and hits the dance floor with some ditsy blonde, someone sits down next to me at the bar and asks if they can buy me a drink. I kindly accept his offer; even knowing he's most likely going to try and get me to leave the bar with him tonight since it's almost closing. Lucky for him my "give a damn" is busted right now.

The stress of Fae assassins trying to kill you, handsome Fae men promising to protect you, and doing a suicidal mission to kill the

Dark Fae King will do that to you. And free alcohol is free alcohol, right? Who am I to pass that up?

The man's name is Dean, and don't get me wrong he is extremely handsome. Most definitely the type of guy who takes pride in his body and works out like it's his job. Pre-Fae Calista would be all over him, flirting and stealing a squeeze of his huge biceps.

However, my stupid mind can't seem to stop thinking of a certain tall, gorgeous, Dark Fae. I probably need to give my therapist a call before I give into my self-destructive thoughts. The fact that he has somehow managed to plague my mind makes me hate him even more.

After Dean has had his second drink, since joining me, he starts getting handsy. Making any excuse to put his hands on me. I'm trying to tolerate it because I know he is just drunk and if it was any other time I would be enjoying the attention. But tonight, if he doesn't reel it in soon, I might go off. I keep taking his hands off me and putting them back in his own lap...what more of a hint can I give him?

"Hey, why don't we take this back to my place and continue to get to know one another?" Dean suggests drunkenly, running his clammy hand up my thigh. I immediately remove his hand and try to grab Seb's attention on the dance floor, but there is no use...his lips are currently devouring the ditzy blonde.

As soon as I remove his hand it comes right back, climbing higher up my thigh. This handsy encounter has me regretting my choice of outfit; short black dress with a blue jean jacket. But I did remember to wear flat black boots in case I had to do any running tonight.

"Will you please stop putting your hands on me, I don't like to be touched." I blatantly lie. I just don't like being touched by *him* right now.

"Oh, it's okay baby, here let me help you relax a little", he says while running his hand up under the hem of my dress. I am two seconds from punching this creep in the face when without warning a strong arm wraps around my waist.

Startled, and ready to swing, I look up into a pair of stormy dark blue eyes...Killian.

I'm instantly overcome with aggravation at the fact that he came here even though I told him not to, which does not bode well for him gaining my trust. But I'm also overcome with a feeling of warmth and gratitude; it's like somehow now that he is here, I feel safe, like I can relax.

Killian's intimidating, yet sexy, deep dark voice comes up from behind. I can feel his breath on the shell of my ear. "I think you should take your damn hands off my wife before I remove them myself...and that won't be pleasant." he threatens.

Killian's words literally make me spit out some of my drink I was in the middle of sipping on. I would have been embarrassed if I wasn't already so aggravated at him for showing up here whipping his dick out and acting so possessive. Alpha-holes, I swear...

"Your *wife?*" Dean scoffs. "Well, you need to keep your *whore* on a tighter leash because she's been throwing herself at me all night", Dean half-slurs, half-spits back at Killian.

Smack

Before I can even register Dean's insult his head snaps back, and his ass hits the floor.

A small part of me can't help but smile at the thought of Killian sticking up for me, but the rest of me is pissed that he just punched a man's lights out in the middle of a crowded bar. Is there no such thing as 'witnesses' where he comes from?

Jumping off my bar stool I turn and push Killian in the chest. "What the hell are you thinking?! Outside now!"

Killian hesitates a moment, staring down at the man on the floor like he wants to beat on him some more. Placing my hand on his arm finally grabs his attention and he reluctantly turns and follows me to the exit.

He can probably tell from me staring daggers at him that I am insanely pissed off.

What is wrong with this man?! I don't know how they do it in the Fae Realm but here in the Mortal Realm you go to jail for physically assaulting people. Even if his actions were justified...in my opinion.

Worse yet, I'm a freaking cop. Am I just supposed to look the other way and pretend I didn't just witness Killian commit assault and battery on that drunk asshole?

Shit!

I must admit that the sight of him tonight stole my breath away. He is always out-of-this-realm handsome, but tonight he looks completely irresistible. I never truly understood the phrase 'I want to climb him like a tree', until I saw him standing there tonight defending my honor. He swapped his usual T-shirt and biker boots for black dress shoes, nice jeans, and a black dress shirt with the sleeves rolled up to reveal the corded muscles of his forearms and a few buttons left undone to reveal his hard chiseled chest. So maybe it's a good thing I'm pissed off at him, or God knows what I would do to this man tonight.

Killian just follows me in silence as I lead us down a dark side alley to give us some privacy. As soon as I am sure no one is around, I let out a *quiet* scream in frustration while pulling at my hair.

"Why are you so upset? He called you a whore...I wasn't letting him get away with that." I can hear how serious and angry he is, but that's still not getting him off the hook.

"You can't just go around punching people, dumbass! You could end up in jail! Hell, I should be taking you there right now. You're lucky that I need your help, or I would be." I yell at him.

Killian closes the gap between us in two long strides. Staring down at me our eyes lock together, and I swear it feels like he is speaking into my soul as he growls out in a low dark voice, "He's lucky all I did was punch him."

His words, so domineering and primal, send a blazing hot bolt of lightning shooting straight to my core.

The way Killian is staring at me puts me in mind of an apex predator closing in on its prey. I began backing away, but with every step back I take he just takes another step forward. Until finally I have nowhere else to go as my back presses up against a cold damp cement wall.

My heart is racing, not knowing what is going on inside that beautiful, dangerous, head of his. However, I can't deny the rush of excitement and anticipation I'm also feeling.

"His hands were all over you and you didn't want that...not like the way you desire to feel *my* hands all over you." Killian speaks slowly. His voice is husky and dripping with lust, as he slowly continues closing the already small space between us.

I blink and open my eyes; to find Killian has me caged in with his hands pressed against the damp cement wall on either side of my head.

I am well and truly *fucked* with no way out.

Even though judging by my body's reactions to my predicament I'm no longer sure I want a way out. But I will be damned if I let him know the type of effect he is having on me.

I can't help but to internally scream at my body to snap the fuck out of it.

Stupid hormones!

"Ha!" I laugh up into his face. I was trying to think of something snarky to respond with but the way my blood is rushing through my head along with the thumping of my heart; laughing was the best I could do.

"You are kidding yourself if you think I want your slimy Fae hands on me." I finally manage to spit back at him. Although, my response doesn't seem to deter him, in fact, it seems to do quite the opposite. Instead of backing away, Killian brings his face down to mine. If I so much as breath too hard our noses will smash together.

Just when I think it can't get any worse; his lips pull up into a mischievous grin.

"Oh, I know for a *fact* you want my 'slimy' Fae hands *all* over you, *little witch*. The smell of your desire is so strong it's making my fucking head spin." Killian quietly growls out, bringing his lips down and brushing them against the corner of my mouth. This small action sends shivers all the way to the tips of my toes.

I gasp aloud.

If you could die from embarrassment, I am positive I would be dead right now. I'm silently praying that the shadows surrounding us right now are concealing my blushing red cheeks.

Killian lets out a low sexy laugh as he realizes his words have left me speechless.

"Not only are us Fae faster, stronger, and more visually appealing than humans...our sense of sight, sound, and *smell* are also enhanced."

"Bullshit" I scowl, trying to maintain my tough girl composure, but instead it comes out sounding breathy.

Killian leans down further. His lips are feather light against mine presenting a silent challenge, "Is it? Then tell me to back off. Tell me *not* to kiss you, Calista. Because once I do, there won't be a soul in all the realms capable of giving you the satisfaction that your lips will hunger for...*crave,* when my lips are done devouring you."

Fuck. Me.

Betrayed by my body's own desire and going against my better judgement; I rise upon my toes, closing the distance between us, crashing my lips into his.

This feeling is like nothing I have experienced before. It feels like so much more than just our lips are colliding together in this moment. It feels like there is this tiny ember of light that's glowing inside me and reaching out to his shadows. The glow seems to become brighter the closer it comes to entwining with his shadows. It's almost as if this glowing ember inside of me recognizes or is familiar with these darkened shadows inside of him.

All I know for certain is that there is still too much distance between the two of us. Without hesitating I reach up and run my fingers through his soft luscious hair...

As my fingers move to drag his head down to deepen our kiss, my phone goes off.

I quickly break off the kiss and pull away; answering the call before Killian can stop me, but not before I hear the frustrated growl he releases. Which puts a wicked grin on my face.

It's just Seb checking to see where I am. I guess he finally came up for air from his dance floor make-out session and noticed I wasn't around. I told him I just stepped out to get some fresh air and that I'm heading back inside now.

Like I thought, tonight was a total bust at finding the assassins here at the bar.

Maybe the guys will have better luck tonight since they plan on staking out her place until morning.

Not even looking at Killian, I turn around and begin walking back to the bar.

"Go back to your assigned post Killian", I yell, glancing back over my shoulder at him.

"Are we just going to ignore what just happened?!" he shouts, standing exactly where I left him. I ignore him and continue to walk away, leaving him alone in the dark alley.

I turn back to face him, still walking backwards towards the bar. I don't trust myself right now to not get pulled back in by his raw magnetism.

Shrugging very nonchalantly I lie right to his face, "Nothing happened Killian, it was a brief mistake." The pained look that flashes across his face when I say those words makes me feel guilty for dismissing him so easily.

Some people can tell a lie so repeatedly that they actually come to believe it's true...and that is exactly what I plan to do.

Lie and deny, my new way of life.

At least until these stupid Fae are out of our lives for good.

'That kiss meant absolutely nothing. There is nothing between me and Killian.'; this is my new mantra that I repeated silently to myself from the time I turned away and left Killian standing in that dark cold alley, till the time I fell asleep.

When this heat between us finally settles down he will realize that in the long run I was doing us both a favor. He is a Fae and I'm a human; from two completely different realms. There is no chance for us to have a future together.

No matter how strong this pull between us continues to suggest otherwise.

CHAPTER 19

KILLIAN

It has been three days since my back-alley kiss with Calista. Three days of her ignoring my calls and texts. Three agonizing days battling against this internal pull between the two of us, that is leaving me with a desperate desire to be close to her.

I keep telling myself it's only because she is the *key* to destroying my father; and if something happens to her, I will be stuck waiting another Gods knows how many years for something to come along and help me destroy him. But deep down I know it's *more* than that.

I'm trying to give her space, because I know she is still trying to process this immense attraction we feel between us. I've given in to my desire a couple times; concealing myself within my shadows so I could see her with my own eyes and know she is safe.

Her sisters, Hazel and Eve, have been over every day working with the guys to awaken and access more of their powers. I can sense most of their power lying dormant within them; however, even when their powers do fully emerge, their full abilities won't even come close to being on the same level as Calista's.

When Calista's power awakens; and she opens herself up to reach her full potential, she will be unstoppable... More powerful than any Fae I've ever heard of...me included.

There is something *more* to her...something *old*. My little witch is something *other* than what she has been led to believe. And I fully intend on discovering the truth.

Both sisters have lied straight to my face repeatedly for days now. Assuring me that Calista is not avoiding me and that she has just been very busy with work and the assassin case. Do they not know that Fae senses are far greater than those of humans? I can hear the slight change up of their heartbeat every time they lie. Their heartbeat speeds up, even if just for a few quick beats.

No matter though...her avoidance *ends* today. Callum and Eve are going to stake out Olivia's apartment in case the assassins decide to make a move. Dante and Hazel, if they don't kill each other first, are going to ride around the city to see if they can pick up any kind of trail that will help lead us to the assassins.

Leaving me to pay my little witch a visit. We will be staying in tonight and working on accessing her powers...since she has been 'too busy' to come practice with her sisters these last few days.

She has a long way to go before she can stand a chance against my father, and each day she avoids training with me puts her at even more of a disadvantage.

Damn! She is a sight to behold, standing there in that cut off shirt. It hangs just below her breast and off one shoulder, revealing just enough of her black lacey bra. Those shorts, if you can even call them that, are practically painted on and show off just the right amount of cheek at the bottom. She is a Gods damn knock out, and all she is doing is standing there chopping strawberries.

I am utterly and completely *fucked* when it comes to this woman. These feelings she awakens in me keep distracting me from my entire purpose of coming to the Mortal Realm in the first place...to use her and her sisters to help defeat my father. She is merely a *tool* to be used for my plan to succeed...or so I keep reminding myself.

"Hey, you." I say, leaning against her living room wall, startling her from behind. Calista whirls around holding up the knife she was using to chop strawberries, ready to strike.

She leans forward grabbing her chest, revealing more of her lacey bra hiding beneath her shirt. "Shit Killian! Don't you know how to knock!?", she snaps. Then she looks at me with one eyebrow raised; like I've come to realize she does whenever she is unsure about something. It's quite adorable. "How did you get in anyway? I know my door is locked." she asks.

"Shadows, remember?" I begin walking over to join her in the kitchen. "I can use them to transport myself wherever I want to go, well, as long as I've been to the destination before."

"Oh...yea...I forgot" she admits, visibly relaxing and turning around to get back to work on her strawberries.

"Sorry I'm still trying to wrap my mind around having a bunch of fairies in my life now."

"Fae! Not Fairies." I immediately correct her, as I lean against the counter next to her and watch her work.

She looks over, staring at me like I have two heads. I find it adorable the way she scrunches up her nose when she's confused about something. And that is *NOT* okay...I need to get my shit together...I have a job to do...I can't let my feelings towards her distract me from my purpose.

She is only a tool!

The guys made sure to remind me of that before they left this evening. Telling me to not go thinking with the wrong 'head'. And that Calista and her sisters are just a means to an end, so I don't need to be forming attachments.

It's turning out to be easier said than done. Especially since I have a very high suspicion that an attachment was already there. Even before the first time I saw her walk into that bar.

I felt it the night she kissed me in that Gods forsaken alley. My shadows somehow recognized the light glowing inside of her, I could sense them spreading out inside of me, yearning to connect with the warmth of her glow.

"Fairies are those tiny little pansy bitches with wings you see in all the storybooks they show you humans, shitting sparkles all over the place." I inform her, giving her a smug smile. And to my complete surprise, she smiles back at me...*really* smiles.

The second I see it I know I'm done for; it is the most breathtaking thing I have ever seen. I could live my life solely off her smiles alone.

And standing here in stunned silence, just staring back at her beautiful smile, I realize I will do *anything* I can to keep those smiles on her face, for as long as she will let me.

"So, you...but minus the wings?" she jokes, bursting into laughter when she sees my annoyance all over my face. And Gods, her laugh is one of the sweetest sounds I have ever heard.

Without thinking, I lunge. I take her by the waist and spin her around, as my other hand slides down over her perfect ass. I lift her up to sit her on the counter, where I place myself right between her long smooth legs.

The little gasp she releases goes straight to my cock.

Even with her sitting upon the counter I still tower over her, and I find myself looking down into her mesmerizing eyes. I could drown in those eyes and would be completely content with that...

Damn it! I am well and truly *fucked*! What spell has this little witch put me under?

Calista's startled reaction is gone the moment she looks up at me. She reaches over, grabbing a strawberry, and slowly places it in her mouth. Her eyelashes flutter shut as she takes the most sensual bite I have ever seen. She follows it with an intoxicating moan. When she finally opens her eyes, she looks up into mine and offers me the rest of her strawberry. I slowly bend down and place my mouth around the berry, never taking my eyes off hers. Even this simple act of sharing a strawberry with this woman feels so incredibly intimate.

She finally breaks eye contact with me, looking over to pick out another juicy berry. I can't stop myself from staring down at her; taking in her every detail...then I see it.

My heart comes to a complete stop. Behind her ear I spot a small delicate tattoo...of a single red *rose.*

"I like your tattoo" I whisper, while lightly tracing my finger along the design behind her ear. As I do, I can feel a little shiver pass over her, bringing a satisfied smile to my face. "Why a rose?"

"It was for someone I loved, a long time ago. I never got the chance to show them though." She says, looking down to avoid eye contact with me, but I can hear the pain in her voice. I just want to wrap her in my arms and keep her from ever feeling such pain again.

"I got it with my aunt on my eighteenth birthday. I remember thinking how cool she was to be encouraging me to get my first tattoo so young, as her gift to me. It was an amazing day; we had such a great time together and I'll never forget it, that's for sure. But after that day I never saw them again...the man I was in love with." When she finally looks back up at me with tears in her eyes, my heart aches for her...and for *him.*

Everything she just said has me thinking that my suspicions I've had from the moment we laid eyes on one another in that bar are correct. And if that's true...my purpose here can be damned.

I must know the truth though before I turn my back on everything my friends and I have risked and set out to accomplish in coming here.

"What are you doing here Killian?" Calista asks, snapping me out of my thoughts. It takes me a second to recall her question before I can finally answer her.

"I thought we were going to work on your magic, while the others are off scouring the town for the assassins? Your sisters said they filled you in on the plan."

"I know that." she playfully rolls her eyes at me. "I mean what are *you* doing *here*...standing between my legs", her voice drops down into a breathy whisper as she looks up at me from under her long lashes, "looking like you want to kiss me?"

As soon as those words leave her mouth, I throw restraint out the window and crash my lips into hers.

Threading my fingers through the back of her hair, I angle her head back, tracing my tongue along the seem of her soft lips, begging her lips to let me in. She moans and I swear I see stars. Her lips part as she glides her tongue along mine allowing me to deepen our kiss. She tastes delicious, like vanilla and strawberries; this sweet combination causes my head to spin.

But this kiss is still not enough to satisfy this burning desire that has ignited a fire inside of me.

Before I can fully process what's happening between us, she breaks the kiss and pulls away. Both of us are breathless as we stare at each other, concern gleaming from her eyes.

"Killian, we can't. I'm sorry, but this wouldn't work," she says, shaking her head and gesturing between us. "We come from different realms. You're Fae, and I'm human." She pushes me back and jumps off the counter and begins walking down the hallway toward her bedroom.

But I refuse to let her walk away from me again.

"I know you feel the connection between us" I exclaim, as I follow her down the hall. "I've felt it since the moment you walked into that bar...and I think you felt it too. Look me in the eyes, Calista, and tell me you don't feel anything between us, and I'll let it go." I know she can see the pleading look on my face when she turns around to face me as she is opening her bedroom door. My eyes search hers, looking for the answer my ears desperately hope to hear.

"Am I attracted to you? Yes! Is that what you want to hear? Because it still doesn't change anything."

Before I can stop myself, I reach out and pull her body against mine. With one arm around her waist and my hand behind her neck I crush my lips to hers. If she wants to play stubborn, that's fine, but I am going to make it very hard for her to deny the truth of what she feels between us.

At first the kiss is rough, desperate, like we fear this may be the last one we ever share, and we want to capture every moment of it.

She has her arms around my neck and hands in my hair, pulling me down into her, deepening the kiss. My arm is wrapped so tightly around her waist; crushing our bodies together perfectly, like they were made for one another.

I'm not sure if I can ever let her go, and even if I decided to, my hand is so tangled up in her hair I doubt I could.

The kiss finally slows...into something *more*, revealing a whole new layer of feelings shared between us. It is soft and tender; filled with an emotion I'm not ready to acknowledge. When she finally pulls away, we are both left breathless with swollen red lips and messy hair. We stand here, just staring into one another's eyes. She can deny it all she wants, but her eyes give her away...she feels it too.

"Goodnight, Killian", Calista whispers up at me before turning into her room and closing the door in my face.

Rejected...well there is a first time for everything.

Here I'm left looking and feeling like a complete fool. I brace my hands on the door frame and hang my head in defeat.

Did I misread her? Does she not feel *that constant pull between us? Maybe I am imagining it?...*

I lift my head and accept defeat, ready to walk away. But before I get a chance to move the door opens. She is standing there, gazing up at me. I don't even care if she sees how defeated I look. This woman somehow possesses the *power* to destroy me, and I have no way of hiding from it.

Maybe I don't even want to hide from it?

Her gaze reveals everything; she feels the same longing and desire I feel whenever she is around. As I prepare to speak, she breathlessly confesses, "I'm not even slightly tired."

I don't know who moved first but before I can register what is happening her lips are locked against mine. This kiss is not gentle, but it is *everything*. All the emotions we have felt towards one another in this short time together are being poured into this kiss. Teeth and tongues are clashing, fingers are grasping and pulling at hair and clothes, and lips are bitten and sucked.

Without wasting another moment, I lift her up by her ass and carry her towards the bed. She releases a tiny whimper as she wraps her sweet thighs around my waist. Before I can stop it a groan of pleasure escapes my throat. My cock is so ready for her it is slightly painful to walk, but I'll be damned if that is going to stop me.

I swear if I wake up and this has all been a dream, I'll ask the Gods to just kill me now to end my suffering. I will never be able to recover from this moment for as long as I live and breathe.

I lay her gently onto the bed, taking my time to savor every moment of this experience. She is more beautiful than words can describe, just laying here beneath me, her hair splayed out like a halo around her head. And she is all *mine*. I could listen to her moan every day for the rest of my life...and the fact that I am the cause of them makes me rock hard.

She makes quick work of pulling my shirt off over my head and tossing it to the side. I simply take her top in my hands and rip it completely down the center...I will buy her a new one later.

She doesn't seem to mind as she grips my hair tighter and pulls me back down to her. I begin kissing her jaw and slowly working my way down her neck to that sweet spot just above her collarbone.

Something inside of me takes over and I let out an animalistic growl before sinking my sharp canines into her soft flesh. She releases a short scream, that turns into a deep long moan of pleasure, as I begin swirling my tongue around and kissing on the spot I just bit. She lays her head to the side inviting me to more of her delicious neck, while simultaneously grinding her center along my straining cock. It is getting physically painful at this point to keep myself from releasing it and driving it home, deep into her heated core.

Working my way back up, I trail kisses along the side of her neck. I nip her ear lobe between my teeth and whisper, *"Mine"*.

Calista breathlessly moans out *"Yours"* in return, which freezes me in place as I stare down at her in complete shock.

I feel like I am having an out of body experience. I can see the two of us laying there tangled up together. Speaking words that have so much more meaning behind them than she even knows. Part of me wants to stop and explain what these declarations mean in the Fae Realm, but the selfish part of me doesn't want to stop what we have started.

Before she even notices the effect her words just had on me, I release another growl and dive back upon her mouth, kissing her *fiercely*.

I'm kissing the tops of her breasts, grabbing hold of her black lacey bra to tear it right off her chest, when my phone begins ringing.

Releasing another growl, I tell her to "Ignore it" before returning my attention to her supple breasts. It would have to be a phone call from the Gods themselves to tear me away from them.

"No... answer it", she laces her hands through my hair pulling my head back up. I know she can tell by the look I'm giving her underneath my hooded gaze, that it is not going to happen.

I try to pull my face back down to where I left off, but she has a death lock on my hair. I would be extremely upset if I wasn't turned on by how strong she is.

"No!" I growl out. "They can call back." I say as I go to kiss her again. Dodging my kiss, she reaches around and shoves her hand down into the front pocket of my jeans to grab my phone. As soon as I hear her breath catch, a devilish grin creeps across my face.

Her hand has found more than my phone in that pocket. The feel of her fingers running along my shaft has me almost coming right then and there. Hell, I'm wound so tightly I think a light breeze could get the job done at this point.

"It's Callum, it may be important", she insists handing me my phone. I'm amazed the screen on my phone doesn't shatter as I swipe to answer his call.

"WHAT!?" I shout into the phone. Making my irritation at his interruption known.

"Whoa dude! What's wrong? Did I interrupt you in the middle of getting your dick wet?" Callum laughs, not knowing how correct he is.

"Why the *fuck* are you calling, Callum?" I growl out.

Callum barks out a laugh. "Ah man...really?! *Shit,* I'm sorry." My anger is only growing at the amusement lacing his voice. "Fornicating is going to have to wait till later. We found something. Meet us at All Souls now.

As Callum gives out another apology for the cock block, Calista is already rolling out from underneath me and heading over to her closet to get dressed. I let my body crash down on top of her bed, already missing the warmth of her soft body beneath mine. I lie there rubbing my hands across my face and wishing I could turn back time.

Ending the call, I just stare over at Cali, taking in every curve of her body...wishing it was back underneath mine. *Fuck!*

From the closet I hear her let out a giggle. What is she laughing at in there? Did I accidentally shout that out loud instead of in my head?

Calista emerges from the closet dressed in tight jeans, a black sleeveless blouse with a golden snake embordered up the side, and gold heels. Looking deliciously edible.

I think she is purposefully trying to drive me crazy.

Pulling my black t-shirt back on over my head, I grab her wrist as she goes to walk past me. Looking down into her eyes I bring my lips to hers, softly, intimately. "This isn't over", I whisper against her lips, but she just smiles up at me and walks off. Leaving me to sit back down on her bed in an extremely uncomfortable situation.

Fuck!

CHAPTER 20

CALISTA

When Killian and I arrived at All Souls, we became the center of attention. Based on the looks we were getting from everyone, particularly my sisters, it was evident that they had all been present during Callum's phone call with Killian. I had to gather all my composure to not shrink up from embarrassment.

The four of them were packed into a booth in the back with two chairs sitting at the end awaiting me and Killian. The booth was normal sized, but it looked comically small with the two huge Fae males taking up all the space.

Killian made it over to the chairs first and took a seat. As I go to take a seat in the chair next to him, he grabs my waist and pulls me down onto his lap.

Mortified, I quickly pull his hands away and jump from his lap, moving around to take the chair next to him. I was already dying of shame on the inside from my sisters' judging stares...I didn't want to give them any more ammo for them to hold against me.

Of course, Callum and Dante would find me publicly rejecting their friend to be hilarious. At least they did, until Killian fixed them with a stare that promised a slow painful death.

After putting them in their place, Killian looks over at me with a confident smirk pulling at his soft lips. The message behind his smirk is clear; I can fight it all I want too but I will eventually give in to my feelings towards him.

"So, what are we doing here?" I ask the group, sounding a little too frustrated for my own liking. I should be grateful they called us here in time before I ended up making a horrible mistake. I obviously wasn't thinking in my correct state of mind before they called.

Maybe there is a carbon monoxide leak in my apartment and it's beginning to impact my brain.

Logical thinking there Cali, I'll call the apartment manager first thing when I get back to have them check...you can never be too safe, right?

The fiendish smile I find on Dante's face when I look over at him makes me feel uneasy. And unfortunately, that feeling won't be going away anytime soon as he reveals to the group, "Hazel here has informed us that you girls have been in contact with another Dark Fae...and that you *also* made a deal with them to help kill the king."

I look over at my sisters in complete shock. I clench my jaw shut to keep myself from saying something I'll regret. Why would Hazel tell these guys this information; especially the one she supposedly can't stand? We don't even know if they can be trusted yet.

Callum turns to address Killian directly and adds, "Maybe you don't know your little witch as well as you think, Kill."

"Fuck you, Asshole!", Hazel spits at Dante. Dante flinches from what I'm assuming must be Hazel kicking him under the table.

She then turns to me with her eyes full of remorse and brimming with tears, "I'm sorry Cali it just slipped out...please don't hate me".

Before I can stop myself, I shake my head at Hazel revealing my disappointment. She is the main reason we are even in this whole mess in the first place, with her insistence on us doing the ritual to find our mothers' killer. I have no clue what is going through her head these days.

And Dante with his smug ass remark. He looks so proud of himself; like he just ratted me out to Killian and was excited to see me get in *trouble.* For being around one-hundred and seventy years old this guy still needs to grow the fuck up apparently.

Killian casually leans back in his chair; studying me with his gaze, "Is this true, *little witch?*" His tone is so uncaring, like he isn't upset in the slightest regarding this new information.

But his eyes give him away; just one look is all I need to see how hurt he is that I lied to him.

Well not 'lied' just withheld important information. And I still fail to see how any of it is his business. Our deal with Cerberus has nothing to do with them.

Seeing no way to perform damage control, I sigh and reluctantly explain everything to our new friends. I start from the beginning with the summoning ritual all the way to the deal we made with the Dark Fae. Though, instead of sharing information about Cerberus, we decide to go ahead and introduce them directly.

Seeing as how we all have the same end goal there shouldn't be any harm in that, right? The more people we have on our team the better...I think.

Back in my living room we all stand around the summoning circle waiting for Cerberus to answer our summons. I find myself happily surprised when he appears *inside* the summoning circle this time; even though he doesn't stay there.

"Well, what do we have here?" Cerberus inquires while looking around and taking in the new members in our group. At first, he seems to be more curious about the newcomers, but as soon as his eyes lock onto Killian, he appears to be angered. "Ladies, do you mind telling me what the hell is going on?", he inquires sternly.

The girls and I just look around at one another confused. I'm unsure of what I should say to mitigate the situation at hand. The last thing I expected was for one of the guys to know Cerberus. I especially didn't expect there to be negative feelings between any of them.

But I think it's safe to assume I was wrong, because Cerberus and Killian currently seem to be in the middle of an intense standoff.

Killian snarls, taking a step closer to Cerberus. "Hello, *Uncle*".

I swear I can feel my jaw hit the floor.

Uncle?! They are family?!

My mind is spinning so fast that the room looks like it is starting to spin with it. Then, just when I think things couldn't get any crazier, Cerberus closes the gap between them and drops another enormous bomb. "Killian...or should I now address you as *Prince?*"

"The Fuck?!"

I must have shouted that out loud seeing as how both men instantly turn to look at me. Looking at my sisters I can see that they are also stunned in silence with their mouths hanging wide open.

Turning my attention to Killian I manage to question him on what all three of us are thinking, "*Prince?!* You are a Prince?" Looking indifferent about the whole ordeal Killian moves closer to me, but I retreat a step. Right now, I need to keep my distance until I can wrap my mind around this information and get some answers.

"*You* are the Dark Fae *Prince?* And you want us to kill your *father*...the *king!?*"

With a pleading look on his face Killian tries reaching out for me again, but I continue to back away. I start to pace around the room before Eve comes up and lays a calming, reassuring hand on my shoulder. "Was this all a set up and you guys really are the assassins sent to kill us? And you what? Thought you would have a little fun with your prey first?" I yell, revealing some of the thoughts that are lining up in my mind.

"NO!" Killian roars out.

His sudden outburst interrupts my spiraling thoughts, allowing me to concentrate and refocus.

"This is too great," Cerberus says, clapping slowly, clearly enjoying himself. "You didn't tell them you were the prince?" He laughs darkly, turning to pin me and my sisters with his serious gaze.

"Why is my nephew and his two goons here?" Cerberus curiously asks us. Seeming to be less than happy about this unplanned reunion.

Callum and Dante don't look happy about being referred to as 'goons' but they continue to stand quietly on the sideline.

I can't seem to take my eyes off Killian's. From the outside it must look like we are having our own private conversation, which we kind of are. His eyes are begging me to trust him...hopefully he can tell mine are just calling him a "dumbass fairy" repeatedly. The ones with wings that fart glitter out of their ass.

Thankfully, Eve steps in and fills Cerberus in on everything that has happened since we last spoke with him a week ago...before we met the guys.

"So, you want to kill your father? Why?" Cerberus interrogates Killian. He seems very taken aback by this revelation and finding it hard to believe.

Killian explains his reasonings behind wanting the king dead to Cerberus, like he did before with us...except this time he added in a few details about the king being a horrible excuse of a father.

"Do you plan on taking the throne for yourself? Or will you right your father's wrong and relinquish the Unseelie throne to the rightful heir?"

"I plan to rule my kingdom proudly and bring it back to all its glory and then some. But seeing that the throne does rightfully belong to you, if you wish to reclaim it and rule as your father once did, I will relinquish the throne and crown to you, Uncle." The honesty in Killian's voice and his eyes cannot be denied. Cerberus must have noticed it as well because he gives Killian a respectful nod. However, I can't help but notice he didn't give Killian an answer about if he would be taking back his throne.

I thought the whole point of us killing the current Dark Fae King was so he could get justice for his father, the late king, and to take back the Unseelie Kingdom that had been stolen from him.

I walk up and place myself between both Killian and Cerberus. Looking to Cerberus I ask, "So can we actually trust these guys?"

He only hesitates slightly before giving us a nod of approval. "Yes, I think we can."

For some strange reason, Cerberus's trust in them helps to slightly ease my worries.

We fill Cerberus in on our plans to train with the guys, and how our search for the assassins is going. He agrees to take a closer look at the prophecy to see if it could give us any clues on how exactly the Dark Fae King is to be destroyed. He is also supposed to ask around to see if any of his contacts within both the Fae and Mortal Realms have any clue as to where the assassins are hiding out while they are here.

CHAPTER 21

CALISTA

The next morning work starts off with my Lieutenant reprimanding me for our slow progress with the serial killer case.

Ever since we released the profiles of our three suspects to WUSA9 News, the local news broadcasting station, the suspects' profiles began spreading like wildfire across social media. Which is exactly what I hoped would happen since nowadays around twenty percent of Americans get their news from social media sites. Now that their faces are plastered everywhere you turn the assassins seem to be laying low.

I still have a couple members of my team tailing Olivia anywhere she goes and posted up outside her residence, in case the assassins decide to show back up to make their move.

Seeing as how there hasn't been a murder in over a week; I will take that as a win. However, the Lieutenant doesn't seem to share my viewpoint.

As much as I hate to admit it, me and my sisters acting as bait for the assassins may be our best chance to catch and eliminate these assholes.

Sebastian finds me in the break room, shamelessly drinking my third cup of coffee since arriving at work less than an hour ago.

We both knew I was going to get my ass handed to me when the Lieutenant called me into his office first thing this morning.

"How bad was it?" Seb asks, while walking over to grab himself a second cup.

"Do I even need to answer that? He acts like we aren't even trying to catch these perps. I've literally exhausted every officer at my disposal to catching these guys." I turn around and push myself up onto the counter next to the coffee machine.

Instantly, my mind can't help but think about what happened the last time I was sitting like this with Killian, and I feel my face start to blush.

"We are keeping the heat on them with their profiles out there now for all to see. They shouldn't even be able to walk into a gas station without being recognized. And sooner or later they will have to go out for food or something, right?" Seb says optimistically, as he easily pushes himself onto the counter to join me, using only one arm...show off. I look over to tell him as much, but he is leaning away from me with his face all scrunched up in disgust. "Did you change your shampoo or something?"

"No why?" I ask. Insulted by the fact his face looks like he just smelled a dead body.

"You always smell sweet, like flowers and vanilla, but today you smell...*weird*." He looks at me again with his nose still scrunched up. "I can slightly smell your usual scent but there is another smell mixed in almost covering it up. Sandalwood. That's it!" He snaps his fingers as he determines the scent.

It's my turn to scrunch my face up in disgust now after that weird description. "Guess that's what I get for finally taking your advice and going on a date with someone from that stupid dating app." I know he can tell by the smile spreading across my face that I am bluffing.

Sebastian burst out laughing, and his handsome smile and jovial laugh has me laughing right along with him. He can always raise my spirits...apparently even when he is insulting the way I smell.

After Seb leaves and I'm left alone again, I try to be as subtle as possible and lean down to sniff my shirt. I smell like I always do, like sweet vanilla and roses. I have no clue where Seb got sandalwood from...maybe he was smelling his own cologne or deodorant on top of mine?

That must be what happened...he's such a dumb ass sometimes.

Another case closed by the unstoppable Detective Calista Adams!

The rest of the workday seems to fly by. Early afternoon we got called in to investigate another murder scene. The victim was female, but the M.O. didn't match up. This female seems to have died from an accidental overdose, given the fresh track marks down her arms. Her body was then dumped into the Potomac River sometime within the past forty-eight hours, judging by the body's state of decomposition.

My guess is that people were probably shooting up together when one of them took a little too much. The other person/persons involved panicked; and with God knows how much or many drugs in their system, thought that tossing the body into the river would be a quick fix of the situation.

Thankfully, I didn't have to waste any more time or brain cells diving into this case. Another team from our sister precinct stepped in to take this one on. This case is low priority for my team seeing as how we still have an active serial killer case on our hands.

The next morning, Killian shows up at my place shortly after I wake up to get ready for work. I was in the process of getting dressed when I heard excessive knocking at my door. Apparently, he couldn't wait for me to meet up with him at the Hive later this evening after I got off work like we had originally planned.

"What are you doing here? We weren't supposed to meet until later.", I question as he steps inside.

"Change of plans, you're not going to work today." he replies as he starts pacing back and forth in my living room. He keeps rubbing his chin; it looks to me like he has some crazy idea, but he isn't sure if he wants to say it out loud. But seeing as how he came all the way over here and decided on my behalf that I'm not going to work today, he is going to tell me what he has going on in that strange Fae head of his. And it better be good!

"Well? Are you going to tell me what you are thinking or are you just going to pace a hole into my floor?"

He whips his head up and finally stops to look at me. He looks upset. "Your powers are taking longer to awaken than I had hoped. If you were forced into facing off with the king today; you and your sisters wouldn't stand a chance. So, I have a crazy theory I want to test out. If I'm right, then your powers will not only awaken but become stronger and more controllable."

He looks more confident now that he has explained where his head is at.

Walking over to me, he reaches out his hand for me to accept, "Do you trust me?" he asks, staring down at me with those eyes I can never seem to get my fill of. He has a slight crease in his brow like he is worried about what my answer will be.

My heart started fluttering as soon as he asked the question and it doesn't feel to be slowing down. That alone tells me all I need to know; I *do* trust him.

I know I shouldn't, not only because we just met but he's also the Dark Fae Prince. I don't even know his last name, but for some reason that I can't explain, I do trust him.

Though I do need him to provide more clarification on what exactly he has in mind; like what this theory of his entails before we go skipping off into the sunset together.

If he thinks I'm going to admit that I trust him though, he has another thing coming. I'm way too stubborn. If he hasn't figured that out by now, he's in trouble.

"Absolutely not" I tell him, before reaching up anyways and taking his hand. I can tell by the grin on his face he can see right through my charade. But before I have a chance to ask what he has in mind we are encased within shadows...and my vision begins spinning before everything plunges into darkness.

What the hell did I just get myself into....

CHAPTER 22

CALISTA

I will not puke...I will not puke...I will not— Oh God I'm going to be sick!
As soon as my feet are back on solid ground I fall onto all fours, dry heaving through the intense nausea I am experiencing. Luckily, there wasn't much in my stomach to begin with, so I don't actually puke my guts up in front of Killian. That would be mortifying.

Slowly opening my eyes, I can see that I am still inside of Killian's shadows. Cocooned in a blanket of darkness; that almost feels...safe?

"Ow!" Slapping my hand behind my ear over my rose tattoo I quickly whip my head around to find Killian standing behind me. "What the F—", my breath leaves my lungs before I can finish.

As soon as I look up at Killian his shadows evaporate, revealing a world I thought had only existed in my dreams. A world of darkness illuminated by a magnificent full moon and dazzling starlight. A world I have longed to return to over the last ten years.

Still clasping my ear, I slowly turn in place, taking in the breath-taking scene before me. The surrounding darkness is filled with beautiful creatures and flora made of starlight, iridescence, and flames.

Beautiful sparkling bird-like creatures with long feathered tails soar across the sky like shooting stars. Deer-like creatures engulfed in orange and gold fiery flames, with three long whip-like tails prance through the forest of shimmering flowers and trees. Flames trailing in their wake, miraculously never catching anything else around them on fire.

Little flying insects light up to decorate the night, they make it look as if the stars themselves have floated down from the midnight sky above to dance around the open field.

Off in the distance, starkly standing out against the surrounding darkness is a flowing river of lava. I recall watching long anaconda-like creatures made of ice slithering through the flowing lava. They sported multiple spikes made of ice that cascaded along their backs. The surreal manner with which the fire and ice coexisted always astounded me.

This world is beautiful and enchanting. Exactly like what I had seen in my dreams all those years ago. Where I always felt at home.

There is no way this is really happening...right?

It was all just a dream...

A magical world created in the unconscious mind of a young sixteen-year-old child, who longed for a place where she could feel like she belonged.

When my eyes finally land back on Killian my racing heart comes to a skidding halt...

Words cease to exist. It's all I can manage to get out a single syllable.

"Y—Yo—" I struggle to speak without my heart working to push blood throughout my body and air into my lungs.

"YOU!" I yell, pointing at Killian.

It was him, but different...

Killian's hair was now a stunning silver, and his eyes were as dark as night and glimmering with starlight; beautiful silver specks that sparkled like the stars in the night sky above. The contrast between his eyes and hair alone took my breath away. His skin was fair like mine but had a sheen to it like it was glowing in the moonlight. Just as I remembered him...

Killian's smile is as bright and full as the moon overhead. "Hey, *Viper*" his voice is low and soft, like he's trying not to scare off a shy animal.

On the inside my mind and heart are racing around like they are competing in the NASCAR Daytona 500.

This cannot be real? Maybe he killed me after all? Or maybe one of his powers is he can invade people's past dreams?

"You're not going crazy. It's really me." he says shyly, finally bringing me out of my stupor.

Slowly, I walk closer to him, taking in every small detail I can from his swaying silver hair splaying across his forehead, to the way he carries himself. "Rose? Y—You're Rose?"

Killian closes the distance between us, taking both of my hands in his and giving me his signature knee buckling grin.

"About time you figured it out.", he reaches up to gently tuck a strand of my hair behind my ear. "You're going to have to be faster than that if you want to keep living up to your name, Viper."

I'm glad he is finding all this amusing because I feel completely bamboozled.

He thinks I'm slow...I'll show him slow.

Crack

I punch him straight in the nose. Striking fast just like a *viper*. He probably didn't even know what was happening until his neck was already whipping in a different direction. Serves him right for keeping all of this from me.

Killian looks back at me, wiping away the blood from his bleeding nose. I thought he would be pissed off but instead he starts to *laugh*. Laughing and smiling! Which is doing absolutely nothing but fueling my anger.

"There's *my* Viper"

His words cause me to lose control over all the emotions I'm feeling. I begin to shout and pace back and forth.

"What the actual fuck, Killian? Is that even your *real* name?"

Thankfully, Killian grabs hold of my arm and brings me to a stop before I begin ripping my hair out. I turn around and glare up at him. Trying not to get lost in his starry eyes and forget how angry I am right now.

I am channeling all the anger and frustration that's coursing through my body into my stare. Hoping my stare alone conveys my feelings of hurt and deceit.

Taking slow deep breaths, I finally calm down enough to ask, "Have you known this whole time who I was? Why would you not tell me?" I can't help but feel a little betrayed by the thought of him having known the truth the whole time and not saying anything to me.

Killian slowly shakes his head. "No, I didn't know for sure it was you until now. I started to suspect it was you as soon as I saw you walk into that bar...but I thought it might just be wishful thinking."

The look he gives me sends chills down my spine.

I know that feeling he's projecting all too well.

The one where you held out hope for something for so long that it eventually turned into sadness; and then when another ember of hope appears, you're afraid to let down your walls that you worked so hard to build, to embrace it.

"Then the night I saw your rose tattoo...I wanted to say something then. That pull between us is one I've only felt one other time in my whole life...and that was also with you, all those years ago."

I can tell by the desperate look in his eyes he is being honest with me.

Suddenly he grabs my hands and pulls me against his chest.

"I didn't want to get my hopes up until I knew for sure if it was you...and it is." He says softly, his smile finally returning along with that confusing flutter in my heart.

Well, now that I know the truth about who he is, the fluttering sensation in my heart isn't so confusing now.

I'm still aggravated that he didn't say anything before we came here, because I've been feeling that pull too.

I thought Rose was all a dream, concocted by my teenage mind years ago.

But he was real...it was all *real*.

I have so many more questions for him; but as I continue to stare up into those piercing eyes sparkling with starlight, I can feel my anger dissipating. In its place my heart is beginning to soar. The only boy/man I ever *truly* loved, even if all this time I thought he was a figment of my imagination, is *real* and he is standing right in front of me.

Maybe I can get my happily-ever-after, after all.

If his father doesn't obliterate me that is.

This is just my luck...I find my soulmate only to then be erased from existence.

"Where did you go ten years ago?" I ask as we stand out under the moonlit sky.

Something about the way the light of the moon feels like it is shining directly down on just the two of us makes this moment even more magical.

"Nowhere. You're the one who disappeared. I took Dante and Callum, and we searched the entire realm for you. Looking back, I guess we should have told one another our true names and where we were from. I just assumed you were from here in the Fae Realm." he explains.

"Oh! I guess I never mentioned it because I thought it was all a dream." Killian gently uses his thumb to wipe away the tears that are now falling down my cheeks. "After I turned 18 the dreams just stopped...I was devastated."

His eyes reveal the sorrow he feels as he recalls the days spent searching for me. Not knowing my whereabouts or what transpired to cause me to suddenly disappear.

At least for me, I thought it was all a dream, just something I created in my mind. But for him it had been real, and he had spent his time scouring this entire realm to find me.

If that doesn't make a girl feel special, I don't know what would.

Killian slowly runs his knuckle over my tattoo. The pained look on his face makes my tears fall faster. I feel both joy and sadness.

I'm happy that after all these years we have finally found each other again, but it's sad to think about all the adventures and opportunities we missed out on experiencing together.

"It was your tattoo...that's why I cut it, sorry." he apologizes as he leans down and places a kiss on my rose tattoo behind my ear. This small action sending goosebumps along my skin. "The ink was spelled and infused with iron. You said you got it on your eighteenth birthday and then your dreams stopped. Someone knew you were somehow visiting the Fae Realm when you dreamt and tried to stop it...and succeeded. Well, that's my best guess at what happened."

I gasp and pull away from him, reaching up to feel the small cut that's now severing my rose tattoo. "My Aunt? Why would she—"

"It's okay now", Killian assures me as he pulls me into his arms and wraps me in a warm strong hug. "We can figure all that out later."

He pulls away just enough so he can take in the whole sight of me. It's like he is seeing a whole new person before him.

"You are exquisite, the most beautiful Fae in all Stellaris. Just like I remembered."

Reaching up he slowly runs his fingers along my ears, all the way up to the tips.

The tips?! Holy shit!

My breath catches as a tingling sensation shoots straight from the tips of my ears all the way down to the tips of my toes.

Killian releases a low chuckle and shines his devilish grin at me.

At first, I'm slightly confused, but then it hits me, and I can feel myself start to blush. I remember something Killian told me all those years ago. I used to love tormenting him in the most delicious ways, and playing with his ears was one of them.

Apparently, Fae have very sensitive ears and even the slightest touch can get their blood rushing to all the *wrong* places...It's essentially foreplay for Fae.

Playing with Killian's ears always led to the best make-out sessions of my life. None of my real-world experiences could compete with the magic I felt with him. And now I know why...he is *literally* magical.

Killian's grin doesn't go away as he continues to admire my ears, "These, however, are new".

"Fae ears!? Holy shit I have Fae ears!"

Killian begins laughing, "Yea you do have *Fae* ears, my little Fae *Princess.*"

I laugh right along with him, too busy examining my new ears to realize that Killian just responded to something I know I said in my head to myself.

"Wait! How did you hear that? Can Fae speak into each other's minds?"

He cups my face in his hands and looks at me as if I am the most precious thing in the world. I can feel myself start to blush just from what his look alone says about his feelings toward me.

Killian's voice enters my mind, tingling throughout at first before returning to normal, and he says, *"Only Fae who are bonded to one another can speak mind to mind. That pull you feel between us...if you focus you can tell it is more like a cord that is connecting the two of us. That cord is what allows us to do this."*

He looks like he has so much more to explain but I have this overwhelming feeling of throwing caution to the wind. Looking within myself, I can see the cord he is talking about; it looks and even *feels* like him. It looks like a starry night sky surrounded by smoky stratus clouds, but on closer examination I can see those aren't clouds at all, they are shadows...Killian's shadows. The more I concentrate on the cord I notice it's not just a 'pull' I'm feeling...I can *feel* Killian on the other end. It feels like a beacon leading me to safety...or home.

He feels like *home.*

Reaching within myself I grab hold of the cord with both hands and speak into Killian's mind. *"Kiss me"* I shamelessly demand.

Before I even finish speaking the words in my mind, Killian is crashing his lips into mine.

This kiss is different. It doesn't feel like just a kiss.

It feels like *everything*.

Killian wraps my hair around his hand; tilting my head back so he can deepen our kiss. I happily oblige, wrapping my arms around his neck and running my fingers through his soft hair.

A feeling of warmth begins spreading over me causing me to finally open my eyes.

Killian has encased us within his shadows.

I love the feeling of being surrounded by his very essence. It's like I can feel him everywhere, and it just feels right.

I jump up, wrapping my legs around his waist. Wanting to be as close to him as possible.

Suddenly I jolt back, breaking our kiss and leaving us both breathless. Killian stares at me like he is in physical pain from his lips no longer touching mine.

Full of hope I ask excitedly, "Nightshade...is he?"

Killian leans his head back and chuckles into the night sky. "Yes, he is real too."

I cannot contain the huge smile that's now taking over my face. I feel like a kid on Christmas morning who wakes up and finds exactly what they asked Santa for under the tree.

"Take me! Take me, take me, take me. Pleeease!". I beg him, throwing my head back and yelling into the sky dramatically. Killian almost drops me from me bouncing my legs around with excitement. But the pure happiness on his face tells me he doesn't mind at all.

Laughing Killian advises, "Hold on tight".

And luckily, I do, because we are again spinning around in a vortex of shadows. This time when my feet are finally back on solid ground the nausea isn't as bad as the first go round. But I'm still glad I don't have anything on my stomach.

We are standing in front of the most elegant I have ever seen. The front is all made up of beautiful grey and white stones, with ivory and wisteria climbing along the exterior walls. If you look closely it looks like a starry night is connecting each stone; like the cement itself is a glittering black.

It's absolutely stunning.

Elegant.

Charming.

Everything I ever imagined...literally.

This is the house that Killian, or *Rose*, and I once envisioned as our future home. It was the place we fantasized about living in after we got married and decided to settle down.

We would lay in a field surrounded by wild luminescent flowers for hours at a time discussing our future home, down to the very last detail. We even carved our names, Viper and Rose, into a beautiful tree with vines of black roses crawling up the trunk, to mark where we wanted the house to be built.

And he built it...

He built our dream home. And right in the front yard is the marked tree.

"How did I do? Do you like it?" Killian softly whispers in my ear as he steps up behind me, wrapping me in his arms. He sweetly nestles his face into the crook of my neck, waiting for my reaction to this beautiful house...*our* home.

I let out a shocked little laugh as I reach back and run my fingers through his short hair. "Like it? Killian, I love it! You remembered?"

He places a soft kiss on my neck. "Of course I remembered, baby. I remember everything about our time together. Even though I couldn't find you, I still wanted to make sure you had the home of your dreams waiting for you if you did ever return."

I turn around and kiss him, slowly, passionately. Pouring all the love I can give him into this kiss. I have always been bad at showing my feelings, but I hope he can feel my love for him through this kiss.

When we finally part I can't wipe the smile off my face. It matches the huge one he has on his face too. He takes me by the hand and pulls me along to the front door.

"Princess" Killian says, scooping me up into his arms at the front door. I squeal like a little girl as I'm taken by surprise.

Is he seriously about to carry me 'across the threshold' into this house he built for me...for us? But I couldn't deny him even if I wanted to, which I don't. I am dying to see the inside of our house we imagined together. And more importantly, Nightshade.

I take in a stunned breath as we enter the house. And damn if he didn't do it...he created our dream home we thought up together down to the very last detail.

The foyer is huge with an eye-catching golden chandelier dangling over white marbled floors with black and gold lines swirling together throughout. Then off to the left is an eloquent dining room with a very large table; large enough to hold at least ten guests. The base is made of black granite that supports the beautiful white and black marbled table top that shimmers under the hanging lights above. The chairs perfectly complement the table, black bottoms and white tops.

Off to the right of the foyer is a massive sitting room with a comfy looking cream sofa and a huge fireplace. There was also a beautiful billiards table off to the side, which I had specifically demanded we must have in our future house. Fae don't even play pool, but I love it! Hustling drunk old men at the bars is one of my favorite past times.

My breath catches when I stare up at the ceiling. Immaculately painted across the entire ceiling is a gorgeous starlit sky, highlighting all the constellations. I literally don't have the words to describe how stunning it is.

The fireplace was already burning, making the room warm and cozy. I walk over to sit on the inviting sofa, admiring the strangely textured black rug...

Wait that's no rug!

Two large bright green eyes slowly open and meet mine.

The next thing I know the large black mass comes charging at me, knocking me straight on my ass. Followed by a gritty wet tongue slobbering all over my face.

"Nightshade!" I joyfully exclaim.

I can't stop the child-like squeals and laughter coming from me. Nightshade is *real*! And he has gotten so big! Last time I saw him he was the size of a Rottweiler, but now he has filled out and bulked up and can pass as a full-size lion...with wings!

I found the chimera when he was no bigger than an overweight shih-tzu. He was injured with a broken wing and hiding from his attacker underneath a tree with a canopy of beautiful gold leaves. As soon as I saw his beautiful green eyes, any fear I had of the strange creature disappeared.

He is fully black but has a sheen that shows every color of the rainbow when he moves within the light of the moon. And he is a mix of three creatures: he has a fuzzy lion-like head and mane that transitions into scales of a dragon-like body, with again, a lion-like tail will a ball of fuzz at the tip, and then the wings of a bird. A very large bird of prey...like a falcon.

Turning my head, I find Killian leaning against the wall, arms crossed, and snickering at the display.

"A little help here, please?" I beg in between my uncontrollable giggles.

He grabs Nightshade by his mane and pulls him off me. "Alright Nightshade, that's enough. We just got her back and you're going to drown her with drool."

Once Killian finally gets him settled down, I crawl over to him on the floor and wrap my arms around his broad chest and snuggle my face into his soft fluffy mane. I'm on the brink of crying again from the happiness I feel building up inside, knowing that Nightshade never forgot me.

I never let people see me cry, I need to get it together.

The three of us sit snuggled around the fireplace for a while reminiscing about all the times we shared together so long ago. In fact, I met Killian (a.k.a. Rose) right after I found Nightshade under the unique tree. I had picked up the small creature to run across the open field into the safety of the covered forest, when his attacker returned to finish off his kill. It was a Jabberwocky, a huge drag-on-like creature with huge sharp claws, and huge fangs with drool dripping from the tips. Its face put me in mind of a catfish with its whisker-like barbels protruding from each side of its gaping mouth. And its eyes were as black as the surrounding sky.

Killian appeared out of nowhere and shoved us right out from under the Jabberwocky's claws, drawing his sword and valiantly fending off the beast until it finally gave up and retreated. He literally saved my life the first time I met him.

It's still bittersweet knowing that we could have been together all these years if someone hadn't sabotaged it.

Even worse, one of the people I truly love and trust most in my life may be to blame.

This whole situation is doing nothing to help with my trust issues, but I intend to get answers as soon as I get back home.

CHAPTER 23

CALISTA

Killian decided it was best to practice awakening my powers in a large open area. Not wanting to accidentally set anything on fire in the house, but also not wanting to harm any unlucky creatures scurrying around in the forest.

That is how I find myself smack dab in the middle of the clearing where I first met Killian.

The beautiful tree with the golden leaves where I found a small, scared Nightshade, still stands tall on the other side of the clearing. The golden leaves stand out so beautifully against the dark, starry night sky.

I can still hear it calling out to me and trying to draw me in to come closer to it, just like it did the last time I was near it.

Killian instructs me to take off my shoes so that my bare feet are touching the ground itself. He told me to try and *feel* the power flowing through the ground beneath my feet. All I am feeling though is the soft, thick grass tickling the soles of my feet as I wiggle my toes. My freshly pedicured pink toenails really pop against the color of the ground.

The grass here is of the deepest shade of green I think I have ever seen. It's beautiful; not only because of its dark coloring and lush texture, but because it serves as a reminder that life always finds a way. Even here where the moon is the sole source of light, the grass has adapted to the absence of sunlight, changing the way it creates the energy it needs to grow and flourish.

So here I am, standing before my handsome Dark Fae Prince barefoot in skinny jeans and a white tank, ready to embrace my abilities. Killian is also barefoot and in his normal human attire of jeans and a tight black shirt, which somehow, he makes look so sexy, it seems unfair for the rest of the male species. Both human and Fae.

"You're not focusing, princess", Killian growls playfully.

"I'm trying! And stop calling me princess! Just because you're a prince that's crazy obsessed with me, doesn't make me your princess. I much prefer Viper."

With a sly grin plastered across his face Killian begins advancing on me ever so slightly.

"Is that right? From here it looks like you might be the one obsessing." he chuckles. "And *now* I prefer princess, *princess*."

Then he lunges forward.

Where did he —?

"Umph" is the only sound I can hear as the air leaves my lungs, and I find myself staring up into the starry night sky.

That dirty cheat teleported! Then kicked my legs out from underneath me from behind.

"Hey that is not fair Kill—"

My words are cut off when he appears in front of me out of nowhere, and before I can move, he grabs my arm and pins it behind my back, stepping forward to tower over me.

In a low voice he asks, "Do you think the king or anyone else who wants you dead is going to play fair?" He releases me and disappears again.

He does make a good point, but how am I supposed to fight teleporting?

"Ooph" I sound out again as I land face first into the ground. This time he kicked my feet out from under me in the opposite direction.

Real creative Fae-hole.

All this is doing is pissing me off, not helping me learn to channel my abilities.

"You Son-of-a-bitch!" I shout down the cord connecting the two of us.

My head then fills up with Killian's sexy laugh. Damn him! Now I'm pissed...and slightly aroused.

"Good use that anger princess. Visualize it and pull it together into a tight ball that you can see and grasp within your mind. Then once you have a good hold on it, release it."

"How do I release it? Are there magic words I need to say or something?"

"Ha!" Killian bellows through my mind. *"Just imagine what you want that power to do, picture it in your mind, then project it out into the real world."*

Digging deep, I focus all my attention on the world around me. Trying to open myself up to any vibration or other sensations the ground or air itself may give out.

Right as I start to release a frustrated scream, I feel something inside. It's very subtle...but there is something. A charged sensation that sends goose bumps along every inch of my exposed skin.

It feels like a combination of static build up and that tingling sensation you feel in your legs when they fall asleep; like ants crawling inside of you. Or in this case millions of tiny fire ants, crawling up through the soles of my feet and into every vein flowing throughout my body, releasing tiny hot embers with each bite. It's hot and slightly burns, but it's welcomed warmth.

I'm entranced by this warm feeling taking over my entire body, until suddenly that feeling gets replaced by another and I release a brief scream. "Ahhh! What the hell is that?"

The surface of my skin now feels like thousands of little needles are sticking deep down. I half expect to find a swarm of bees attached to every part of my exposed skin when I reopen my eyes. But there is nothing there to see...this is just the raw power that freely flows throughout the air in this realm.

After the initial shock of the stinging sensation passes, it begins to feel like my skin is alive and *buzzing*.

And damn if it doesn't feel amazing!

It's like I'm a warm electrical charge that is ready to destroy anyone who gets in my way.

Doing as Killian instructed, I focus on this newfound power that I can feel pouring inside of me. Coming not just from the ground but also from the air that surrounds me. I try my best to visualize using my hands to gather up all these little particles of energy flowing throughout my body, rounding them up into a ball of pure energy...power.

Next, I slow my breathing and focus solely on my new Fae hearing. Trying my best to pick up on each sound Killian makes when his feet retouch the ground after he teleports. Then, I try to feel for his power and how it moves each time he teleports. It's almost like it leaves a ghost-like trail of itself between point A and point B. This might only be possible to do because of the cord that connects us, but I guess the only way to find out is to test it on another Fae who can teleport one day.

I try my best to focus on using all three abilities: hearing, feeling Killian's magic, and controlling my own power. Then I wait for him to move in to make his next strike.

Killian's feet hit the ground to my left. I roll forward, landing in a crouch. I glance back and see a surprised look on his face, maybe some pride too.

"There's my Viper." He winks at me, and then 'poof' he's gone again.

Focus

I can't let myself get too excited from that small victory. Excitement leads to distraction and distraction leads to getting the air knocked out of my lungs.

I'm ready to knock him on his ass for once.

I can feel the ball of power I'm holding onto internally grow larger, as I wait for Killian to make his next move.

There! I can feel him before I even hear him come up behind me. I turn around and this time I throw my arms out towards him, willing my power to knock him back off his feet.

BAM!

I release an ear-piercing scream. I didn't even know I could make the sound I hear coming from my own throat.

I knocked him on his ass all right! Only about fifty yards further than I meant to! I'm running to him as fast as I can and calling out to him, but he is not moving.

I killed him! I fucking killed him!

This is why I have kept a metaphorical lock on my magic all these years. Ever since that incident with the school's janitor I never cared to know how deep my abilities ran. I wanted them to go away so I could live a normal life. Not having to worry about burning someone alive from the inside out every time I touched them.

He is laying there lifelessly upon the dark grass; just a few more feet to the left and he would have slammed into the tree. I fall to my knees when I finally reach him. Thankfully I can see his chest inflating just fine, but I most definitely knocked the air out of him... and maybe gave him a concussion?

"Killian! Killian! Wake up! Can you hear me?!" I gently shake him, not wanting to injure him further if he has a spinal injury from the landing.

His eyes begin blinking slowly until they are fully open and he is staring up at me. I release a sigh of relief.

"Am I dead? Is this the Flaming Hollows? Because I could get used to this view.", he jokes with a smile spreading across his face.

How is he cracking jokes right now!? I could have killed him!

I gently shove his shoulder. "Shut up! I thought I killed you! Are you okay?! I'm so sorry...I didn't mean to."

He raises his hand and presses his fingers against my lips to shut me up.

"Shh! I'm fine...my ego on the other hand...", he teases smiling up at me. "You did amazing! Once we get that power of yours under your full control you will be a force to be reckoned with, Viper"

I think it is safe to say I impressed him.

I sit back on my heels with my face buried in my hands, trying to calm my nerves from all the excitement of the last few minutes. However, a moment of peace and quiet seems like too much to ask for when sitting next to this tree.

I stare up at the tree, shaking my head.

"Does this tree ever shut up?"

Killian gives me a strange look; then begins looking back and forth between me and the tree.

"You can hear this tree?" Killion's face is etched in confusion.

Suddenly I'm hit with deja'vu.

I had asked Rose that exact same thing right after he saved us from the Jabberwocky attack. He had looked completely shocked by my question and began to stare at me curiously, like he was studying me. "What?!" was his only response to my question. All I could think to myself was 'great now he thinks I'm crazy'. So, I tried to play it off by saying, "Never mind, the stress of running for my life must be playing tricks with my mind."

But I'm not letting my question go this time around.

"Yeah, can't you? That's how I found Nightshade the day you rescued us. The tree was calling for me to come closer and my curiosity won out, but when I got under the canopy, I found him lying there injured and scared. I thought maybe it was calling for me to come help the injured creature, but it kept insisting that I touch it. To touch the tree, I mean. And like now, ever since we got here today it's been calling out for me to come closer and touch it. Kind of creepy if you ask me..." I explain, standing up and offering Killian my hand to help pull him off the ground.

"No, I can't hear anything...it is rumored to be only one person who can hear this tree." I look at him, now very confused myself. If that is so, then why can I hear it?

"There is a legend here in the Fae Realm about the tree with leaves of gold." he says, pausing to look up at the tree.

I'm already looking at him wide-eyed and intrigued, ready to hear more about this legend, but he just keeps staring at the tree like he is entranced by it. "Well?" I ask aloud, trying to draw his attention. "Are you going to tell me about the legend or just stand there staring at the tree?" I tease.

Moving closer to check on him, I take his hand in mine, and he finally looks over shaking his head as if in disbelief of something. I don't even think he realized that he had zoned out mid story.

Killian rubs the back of his head, "Shit, sorry...I guess I hit my head harder than I thought." Pulling me closer, he places a brief kiss atop my head and then begins telling me the story about the tree.

"Sisters, Selenity Goddess of the Moon and Alektra Goddess of the Sun, once ruled over the Fae Realm together, in harmony. There was no Unseelie and Seelie divide between the realm; all was united, the sun rose and set giving rise to the moon everyday throughout the lands. However, Alektra's husband Pyroneous, God of Fire, had a wandering eye for her sister Selenity. On the eve of what we now call The Great Divide; Alektra paid an unannounced visit to her sister's chambers. Catching both Selenity and Pyroneous tangled up in the throes of passion.

"Alektra's anger was so strong the days started to become longer, leaving Selenity pushing against her sister's powers daily to raise the moon. Some days both the sun and the moon would be high in the sky, leaving the sky in a swirling battle between twilight and dusk. When the Fae and other creatures of the realm began to complain, the sisters decided it best to divide the land into two new separate kingdoms. Unseelie for those whose powers thrive in the moonlight, and Seelie for those whose powers are driven by the rays of the sun."

Killian pauses to give me a moment digest everything he's telling me. He can't seem to help but smile and shake his head at whatever look he sees on my face. Most likely amazement, because this 'legend' is so interesting. I wonder if there is really any truth to it?

"What does any of that have to do with the tree though?"

"Whoa, chill out, we are getting there." He smiles. "Someone's impatient I see."

I slap him across this arm, scrunching my face and sticking my tongue out at him. This gets me one of his full-blown laughs that sends butterflies zooming around inside my stomach.

"Alright before you resort to violence I'll continue."

I move to slap him again, but he jumps back laughing and holding his hands up in the air in submission.

"Well, as you know, the realm remains divided to this day. The sisters never had the chance to reconcile their relationship before the Gods disappeared from the face of the realm. This event is now known as The Deafening Silence. The reason for their sudden disappearance is unknown, but according to legend, this tree was the last gift the sisters left to the realm. The sisters understood that all life requires balance, and without both light and darkness, the realm would collapse. They decided to put aside their differences and pour their lifeblood into this very spot of land. And from it rose the tree with golden leaves, which became known as the Tree of Resurrection.

"As long as the tree stands strong so does the realm itself, for through its veins both darkness and light flow. Seeping out through the roots and spreading out across the lands. If you listen closely, you may just hear the tree calling out, while patiently waiting and searching for the true heir of the realm to return home. Or at least that last part is what all the elders tell the kids to get them to shut up from time to time," he chuckles, "but the real legend says that the Tree of Resurrection is waiting for the true heir to return home and rise to power, and only the true heir can hear its call." Finished he turns to face me.

I stare back at him dumbfounded with my mouth hanging wide open. He must be pulling my leg, right? I can hear the tree, so does he expect me to believe I'm some powerful moon goddess heir?! Ha, ha, nice try Killian. I just sprouted Fae ears earlier today and now I'm supposed to believe this too? His chuckle has now turned into a full-blown laugh from the look still plastered on my face.

"Oh, so I'm supposed to believe that I am the lost heir? Wait, and of whom?" I ask him.

"Rumor has it that Pyroneous and Selenity had a secret child. The moon goddess sent the child away after birth, not being able to bear the thought of causing her sister more pain. Where she sent this 'heir' nobody knows. I don't think Pyroneous even knew she was pregnant given he was banned from the realm by Alektra after she discovered the affair."

"No wonder I knocked you on your ass so hard! I'm a descendent of not only the goddess of the moon but the god of fire too!" I say jokingly, while walking over to stand next to the tree.

All joking aside though, I can really hear this tree speaking. Maybe if this tree *truly* has goddess blood flowing through it; the tree itself has become sentient?

Oh gosh, I must be losing my mind if I'm buying into all this crap.

"Well then let's see if it's true then..." I drag out the suspense as I move slowly to place my palm against the bark. "Ahhhh!" I playfully scream, acting like something crazy is happening and the tree is trying to suck me inside.

Killian just rolls his eyes and then lunges after me. I try to run but he is too fast as he scoops me up over his shoulder and spins me around. I can't stop laughing and screaming. I wish I could just bottle this moment up and relive it whenever I want.

We spent the rest of the evening practicing control over my magic along with other skills. I can now channel that inner fire that runs through my veins to form outside of my body. Creating a physical flame in my hand or a small ball of fire.

We need to keep working on my ability to control where and what my fire ignites though. Learned that the hard way; but it gave us the opportunity to learn that Killian's shadows can smother out my flames...keeping me from burning down a small chunk of forest on the outskirts of the clearing.

CHAPTER 24

CALISTA

Later that night I find myself sitting in front of the cozy warm fireplace on our makeshift bed comprised of soft pillows and blankets. Snuggled up between Killian and Nightshade, right where I belong. I don't think my heart can get any fuller than it is now at this moment. I just keep rethinking about how everything I thought was a dream back when I was a teenager was all real. They weren't dreams at all. I have no idea of how I ended up in the Fae Realm when I would fall asleep, but I'm hoping Aunt Ellie can enlighten me with that information.

"You're incredible, you know that?" Killian praises, as he reaches over tucking a string of my long brown hair behind my ear.

"You're not too bad yourself." I say teasingly, bumping up against his shoulder.

Killian lets out a low chuckle, shaking his head. I think he enjoys us teasing one another. I know I do. It's just like old times.

"No really. Your power has grown to a level today in what I thought would take weeks for it to get to." He says in all seriousness. "I guess my theory was correct. I thought bringing you here might help. Getting you back to your Fae roots." Grinning he grabs my hand and gently kisses my palm. Even a gesture as simple as this makes me feel all giddy inside.

"What do you mean my 'Fae roots'? I'm not Fae, my mother was a witch. That's where my powers come from."

He barks out a loud laugh and gestures to his ears. "Then how do you explain those new ears of yours?"

Holy Shit! I reach up and touch my ears; gasping as I recall they are now elongated with pointy tips. My mind was so overcome earlier with the realization that this entire world was real...that Rose was real...I had completely forgotten about my newly tapered ears. My thoughts had gone straight to how I used to love to tease Rose by fooling around with his ears when we were together all those years ago. Leaving me to forget the most important question I should have asked right away; 'Why the hell do I have Fae shaped ears?'

"What about your father? Could he have been Fae?" Killian's question pulls me from my spiraling thoughts. It's like he's trying to casually throw out information for me to consider. Not realizing that I'm still trying to process the fact that I never thought to wonder *why* I've been walking around with pointy Fae ears all evening. Oh, and I can't forget the enlarged canines, which I discovered when I accidentally bit the shit out of my tongue earlier.

The 'mind exploding' emoji on my phone is the perfect picture example for how I feel and possibly even how I look right now.

Of course, I had considered that possibility before, but I guess I just let it go after all these years. However, now with these new ears and sharp canines coming into play as evidence, I think it's highly probable that my father is a Fae.

"I don't know who my father is. If he's a Fae, can we find him?" I scold myself for feeling hopeful. He has had twenty-eight years to look for me if he wanted to, assuming he even knows I exist. He either doesn't know or chose not to be a part of my life.

"I think we should ask my uncle when we get back."

"You think he could find out?" I ask skeptically.

"He knows a lot of people both human and Fae, so it's worth a shot."

I can't fight the small smile that begins to spread across my face. And again, I internally scold myself for even entertaining the idea that there is even a small chance of finding my father.

Finding him would be a dream come true. A dream I had given up on years ago. So instead of shooting down Killian's idea I nod my head in agreement that we will talk to Cerberus about it when we get back.

"Hey, can I ask you something kind of embarrassing...?" I ask shying away from his gaze.

"Don't be embarrassed princess, you can ask me anything."

"Are you...I mean are we..." I stop, releasing a frustrated sigh. "Are you, my mate?" I can't help but cringe on the inside. I feel so embarrassed for asking such a stupid question.

Killian's eyes go wide, and his lips slam shut. All I can do now is sit here listening to the crackling of the fire and Nightshades muffled snores; praying that I didn't just scare Killian off.

Just as I start to accept that he is not going to respond his lips finally peel apart, "Why do you ask?"

"I know I was playing around, but when I touched the tree today it really did start whispering something different in my mind over and over, "Mate, mates, he's your mate...? It sounded like something along those lines. The voice was fuzzy this time and harder to make out."

If I thought his eyes were wide before, that was nothing. If he was a cartoon character they would be bulging out of his skull.

"Holy shit!", he whispers sitting up straight. "So, the tree really does speak to you?" It's more of a realization than a question as he continues to look at me in shock.

"Yes! I told you so, did you not believe me? So, does that mean the tree was speaking the truth? You're my mate?" I think deep down I know it's the truth. If I had any doubts, which I did, those flew out the window from seeing how he just reacted to my question.

Why wouldn't he have told me this sooner...or did he, back before the dreams stopped?

"The hand thing...when we sliced ours and held them together?" I recall, looking back over at him. Starting to remember bits and pieces of what he told me the whole purpose was behind what we were doing way back then.

Killian slowly nods in confirmation. He looks like he is bracing himself for what my reaction will be; like he is expecting me to be angry or upset in some way.

He positions us to face one another and takes my hand. His voice deepens as he explains, "The night of your eighteenth birthday, we chose to solidify our love through a mating bond ceremony. I told you that you were my mate and explained how fortunate we were to have found one another. Some Fae live out their entire lives without finding their mates. Although, they can still fall in love and create a symbolic bond through marriage, they will never experience the all-consuming love that mates feel towards one another through the mating bond. It's a love like no other. Once the mating ceremony is completed, mates can sense each other's emotions, share power through the bond, perceive each other's presence, and communicate telepathically. Some may even see glimpses of what their mate sees. Mating bonds are so rare that there are undoubtedly abilities that mates possess which remain undiscovered."

His eyes search mine with a silent plea, hoping that I will say I remember...and I do.

While he was recounting that day everything came back to me; like a tidal wave washed over my mind and pulled back the sand to reveal in detail the memories I had of this moment. Our love we shared for one another, being overjoyed at having found *my* mate, and having been indubitably ready to perform the mating ceremony to take Killian as my mate. We had to slice our palms and hold hands to combine our blood, and then we had to recite a few words.

I turn and place my hand on Killian's cheek, making sure his eyes are locked onto mine.

Then I recite the vow I recall from all those years ago, "I am yours and you are mine".

A contagious smile spreads across his face, and I gasp as he pulls me onto his lap and steals my lips for a slow intimate kiss.

Releasing my lips he looks down into my eyes and quietly whispers, "You are mine and I am yours". Then his lips are melded with mine once again.

This moment is beyond what any words could describe. Magical? Incredible? Mind blowing? Hell, even life altering doesn't seem appropriate enough.

The thought of coming home from work to him every day and getting to wrap myself up in his scent and kiss his soft lips...

Now that I know it's possible, it's everything I want.

He is my happily-ever-after I've always secretly dreamed of but didn't dare to wish for.

And one that I know I shouldn't bank on now. Life is never this easy, and the logical part of my brain is screaming that this is too good to be true. That *he* is too good to be true.

I have let my trust issues influence every part of my life since I was a very young child; I think maybe it's time to get out of my head and let myself try to find happiness.

At some point in the middle of kissing the man I love and my mind running wild with all the ways this will end badly, Nightshade decides to interrupt us by making a sound of what I can only hope is approval. Given the huge drooling smile on his face, and the wet slobbery kisses now marking the sides of our faces, I think it's safe to say he's happy we are all back together.

Turning back to Killian I ask, "So we have been mated together this *whole* time? Is that why there is that crazy pull between us?"

His brow furrows and he shakes his head. "Yes and no." As soon as he says no, I feel my smile deflating. "Yes, that is why there is that cord that connects us. No, because although we are mates, we never officially completed the ceremony." he explains.

I stare up at him quizzically.

"In order for the mating bond to be complete we have to...as you humans say...consummate the marriage." Killian goes silent and my eyes go wide.

The two of us sit there, staring silently at one another.

"Oh..." I say, feeling my blush creeping up onto my cheeks.

Is that the best response I can come up with? Get it together woman... you have been pining over this man for years. And now you know he is real, he is right in front of you, and he is your mate. Woman up and go finish what you started ten years ago.

After that inspiring mental pep talk, I loop one of my arms around his neck, running my fingers through his hair, and slowly I lean in until my lips are just shy of his. Placing my other hand against his chest I quietly ask him in a soft sultry voice, "So, Killian...will you *officially* become my mate?"

As I gaze up at his beautiful face from under my long lashes, I see his devilish grin forming right before my eyes.

"Fuck yes!" is his only reply before he is grabbing my neck and pulling me into a toe curling, life altering kiss.

We don't even bother taking it to the bedroom.

That would involve breaking our kiss and that is not happening. Killian grabs one of the couch cushions we were using on the floor in front of the fireplace and tosses it at Nightshade, telling him to get out and give us some privacy.

I'm pretty sure he just went into the bedroom and jumped onto the luxurious king-size bed and made himself comfortable. He might as well since we aren't planning on using it anytime soon.

I pull Killian's tight black shirt over his head, revealing his chiseled abs. I swear I could run my fingers up and down the deep grooves of his abs all day and never get tired of them. This man was created to be in a spotlight; his body looks like it has been chiseled out by the

Gods themselves. All the way down to those delicious 'V' cut muscles that lead my eyes further down to the massive bulge begging to be set free from inside his jeans.

My mouth suddenly goes dry at the thought of what I might be getting myself into.

My shirt quickly joins Killian's on the floor. He begins moving his attention to my neck; placing soft kisses as he slowly moves lower. A shiver runs down my spine when he kisses that sweet spot right above my collarbone, and Killian's low chuckles sends small vibrations over skin. Killian wraps his arm around my waist and pulls me closer. Then suddenly he flips us around; placing his hand beneath my head as he lays me down underneath him.

His lips crush mine again with such need; like the taste of my lips is the only thing keeping him alive. I kiss him back just as fiercely, tangling my tongue with his and biting his bottom lip. The growl I hear leaving his throat only stokes the fire that's fueling this insatiable desire between us.

This kiss is devouring.

Like we are ravaging animals that have been starved out for years...and now a feast is laid out before us. And we are both greedy for the taking.

Killian raises up and cups my breast beneath his large strong hands, squeezing, causing my back to arch off the floor. Without releasing, he grips the thin black lace of my bra and rips it in half. My breasts are now on full display, and all his for the taking.

"I've been dying to do that...and this" Killian growls out.

I release a loud moan as Killian takes my hardened nipple into his mouth, sucking hard and then *biting*. I scream but it quickly becomes a moan as he slowly rolls his tongue around my nipple. Turning the pain into a delicious pleasure.

I've never experienced that before, but I think I just became a fan of it.

He places slow tender kisses on my breast before he continues trailing nips and kisses down towards my core.

He makes quick work of my jeans. Reaching back down to trace his fingers along my thin lacey thong; feeling how wet he's already made me. The sound of approval that comes from deep in Killian's throat sends a spark of desire shooting straight to my core, causing my panties to dampen even more. He circles the lacey material against my clit, the added friction from the lace has me moaning and writhing underneath him. The thin material might as well have not even been there with how easily Killian rips them off my hips.

Killian pauses to take in the sight of me laying naked beneath him. As his eyes devour my entire body, that is now at his complete mercy, I lay here feeling more vulnerable than ever. My pulse is racing so fast if he doesn't make a move soon, I feel like I will die from the anticipation.

"Gods Damn, you're magnificent." he whispers, staring down at me.

He teases me, taking his sweet time trailing his tongue higher along my inner thigh. Grinning up at me as I buck my hips, a silent plea for him to hurry closer to where I need him most. And he knows exactly where I want him, but he is taking his sweet time getting there.

Finally, after what seems like the longest thirty seconds of my life, he drags his tongue along my core until he is focused in on that little bundle of nerves. Swirling his tongue around and around in long slow delectable circles; pushing me closer to the brink of pure ecstasy. I arch my back lifting my hips as I run my fingers through his hair, shamelessly riding his face to chase my pleasure. I can tell he approves of my actions from the primal growl he releases in response.

I am so close to my release when Killian slides two fingers into my core. Fucking me with his fingers while his tongue continues to play with my clit. Stars explode in my vision! My back comes off the floor as I arch into my release, screaming his name as intense pleasure racks my body. He continues his actions, riding out my entire orgasm, until I am completely spent and shaking underneath him.

He finishes dining on my core with one last luxurious lick along my entire center. Then slowly he begins to climb back up my body.

"You taste like heaven. I want to taste you every day for the rest of my life. Fuck, I want to die with the taste of you on my tongue." he growls, making fast work removing his jeans. Allowing his huge bulging cock to spring free of its tight confines. The enormous size of it steals all the air from my lungs as my eyes take their fill. It is throbbing with need and ready to take me.

"See something you like, princess?" Killian jokes, as he watches me staring at his cock.

A shiver from both excitement and a little worry, shoots through my body as I continue to take in the sheer size of him. There is no way he is going to fit; he is going to tear me in half.

I don't even think my hand could completely wrap around him if I tried.

With my mouth bone dry and the air gone from my lungs; the only response I can give him is a nod of approval. This rewards me his deep sexy laugh.

I thread my fingers through his silver hair as I pull him down for another kiss. Licking myself off his lips as I go. His groan of approval makes my toes curl.

As I wrap my legs around his waist, I feel the head of his enormous cock pressing against my core.

He pauses, staring into my eyes as he gently runs his hand through my hair. "Are you sure?" he asks. Completely making sure that I am ready to take this next step with him.

"Absolutely", I confirm breathlessly.

We take a few more seconds to just stare deep into one another's eyes. Cherishing this moment. A moment that has been twelve years in the making, if you count from the first time we met.

Running his thumb along my cheek he smiles down at me and says whole heartedly, "You are mine and I am yours, Viper."

Smiling up at him I say undoubtedly, "I am yours and you are mine, Rose".

He leans down taking my lips in his and begins to slowly push himself into my core.

"Fuck you're tight", he groans, fisting his hands on either side of my head.

I know he can see the look of pain on my face, but I don't want him to stop.

"I can take it", I assure him as I look up at him. He nods, and again his lips are devouring mine. This kiss isn't sweet...it's rough... it's possessive. And I love it!

"Ahhh!" I scream as he drives his cock into my core with one thrust. He pauses, searching my face for any sign of lingering pain; and allowing me time to adjust to the size of him. Then slowly...ever so slowly the pain begins to turn into pleasure. I release a breath and nod, assuring him I'm ready to continue.

"More", I moan as he breathes heavily against my neck.

He thrust one last time, finally, fully seating himself inside my core. I release another scream that quickly turns into an intense moan of undeniable pleasure.

It's then that I realize, as I come down from the sensation, that he has his teeth sunk in my neck. He bit me! And damn if it doesn't feel amazing!

I moan thrusting my hips up and taking him deeper. He moans before he finally releases my neck and stares down at me. I think I see worry on his face...like he thinks I might be frightened at the sight of him with my blood running off his lip. It's quite the opposite though...something must be wrong with my brain because I think he looks sexy as hell right now.

I lean forward, taking his lower lip in between mine and slowly suck and lick my blood from his lips and the corner of his mouth. His pupils dilate and his eyes darken, then he is thrusting his huge cock in and out of me mercilessly.

I can't help but to cry out his name as he pounds into me over and over. I am so filled up my mind can't even think straight. Every inch of me is filled up and each thrust is quickly bringing me to the brink of ecstasy once again.

The pleasure he is wringing out of me is mind-blowing. I'm glad he is my mate because I don't think another man could ever satisfy me sexually ever again.

The moans of pleasure I bring out of him as I thrust my hips up and meet him stroke for stroke fills me with such confidence and pride. I want to forever drown myself in the sounds of his moans and growls.

He lifts my leg up over his shoulder, this new angle allowing him to go even deeper, hitting that perfect spot.

"Killian don't stop" I plead breathlessly, "I'm so close...Oh yes! Right there!"

He reaches down between us circling my clit with his thumb, "Come for me princess."

"Killian...", I scream out in pleasure as if on his command as my orgasm hits.

I can tell from the feel of his cock thickening inside of me that his is not far behind.

Killian begins thrusting harder and faster chasing his own release.

I lean up, still riding out the high of my own incredible orgasm and sink my new canines into his neck.

Killian roars and bucks deep inside me, all the way to the base of his cock, once, twice...then he follows me over the edge finding his release. Filling me completely up.

We lay there in front of the cozy fire with Killian still inside me; gently placing loving kisses along each other's necks.

"So, you're into biting, huh?" I finally kid him, breaking the silence.

He gives off one of those sexy deep chuckles I love of his. He gently nuzzles his nose against mine, this sweet act making my heart flutter.

"Fae will often bite their mates to stake claim to them. Other Fae can sense when another has already been marked. It acts as the one and only warning for any other male to stay away from what's *mine*." As he stakes his claim, he playfully pulls me closer. His shy smile melts my heart, I think he is waiting for me to argue about him being so possessive, but I like the idea of being *claimed* by him. That still doesn't mean I won't tease him for it.

"So, you are one of those over possessive Alpha-holes." I tease. He reaches up and flicks my nose playfully.

"Well, that better work both ways, because I'll kill any woman who tries to steal you away from me." I roll us over so I am now straddling him. Throwing my head back with a soft moan as his cock buries deeper inside of me.

Killian sits up and begins running his fingers down the length of my long dark hair. The way he looks at me makes me feel like I am the most important person in all the realms. I can't get enough of how happy he makes me feel.

Through all the darkness in my life, he is my light. Which seems ironic given the fact that he is a Dark Fae that lives in a kingdom shrouded in darkness.

"I love you, Calista", Killian tells me, as he trails his fingers down my neck.

I'm suddenly not sure if I'm still breathing, and my heart is pounding out of my chest. I know we just reconnected after spending years apart but the way I feel towards him has never changed. And he isn't just Killian, the Fae I've only known for a few weeks; he's Rose, the guy I gave my heart to twelve years ago...and left it with him. And though my sisters are probably going to think I've lost my mind, I know what we have with one another is real...and true.

"I love you too, Killian". I can't contain the huge smile that spreads across my face. I know it mirrors the one shining back at me on his handsome face.

My heart is filled with so much happiness it may just explode.

Cupping his face with both hands I lean in and kiss him with everything I have. I can feel him instantly get hard again and my eyes fly open. Killian erupts with laughter.

"Fae have really good stamina", he brags with that cocky smile of his. And damn if I'm not impressed, but I'm not going to tell him that. Instead, I just roll my eyes and bring my lips back to his.

This is going to be a very long night...

CHAPTER 25

CALISTA

When morning finally rolls around, I wake to find myself wrapped up in Killian's strong arms. Neither of us got much sleep last night. Any time I did fall asleep I would find myself awoken shortly after by Killian placing sweet kisses in *all* the right places. The few hours of sleep I did manage to get, though, was the best sleep I've had in ages. I was just absorbed by a feeling of peacefulness and contentment while being wrapped up with Killian.

I don't want to wake him, but a relaxing hot shower is calling my name.

Right as I attempt to lift one of his heavy muscular arms to sneak out of his embrace, he begins trailing his fingers up and down my spine. I tilt my head up to find him smiling down at me, sleep still heavy in his hooded eyes.

"Good morning", he leans down placing a kiss on top of my head. His voice sounds gravely from just waking up.

I rise so I can lean over and plant a proper kiss to his lips when something catches my eye.

On the left side of his chest where my face was just laying sits a large tattoo. One that I know did not exist last night when we finally let sleep claim us.

And we explored every single inch of each other's body last night so there is no way in hell that managed to get past me.

But now, as sure as I live and breathe, there is a beautiful tattoo covering his left pec muscle all the way up to his collarbone. There is a vine of deep dark red climbing roses with a large black snake with striking gold slitted eyes acting as the vine, coiling in and around the roses themselves.

On second thought that isn't just *any* black snake...it's a *viper*.

I look up and find Killian looking down at what snagged my attention. His brows are knitted together in confusion, but other than that small sign of concern he doesn't seem to be that taken back from this new development.

"Where did—" My question doesn't even make it past my lips. My eyes are now the size of saucers as I stare down at another tattoo. My tattoo!

As I reached up to trace my fingers along the new artwork on Killian's skin, I discovered that I also have a tattoo now...climbing up my entire left arm.

I think I'm frozen in shock because I can't pull my eyes away from what I'm seeing. I've never been much of a tattoo person. The rose behind my ear is the only one I have, and I only got that because it had meaning behind it...and because of my aunt's unrelenting peer pressure to get one for my eighteenth birthday.

Which now I know was because she had an ulterior motive.

"Oh shit!" Killian exclaims, sitting up and taking hold of my arm to get a better look at the tattoo that now marks my skin. I still can only just look at it and nod in agreement at his choice of words.

I thought Killian's tattoo was large, but his pales in comparison to mine. Mine takes up my *entire* arm! All the way from my thumb to my shoulder. The only way for me to see the whole tattoo is for me to fully rotate my arm from side to side.

Climbing and winding around my entire arm, starting with the tip of the tail running along the top of my thumb to its head wrapping around and stopping directly at the top of my shoulder, is another black viper. Surrounding the viper's head are these simple but beautiful flowers. There are two circular rows of black pedals that surround light yellowish-white stamens. I've never seen a black flower like this, but they're lovely.

"Extraordinary", Killian breaths, while looking back and forth admiring both of our tattoos.

After I'm done staring in amazement, I finally ask the question that has been screaming inside my head, "Care to explain why we both are waking up to tattoos? Especially why they both have a viper?"

Wow, I always thought I would be asking this question after a long night of drinking out on the town with my sisters. Intoxication and impulsive questionable decisions are kind of our thing sometimes. But never from waking up after a night with zero alcohol and a full recollection of the night's activities.

I like the way he scrunches up both his eyebrows when he's thinking; it's super cute...in the sexiest way possible, of course. "I think these are our mating marks." he finally answers.

Like that tells me anything. Seeing my confusion he keeps on explaining.

"Before The Deafening Silence, fated mates would receive mating marks after the completion of their mating ceremony. They were said to be a gift from the Gods for having found and come together with your mate. I've never seen or heard of one appearing on mates since then. When the Gods disappeared, they took with them the gift of mating marks...and our wings."

I gasp. Looking down at him with so many questions running through my mind.

"Wings? So, wait...does that mean I was right, and that Fae are fairies? And you just call yourself Fae now because you are just pissed off that you no longer have wings to fly around and shoot sparkles from your ass?" Killian's eyes darken into an evil gaze, and I burst out laughing.

My laughter becomes a shriek, as Killian grabs my waist and flips us around. He brings his head into the crook of my neck and begins tickling my neck with his nose, growling in my ear "When I'm done with you, I promise you'll never question if there is a difference between me and a fairy ever again." Then he bites my earlobe making me shriek out again.

He begins kissing my neck, but I stop him before I can no longer think straight. He pulls back with a smile still on his face from making me laugh so hard.

"So, do these marks mean that the Gods are back? And how would they know we call each other Viper and Rose?"

He runs his fingers over my lips to make me hush.

"I have no clue how or why we got these specific mating marks. All I do know is that it is an absolute honor to have this," he places his palm over the mating mark on his chest, "and you." He leans down and sweetly kisses the tip of my nose.

I smile up at him. It's hard not to when his words make my heart swell and flutter.

"Mine is pretty 'bad ass', I guess." I say before leaning up to kiss him. "Wait," I pull back concerned, "how am I supposed to go back home like this?" I point to both my ears and tattoo, "I'm pretty sure everyone will notice I now have pointy ears and a big ass tattoo!"

Not to mention my large canines...I can hear Seb now going all Little Red Riding Hood on me, "Wow what big teeth you have, Cali".

He smiles running his finger along one of my ears, causing me to shiver. "You can glamor them, I'll teach you."

Relieved, I smile up at him. "Okay, but right now I hear a hot shower calling my name so..." I quickly sneak out of his grasp and head for the shower.

I yell out and tell him to go make us some coffee as I turn on the shower; and wait for the water to heat up. This bathroom is gorgeous, with the swirling black, gold, and white marble theme that flows throughout the house. The shower is large enough to hold several people, it also has a large bench, and multiple shower heads. But my favorite thing—no surprise—is the humongous golden claw foot tub, that sits directly underneath a large skylight, allowing the light of the moon to shine down and illuminate the entire space.

I stand directly underneath the hot water pouring out from the rainfall shower head; letting it run down from head to toe. Thinking back on everything that has happened the past twenty-four hours, when suddenly, two strong arms are wrapping around me from behind.

This mate of mine really is insatiable. Not that I'm complaining.

I feel his already hard length against my ass as he leans down and begins kissing my neck. Before I can tell him I'm still sore from last night, his fingers are trailing down between my legs to my already wet core.

My body's instant reaction to him is unfair and makes it impossible to turn him away...not that I would ever want to that is.

I guess coffee will have to wait...because this shower just became way hotter.

CHAPTER 26

CALISTA

Nightshade's slobbery kisses are the best. He has been breaking my heart with his huge lion-sized puppy dog eyes since I told him I had to go back to the Mortal Realm for a while, but I promised that I would be back as soon as I could.

I would stay around a little longer but apparently Fae don't drink coffee, and I don't like tea, so Killian is taking me back home for a proper cup of coffee.

It's the least he can do since he interrupted my shower this morning; pressing me against the cold white tiled wall while he took me from behind.

Who am I kidding, it was amazing! I am all for that becoming a permanent addition to my shower routine.

"So, what type of flower is this?" I ask pointing to my mating mark.

"Midnight Hellfire or as some call it Moonlight Vipers."

"Vipers?"

"The Goddess of the Moon loved the flowers, and the vipers that live in the fields where these flowers bloom loved the goddess. The goddess was said to have taken some of the vipers as familiars, and she would wear them around on occasions, like a piece of jewelry. She was immune to the viper's venom. A venom so toxic that it burns its victims alive from the inside out; hence where the name hellfire came from. In all the depictions of the Goddess of the Moon she is seen with a large black viper wrapped up along her arm." He lifts his eyebrow staring from me to my mark. Insinuating that this is more evidence of me being the heir to the moon goddess.

I roll my eyes dismissively. "Shouldn't I have a rose though to symbolize you being my mate?"

"Not if this mark is meant to tell you something else..."

"Ahhh, you're impossible." I grumble, removing Killian's over-sized shirt I put on after getting out of the shower.

The next thing I know the floor is being covered with tea spit out from Killian's mouth, like something just startled him.

I stare at him concerned as he begins walking over to where I'm standing. Ever so slowly, he reaches up and runs his thumb along the underside of my right breast, and down over my ribs. I look down to see what has grabbed his attention and I see it. A single dark red rose just like the roses in his mark.

I follow him and begin tracing my fingers along my *second mark...* second mark?

He can see the question in my eyes as I look up to stare at him. He just shrugs his shoulders, having no clue as to why I ended up with two marks.

Before this mystery drives us both crazy, I decide to put an end to this 'I'm the *very* far off great grandchild descendent of the disappearing moon goddess' suspicion. "Take me back to the tree", I demand.

Killian looks at me as if he's trying to tell if I'm serious or not.

"Now please, Killian, before I change my mind."

As soon as he realizes I'm dead serious about my request, a moment later we are swallowed up in his shadows being carried away to the tree with golden leaves, the Tree of Resurrection.

Here I find myself again, for the third time, under this beautiful canopy of golden leaves. *Third time's the charm, right?*

As a detective I always use clues to solve my cases. Be it a physical clue that I can really see and touch, or maybe just a sign or a gut feeling I have that helps lead me to my next clue. All finally coming together in the end to lead me to the answers I am searching for. Why would I do anything different here in the Fae Realm?

First off, I have heard with my own ears the tree before me speak, it seems to be communicating with me specifically, and only the 'true heir' is supposed to be able to hear the tree speak.

Next, not only did I receive one mating mark but *two*. One of which is of a viper climbing up along my arm, which matches the description of the moon goddess's arm that's portrayed in this realm. My mark also has her two favorite things together: a black viper and the Moonlight Vipers flower, also called Midnight Hellfire.

Lastly, the viper's venom can burn a person alive from the inside out...much like I did to that Fae janitor years ago. And the moon goddess was immune to their venom...and my gut is telling me if I was bit by one of these vipers, I would be too. However, I am not testing that one out...not yet at least.

Where there is smoke there is fire, and as I sit here and run all this information over and over in my head, I feel like I'm dizzy and fighting for air from breathing in all the smoke from this blazing hot inferno.

I reach over and ask Killian to hand me his knife. He raises his brow in question as he digs it out of his pocket and hands it over to me.

His question is quickly answered as I take his knife and place the blade against my palm. "Blood is power, right? It can summon entities, activate spells, and form unbreakable bonds between mates."

He silently confirms with a nod, following along with my train of thought.

"Being blood related and touching the tree is not enough...the tree needs blood...*actual* blood." With that I slice my palm, allowing blood to gather and drip off the sides of my hand. I glance over to

Killian one last time and then before I can change my mind, I close my eyes and slam my palm up against the smooth trunk of the tree.

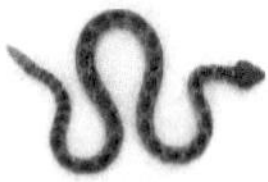

I slowly reopen my eyes, keeping my bloody palm planted firmly against the tree. Nothing *feels* different, and my surroundings look precisely the same.

So much for that blazing inferno...looks like it's all just one big coincidence. I am so glad I missed the mark with all those 'clues' though, because I do not want to have the responsibility over an entire realm sitting on my shoulders.

Now that we have proof that I am not the heir to the Fae Realm, Killian can now take me back home.

As I begin to remove my palm from the tree, movement on the outskirts of the field catches my eye. In the distance I begin to make out two figures emerging from the forest and walking across the clearing, heading right for us.

I quickly look back over my shoulder to ask Killian what we should do. Should we run? Should we act normal and see what they are doing here? Maybe they just wanted to come here to sit underneath the tree with gold leaves. It is a very beautiful spot to sit down and relax.

However, as I look back to where Killian stood a moment ago... he is now gone. Shock and fear overtake my attention. *Did he just leave me here all alone?*

I audibly gasp when I turn back around to get a better look at the beings coming *my* way...the tree I was holding my bloody palm against is also nowhere to be seen. It seems it just disappeared along with Killian; or maybe neither of them has come into existence yet...

Everything begins to click into place. My blood was the *key*. The key to what exactly I am still not sure, but apparently the tree wants me to see this vision from long, long ago. Before its roots were ever seated to this spot.

If the tree has yet to exist, that means I am seeing back to when the two sisters ruled over the Fae Realm. Back before the Gods and Goddesses vanished from the realm. Before The Deafening Silence.

Focusing back on the two beings getting closer to where I stand, I am quite sure I know who they are and why they are here. Walking towards me are the two sisters: Selenity, Goddess of the Moon and Alektra, Goddess of the Sun.

The closer they get I can start to make out more of their features, and they are indescribably beautiful. Flawless. Elegant. Glorious. My skin begins to tingle as if it can literally feel the power radiating off them.

It's easy to tell them apart. Selenity, Goddess of the Moon, has long raven black hair that flows all the way down to her waist. She has flawless pale skin from the lack of sunlight in the Unseelie Kingdom, and the most captivating emerald, green eyes I have ever seen. It's like her skin is covered in starlight, every time she moves, I can make out a slight sparkle radiating off her. It reminds me of Edward Cullen from the *Twilight* movies; when he removes his robe in the sunlight for everyone to see him *sparkle. Maybe Edward wasn't a vampire at all... maybe he was a Fae in disguise.*

Alektra, Goddess of the Sun, has shimmering golden hair that lights up the darkness of the everlasting night surrounding her. It would be very useful in the event of a power outage. *Just saying.* Her skin is a beautiful golden brown, like how my skin got that one summer I laid out by the pool every day for hours on end. The length that she wears her stunning gold locks, and her green eyes seems to be the only things the two sisters share. However, her green eyes are a light lime green like peridot; the gem used to represent August's birthstone in the Mortal Realm, where her sister Selenity's eyes are a deep dark green like a sparkling emerald gem.

It appears that they can't see me standing right next to them. Eavesdropping on their conversation. As they come to a stop directly on top of the spot where the tree should be.

"Here, this spot will suffice. Time is of the essence and enough has been lost." Alektra says in a rush as she turns to face her sister.

"Are you sure of this plan? We cannot know for certain that an heir will ever return. Luna is but a small child; she may not live long enough to bear children. Same for the next child and the one after that." Selenity asks, as tears begin to fall from her eyes.

Luna must be her daughter that she gave up in hopes to keep her safe and out of Pyroneous's grasp.

Alektra takes her sister's hands in her own. "We mustn't lose hope, Selenity. Luna is born of strong blood from both her mother and father. I have faith that she will not merely survive but thrive. She herself may one day return to place her claim on this realm, or her blood shall continue to be passed down through generations to come. Still giving hope that an heir will return and bring peace to the entire realm. Healing the divides that separate all beings throughout Stellaris."

Selenity reluctantly nods, accepting her sister's words.

"We must make haste...give me your blade." Alektra orders, taking the sharp blade Selenity offers her. Alektra slowly drags the blade along her palm. Blood mimicking the golden rays of the sun begins pooling into her cupped hand instantly. Selenity then reaches out, taking the blade back from her sister and quickly mirrors the cut onto her own palm, revealing blood as black as night, spilling out from the wound. They both stand there letting their blood gather into their cupped hands. Selenity's black blood and Alextra's golden blood, both contrast and complement the other. Truly representing each sister and the celestial body they rule over.

Selenity finally breaks the silence, staring over at the long black viper that is wrapped around her arm.

I can't believe what I'm seeing. This whole time I thought I was staring at a tattoo of a viper on her arm, almost identical to mine. I had no clue it was an actual *living* snake wrapped around her arm!

"Drax, my oldest and most loyal friend, are you ready?"

Then, I shit you not, the viper slithers up her arm and sticks out its tongue against her cheek. As if he is kissing her goodbye.

The sisters join hands, uniting their powers through the mixing of their blood. Slowly, they bend down and place their bleeding palms to the ground. Keeping their fingers interlinked; to not break the bond they just created between their powers.

Both sunlight and shadows rise from the ground beneath their hands. Twirling and climbing higher and higher, working together as one, reaching out from the top and straying in different directions.

They are creating the Tree of Resurrection. No wonder the tree seems to be sentient, it was created by the blood and power of two living beings. Well...not just beings, but Goddesses. Strong, intelligent, beautiful, exquisite Goddesses.

And one may be my great grandma and the other my great aunt... very heavy emphasis on the word *'great'*.

I cannot look away from this magical display before me. Slowly the tree I am currently holding my bleeding palm against back in the present, is being created right in front of my eyes. The golden canopy of leaves is taking shape right above where I'm standing.

The tree is almost entirely complete, except for a large oval opening in the center of the trunk. The tree is still shimmering from the contrast of shadows and sunlight along its entire surface. I am still completely transfixed with the scene before me when suddenly the viper begins uncoiling from Selenity's arm. She holds her arm out to the hole in the trunk of the tree, and it appears like the snake is planning to go inside the tree itself.

Right before the viper enters the hole, he turns to face Selenity. Tears are running down her face and a sob escapes her throat. "Watch over and guide them once they return, Drax. You will always be here." Selenity places her hand to her heart. "See you in the next life, old friend." The viper visibly nods, accepting the task placed upon him, while also returning her sentiment.

Turning, the snake slithers off and disappears into the hole in the trunk of the tree. When he is completely out of sight the hole begins to close, until it is completely sealed with no way to open it. Or at least none I can see.

Selenity begins to sob but Alektra grabs her by the arm insisting they must leave. They begin to walk back the way they came from...

Selenity continues glancing back over her shoulder at the tree that now holds something very close to her heart.

Drax, the black viper.

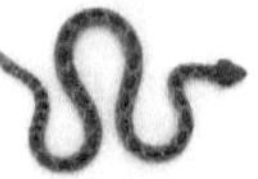

As I continue to stand beneath the canopy of golden leaves, trying to make sense of everything I just saw, my current surroundings come back into view. Turning around, I find both Killian and Nightshade staring at me like I've grown a second head.

I wonder what they saw while I was getting a glimpse into the past? Did my body remain here where they could still see me, or did it disappear from their sight? Whatever they witnessed while I was 'gone' must have been strange because I've never seen Killian look so dumbfounded like he does now.

"Are you two, okay?" I ask them, which seems to do the trick in snapping them out of whatever trance they were in.

Killian shakes his head but before he can respond Nightshade slams into me like a bulldozer, knocking me to the ground, and slathering me with kisses.

"Us?! Are you okay?!" Killian asks as he comes and squats down in front of me and Nightshade. He brings his hand to my cheek with a look of concern on his face. "You were the one encircled in a swirling vortex of shadows and sunlight. Even some small flames made an appearance."

I just stare back at him in complete shock. I didn't feel any different while my mind was away; seeing what the tree wanted to show me from the past. Were my powers awakening and causing that to happen? Or maybe the tree was putting up a protective barrier around me while my body was standing out in the open defenseless? I am going with the latter, even though this strange new humming inside my body is telling me I know the correct answer.

"I tried to get inside to you, but I couldn't break through. Even my shadows we no match against the strength of all that raw power encircling you." he explains, as he lays his forehead against mine.

I take his face in my hands as I pull back to stare into his two pools of starry night skies. They bring a strange comfort to me I can't quiet place.

"It worked...", I smile at him, not breaking eye contact.

This seems to assure him that I'm alright and his eyes finally begin to gleam with excitement and curiosity before he leans forward and kisses me deeply.

We sit there under the tree as I recap everything I saw and heard for Killian. The whole time his face is filled with such wonder; learning that the lore he grew up hearing his whole life wasn't all hog wash.

When I finally finish and have answered as many questions as I could from Killian, I inform him that I need to get back before I'm late for work. Work is the furthest thing from my mind right now, but I know my Lieutenant will have my ass if I show up late. Especially, in the middle of such a high-profile serial killer case.

Plus, although evidence has shown that I am most likely the rightful heir to Stellaris, I'm nowhere near ready to cut ties with my life in the Mortal Realm. Hell, I don't know if I will ever be. That's where my career is that I worked my ass off for, my friends are there, and most importantly, my aunt and sisters. I can't just up and leave everyone and everything I worked so hard for.

Besides, I have absolutely no desire to be Queen of *anything*...let alone a whole realm!

After giving Nightshade some good belly rubs and more slobbery kisses goodbye, I place my hand on the trunk of the tree to help myself up. It's then that I feel it, the trunk is no longer dry...but wet. Before I can look over to see what my hand just touched, my eyes stop on Killian. He stood up first so he could give me a hand up, but now he is wide eyed with a look of amazement on his face, staring not at me but at the tree I'm touching.

Following his line of sight, I gasp and fall back from the tree.

I can't believe what I'm seeing.

Golden liquid is now flowing down the trunk of the tree.

The hand I placed against the tree is now covered with the golden liquid. However, it isn't sticky like sap...it's smooth like water.

"Crying tears of gold

When the true heir returns home"

I look back up to find Killian staring at me after blabbing something about tears of gold.

"I can't remember the rest of the prophecy...but..." he cuts himself off by shaking his head and smiling in awe of me.

I can't help but stare back at him with understanding of what he now believes to be undoubtedly true.

Shit, I think we just closed this case.

Rising, I walk over and take his hands in mine. I guess it's time for me to accept what's right in front of me. Looking up at this handsome Fae of mine, I speak into his mind.

"I am the heir of Stellaris"

CHAPTER 27

KILLIAN

My mind was still reeling from the fact that *my mate* is the long-lost heir to Stellaris when we returned to the Hive. Yesterday was the happiest day of my life; Cali and I were finally able to seal our mating bond after ten years of thinking I would never find my mate again.

I spent most of the night and this morning showing her just how much she means to me.

My world now fully revolves around her.

She is the air my lungs need so desperately to breathe, and I will do whatever's necessary to make sure she is never taken from me again, until my last breath.

We found Callum and Dante sitting around a laptop at the kitchen bar. When they heard us arrive, they spun around ready to fight until they realized it was us.

Callum was the first to welcome us back; running over and slinging his arm playfully around Cali's shoulder as he asked her what she thought of the Fae Realm.

This brought a huge smile to my mate's face, and I suddenly found myself filled with anger. Both my fists were clinched tight by my side as I tried to calm down my emotions. I know Callum isn't a threat but for some reason the sight of him touching her has my blood boiling. Before I can get a grip on myself a deep growl escapes from the back of my throat getting everyone's attention.

Callum's smile falters as he raises his eyebrows at me in question, but then his eyes light up and he leans down and sniffs *my mate*.

Mine.

Before I can stop myself, I have Callum pinned up against the living room wall growling in his face, "Mine".

He raises his hands in the air showing he means no harm, but then a shit eating grin spreads across his smug face.

"Oooh shit!", Dante shouts bringing his fist up to his mouth like he is trying to make himself shut up before I turn on him next.

I turn back to Callum who is still in my grasp pressed against the wall where his shit eating grin has now turned into a full-blown smile.

"Looks like Kill has found his mate.", he says smiling and keeping eye contact with me. He moves his head to look over my shoulder where Cali is standing. Even this small action gets a rise out of me and my grip on Callum's shirt collar tightens.

"Don't look at her", I growl out what sounds like a threat.

I don't even recognize myself right now. I know Callum and Dante would never betray my trust. Hell, if I told them to protect Cali with their life they would happily die doing so. That's how deep our bond goes; they aren't just my friends...they are my brothers.

Cali steps up to my side and places her hand on my arm that's still gripping Callum. "Killian, what the hell are you doing? You have hit a whole new level of alpha-hole." When I don't respond she glances around at the three of us waiting for someone to enlighten her on the situation. "Does someone want to explain what's going on here?"

Dante walks up to stand next to Cali and I quickly turn around and give him a look that tells him that is not a good idea. He slowly backs away and comes to stand on my other side.

"After Fae males complete the mating bond, they become super territorial over their mate. Challenging and fighting any male who gets too close." Dante informs her while he smiles and shakes his head at me in disbelief.

I look over at Cali who now has this look of horror on her face. I slowly release Callum and reach over to take her hand that still rests on my arm, but before I can apologize for my actions Dante cuts back in.

"Don't stress too much Calista; he should be back to his normal level of alpha-hole in a week or so...three tops."

"Three!?" Cali shouts, looking at me with her eyes on the verge of falling out of her skull. "I work in a male dominated workplace... my partner is a male! And he loves to tease and poke fun at me, so how the hell am I going to stop you from killing them for possibly three whole weeks?!" She releases me, obviously stressed out and starts pacing back and forth.

I stop her, taking her face in both my hands so I can stare into her beautiful eyes. "Hey, it's all going to be fine. I'm sorry that happened and I'll do everything in my power to make sure it doesn't happen again. Okay?"

Her shoulders visibly relax, and her eyes soften as she gives me a nod. Just standing here next to her has my heart working overtime. Knowing that my actions haven't scared her off and that she trusts me to handle this raging beast I am currently fighting off inside means a lot to me.

These next couple of weeks are going to be Hell though.

I slowly lean down and place a kiss on her forehead. Basking in the unspoken words passing between us that are filled with love and devotion.

Callum walks around and pats me on the back, it's our way of saying everything is good between us, before he takes a spot on the couch.

"I should have known the moment you got back...you both stink of one another." Callum teases.

Cali leans over and sniffs me before looking back at Callum like he is pulling her leg. "I don't smell anything".

We take the next few minutes explaining to Cali that once the mating bond is complete the two being's scents merge into one. Which is another way for both male and females alike to know that Fae is already spoken for.

The guys also inform us that nothing happened while we were gone, and that Hazel and Eve checked in this morning before they left for work. As of now, everyone is safe and accounted for.

Now if only we could locate my father's damn assassins.

I apparated Cali back to her place so she could get ready and head out to work. I am secretly looking forward to the day she can leave this place and come back to Unseelie as my queen.

The thought of her being surrounded by all those males at her work was beginning to make me see red. I desperately needed a distraction to keep my mind off it. I never thought I would succumb to such behavior brought on by the mating bond, and now that I am experiencing it firsthand it cannot wear off soon enough.

I pinned one of my oldest and most loyal friends up against a wall for touching her and making her smile. The Gods only know what I would do to a stranger.

After I was finally able to pry myself off Cali, I returned to find Dante and Callum lounging on the couch looking anxious. They seemed fine when I left so I have no clue what could have happened in the last fifteen minutes to upset them.

They both look up to stare at me as I walk over to where they're sitting. The look they're giving me is telling enough...for whatever reason, I'm the current cause of their stress.

I shoot my hand up to silence them before they even start speaking. My vision is still outlined in red, and something is telling me that whatever they are about to say would only set me off. They don't fight me on it; most likely because they can sense the rage I am desperately trying to smother. I use their silence as an opportunity to head straight to my room and slam the door shut behind me.

My skin feels like it is literally on fire from the thoughts of *my mate* being surrounded by men all day without me there to keep them in their place. That place being far, far away from Cali.

I decide on taking a cold shower to help extinguish the fire blazing inside me and sooth my burning skin. I know I can't avoid the guys for long, but they can wait long enough for me to calm down... before they inevitably piss me off again.

With that I take off my clothes and step into the shower, turning it to the coldest setting possible. Hanging my head under the cold spray I look down at the new ink that marks my chest, my mating mark. After losing her ten years ago I never thought I would have one of these. It is extremely rare to find your mate in the first place, and the fact that I lost her then found her again all these years later is still unbelievable.

I can't fight the huge smile that overtakes my face as I look down at my mark and how it represents the two of us perfectly...the Viper and the Rose.

CHAPTER 28

CALISTA

It's already a quarter to noon as I find myself rushing back over to Hotel Hive.

After Killian dropped me back off at my place earlier, I quickly showered and got ready for work. However, as I went to text my sisters to check in with them and let them know I was on my way to work, I realized I didn't have my phone with me. It must have fallen out of my pocket when I was sitting on the couch talking to the guys this morning.

My first reaction was to reach for my phone and call Killian to find it and bring it to me, only to realize I was in this conundrum because I didn't have my phone in the first place.

This new mating bond has my emotions all over the place making it hard to even think straight...I'm so glad this is only temporary.

I decided it would probably be best if I at least show my face at the office first. Versus being late and having my boss bust my figurative balls. Luckily, I wasn't on the schedule to come in until noon today, so I still had plenty of time to get there. I would just get Sebastian to drive me over to the Hive after I make an appearance at the precinct.

As the elevator doors open for me on the ground floor at work I come face to face with Seb. He must have been dropping off some new evidence or checking up on existing evidence since the elevator was coming up from the basement where the lab is located. When he first looks up and sees me standing there, I swear a look of surprise flashes across his face, before he throws on his charming smile.

He's probably as surprised as I am that I made it in on time today.

"Look who decided to grace us with her presence." Seb jabs at me teasingly as I push him over to let me in the elevator.

With a pouty smile I sarcastically reply, "Ha, Ha!"

"Hey, just saying you are cutting it close." He says pointing down at his wristwatch. "Made it with four minutes to spare."

I shove him playfully over to the opposite wall inside the elevator.

"No seriously, Daniels would have had your balls if you were late. I swear yesterday I saw smoke coming from his ears during our afternoon debrief when he had to tell captain that it seems like our serial killer case has gone quiet."

I throw my head back with laughter. "Damn I would have paid good money to see that."

"Then don't call out and leave your partner solo and desperate. Daniels put me with Ortega...I can't stand that hippie freak. He took us to some Peace, Love, and Tofu place for lunch where I then had to force down a tofu salad, Cali. *Tofu*! I'm going to be shitting rabbit pellets for days."

I feel sorry for him, but I can't stop myself from rolling with laughter. By the time the doors to the elevator finally open to our floor I have tears streaming down my face from laughing so hard. Seb just stands there shooting me his 'I hate you' stare until we finally step out of the elevator.

Wiping the tears from my face, I tell Seb to grab the keys to the squad car because I need a lift to Hotel Hive. When he starts to ask 'why?' I just tell him that I left my cell phone there this morning before I did a walk of shame back to my car. That stops him from asking any further questions, but it doesn't stop him from saying, "Oh, that explains why you smell weird again today."

Normally I would retort back with something snarky, but after the events and conversations with the guys this morning it makes sense. I just had no idea humans could also smell the change in someone's scent once they bonded with their mate. *Strange.*

After I sit my laptop bag down at my desk and clip my badge to my belt, I turn around to the sound of keys jingling. Seb has returned holding the keys up in the air and sporting a huge smile; like he's so proud of himself for successfully completing such a *hard* task. I just roll my eyes and shake my head at him.

"Hurry up", I yell at him.

"Fine, but make it fast I have a hot date for lunch." He informs me, shooting me a playful wink.

"What have I told you about those dang dating sites? I don't want to hear it when you end up with an STI."

Before he responds, Officer Ortega turns the corner and heads towards us. I stifle a laugh as Seb curses quietly.

"Hey Seb! Glad I caught you; do you want to grab lunch with me again today? There's this really great—"

"Sorry, Ortega. Adams here needs me for important business." Seb says cutting him off. Leaving me in suspense as to what new tofu restaurant he has found for the two of them to try.

Seb looks over at me with a pleading look, wanting me to confirm his excuse to Ortega.

Taking pity on him, I tell Ortega he is busy today...but *tomorrow* is another day.

"But if he is free tomorrow, he's all yours." I smile over at Seb and pat his shoulder; trying my best not to break out into another laugh when his face drops into a frown. "He hasn't stopped raving about that place you took him to for lunch yesterday."

Ortega gives me the biggest smile before nodding excitedly at the possibility of having Seb as his lunch buddy again tomorrow. Then he excuses himself and heads off to leave Seb and I to our 'important business'. I look up to find Seb shooting death rays at me through his gaze. I would be kind of scared if I wasn't secretly dying of laughter inside.

We head to the elevator and as soon as the doors are completely closed, I turn to find Seb *still* giving me an evil stare. I erupt into laughter, unable to help myself. Seb is trying and failing at staying mad at me, because by the time the elevator opens back up on the ground level my contagious laugh has spread to Seb.

We find ourselves laughing and making tofu jokes the entire drive over to Hotel Hive.

CHAPTER 29

KILLIAN

After what felt like hours sitting under the cold shower, I finally feel calm and in control of my emotions.

I throw on a pair of jeans and a grey T-shirt before dropping onto the bed and checking my phone to see if Cali has messaged me. I feel like a weak pathetic human the way I'm sitting around pining to hear from her. Battling an internal war to keep myself from blowing her phone up to check on her.

These new mating bond emotions need to get themselves in check sooner rather than later; especially if I don't want to cause bodily harm to any male who gets too close to my mate.

Callum and Dante are still posted up on the couch waiting for me to join them when I finally emerge from the bedroom. They look even more frustrated and pissed off then they did earlier.

I can't help but grin because I know I took my sweet time in the shower trying to cool off. I don't even feel slightly bad about it either.

As soon as they notice me coming into the room, they both rise and walk over to stand directly in my path. I was planning on joining them on the couch, but I guess they just couldn't wait the additional ten seconds it would have taken me to get there.

I quickly reinforce my mental shields in hopes that they may help to keep my emotions from getting out of control again; especially if the guys are about to bring up what I think they are.

"Can I help you?" I say dismissively, like I couldn't care less about what has crawled up their ass and died today.

Dante's eyes flare open in both shock and anger at how disrespectful I'm being towards them. We have been friends for more than a century, and I can count the number of confrontations we have had between the three of us on one hand. "Hell yes, you can help us! By telling us what the fuck you were thinking completing the mating bond with that witch?!" he shouts at me in anger.

Before it even registers to me what I'm doing I have Dante pinned up against the wall; my arm pressed against his throat and growling in his face. "That *witch* is my mate, and she has a name. I highly suggest you think carefully about what you say next, or I may have to come up with a story to tell your father about why his son is never returning home again."

He dares to growl back in my face as a challenge, and my vision begins to close in. The color red is bleeding in from all sides leaving a clear view of Dante directly in the center of my tunnel vision.

"At ease soldiers!" Callum commands, as he tries to pry us apart from one another. "We are brothers. Killian stand down...now." he finishes, growling out the last word.

I glance over at Callum, and I see the desperation in his eyes. Turning back to Dante, I slightly apply more pressure on his throat before I finally shove myself off him. Leaving him to take in a full breath of air.

"There that wasn't so hard." Callum says looking relieved, and I turn to face him, snarling at him in response. "Let's sit down and try this again." We both stare at Cal like he has grown a second head before we resign and sit down on opposite sides of the couch, leaving plenty of space between us.

"Kill, this news just makes shit a lot more complicated and we need to know where your head is at now that Calista is your mate."

Callum calmly states. Now why couldn't Dante have spoken like this instead of coming off so threatening towards Cali.

"I don't know." I admit, lowering my head in defeat. "Fuck!" I scream out, fisting my hair in my hands. I feel torn, knowing that the guys are right and this new development has put a kink in our original plans we made before we set out on this quest to dethrone my father and place the crown upon my head. "I had no clue one of the witches we came to find was going to be my mate. We searched all over for her for years; you should have known that once I found her, I couldn't let her slip away again. As for our plans..." I drop my head into my hands again and pull at my hair. "Shit! I don't know what to do."

Everyone is quietly waiting to see who is going to speak up next. Dante looks over at me slowly and I guess what he sees in me gives him the courage to speak up again.

"Originally the plan was to find the witches, have them kill your father so you can take his place, and then dispose of the witches so they aren't a threat to *your* reign. We never decided if we were going to kill them, imprison them in the dungeons, or just negotiate with them to never step foot in Stellaris again..." Dante never takes his eyes from mine, waiting for me to say something in response to our original plans he just recited.

I can't be upset with him because he is just stating the facts. That was our original plan, even though we never came to a definitive conclusion on what to do with the witches after they were no longer useful to us. However, none of us imagined one of those witches would end up being my mate, the very girl we searched for years ago. They knew about Viper from the beginning of our relationship, but I never brought them to meet her. I cherished the time we had together, and I didn't want to share any of her attention. After she disappeared, Cal and Dante didn't hesitate to drop all their other responsibilities and set out with me on a quest to find my missing mate. Even knowing we would all be facing the consequences once we returned to our kingdom.

That's the kind of friends they are, and I know they would never do anything to intentionally hurt Calista.

In all my waiting around like a lost puppy for Cali to message me this morning; I forgot to inform the guys about the most important information that was unveiled during our little rendezvous in Stellaris.

This was game-changing information; even if Calista wasn't my mate we would have to stop and rethink our plan of action after making this discovery.

I can't stop the grin spreading across my face as I prepare to tell the guys what we uncovered. The looks they are giving me is a mix of curiosity, worry, and excitement.

"None of that matters now because everything has changed." Both Cal and Dante lean in closer giving me their full attention.

"Calista isn't some *witch*...she is a full-blooded Fae. And once she learns to harness and control her powers, she will be more powerful than any Fae in the entire realm."

"Shit" Cal says, running a hand over his face. I turn to Dante to find a look of complete shock on his face.

"Yeah, she sent me flying, landing on my ass during our first training session...and her ears emerged." I say with a shit eating grin.

"What makes her so special? Everyone we know except a slight few are full-blooded Fae." Dante asks. Causing my anger to begin to rise again from the tone of his voice as he questions the strength of my mate.

I close my eyes and release a slow breath as I stand. Looking at my friends I reveal to them, "Divine blood runs through her veins..." Now it's their turn to look at me like I have just told them something insane; like that I am actually a werewolf or some shit.

I pause as both men release a few gasps and curses under their breath. Dante's look of shock has now turned to pure horror.

"The tree speaks to her—" I try to explain until Callum interrupts.

"Wait! You mean *the* tree? The Tree of Resurrection with its golden leaves that the prophecy speaks of? That tree?!" he is clearly starting to freak out on me.

"The one and only", I confirm.

"Fuck me...", Dante mutters, his tone as dry as a desert as he stands and walks over to look out of the window.

"Yeah...that's not even the craziest part. When her blood made contact with the tree, she was sucked into a vision of both the sun and moon goddesses creating the tree itself. And when the vision ended, golden liquid began to flow down the trunk of the tree... 'crying tears of gold'." I stop to give them time to take in this realm changing information. It's a lot to process, especially when you have grown up your whole life believing the prophecy to be nothing more than a myth.

Cal and Dante both continue to stare at me with wild wide eyes. I attempt to recite the prophecy everyone throughout the entire realm has heard since birth...almost as if it was a nursery rhyme. Struggling, Cal steps in to help, reciting it perfectly as if he has it memorized.

"The Tree Will Bleed
When Serpent and Seed
Become One Beneath Its Leaves
Crying Tears of Gold
When The True Heir Returns Home"

There is a second stanza to the prophecy, but this part in particular is the most well-known. Plus, I have no clue how the other part pertains to our current discovery, so I am just focusing on this for now. One step at a time...

Dante sits back down, leaning forward with his head in his hands as his fingers massage his temples. This new development obviously has him worried. He speaks quietly, almost in a whisper, as the realization sinks in, "Calista is the long-lost heir to all Stellaris."

Callum shoots out of his seat cursing before turning and looking at me dead in my eyes, as if he wants to make sure I'm not pulling his leg. Once he realizes that I am serious he walks to the refrigerator and grabs us each a beer. When he sits back down, I tell them both about everything that happened over the last twenty-four hours. Well not *everything*.

By the time I am finished they are both staring at me with their mouths wide open in full disbelief.

"Holy Shit!" Dante rubs his hands over his face and overtly points out the elephant in the room. "So, you're basically screwed. If the Fae finds out who she is she will take your throne. You will only be a Prince Consort if you wed, not even a king, and she will hold all the power and say over not only our kingdom but all Stellaris. Are you really going to be okay with that? Putting our kingdom, as well as the entire realm, at risk by allowing a 'human' to act as their queen? Because the fact is mate or not, she has been raised as a human, and she knows nothing about our realm, Killian." Dante may be blunt, and his words may piss me off, but he is right.

I'm no idiot. Of course, the repercussions of Cali being the lost heir of Stellaris crossed my mind. But those were pushed aside and overlooked by my thoughts that came along with Cali turning out to be 'Viper', my mate; and us completing the binding of our mating bond.

Now that I know she is the rightful heir to Stellaris, I must selfishly ask myself...

Am I okay with that? With her becoming the queen? I have been waiting for the day that I take the throne and become the King of the Unseelie Kingdom. Determined to bring the kingdom back to its former glory after the disgrace it has become under my father's reign.

Can I just throw away all I've worked towards and look past it for Calista? She's my mate but Unseelie is my kingdom. Cali knows nothing of the Fae Realm, least of all how to rule as a queen.

Maybe, the Gods will work in my favor and Cali will be satisfied to rule by my side as Queen Consort...

"Well," Callum's voice breaks me out of my train of thought, "I think we can all agree that after spending time with the ladies they have grown on us –"

"Speak for yourself" Dante scoffs, cutting Callum off before finishing the last of his beer.

Callum rolls his eyes at Dante, calling bullshit on how Dante pretends he can't stand Hazel. And I have got to agree with Callum; Dante does seem to enjoy arguing and getting under her skin, just to get a rise out of her.

Dante moves to lunge himself off the couch towards Callum, but I'm quicker, as I place myself between them with a hand to Dante's chest holding him back.

When the two of them finally back down I sternly instruct them on what needs to be done next. "Look, let's just table this discussion for now. The three of them are nowhere near ready to face my father. Focus on awakening and strengthening their powers; then we can decide on what to do about them. And for fucks sake, find those damn assassins!"

The guys nod in agreement and I can almost instantly feel the tension in the air beginning to dissipate. I know we have some big decisions coming up, but for now the most important items are to get the girls trained *and* eliminate the assassins sent by my father to kill them.

Ding

What was that?

The guys and I move towards the couch looking for the source of the sound.

"Yo!", Callum says, holding up a cell phone that he pulled out from behind one of the couch pillows.

Moving closer I realize I recognized that phone.

"Shit" I say taking the phone from his hand. "This is Cali's, she must have forgotten it this morning." No wonder I haven't heard from her. I guess she won't mind if I show up at her work to return it to her? Besides, it gives me an excuse to show all the men in her office that she is spoken for and to back the hell off.

CHAPTER 30

CALISTA

My heart is pounding uncontrollably as I stand in the hallway right outside the door to Killian's suite in Hotel Hive. I arrived a few minutes ago and had been just about to knock when I heard Callum, at least I think it was him, yelling in military fashion. It sounded like he was trying to break up a fight, and once I heard him yell at Killian to 'stand down' I couldn't help but to indulge in a little eavesdropping.

I really regret that decision now though, as I stand here with my heart shattering into a million pieces.

It was hard to hear them clearly at first over the sound of my heart pounding so loudly in my ears. But as soon as I tapped into using my Fae hearing, I was able to make out everything they were saying clear as day.

And they *clearly* have been deceiving us from the start.

I absolutely hate the fact that I even feel somewhat surprised right now; seeing as how I've repeated to myself and my sisters over and over, since the first day we made a deal with the guys, that we could not allow ourselves to fully trust them.

I let my guard down with Killian. Hell, he tore my walls down like they had been made of tissue paper as soon as I realized who he

213

was and that he was my mate. *My mate.* So much for that meaning much of anything; seeing as how I just stood here listening to my mate tell his friends that they can decide what to do with me and my sisters *after* they get what they need from us.

Well screw him and his friends. If they want big bad daddy gone, they can do it themselves.

Why in the hell would I let my sisters, and myself, risk our lives facing this bad son-of-a-bitch when my own mate might kill me or lock me away in the dungeons afterwards?! No, absolutely not! We are through with this deal we made with them. There must be some way to void it since it was made with ill-intent, right?

As for the assassins...let them come for me. If I truly am the heir to the Moon Goddess and the God of Fire, then they should be afraid of me. At least this is the pep talk I am going to continue giving myself as my world continues to fall apart all around me right now...

I've always kept a lock on my emotions; mostly by keeping my heart surrounded and protected by a wall made of reinforced steel. Well now that this wall has melted away by the fire Killian stoked within me, with both lust and anger, I'm finding it difficult to keep it together right now.

It must be that stupid mating bond making my heart feel like it is literally being burned to ashes within my chest. I've never felt heartache like this before; not even the first time I lost Rose, a.k.a Killian.

The first time I was young, and it was devastating; leaving me with lifelong relationship issues. I never let anyone get too close because I didn't trust them to not just up and disappear on me one day taking my heart right along with them. Not that I really had a heart left to give them anyways after I lost Rose that first time. But now, knowing that Rose was *real,* and having completed the mating bond with him, makes the pain of losing him again practically unbearable.

This won't break me though; I won't let it.

I refuse to become some damsel that thinks she needs a man in her life to take care of her and make her happy.

I am and have always been a strong independent woman that can kick ass and find pleasure and happiness in more ways than one. I've never needed a man to feel complete or accomplished in life. Hell, one of my all-time opinions in life is that 'men are more trouble than they are worth'. And here I am once again feeling the truth of that opinion.

I've never been a big fan of those dainty Disney princesses like Cinderella or Sleeping Beauty. I've always thought of myself as more of a Xena Warrior Princess.

Hold my glass slipper, bitch. I will be my own damn Prince Charming.

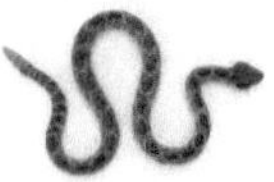

I grab a taxi outside of Hotel Hive once my mind stops spinning long enough for me to fully focus. It is times like these that I need my sisters most. Besides, I need to warn them to stay far away from those conniving Fae-holes.

Everleigh had told Seb she was going home for lunch to take a nap when I had asked him if she was in the lab earlier, so that's where I plan on heading. I hate to interrupt her rest; because I know I hate when mine gets interrupted, but this is super important, and I can't even begin to guess where to find Hazel right now. Eve can just text her to come and join us so I can explain everything to them.

My sisters and I are so used to letting ourselves into one another's places that I just take out my key to let myself into Eve's apartment out of habit. Normally we at least shoot each other a text that we are heading over before we just show up and let ourselves in, but my phone is still back with Killian.

Now I know why that small detail of sending a 'heads up' text is *very* important! It could have saved me from the scene I catch myself walking in on.

Crying out in alarm, I quickly slam the door shut to Eve's apartment. Standing in the dimly lit hallway in front of her apartment door I keep blinking rapidly to try and erase the image I just walked in on from my mind. My mind is reeling as I stand here trying to come to terms with what I just saw.

I seriously feel like I'm going to be sick...

I don't know how this day could get any worse.

Knocking on the door, like I should have done in the first place. Yes, it was my bad, I guess. I wait until Eve sounds the 'all clear' before slowly reopening the door. I keep my eyes closed until I am fully inside her apartment before slowly peaking them back open.

Standing before me like two guilty kids who just got caught having sex by their parents is Eve and *Sebastian!* Yes, the basically like a brother to us, Seb...that guy. Or better yet...*my partner,* Seb.

What sweet hell did I come back to today? I leave for one day and come back to discover one bat-shit crazy, life altering thing after the other.

I should have stayed in the Fae Realm.

I guess *my sister* was the 'hot date' Seb had lunch plans with today. Although...I'm not sure what I just saw him *devouring* can truly be considered 'lunch'?

Eve cannot make eye contact with me as she continues to just stare at her feet; Seb just looks worried, but it's not directed at me or how he thinks I might react, but at how Eve is feeling right now. He must really care about her...which means this must have been going on for some time now. It isn't some new development. I'm not sure which I would have preferred it to be if I'm being honest.

Shit I wish I had never discovered this...

What if something happens and he breaks her heart or vice versa? Can we still be friends? Partners? Can I even work in the same department as him?

No, there is no way...it would be way too awkward.

Seb steps forward with his hands raised; like he thinks I'm going to shoot him or something. Hell, maybe I would if I had my gun on me right now...

"Cali, look we're sorry. We should have told you back when we first started seeing each other. Blame me, okay? Eve wanted to tell you, but I was too worried it would mess up the vibe between you and me at work—".

"No" Eve steps forward, placing herself in front of Seb. "That's a lie...and now that this is out, I am done with the lies." she confesses, looking back at Seb. Turning back to face me Eve admits, "He wanted to tell you...I was the one that begged him not to. I was afraid you would be angry with me, and I couldn't continue seeing him if I knew you didn't approve."

Trying my best to remain calm, I take in and release a deep breath. "How long?" I ask flatly. When they just stare at me without answering I probe again. "How long has this been going on?"

"Two years..." Eve shamefully admits, averting her gaze again.

My eyes fly open in shock. They have been seeing each other for two years and neither I nor Hazel knew? Well, I'm assuming Hazel doesn't know anyways?

Eve must see my train of thought because before I can ask, she takes a step forward and tells me, "No, Hazel doesn't know either. Please let me tell her. I'll do it as soon as I see her, I promise."

I know I shouldn't be angry...well at least not as angry as I feel, but I currently have a lot of emotions running haywire throughout my entire body right now. When I arrived here my heart felt like shards of broken glass scraping around inside my chest, and now on top of that my brain feels like complete mush.

I'm pissed that out of all the men out there my sister decided to sleep with *my* partner. With seemingly no concern about how this could affect our working relationship. If they split up, she works on a completely different floor and would rarely have to see him; I on the other hand will be stuck in very close quarters with him daily.

Somewhere deep down, I am happy for her...and Seb. They are both great people and deserve to find happiness; it's just a little strange that they found it with each other.

All the family gatherings he's attended with us, all the hang outs, vacations...and I still hadn't put two and two together. They were super slick about keeping their relationship hidden that's for sure. I'm a detective for fucks sake; I should have seen this coming a mile away.

I want to be happy for them, and I know I will...but right now all I feel is anger and betrayal. And not just toward them but towards Killian regarding everything that I was on my way over here to tell Eve in the first place.

As I stand there taking in the two of them coming together to hold hands, my tears begin to fall again. Both know me well enough though to know I am not one to cry tears of sadness in front of *anyone*. When you witness tears falling from my eyes you had better run the other way, don't try to console me, because I am pissed beyond control. It's just a matter of moments before I fly off the handle on someone.

Shaking my head with disappointment I open the door to leave. Before I can shut the door, I turn back around and look them both in the eyes.

"Well sis, promises mean jack-shit to me today."

Then I slam the door behind me and sprint off back towards my apartment. The boss can have my balls later, but right now I need to be alone.

CHAPTER 31

CALISTA

By the time I make it back to my place I feel like everything is blowing up in my face.

I lean back against the front door once inside; trying to take a moment to catch my breath and process everything that happened over the last hour. I still have dried up tear stains running down my cheeks and can't help but shudder every time I think about what I walked in and saw going on with Eve and Seb.

I feel like I have been betrayed by four out of the five people I trust most in this world. Well one coming from the Fae realm, but still. Killian, Eve, Seb, and Aunt Ellie.

Killian was planning on possibly betraying me soon, Eve and Seb are currently betraying my trust, and Aunt Ellie betrayed me ten years ago when she had me get a bewitched tattoo. The only person in my life who hasn't betrayed me yet, that I know of at least, is Hazel. And with the way my day is going, who knows what else I will find out today?

Crap, I still don't have my phone.

My eyes begin to wander around my apartment as I try to brainstorm up a way to contact my boss and let him know something has come up and I'm not returning to work today. I took my laptop to work with me this morning so that option is off the table.

AHA!

I see my tablet lying on the coffee table. I will just shoot Lieutenant Daniels an email with some shameless excuse as to why I will not be returning to the precinct today. If he has a problem with it then he can bite me!

Always have a back-up for your back-up!

But first, I need a drink! I don't even care that it's only one o'clock in the afternoon. Today of all days calls for some good ole fashioned day drinking. Maybe if I'm lucky I can drink until I forget everything that happened today.

Looking through the fridge I find an unopened bottle of Moscato, one of the girls must have brought over for our last movie night.

Don't mind if I do.

My pour is very generous. I take a big mouthful of the sweet, delicious wine from my glass, and then top it off before I turn my attention back to the task at hand. Sending an email to my Lieutenant explaining why I will not be coming back into the office today.

Squeezing myself between my large cozy couch cushions and kicking my feet up onto the coffee table; I power on my tablet to compose an email. All I must do now is think of a good reason for not coming back today.

Something creative

He saw me when I arrived earlier so I can't pull the sick card... but he hasn't seen me since lunchtime so maybe food poisoning?

Yes, explosive diarrhea! No one is going to question that excuse.

I'm not completely certain if food poisoning can happen that fast...but today it can!

A small smile pulls at my lips as I begin to compose this ridiculous email to my boss. I can just see his face turning blood red and steam coming out of his ears when he reads this email.

Chuckling to myself I hit send.

Now time to sit back, relax, and get white girl wasted.

Ten minutes later, I haven't moved a muscle as I sit here in a state of relaxation bliss. I feel cheerful even as I sit here and laugh my head off at adorable animal videos. I could totally imagine Nightshade getting into some of these antics.

A pang of sadness hits me at the thought of my goofy, fun-loving chimera. I wish I could bring him here to live with me but there is no way he could pass for a dog. Plus, I work too much, and he loves the freedom he has to run and explore the enchanting iridescent forest around his home. I couldn't take all that away from him...it would be selfish of me.

Well so much for feeling cheerful. I pretty much shot that in the foot. Now that I have been to Stellaris I can't imagine never going back. Something deep down inside of myself awoke, and I felt alive there...like I was always meant to be there.

And I guess I was always destined to go there. At least if what we believe is true and I'm descended from Luna, the daughter and long-lost heir of Selenity, Goddess of the Moon and Pyroneous, God of Fire. Destined to return to Stellaris and bring peace throughout the entire realm.

Ha! I can barely keep my own life straight. Who in their right mind would want to put the future of an entire realm into my hands?

Shaking off my insane thoughts, I finish my entire glass of wine in one go. I'm ready to relax and watch some more adorable animal videos. But suddenly...

What the fu—

I catch a glimpse from the glare on my tablet screen. Someone, a huge someone, is standing directly behind me.

Before I can react, I'm thrown into the air and crash into my living room wall with full force.

I'm trying desperately to draw air back into my lungs while also trying to not give into the blackness that is creeping into my vision.

If I pass out, I'm dead. At least if I stay awake there is a 48% chance, I might live to see another day.

With my eyeballs safe in their sockets where they belong.

My head is spinning as I try to look around for my attacker. The pain from the impact is shooting through my entire body with every little move I make to try and sit myself up.

I can outfight all the men in my precinct, and I've taken many beatings in my line of work, but I don't think I have ever been knocked down this hard.

Despite my best efforts to resist it, the only thought I seem to have right now is 'this is it'.

I have no phone to call for help, and if there is more than one assassin there isn't a prayer in the world that can save me now. I know I am powerful, but I have only skimmed the surface of my abilities; and these are highly trained Fae killing machines.

But I have never backed down from a fight and I don't intend to start now. No matter if they want to catch or kill me; they are going to have to work hard for it.

Fuck my life! This day just keeps getting better and better...

At first glance I begin hoping that my vision is still spinning, causing me to see multiple, but no such luck...three humongous Fae stand before me. All three men are at least six-foot-four, are as broad as they are tall, and their shirts look like they are working overtime to hold in their bulging muscles.

Basically, I have three beautiful Adonis-looking Fae warriors standing in my living room.

They seem content to just stand there and watch me as I try to rise and regain my footing. Which unfortunately for me means they probably like to play with their prey before they go in for the kill.

"What's so special about this one? Seems like a waste of power if you ask me?", the red-haired Fae with bronzed skin asks his accomplices. He has a scar trailing down from his forehead to his cheek. The other two look very similar to one another, unfairly gorgeous, with one having slightly darker brown hair.

I don't know why my brain is sitting here profiling them when I'm not going to make it out of this fight. Maybe if I stand here and keep my mouth shut, and don't antagonize them, they will go easy on me...but then that just isn't me.

The longer they just stand around criticizing and judging me, the more time they are giving me to dive deep within myself and reach into my well of power. I can feel the burning of the fire flowing through my blood; and it feels intoxicating. It feels as if my power knows I'm in trouble and is readying itself for the fight. Giving me the courage I need to cut in and make my move.

"Hey, Scarface!", I yell to the red head with the scar. He turns my way with a glare that promises my imminent death. "Say hello to my little friend."

Before I even finish the sentence, two fire balls blaze to life in each hand. I throw them as quickly as possible at Scarface, and Ass-Butt #1.

Labeling them helps me keep track of their movements in my head. So why not keep it simple?

Both fire balls go wide, missing my targets, and now I have lost my element of surprise. But at least I managed to wipe the arrogant smug look off all their faces.

Ass-Butt #2 shoots over and grabs me, while his companions are busy dodging my fire. He moves so fast he has me pinned up against his chest in two blinks of an eye. He begins to squeeze, slowly crushing me with the strength of his huge, ripped muscles.

Focus Calista! Now isn't the time, I can admire his muscles once he's lying dead beneath my feet. Until then...Oh shit...

His friends are slowly walking towards me laughing at my failed attempt to light them up with my fire.

Scarface steps up first and grabs me by my shirt. He pulls his fisted hand back and throws it right into my face. Hitting my left cheek with the force of a Mack truck.

I release an ear-piercing scream, but I can barely hear it over the 'crunching' sound of my cheek bone shattering.

I am literally blinded by the pain in my face. I want to scream for help but when I go to open my mouth the shooting pain throughout the left side of my face has me snapping it shut.

This monster of a Fae behind me still doesn't release me. It appears that they plan to draw out my suffering as long as possible.

As I'm still trying to recover from the blinding pain in my cheek, Ass-Butt #1 steps up and kicks me right in my torso, sending all my breath shooting out of my lungs, and my legs falling out from underneath me. I'm doubled over, dangling like a rag doll, and completely dead weight, in the arms of my captor. I am desperately trying to pull air into my lungs. But every small breath I manage to take results in a sharp pain beneath my ribs.

I most likely have a couple broken or cracked ribs to go along with my shattered cheek.

As I hang here helplessly in the Fae assassins unrelenting crushing hold, the power deep down inside of me begins to awaken and make its way to the surface of my flesh. It feels like static electricity is running along my skin, causing goose bumps to rise along my arms.

What follows in its wake is a beast, devouring every red blood cell in its path, as it flares through my veins to the surface of my skin.

Power so deadly that even I fear it; even though it is a part of me. I can practically hear it screaming at me to give in and set it free. To let the fire burn and consume the dangers around me.

Seeing as how I'm not going anywhere anytime soon, and this may be my only hope of making an escape, I decide to give in and embrace the beast within myself.

I close my eyes as I feel this rush of energy, or power, flow through my skin. It's like the fire inside of me is slowly evaporating out of my body through the pores in my skin...and judging by the sudden screams coming from the Ass-Butt #2 who is still crushing me in his arms; I think it has found its target and is seeping into his skin.

An internal inferno, burning him alive from the inside out.

He tries to release me as my flames take root deep inside, but I wrap my arms around his with all the strength I have left refusing to let go. His friends come to his aid trying to pull me from his arm. I jump and kick out both feet as hard as I can, landing a dropkick into the lower abdomen of Ass-Butt #1 and knocking him down. The other one, Scarface, tries to grab hold of me to pull me away from his friend but as soon as his hand encounters my skin, he releases a yell, jerking his hands away from me as he stares in disbelief.

"Her skin feels like fire...we can't touch her without getting burned." Scarface cries out to his friend who is now getting back on his feet and scrambling around trying to find something to use that will allow them to touch me without getting burned alive.

"Release her Kia!" Scarface yells while frantically joining his comrade in search to find something to grab me with. "Just let her go for fucks sake!"

I can feel my power slowly returning to me and the Fae's grasp on me now is only from his muscles having locked up from the intense pain. His screams weaken into whines as he slowly falls to the floor, taking me with him.

As the last ember of my power returns to me I know the Fae who holds me is no longer alive.

So long Ass-Butt #2

I quickly pry myself out of his grasp as his two friends stare down at me in horror.

"Kill her!" they roar in sync before they start to unleash their powers at me.

I dig deep to channel my newfound Fae abilities to the surface. Using my Fae speed is the only way I'm going to avoid their attacks.

Daggers are flying towards me along with a ball of raw energy as I move to speed off and find cover. Unfortunately, my plan falls short. As I take my first step a sharp, searing pain shoots through my side. I hit the ground hard, letting my knees take the brunt of the impact, as I grab my side shrieking out in pain. I undoubtedly have a few broken ribs.

The pain in my face has my jaw clenching up so tight I can't even begin to scream out.

At least the assassins weren't expecting me to hit the ground, so their attacks went flying over my head...barely. That was a close call... too close.

I try to go on the offense and shoot off two fire balls back at my attackers, but I can barely hold myself upright on my knees enough to aim. Ass-butt #1 uses this moment to advance, grabbing me by the arm and throwing me across the room, like I weigh less than a loaf of bread. My back slams into the pantry door in my kitchen, and this time the pain is so *all* consuming that I manage to open my mouth enough to release a sharp ear-piercing scream.

I turn my head around to find my attackers, and my eyes fly open as I see a dagger soaring through the air straight towards my face. On instinct, I throw my hand out in front of my face to shield myself. Another scream tears from my aching face, as the dagger lodges itself straight through the palm of my hand. Now staring me in the face is the blade of the dagger protruding from the backside of my hand, the tip of it is less than two inches away from my nose.

My hand falls to the ground by my side in defeat. I think I stayed alive a decent amount of time having gone up against three trained Fae assassins; especially with me having so little training in using my powers.

As I lean back against the pantry door and close my eyes, a bright light shines through my eyelids, followed by loud yelling from my attackers. With my remaining strength, I open my eyes to see what all the commotion is about.

What I see makes me think I might already be dead...

Sebastian is standing in the entryway of my place, and he is...glowing. Like the sun itself is being held captive beneath his skin and it's trying to set itself free.

Looking around I see Scarface rising from the floor, and next to him, laying on the ground is a crispy-charred corpse. I'm assuming that must be the other Ass-Butt.

Scarface pulls a large, jagged blade from his belt and charges at Seb. The two of them begin fighting right before my eyes, and I swear...maybe it's the couple of knocks on the head I've taken, but it looks like I'm in the fight scene of a Mortal Kombat video game. I've gone up against Seb more times than I can count, be it in training or just for fun. But I have never seen him move or fight like this before. He is a whole new level of savage. His movements are so fast I can barely follow along with what's happening. I would say he is *inhumanly* fast, but I think the Kentucky Fried Fae on the ground next to my dining table is already telling of that.

Seb finally lands an uppercut to Scarface that sends him flying up into my ceiling. I'm sure my upstairs neighbors felt that if they are home right now. When he crashes back to the ground Seb slings him across the room sending him headfirst into my back living room wall. Luckily, he didn't make impact another foot to the right, or he would have gone flying through the window.

I cringe at the sound of bones crunching as he slams into the wall. He must have broken his neck on impact...there is no way that sound was anything but his neck snapping in two. He hasn't moved or so much as opened his eyes since he landed.

Seb must not want to take any risks. He sends two huge golden whips shooting from his palms and wrapping around Scarface's legs and arms. Keeping him tightly bound just in case he's still alive and wakes up to rejoin us.

I just stare back and forth between Seb and his handy work in amazement. The ropes that now bind my attacker look like they are made of rays of sunlight, glimmering in the sun that's peering through my windows.

Before I can ask any questions Seb comes running over to where I'm laying up against the pantry door, looking highly concerned. He gently places his glowing hand on my cheek to try and get a better look at my face, but he quickly releases me when I let out a sharp hiss of pain.

Looking me dead in my eyes with a frown on his face he tells me, "I can explain". All I can do is stare back up at him and give him a small nod before leaning my head back against the door and closing my eyes to rest. Everything hurts.

A female scream has me jerking my head up right away. It looks like Eve wasn't too far behind Seb's arrival, and the look of surprise on his face must mean he didn't know she was coming over here either.

"Oh my God! Is she okay?! What happened?!", my sister cries out in a panic as she comes rushing over to my side.

"There was a break-in, but I got here just in time." he says looking back at me still sporting a frown. "Go grab some wet washcloths and any first aid supplies she has."

My sister nods and quickly rushes down the hall towards my bedroom to find some supplies. With her gone I lay my head back again to try and rest my eyes.

Swoosh

Suddenly my hair is flying across my face as if a gust of wind flies by, followed by a hard thump.

I open my eyes again to find Killian holding Seb up against the wall with his hand tightening around his throat.

"You're a dead man", Killian spits out, but Seb releases a rush of air that throws Killian across the room and right into my TV. I cringe, but not so much from Killian getting thrown around like a tossed salad, but from my nice flat screen TV getting wrecked. Priorities...I'm going to need my TV to binge watch horror movies to help heal my heartache that both Killian and my sister caused.

After Killian stands back up both men square off to one another in the middle of my wrecked apartment, preparing for what looks like an intense face off. I wish my jaw would work so I could cheer for Seb.

They look like two opposite sides of a coin; Seb has golden rays of light surrounding his raised hands, while Killian's fists are covered in shadows.

Before they can get started killing one another, Eve runs into the room screaming at them to stop. Her entrance gives Killian enough pause as he looks back and forth between her and Seb. She runs to place herself in front of Seb to block him from Killian, but Seb takes his arm and moves her behind him...such a gentleman.

Killian finally lowers his hands as he looks over at me lying on the floor. There is such indescribable pain on his face that it makes my heart hurt. Why would he look at me like that if he was planning on possibly killing us or locking us away this whole time?

Oh, probably because he needs me in top fighting shape to destroy his father for him. And right now, I'm broken and battered.

He runs over and drops down in front of me. He puts his hand beneath my chin to examine my injuries and gets the same hiss of pain that I gave to Seb when he touched my face.

"Who did this to you?", he growls, his voice a low gravely tone that is fueled with rage and vengeance.

As I stare back into his eyes, I can see that his pain and worry are real, and my heart feels like it is being pulled in two different directions. I feel torn between desperately wanting to believe that he loves me with his entire being and that he would never let anyone harm his mate, not even himself. I would love to give in and curl up into his strong arms. But only a couple hours ago I literally heard him talking with his friends about how they were planning on betraying us from the beginning and may still do so. That betrayal is gut wrenching and I'm not sure if we can come back from it.

In this moment I'm not sure if I want to kick him in the balls or go ahead and wrap myself up in his arms.

For now, the only look I can give to him in return is that of indifference. I must keep my guard up until I get some solid answers, and even then, it's going to be hard if not impossible for me to ever trust him again. I feel stupid for letting my guard down in the first place.

He leans down placing his forehead to mine and I feel a soothing warmth spread beneath my skin. Slowly, the pain starts to ease off and I can begin to move my jaw back and forth and take in full breaths of air without the stabbing pain in my side. My hand that was impaled by the dagger no longer has any trace of ever being damaged. Though it did hurt like a bitch when he had to pull it out to heal it.

After I'm miraculously all healed up, Killian lifts me back onto my feet. He reaches out to pull me in his arms but before I can even consider going back down that road again, I push him aside and run into my sister's open arms.

I nuzzle my face into her neck and whisper to her, "I'm sorry. I thought I was going to die without you knowing that I am happy for you. I just had to get over feeling betrayed first." I chuckle into her hair, and she joins me.

"I'm so sooo sorry! I should have told you from the start." Pulling me back, she grabs my face and looks me dead in my eyes while tears run down her cheeks. "No more secrets, I promise."

Staring back at her with love shining in my eyes I nod my head in agreement, "No more secrets".

"Great, now is someone going to tell me what the hell happened here?", Killian demands, killing the moment.

CHAPTER 32

CALISTA

Everyone was sitting around my living room anxiously waiting to hear about what exactly went down between me and the Fae assassins who attacked me.

The guys had relocated the two dead assassins, so I at least didn't have two dead bodies just chilling in my apartment for this conversation.

I would find out where they had taken them later, but right now I honestly don't have it in me to care.

My sisters and I sat on the couch, Killian sat in an armchair he pulled up next to me, and the other three pulled over bar chairs from my kitchen island. Amazingly none of my furniture was damaged other than my TV. It was mainly my walls that took all the hits.

Nothing some good spackle and a paint job can't fix though.

While we had been waiting for everyone to arrive, Killian confirmed that the two dead Fae and the one unconscious one that were spread around my apartment, were in fact the three assassins his father had sent to find and kill me and my sisters.

He couldn't really identify the charred corpse; but seeing as how he identified the other dead and unconscious Fae, Kai and Raidus respectively, I think it's safe to bet that the crispy fried Fae is none other than his friend Sedrik, the infamous tracker they told us about.

I did my best to recount the entire encounter I had with the three assassins. Everyone just listened, wide eyed and slack jawed, obviously surprised that I was still sitting before them right now to tell this story.

Killian keeps incessantly apologizing for not being there, and as much as I want to blame him, I know it wasn't his fault. He thought I was safe at work; he had no idea I was moping around at home making myself a sitting duck.

This was a terrifying experience and has lit a fire under my ass to practice using more of my abilities, in hopes that I will never find myself defenseless like that again.

It is, however, reassuring that we no longer must keep looking over our shoulders waiting for the assassins to make their move. Now we can keep all our focus on the devils we know; the ones that are currently sitting directly in front of us.

After I finish my recounting of events I turn and pin Seb down with an accusative stare.

"Now it's time for you to explain why it suddenly appeared like you literally had the sun shoved up your ass..."

He smiles that charming smile of his, trying to come off like this new development is no big deal. "I'm a Light Fae from the Seelie Kingdom. The sun is my source of power...unlike the *little* shadow prince over there who uses the moon as his power source." he says, nodding his head at Killian.

Killian releases a threatening snarl at Seb's words. Obviously, for some reason or another there is no love lost between these two. I will have to figure out more about their relationship at another time though. Right now, we have bigger fish to fry.

"I honestly can't believe the universe is cruel enough to choose him as your mate. I should have recognized his smell on you the minute you stepped into the elevator this morning." Seb continues, looking over at Killian in disgust.

Even though I am upset and conflicted over my feelings towards my mate right now I still feel this overwhelming need to defend him. Narrowing my eyes at Seb I release a growl of my own, indicating for him to back off from insulting my mate. I chance a glance at Killian and see he is smirking over at Seb like he won this round...but little does he know his ass is about to get handed to him momentarily.

The entire time he has been here I swear I can feel him through our bond. It feels like he is literally caressing the cord that binds us together, running invisible fingers along it to try and soothe my emotions.

He also keeps glancing over at me with a look of concern.

I wonder if he knows there is more to how I'm feeling right now; and that it is non-related to the attack I just went through?

Eve releases a sharp gasp right about the same time as Hazel cries out, "What?!"

With all that's happened today, I haven't even had a chance to tell my sisters about my trip to the Fae Realm and all that I discovered. Not only about me now having a mate, but also that I am the heir to the *entire* Fae Realm.

"Yeah...we have a lot to talk about. Impromptu girls' night?" I smile over at them knowing they would never be able to say no to a night of sisterly bonding. Especially since they almost lost one sister today.

They both nod excitedly.

"But wait! You have to give us something in the meantime," Eve insists, batting her big blue eyes at me.

I look over at Killian to find him staring back at me; I guess he's waiting to see how I want to go about sharing this life-changing news with my sisters.

Such a gentleman...oh wait, that's right...he's currently planning the best way to rid himself of me and my sisters.

I turn to him and shrug. "I'll show them mine if you show them yours?" I challenge him playfully.

He gives me that sexy devilish smirk he knows I'm a sucker for. Standing he pulls his shirt up over his head, revealing his smooth chiseled chest that now has a beautiful tattoo of a viper twining up a flourishing rose vine.

The room is so quiet you could hear a pin drop.

I rise and stand next to Killian, lifting my shirt enough to pull my left arm free from its sleeve.

The silence in the room is broken; filled with gasps and whispered curses as they take in the enormity and detail of the viper climbing around my arm surrounded by the beautiful Fae flowers; moonlight vipers. I also raise the right side of my shirt to reveal the rose tattoo along my ribs right under my breast.

As everyone is taking in the similarity of our new markings, I explain to my sisters that Killian is my mate and how these markings appeared after him and I completed our mating bond ritual.

While I'm at it I go ahead and inform them that Killian is Rose; the guy from my dreams all those years ago, and that I didn't recognize him because he is glamoured here in the mortal realm.

Of course, there is so much more for the three of us to discuss, and I promise them that I will explain everything in more detail tonight over pizza and wine. Lots and lots of wine...

Seeing as how Seb is now involved in our mess, I have my sisters and the others catch him up on everything else that has been happening. Including the deals we have made with both Killian and Cerberus.

By the time everyone has finished catching Seb up and answering most of his questions he is just staring between me and my sisters with a mixture of relief and horror all rolled into one.

Curious of his reaction, I ask him why he seems to look slightly relieved. He said it feels like a huge weight has been lifted from his shoulders. He no longer must keep his Fae identity a secret from me and my sisters, and now he can help us carry out our end of the deal... killing the Dark Fae King.

I know the four of us; myself, Seb, and my sisters need to sit down and have a long talk about why he has kept his identity a secret from us the past five years, but right now I want Killian to look me in my eyes and swear to me that he has no intention of harming my sisters and me in any way.

When all the conversations begin to calm down over everything that has come to light in the last half hour I decide now is just as good as any to make my move.

I can't wait to see the look on Killian's, Callum's, and Dante's faces when I reveal to them that their traitorous plans have been uncovered.

"Uh-um", I clear my throat to get everyone's attention. Once all eyes are focused on me, I slip on my metaphorical detective hat as I begin to interrogate the three Fae males sitting before me; excluding Seb of course.

"So, if you can believe it, getting attacked by three psycho Fae assassins is not even the *worst* part of my day so far." Eve turns to me looking remorseful; thinking that the blame is going to fall on her and Seb, but that discovery was just the sprinkles on the cupcake. The cherry on top was finding out my mate was going to betray me.

Besides, her and Seb's relationship is theirs to tell, but I will be making sure that she comes clean about it to Hazel tonight.

I walk over and stand next to the hole in my wall where my TV should be right now and reveal my findings, "Imagine my shock this afternoon when I arrived outside the door to my mate's fancy suite at Hotel Hive to the sounds of yelling. In what seemed like a disagreement between the three of our new Fae *'allies'*." I make air quotes as I spit out the word like it literally puts a bad taste in my mouth.

Slowly one by one the look of realization comes over them; followed up with a look of alarm.

The girls must have noticed the shift in the guys' demeanor because my sisters are now staring at me completely intrigued; waiting patiently to hear where this story is going.

"I went there with the intention of hopefully finding my cell phone, but what I found instead was the three of them arguing about what they were going to *do* with the three of us *after* we destroy the Dark Fae King for them.", I say motioning between the three of us.

Killian immediately jumps up and starts trying to explain, but I quickly cut him off and keep going. He is not going to stop me from revealing all I heard to my sisters.

"So, pay attention girls because apparently these are our three possible fates the guys will be choosing between." I hold up my fingers, counting, as I disclose the options. "One, ban us from ever returning to the Fae Realm. Two, lock us away in their dungeons, or three, my personal favorite...*kill us.*"

As soon as the last words are out of my mouth everyone is on their feet.

Seb is standing off against Dante and Callum, with Eve and Hazel closing in on his sides for backup.

Killian makes a move to grab my hands, but I quickly jerk them away as I snarl at him, "Do. *Not.* Touch. Me!"

He looks at me like I've just driven a knife through his heart. His pain is real; I can feel sadness and guilt coming from his end of our bond. Just as I'm sure he can feel the heartache flowing from my end.

He deserves to feel the pain he is causing me; I want him to feel it. Even if it breaks me even more to sit here watching and feeling his own pain.

Seb is over there buffing his chest out and squaring up against Callum and Dante, he looks to be two seconds away from eviscerating them with his crazy sun powers. "If you ever lay a hand on them, I swear—"

"It's a little late for that" Callum says arrogantly, cutting Seb off mid threat. Releasing a low dark chuckle, he starts moving slowly toward Seb. He continues stalking towards him like the predator he is, until there is barely any space between them now.

I swear the more power everyone keeps building up inside themselves in preparation for a fight is stifling the air from the room and making it harder to breathe.

I don't regret calling the guys out on what I overheard, but I also don't want there to be any more bloodshed today. I've already shed plenty for all of us...

"Enough!" I yell, hoping to draw everyone's attention to me and away from one another. Once I finally have everyone's attention, I demand for them to sit the fuck down so we can figure out where to go from here.

Hazel remains standing after everyone else sits back down, seeming very upset.

She focuses her attention on me and Eve and admits, "Look I know this is an upsetting revelation; but before we accepted this deal with them, all three of us agreed that we were not going to trust them in case something like this was to happen, right?"

She does have a point. I'm the idiot who didn't practice what I preached.

Both Eve and I nod our heads, reluctantly agreeing with her. "We made deals with both them and Cerberus to help destroy the Dark Fae King. So, even if we could get out of the deal we made with them through some technicality, now that we know they mean us harm... We are still going to have to go up against the king because of the deal we made with Cerberus. And I don't know about you two, but I am nowhere near ready for that."

"So, what are you suggesting we do then?" Eve mutters dryly

"We make another deal..." Hazel bravely suggests, rising to her full height.

I can't even respond to that...all I can do is stare back at her like she has lost her damn mind. She wants us to get ourselves tangled up with these conniving Fae-holes more then we already are?

Once Hazel realizes that neither me nor Eve are planning on responding to her insane suggestion, she turns her attention to Seb and starts trying to pick his brain on the idea. "Seb...?" Knowing what she is about to ask, he immediately releases an annoyed groan and drops his face into his hands, "Can deals with Fae be revoked?"

"Uhh...no" he grunts, shaking his head. "Once a deal is made you are bound to it until the deal is completed."

Killian shoots back out of his seat and rushes over to me. His sharp movements reveal how agitated he is with this entire situation.

"Look, this is ridiculous! You know I would never hurt you in any way...I love you; you are my mate!" he pleads, his brows furrowed as he studies my face for any reaction. Then he reaches down to take my hands in his.

I bat his hands away and step forward until my body is almost flush against his. We are so close my breasts are raking against his chest with every breath I take. Being this close to him is intoxicating; my nipples have already hardened from this small amount of friction, and heat is beginning to spread through my core with need from being this close to my mate.

"That doesn't mean you won't do something to my sisters!"

Cupping my face with both hands he leans down, placing his forehead against mine and staring deep into my eyes. It feels like his gaze possesses a power that allows him to see into my very soul.

Being this close to him almost has me forgetting I'm mad at him...*and* that we are not the only people in this room. A very important thing to remember in case I lose my self-control, and we begin ripping each other's clothes off.

I can feel the bond between us tighten as he speaks directly to me, *"Your sisters are a part of who you are; harming them in any way would cause you pain and suffering. I swear to you, my mate, my love, that I will sacrifice myself before I let any harm befall you and your sisters. Always."*

He's telling the truth; I know it in both my heart and soul. The way his words caressed our bond, felt as though the love we share for one another is the most precious thing in the world to him.

I knew at that moment that he meant every word he said to me. He loves me with his entire being as I do him. No matter how angry I am with him I could never cause him harm in any way, shape, or form. Even the pain he's feeling now; though it's due to no fault but his own, still feels like I am cleaving a piece of my own soul from my body and tearing it apart.

Though I know this deep in my heart I'm still not ready to speak to him quite yet. Blinking up at him I nod slowly, which brings a faint smile to his lips. He can feel my love reciprocated through the bond, so he knows I believe every word he just said.

"Right", I say stepping back around to face my sisters, "I believe him. But continue to keep your guards up; just in case..."

"So, we keep training. Become strong enough to face the king and come out alive...hopefully. And make sure we don't get too comfortable around our new *'frenemies'*." Hazel concludes, seemingly hopeful about our situation.

"No problem there...does anyone want to swap partners though? Mine is kind of stale...?" Dante deadpans, looking over at Hazel.

Hazel rolls her eyes and looks away, flashing him her middle finger as she walks off into the kitchen. She bends down and begins digging around in my refrigerator until she comes back up with a new bottle of wine in her hands.

I guess she can't wait until our girls night officially starts.

"Oh wait!" Eve pipes up excitedly. "There is one condition...we all get to train over in the Fae Realm like Cali did."

The look of excitement on her face is priceless. The overhead lighting gives her blue eyes an entrancing glimmer, making it hard to say no to her stipulation.

"Deal" Callum agrees, seemingly captivated by Eve's stare.

He agreed so hastily, none of us had the chance to think of a reason to object. However, if there is even the slightest chance that being there can help awaken their magic like it did mine, then we need to go there and find out.

"Now...what do we do about Scarface over there?" I ask, pointing over to the Fae assassin on the floor who just started groaning like he's beginning to regain consciousness.

CHAPTER 33

CALISTA

Scarface is one tough son-of-a-bitch, I'll give him that. Six out of his ten fingers are sticking in all different directions, and he still isn't giving up the information we want.

Killian apparently wants to get any information out of him that we can to use against his father. Guard rotations, weaknesses in his defenses, etc. Callum knows most of this information, but since Scarface is under the command of Callum's father, he may have had access to more detailed information and know of other covert plans the king has going on the side.

To say Scarface—or excuse me—Raidus, was shocked to find Killian, Callum, and Dante helping us is an understatement. He spent the first ten minutes after he regained consciousness and realized they hadn't come to rescue him; cursing at them and calling them every name in the book.

Including some in Fae that I have no clue what they meant, but they sounded anything but pleasant.

An hour later we still have nothing to show for the torture the guys are putting Scarface through, and his screaming is giving me a splitting headache.

From the looks of it I don't know how much skin the man has left to slice up that hasn't already been. Obviously, this tactic isn't working so why not try something a little more humane? Something that I happen to be very well-trained in...

I nudge Seb in the leg and signal for him to follow my lead. Heading over to where the guys have Scarface splayed out and restrained on top of my small kitchen table.

It's slightly comical looking with his head hanging off one end and his legs hanging off the other. I'm sure he is restrained here on purpose, because this position he's in is its own form of torture.

I position myself next to his head and Seb joins me taking the other side. I look over at Killian who is now staring at me in question with his raised brow.

Callum and Dante have a look of blood lust in their eyes; like I'm interrupting their favorite game. But sorry not sorry, their way isn't working so now it's time to try mine.

"The professionals are going to take it from here, boys" I mock, shooing them away.

Dante and Callum move to step forward like they plan on fighting me for dibs on who gets to torture Scarface, but Killian throws out his arm stopping them in their path. A look of betrayal flashes across both men's faces.

They stare at Killian with a mix of confusion and anger before they finally yield and stand down.

I turn and place my ass right on the edge of the table. This allows me to look straight down into my target's eyes, increasing my intimidation factor. His inferior position allows me to take charge and have more control of the situation.

On my signal Seb takes Scarface's head and raises it up; allowing him to get a better look at me, as well as giving him some relief from the pain I'm sure is radiating down his neck.

We are playing a little good-cop, bad-cop like we have done hundreds of times before. If Raidus cooperates Seb will keep holding his head up. If not, Seb will let it drop, causing pain to shoot down his spine.

Calista Adams- Lead Detective for DCMPD- Reporting for duty.

"Cut the shit Raidus...or do you prefer Scarface?" I question intimidatingly. I know this will get a rise out of him and that's exactly what I want. Anything to get him talking again.

"Fuck you" he spits at me. *Too easy.* I glare back at him with a sinister smile crawling along my face.

"I'm going to kill your king", I deadpan looking him straight in his beady green eyes. "Do you *really* want to stop me?" I take a pause to allow my words to sink through his thick skull. I'm hoping that my next words will really drive home the point and allow me to get a read on him. "Or would you rather *assist* me in killing him?"

His eyes widen in surprise. I can see the gears turning in his mind and I know he is questioning my intentions. But for a second, hell maybe half a second, I saw a spark behind those green eyes. A spark that tells me the thoughts of him having a hand in taking down the king piques his interest. Just like I hoped it would.

If the Dark Fae King is as bad as they say he is, I figured there was a high chance that most of his followers are ruled by fear over respect and admiration. Fear that if they defy him in the slightest way they will face extreme punishment, most likely death. And this may work in our favor...my sisters and I will have a better chance at going head-to-head with the king and coming out on the other side alive *if* we can bring some of his followers over to our side.

Maybe Scarface knows of others within the king's army that would be willing to take a stand and join us.

Maybe the king's shock alone at witnessing his soldiers move over to our side of the playing board to stand against him, will give us the opening we need to make our move.

I smile and nod knowingly, as he continues to stare back at me in shock. "Look me in my eyes and tell me you like living under the rule of your king. That if given the chance you wouldn't stab him straight through his black heart?"

He continues to silently stare...

His eyes keep jumping back and forth between me and Killian.

He most definitely thinks this is a set up; a trap set up by Killian to convict him of treason against the king.

"You can't, can you?" Grinning, I look around the room to see how everyone else is reacting to this interaction. The guys just look stoic, like they could care less about how he may respond.

I think they are butt hurt that I got him to talk in less than two minutes, where they were going on an hour with no such luck.

"Join us...help us to defeat him. Be part of the movement that will free your kingdom from his appalling reign. If not for yourself, then for others who suffer at his hand..."

His voice comes out raspy from having screamed so much earlier, as he lifts his head slightly closer to mine and warns, "You will meet your end if you go up against him. He is indestructible. His powers outmatch all the Fae in our lands."

Darkening my gaze, I squat down until my chin is mere inches from his and fiercely reply, "No one is un-killable. Everything eventually dies. And I am no *ordinary* Fae...I am his *ruin*. Destined by the Gods of your realm to be his reckoning." My eyes narrow as I lean in closer to consume his vision. "Why do you think he sent you here to kill me and my sisters? He is *afraid* of us."

Silence...

I am met with silence.

I rise and nod at Killian, signaling that it's time to go back to their way of retrieving information and answers.

The boys move forward to reconvening the torturing. Stepping past them I can almost feel the excitement buzzing from them. The thrill they get from torturing Scarface sends a shiver down my spine.

That is definitely some messed up shit.

The words are so faint as they reach my mortal ears that I can barely hear them.

"I'll help you kill the bastard" he says flatly, allowing his stare to reveal so much more when I turn back to face him.

This is a man who has been deeply yearning for retribution against his king. I do intend on eventually figuring out why he despises his king, but for now getting him to join our side is enough of an accomplishment for today.

I release a long breath I didn't realize I had been holding, allowing the tense muscles in my neck and back to relax.

This could be the turning point we need to bring us that much closer to taking on the king and living to talk about it.

It seems like King Erebus has been a Tyrant for far too long, and all the evil and suffering he continues to allow throughout his kingdom may end up working in our favor...

If Scarface is willing to turn his back on the oath he swore to protect and serve his king, maybe there are others throughout the Unseelie Kingdom willing to join our cause.

I can't contain my smile...hell I don't want to.

Maybe we can pull off a win against the Dark Fae King. We still need a substantial amount of training, but the day will come when King Erebus meets his fate...

CHAPTER 34

CALISTA

At long last, after this shit storm of a day I've had I can finally sit down with my sisters and unload my stress.

Killian took Scarface back to their suite to keep an eye on him. They promised not to torture him anymore since he agreed to help us defeat the king...well unless it is absolutely necessary.

However, dealing with our 'prisoner' is a whole new stressor that I can wait till tomorrow to deal with. Right now, I need some sister time.

The three of us really haven't been able to hang like we normally would, since we started using up all our free time to train with the guys. I need to catch up on how everything is coming along with their abilities and fill them in on everything that happened while I was in the Fae Realm.

I allowed Seb to stay here with us so he could get caught up on everything as well. Plus, he owes us more of an explanation as to why he kept his identity a secret from us for so long; and any other questions we can think of.

After we finish milking him for information though, his sneaky Fae ass is getting kicked to the curb so we can continue with our sisters' night.

After Pizza arrived and Seb returned from a much-needed beer and rum run; we all grabbed our food and drinks and settled back down around the living room for 'sharing' time. I didn't miss how Seb made sure to grab a spot next to Eve or all the stolen glances they were stealing from one another.

Now that I know their secret I can't believe I didn't put two and two together long before today. Some detective I am...

Seb was the first to share his story with the group. Apparently, he has been in our lives a lot longer than we knew of. When I was sixteen and my powers began to manifest, not only were they awakening inside me, but somehow Seb also felt something come alive inside himself.

The way he describes it almost sounds like the pull of the mating bond between Killian and me.

He followed that pull all the way into the Mortal Realm until he found its source...me.

He keeps assuring me that we are not mates and that the bond between us is something different... He calls it a warrior bond. Apparently with this warrior bond shared between us, one of his sole purposes in life is to watch over me and keep me from harm.

As I got older, and my abilities became stronger, the bond grew even more powerful...to the point where his other duties got put on the backburner.

We asked him what those other duties entailed. Thinking maybe he was a warrior in the king's army or a blacksmith...but no.

He is the Seelie Prince! The. Seelie. Freaking. Prince. What is it with me drawing in all these powerful Fae princes?

This, in my mind, only helps support the evidence that points to me being the lost heir to Stellaris.

A freaking princess! One who apparently likes to be surrounded by the attention of hot chiseled princes. *Gag!*

I'm no damsel in distress...never have been...never will be.

His father...the Seelie King, threatened to disown him if he left his duties to come live in the Mortal Realm. Even though he explained to him that he could not refuse the pull of the warrior bond. He would become physically ill the longer he was away from me, but his father refused to accept it. And Seb refused to go against his purpose that the bond had instilled within him.

So here we are. Twelve years he has been in our lives, and we didn't even know it. He was just a figure in a crowd watching us from afar for years. Until he finally got the opportunity to follow me into my line of work, where he used his Fae abilities to pass with flying colors and land himself right next to me as my partner.

By the time Seb was finished telling his story and answering all our questions my jaw was sore from hanging open for so long.

The only thing he really couldn't answer was why he was called to look over me...but he thinks maybe it has to do with helping us defeat the Dark Fae King.

He did show up right in time to save me from those Dark Fae assassins.

Thanks to him having decided to come over and talk with me more about his relationship with Eve, after I had stormed out of her apartment in anger. And thanks to the bond between us which helped save precious time... The pull between us let him know where I was, and as he got closer there was an urgency in the pull which let him know something was wrong. Thankfully that kicked his ass into gear and got him moving at Fae speed, and he got here just in time.

A second or two later and I honestly don't think I would be here right now.

After our discussion with Seb, Eve spoke up and told Hazel about her and Seb's relationship.

I still can't believe I didn't pick up on it sooner.

Hazel was a little shocked about it, but she handled it way better than I had.

In my defense, I did just hear my mate debating with his friends over whether they were going to imprison or kill us in the coming future...

In the end we all shared hugs and congratulated the happy couple. They both shared matching smiles, and you could see the relief they were feeling at finally not having to keep their relationship a secret anymore.

I guess that means it's my turn to share all my crazy news in our little sharing circle...

But before I can even begin, Seb looks over at me with a raised brow and states, "I guess congratulations are in order for you too? You did basically get hitched yesterday."

Wait! What!? He's joking, right?

I'm speechless as I sit here trying to comprehend what Seb just told to me.

"Hitched...like Married?" I squeal out in question.

A question I already know the answer to, if I'm being honest with myself. I can feel in my heart that what he's saying is the truth.

Completing the mating bond in the Fae Realm is equivalent to getting married here in the Mortal Realm. I guess it's just slightly jarring to hear someone else confirm it aloud.

And here I am, I haven't even been married for twenty-four hours and I'm already wondering if you can file for an annulment with a matting bond?

"What?!" both Eve and Hazel shout out at me.

"You got married?" Eve yells, angrily pointing her finger at me. "And you got pissed about Seb and me just dating?!" She waves her arms around gesturing at the two of them.

"Yeah, excuse me?" Hazel heatedly inquires.

"Whoa, hold your horses." I call out, raising my hands in surrender. "Yes, technically in the Fae Realm, completing the mating bond is equivalent to getting married here in our realm. But...I feel like sealing the mating bond is different in that it should be more intimate and private, just between mates. I promise if I decide to stay with the conniving bastard, we can have an actual wedding, and you both can plan the entire thing. Deal?" I explain smiling sweetly, hoping the promise of them having free reign over my wedding will get me back in their good graces.

Seb, you damn Fae, trying to start drama on my sisters' night...which he shouldn't even be here for.

My sisters share a look with one another before turning to me with huge smiles on their faces. "Deal!" they practically scream at me as they suffocate me with hugs.

I guess their sudden change of attitude means they forgive me?

"Oh, and we get to pick your dress" Eve adds, looking at me with that puppy dog look she knows I can't stand, but I also can never say no to.

"Fine", I grind out. Hoping we can now move on to other more important information.

I tell them everything that happened yesterday...well almost everything. Some stuff should stay in the bedroom...and living room...and shower. I digress...

I especially take pride in the fact that I was able to knock Killian on his ass a couple times.

The excitement on my sisters' faces brings a smile to mine. They are so excited to get to the Fae Realm and see if their powers will awaken like mine did, and I really hope they do. I can't stand the idea of them visiting those magically enchanted lands, only to become too disappointed to take it in and experience the beauty and magic that surrounds them.

By the time I am finished explaining to them that I am possibly the long-lost heir to the entire Fae Realm; they all are staring back at me with wide eyes and jaws to the floor. They are shocked beyond belief; just like I still am.

"But there is still a chance that the tree, and the vision, and the golden sap is all just a coincidence. I'm not believing anything until

I'm one-hundred percent sure." I throw that in there before they start losing their minds.

My sisters finally begin to blink again; rejoining the land of the living, but Seb is still just staring at me with something like 'understanding' on his face. Like he has finally figured something out.

Seb suddenly starts laughing. His unexpected outburst has me jumping in my seat, catching me off guard. He comes to stand right in front of me, giving me that charming smile of his. "Gods you are stubborn!", he states as he runs his hand through his shining blond hair. "What more evidence could you possibly need to confirm you are the rightful heir, Cali?"

He paces away from me before striding back and taking a knee right in front of me so he can look me dead in my eyes. "This explains everything...my purpose is not to just protect you and help you defeat the Dark Fae King...it's to help guard and guide you...to help you claim your throne, *princess*."

Seb slowly bows his head before me; and although I'm touched by his actions, it still makes me uncomfortable. I have no desire to be a princess, sitting on a throne all day and bossing people around. I am satisfied with my life I have here...or at least I think I am.

Then again, I guess there is a difference between feeling satisfied with your life and being happy with your life. Living a satisfied life sounds like you enjoy your life, but somewhere along the way you became stuck and gave up on finding your true purpose and happiness.

Maybe if you kept striving for something *more* to add to your life or tried something completely different, you could achieve your true happiness. So, feeling satisfied is good, but finding your happiness is something worth striving for. Finding happiness is worth the blind faith and risks you must take to get there.

Do I settle with being satisfied or take the risk to try and reach my full potential? I honestly am not sure.

I stand, grabbing Seb's arm to pull him up with me as I go. "Please don't do that...I'm no princess...or even if I am I still don't want anything to change between us, okay? I don't even want to rule over a kingdom, plus I would never leave my sisters here."

"You must claim the throne. Your return was prophesied to restore peace to Stellaris. Without you, the realm will fall into perilous darkness." His desperate look has my heart racing. Does he truly believe I can bring peace to the realm? Besides if the Fae Realm hasn't fallen into darkness after all these centuries, what makes him think it suddenly will now that I know the truth about who I'm meant to be?

Yeah, I'm going to need a stiff drink...or three to get through this night.

CHAPTER 35

CALISTA

I was feeling good and tipsy by the time Seb finally left us to our sister's night.

The girls filled me in on their training and how they were getting along with the guys. Apparently, Callum and Eve were getting along fine. Other than him being overbearing at times; but he is an army General, so it is in his nature to be commanding. When I started joking with her and telling her not to let Callum try and steal her away from Seb, she started blushing a little too much.

"Oh no! Have you joined me over on the dark side?" I laugh hoping she gets my joke. I guess we are on opposing sides in the bedroom when it comes to men; I am mated with a Dark Fae, and she is dating a Light Fae.

"Shut up!" she laughs, throwing a couch pillow at me. "You can't blame me for enjoying the scenery...he is *fine* with a capital F."

We all bust out laughing uncontrollably. But she does have a point. I've been in this realm for twenty-eight years and our three new acquaintances are rare specimens indeed. Looking like they were carved out by the Gods themselves, with their sculpted abs, straight noses, and chiseled jaw lines. Seb also fits the description, but now that we know he is Fae it makes total sense. I guess there must be something in the water over in the Fae realm that makes everyone drop-dead gorgeous; and not just the men, the few women I've seen have been heart stoppers, as well.

"They may be nice to look at, but Dante has the personality of a Tasmanian Devil. I can never do anything right according to him. I want to punch him in his stupid smug handsome face." Hazel says finishing off her third rum and coke. "Can one of you pleeease trade partners with me?"

"Put those puppy eyes back where they belong" Eve demands. "Maybe the both of you just need to hate-bang one out to put yourselves in a better mood when you're together."

I spew my rum and coke from my mouth at Eve's unexpected suggestion. The only time Eve is ever this bold is when she is drunk, so it may be time to cut her off for the night.

Laughing my ass off I turn to Hazel before adding to Eve's point; "Yeah I've heard hate sex is amazing!" She just rolls her eyes at us, not having any of our teasing. "But in all seriousness" I turn to her with a straight face making sure she is paying attention to what I'm about to say. "Be careful...", I lean back against the couch and hold my hands up with a good ten inches in between them; "Because Fae men are well endowed."

Eve and I are rolling on the couch with laughter. Hazel leans over and slaps me in the leg, but then she is dying of laughter right along with us.

God, I love my sisters.

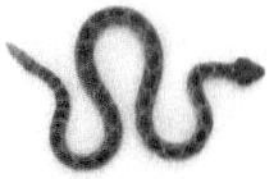

Cerberus is looking dashing as usual as he sits in the chair across from us with his ankle crossed over his knee. Giving off the sense that he doesn't have a care in the world right now. What I wouldn't give to feel that way.

The girls and I decided to go ahead with our plans on summoning him here tonight to ask about how he's coming along in finding our mothers' killer, as well as, if he would be able to find out who my Fae father is.

However, as I sit here across from this powerful Dark Fae, I'm beginning to regret that last rum and coke I drank.

The rum is finally starting to take effect and is causing my brain to feel all fuzzy inside. And if there is ever a time I need to have my wits about me, that time is now.

"How is your training coming along?" Cerberus inquires to no one in particular.

"We have gained more control over our abilities since we last spoke with you." Eve explains. "Cali has made tremendous progress though; she went to the Fae Realm with Killian and her powers awakened. Not only that, but they also seemed to have flourished. The guys promised to take me and Hazel with them next to see if that realm can help with the progression of our powers as well."

"Is that so…" he says lifting his brow as his focus shifts to me. I hate when he does that; I feel like he is judging every single piece of me.

The girls are looking at me to respond. I can tell they aren't sure how much I want to share with him about what all I discovered while I was in the Fae Realm.

To be honest I'm not sure how much I should tell him either… I don't trust him, but he is essential to our plans moving forward.

He could help us until it no longer benefits him and then turn around and stab us in the back, just like the guys had planned on doing.

Before I can even decide what all to share with him, his eyes narrow as he continues to stare at me. It appears like he's studying me and trying to figure something out. Maybe he is trying to see if anything about me looks different since being over in the Fae Realm, or—

Cerberus takes a subtle sniff of the air then immediately tries to hide his agitation at whatever he smelled.

Oh no! He isn't looking for anything different about me…he smells something different about me. Damn Fae and their superhuman senses.

"It appears that you ran off to another realm and found yourself a *mate*." His last word is laced with disgust. He is not even trying to hide that he is appalled at this revelation. He keeps staring at me, cocking his brow, as he waits for me to confirm if he is correct. But last time I checked that type of information is absolutely none of his business, nor is it relevant to the deal we have with him.

Obviously, we need to set some clear boundaries with this guy.

Keeping my chin held high I do my best to appear unphased by his accusation. If I let him see his statement rattled me, then I am basically confirming his suspicion.

"My personal relationships should be of no concern to you; so, if I did or didn't take a mate it is none of your business." The sternness in my voice seems to do the trick because he finally releases me from his stare and looks away.

With that handled, I go on to tell him everything that happened regarding my training and my abilities. I do not share with him that I indeed have a mate, or what our suspicions are of me being the heir to his entire realm.

He is the true Dark Fae King after all, so if he sees me as a threat to his precious throne, he could kill me right here where I stand.

"So, my step-nephew truly believes you to be a full-blooded Fae; not a halfling?" he inquires, seeming genuinely fascinated by my genetic makeup. Which to be fair may come as a surprise to him seeing as how we told him our mothers were witches, and we have no clue who our fathers are.

Here he thought he was relying on three half-witch, half-human women to defeat the king for him, but now he may have the power of a full-blooded Fae behind him.

Or in front of him is more accurate...since he is sending us to the front lines to do the dirty work for him by killing the king ourselves.

"Yes, he believes both my mother and father were Fae...well my mother was part Fae. He thinks she must have been descended from a Fae bloodline."

The look he is giving me as I share this life-altering news with him is that of indifference. This level of detachment looking back at me through his eyes is one I am overly familiar with. I see it time and time again in about every interrogation room I step foot inside. *Guilt.* When guilty people are apprehended, they try to pull off this blank look that doesn't reveal any emotions they may be feeling. However, as uncaring as it may seem, this look is fueled by purpose, and it takes a lot of concentration to pull it off.

Concentration that I can spot a mile away thanks to my years at the precinct.

I jump off the couch and point my finger at him accusingly, "You already knew that though, didn't you?!" My jaw clenches as I try to keep my frustration under control. "What the hell else are you keeping from us? Let me guess, you know who my father is don't you?" I yell at him; sarcasm bleeding through my words as I throw my hands into the air.

Then I remember what Killian suggested after he determined my father must also be a full-blooded Fae. My mind has been so focused on him and his betrayal I completely forgot he told me that I should ask Cerberus if he has any clue as to who my father might be, since he has so many connections in both the Mortal and Fae Realms.

Once I'm finally able to reel my thoughts and emotions back in I find myself breathing heavily and looking over at Cerberus who still appears to be as cool as a cucumber.

Catching my breath, I move around the coffee table until I am standing directly over him. "Y-you know don't you!? You know who my father is..." My voice trembles with the accusation. *Way to be intimidating Cali...*

He doesn't look away; in fact, it feels like he is staring at me more intensely, if that's even possible. Slowly, ever so slowly, a smile begins to pull at his lips. This is the first hint of emotion he has shown since he got here. I can't even smile back. I just stand there with my brow scrunched up feeling overwhelmingly confused, waiting for him to give me some answers.

I really hope he tells me I'm right, but luck has not been on my side today.

Cerberus rises to stand before me, leaving mere inches between the two of us. I'm bewildered when pride instead of anger appears on his face. He releases a low chuckle as he looks down upon me and confesses, "So you figured it out? Took you long enough...".

My sisters who have been sitting there slack jawed since I began going off and throwing accusations at Cerberus finally stand, cursing beneath their breath.

"Cali, what the hell is going on?", Hazel asks, walking over to stand by my side. Eve is right on her heels, putting all three of us standing before Cerberus...waiting for him to provide us with some answers.

"He knows who my father is." I hope they can hear me because the shock I'm experiencing right now has my voice coming out in a whisper. Even hearing myself speak those words out loud seems unreal.

I resist the urge to shove him in his chest as I scowl at him, "Were you just not going to tell me? Or did I have to specifically request for that information when we made our deal?" I deadpan.

This right here is exactly why Aunt Ellie always preached at us to never trust a Fae; 'they are all just a bunch of sneaky, slimy, lying tricksters', she would say.

Cerberus takes his hands and gently pushes the three of us to the side so he can walk by. Casually he looks around like he is taking in all the details inside my apartment; apparently in no hurry to answer my probing questions.

Sick of him wasting our time I move to go over and block his path, but Eve grabs my arm, shaking her head discouragingly when I look at her. Sensing her fear, I relent, jerking my arm free of her grasp.

As though he senses my impatience he finally begins to speak as he walks about. Still looking at anything he can to keep from having to look at us.

"I felt that he was not worth mentioning. That piece of information would have been a distraction, and I need you focused on completing your end of our bargain. Besides that, I was doing you a favor. Consider yourself lucky for not having known him, he is not a good person..." he admits darkly.

Not accepting Cerberus's bullshit response, him and I go back and forth arguing about him withholding more information about who my father is.

After several minutes of getting nowhere with him I accept the fact that Cerberus is one hell of a stubborn Fae. I can tell he is not going to give in to my insistent nagging, so instead I suggest that we come to an agreement.

If we defeat the Dark Fae King and live...he will reveal my father's identity to me.

After all, I've lived my entire life just fine without knowing who my father is, so I guess a little while longer won't hurt...

Moving on from the subject of my father, Cerberus offers up some important information regarding our mother's case.

"Your mother's suspicions were correct in that their High Priestess was working with King Erebus. In fact, your mothers were correct about everything. The High Priestess is only one of many who are involved in a rare type of mortal trafficking. King Erebus has been enlisting more humans over the years to help him bring other human beings across the veil. Offering up a plethora of different deals to those who aid him.

"I'm not quite sure what the High Priestess was receiving in return for her assisting the king. But seeing as how one of her most recent photos I've found shows her looking in her late thirties when she is biologically pushing ninety, makes me think she is receiving eternal youth for her service.

"My best guess is that the High Priestess was threatened by your mothers' investigations. They potentially were getting too close to the truth for her liking. However, not wanting to get any blood on her hands; I believe she convinced King Erebus to take care of them for her.

"Next time you see me I intend to have the answers you summoned me for. Completing my end of the deal." he states rising from his seat and turning to leave. Not even giving us time to process all this information and formulate any questions we may have.

I open my mouth to stop him from leaving, but before I can speak, he looks back over his shoulder at me with a knowing smirk. "Pass on my congratulations to Killian, will you? Finding your fated mate is such a divine moment." With his words leaving me speechless, he shoots me a wink and then vanishes before our eyes.

Moments later I still find myself staring wide eyed at the spot where Cerberus was just standing. I'm not bewildered at him vanishing...which I don't think I'll ever get used to that. No, I'm more upset that he knew who I had taken as my mate this whole time; while he sat there and let me think otherwise.

Dang Fae and their incredible sense of smell.

CHAPTER 36

KILLIAN

I really hope today goes better than yesterday...

I cursed at Callum and Dante without pause after we left Calista's yesterday evening. I didn't let up until I lost my voice, and then after that I threw a few punches at their faces for good measure. They didn't even fight back. They just stood there and took anything and everything I could throw at them. But as much as I wanted to put all the blame on them for causing Calista pain, I knew I was just as responsible for hurting her.

It had been my idea to come into the Mortal Realm to find them in the first place. And when the guys asked me what we would do with the witches after they defeated my father; it was *me* who offered up the ideas that she overheard. *Me* not them. And it was *me* who should have shut that shit down the moment I thought there was even the slightest possibility that she could be my mate.

The very same female that they sacrificed their personal lives and duties to help me search for all those years ago.

I guess I had assumed that when I told them who I thought she was a few weeks back; they would have realized that if it turned out my suspicion was correct, then our original plans regarding the witches would have to change.

I would never do anything to harm or betray my mate.

We will not be banishing, imprisoning, or killing my mate. Just thinking those words releases a growl from deep within my soul.

However, convincing Calista to trust in what I'm telling her is proving to be extremely difficult. She always had trust issues to begin with and now with all that has happened I feel like her and I are back at square one.

I couldn't even manage to keep my mate happy for a full day before I screwed everything up.

Usually after a mating ritual is completed the two mates must drag themselves out of bed long enough to at least eat to refuel and see to their bodily needs. Fae usually take two weeks off from their duties, if possible, after sealing the bond. This is because they will be otherwise 'occupied'.

And here it is day two and I am having to beg her to be within two feet of me. It literally feels like if I don't have her soft warm body pressed against mine soon, I'm going to meet my true death. My body will just disintegrate piece by piece into the air itself before passing beyond the veil into the Immortal Palace.

The Immortal Palace is where most all Fae wish to be granted entrance after their death. This divine place provides our souls a lifetime of peace and rest after death.

Those Fae not so lucky, who are deemed unworthy of finding peace after death, will find themselves reawakening to an afterlife full of pain and torment in The Flaming Hollows. This dreaded place beyond our veil collects the souls that are deemed to come from the most detestable and treacherous Fae.

I couldn't stop myself from messaging and calling her repeatedly last night begging her to let me stay over at her place. I even relented to offering to sleep on her couch...I just needed to be close by to know she was safe. Plus, the bond was causing such discomfort from being away from her so soon after becoming mates.

However, being the stubborn woman she is she refused my offer. Assuring me that she was snuggled up between both of her sisters in her large bed, safe and sound.

The jealousy I found myself feeling towards her sisters was testament to how all consumed I was with the need to be by her side.

No matter though because today is a new day, and I am fully determined to win back Calista's trust. Apparently, she told her Lieutenant that her 'food poisoning' from yesterday turned out to be a 'stomach virus' and she was going to be out sick with it again today. Her sisters called and provided their superiors with the same excuse for missing work today.

We all just arrived here in the Fae Realm; with the hope that Eve's and Hazel's powers will awaken like Cali's did when she first came here.

Cali's smile and the sound of her laughter fills me with hope that if I play my cards right, I may be able to lie in bed tonight with my mate wrapped up tightly in my arms. Where she is always meant to be.

We have been training for a few hours now and I can already tell that the girls' powers are coming along faster within this realm. Cali's powers are still evolving at a rapid pace, more so than her sisters, but they too are slowly getting there.

It took Callum and Dante a good half hour into training to get Eve and Hazel to fully focus on awakening their powers. They were too captivated by their new 'pointy Fae ears' to be bothered with concentrating on anything else. But the quiet giggles I caught Cali releasing every time she heard the guys yelling at them to stop fondling their ears and focus was music to my 'pointy Fae ears'.

Cali's abilities keep astounding me. The more she dives into the well of her power she discovers even more abilities she didn't even know she was capable of, nor did I. Her attacks are becoming stronger and faster, as well as her ability to control them. She can now hit her intended target seventy percent of the time...as long as it's stationary or moving at a very slow pace.

I don't foresee her facing off against any vampires with their lightning speed anytime soon, so we have plenty of time to work on that skill.

When she is finally able to combine all her powers alongside her newfound Fae abilities, like speed and strength, she will be a force to be reckoned with.

She even got lucky and knocked me straight on my ass more times than I would like to admit today. Which unsurprisingly was followed up with Callum and Dante yelling out and teasing me from across the field about how I was getting my ass kicked by a girl.

The only reason I didn't send my shadows out to suffocate the life from those arrogant assholes was because with each jab they shot my way the bigger and brighter Cali's smile grew.

Callum had made some progress with Eve by the time we decided to call it a day. She demonstrated for the group how far along her abilities have come since she began training with Cal. When she lay her hands upon the ground, flowers of all types and colors sprang to life. Chrysanthemums, daisies, and my favorite...red roses.

Her most impressive show took place down by one of the small lava streams that flows nearby. Using both the elements of fire and water, she was able to fuse them together to create a school of small fish made of flames that leapt from the burning lava and swam about. They were fun to watch; looking like small glowing sprites, in this case I guess we would call them 'lava sprites' since the lava is acting as a body of water.

Eve was still practicing controlling their movements. Leaping from the water in all different directions and some landing on shore. But the best was when one shot out of the lava heading straight for Dante's head. He was caught off guard and screamed like a little bitch; luckily, he swatted it to the ground right before it landed upside his face. The surrounding forest echoed with all our laughter at Dante's expense. Eve tried to act like it was a complete accident but the smirk I saw lighting up her face when she thought no one was watching gave her up.

Dante and Hazel...well they managed to not kill one another so there's that. He refuses to just sit around and let Hazel practice her telepathy on him. Instead, she must try to gain more control over that ability while either fighting in hand-to-hand or sword combat, or while simultaneously using her telekinesis to throw stuff at him.

I will hand it to her though; she may be small, especially when standing next to Dante the giant, but she knows how to take a hit and get back up. She's a tenacious little thing.

It must run in the family.

I swear the harder she hits the ground the quicker she gets back up. The aggravation it's causing Dante is hilarious. If you pay close enough attention, every time she gets back up you can see the vein on the side of his forehead throb in frustration.

I swapped out with Dante to work with Hazel on her telepathy before they could start trying to kill one another. By the time I tagged Dante back in I could feel her trying to break through the shield around my mind. I even caught myself flinching once; it felt like sharp claws were raking down my skull. Not a pleasant feeling at all.

With more practice it won't be long until she is able to pose the threat of breaking through my mental shields.

We are all gathering up to leave when Calista clears her voice to get everyone's attention.

I turn around and see her standing there with her hands on her hips and a sly smile directed at me, "I challenge pretty boy to a fight... unless he's too chicken shit?"

Gods I love this woman!

Everyone begins cheering and yelling in excitement, spurring me on to accept her challenge. Which of course I'm going to accept... did they really think there was a chance in hell I wouldn't?

I walk over towards her with a large grin on my face. "So, you think I'm pretty?" I joke, shooting her a little wink.

She rolls her eyes at me, but I can see her fighting back a smirk. "You forgot the part where I called you a chicken shit."

I throw my head back shouting out an exaggerated, "Ha!" just to rile her up. "Show me what you got then, *princess*." She hates when I call her princess and it's because of that I can't resist. I can hear her grinding her teeth together all the way over here.

I throw my arms out to the sides leaving myself wide open for her to strike.

Her power takes me by surprise; in the blink of an eye, she has produced a ball of fire and it's flying right for my face. I teleport away at the last second right before I would have taken a fire ball to the chest.

I have a huge smile on my face when I reappear off to her right side.

I am very impressed at how fast she was able to bring forth and shape her power. Usually, it takes her a couple seconds, but she had a fireball flying at me so fast she almost had me.

She scrunches her face up in frustration, which is quite adorable. "Aw, what's the matter? Is the little princess angry she missed?" I know I'm baiting the bull, but I can't help myself. I love getting her riled up.

In another blink of my eye, she is standing right in front of me with her fist flying for my face.

Holy shit! I didn't know she could teleport that quickly and precisely. I need to focus before she does knock me on my ass hard like she did that very first time...the guys will never let me live it down if they witness it firsthand.

Using my Fae speed I'm able to lean back, just barely dodging a hit to my jaw. It is such a close call I can feel the breeze from her fist flying by my face.

"Shit" I curse out in surprise, causing both of us to pause and take one another in.

She has a spark in her eyes; she knows I've had two close calls now and she doesn't look like she's done with me yet.

She looks up at me through her long lashes, distracting me with those beautiful eyes. My eyes move to her lips just in time to notice her devilish smile; a smile that promises my defeat. I grin back at her, trying to come off unphased and unimpressed by her actions so far.

So, before she gets the chance to take another swing at me, I make the first move.

I begin teleporting back and forth all around her. Causing her to have to rely on her Fae abilities of sight, speed, and sound to keep me from landing a hit on her. I am coming at her with my fists and shadows, but damn if she isn't doing an impressive job of blocking all my attacks. As soon as she hears me reappear, she uses her speed to turn and block my physical blows or to jump out of the way of my shadows I'm attacking her with.

I notice that the longer we keep at it the slower her response time is becoming. I'm wearing her down by keeping her on the defensive.

Right as I'm thinking maybe I should call it, I appear right behind her, but she isn't fast enough this time to block my attack. Getting her a solid right hook to the face.

I teleport about five yards away; doubled over and clenching at my chest as an agonizing pain shoots through the mating bond. Even though she's the one who asked for this fight, and I was just giving her what she asked for, the bond is punishing me for causing my mate harm. *Son-of-a-bitch, that hurts.*

"You running away from our fight, pretty boy?", I look to see my mate standing there with blood dripping down her chin from what looks to be a busted lip. A busted lip that *I* gave her. Pain shoots through the bond again from knowing the blood that is now staining her chin is all a result of my doing. "If I'm still standing then we are still fighting!", she yells; trying to provoke me.

When the pain in my chest subsides and I'm able to stand up straight again, I look over at her again, and she is smiling. *Smiling.* This beautiful, intelligent, strong mate of mine is standing there with a busted up bloody lip, and yet she's still begging me for a fight. And damn if I'm not going to give her one.

We go back and forth another round. Calista even went on the offensive this round. Teleporting as close to me as she could and not holding back on her swings or her magic. She gave me a few close calls and even managed to land her own punch, straight in my gut.

Right now, I have her back on the defensive and her energy looks to be lagging again. I teleport all around her, not even going in for an attack, but making her use her increased Fae senses to detect my movements. I figure this might throw her off, giving me the opportunity to swoop in and knock her on her ass when she least expects it.

Finally, I see my chance and I take it. Hoping to end this fight once and for all.

She is looking off to her right side and I take this moment to teleport until I am right in front of her. I am leaning over with my shoulders aimed to catch her in her stomach and tackle her to the ground, but right as I'm one second away from closing the distance between the two of us my world suddenly flips upside down.

This cunning little creature of mine was ready for me, turning my direction at the very last second and hooking her right arm under my left shoulder. She drops to the ground and uses her body weight and momentum to flip me completely upside down, releasing me halfway through so I am left to free fall flat onto my back. *Umph.* Is the only sound I can make as the air rushes out of my lungs.

When I open my eyes, Cali is straddling me with her hands pressing down on both of my shoulders, keeping me pinned beneath her. *Damn I love this mate of mine.*

"Yield", she commands as she presses more of her body weight on top of me.

She doesn't weigh anything at all, and I could probably flip her off me, but she earned this win fair and square so I'm going to let her have it. Even knowing the guys are never going to let me hear the end of it.

Looking up into her beautiful green eyes, I proudly smile as I admit my defeat, "I yield, Viper".

Along with her victory a beautiful smile lights up her face. I reach up slowly and lightly trace my fingers over her busted lip, healing it with my power. With a slight frown and furrowed brow, I keep my eyes set on her freshly healed, soft pink lips. Even though healing her lip was an easy fix, I still feel guilty about causing the damage to her in the first place. "I'm so sorry", I apologize.

She tilts her head to the side, looking down at me as if she doesn't understand. "Why? I asked for it." she replies with a smile. She leans down and nuzzles her cute little nose against mine; a simple act that sends my heart racing. "I forgive you, Rose".

The smile and laughter coming from her after her well-earned victory, gives me hope that we are going to be okay.

As soon as I stand back up the taunting begins. Callum and Dante have already started mocking me and cheering, "Killian got beat by a girl" ...on repeat.

But screw it...if my mate is happy then I'm happy. She can kick my ass every day if it keeps that smile on her face. My pride can take the hit...I think.

CHAPTER 37

CALISTA

My sisters and I had a great time yesterday training with the guys over in the Fae Realm. It brought me so much joy to finally get to share the place I visited in my dreams as a teenager with them. They were completely in awe of the beauty and magic of the Unseelie lands.

It only took them a few minutes to adjust to the surrounding darkness and allow the moonlight to cast its light upon a whole new beautiful world. I couldn't get enough of their smiles and laughter as they took in everything from the rivers flowing with lava, the beautiful star filled sky, and the glimmering forest filled with a wide variety of luminescent plants. It was absolutely magical.

The best part though was seeing my sisters' reactions to the appearance of their tapered Fae ears. Which the guys believe to be proof enough that Eve and Hazel are also half-Fae. So maybe Cerberus knows all our fathers?

Luckily, I had a compact mirror in my bag I brought along so they could pass it back and forth to check out their ears.

Which reminds me I need to get my mirror back from Callum. He confiscated it when my sisters kept getting distracted by looking at their ears rather than focusing on training.

I had to keep myself from laughing my ass off every time I looked over and found one of my sisters shivering or fluttering their eyelids when they would reach up and stroke their fingers along their ears. I was hoping that after a time or two they would realize that the sensations they were feeling every time they touched their ears were linked to their arousal. After we got back last night, I explained to them that playing with a Fae's ears was basically foreplay for most Fae.

They both turned a hilarious shade of beet red.

That information caused Hazel to have an epiphany that she decided to share with us; "Maybe that's why Dante's enormous ego and boring personality didn't drive me as crazy as it normally does? And I think I only considered death to be a more appealing option than spending another minute with that baboon like once. Usually, it at least crosses my mind five times per training session." Hazel's insight had me and Eve rolling with laughter.

I swear one day I'm going to receive an invitation to Hazel's and Dante's wedding.

I've always heard there is a fine line between love and hate, and seeing as how much these two appear to 'hate' each other; they either really can't stand one another, or they are just sexually frustrated from trying not to rip one another's clothes off when they are together.

My bet is on the latter.

My sisters stayed with me again last night even though our assassin problem was thankfully solved. We were having too much fun discussing the day we just had. And we were heading back to the Fae Realm with the guys first thing in the morning anyways. The boys decided sword fighting would be an essential skill we may need when going up against the king, so that is on tomorrow's agenda.

The three of us are planning to milk our 'stomach bug' excuse to get us out of work for as long as we can. At least for another day or two. The natural magic in the Fae Realm really seems to be helping all of us expand and hone our powers faster than if we just stayed here in the Mortal Realm and practiced.

After spending the past three days training our asses off over in the Fae Realm, I figured I better head back into work before I get fired.

Seb has been keeping me up to date on everything happening at the precinct. Threatening to blow his own head off if Ortega drags him to anymore and I quote 'tofu eating, organic growing, PETA loving' places for lunch. So, I figure it's only fair for me to cut him a break since he did save my life earlier this week.

I also want to talk to him about the information Scarface gave us last night. There isn't much to go on, but my nerves have been on edge ever since hearing it.

"Hey! Look who was finally able to get off the shitter!", I scowl looking up from my desk at the precinct to find Sergeant Raynard trying to rile me up from across the room. *Asshole*. Sadly, his joke does not fall flat and earns me an earful of laughter and jokes from my colleagues. Right as I'm about to tell him where he can stick it Seb comes up behind me laughing right along with everyone else.

I quickly spin around and kick him in his shin.

"Shit!" Seb shouts, as he throws up his hands in surrender. "Sorry, but it was funny" he quietly teases only loud enough for me to hear.

I just roll my eyes at him before turning back around to my desk and the mountain of paperwork I need to get through today.

"Walk with me to get coffee?" I ask him before I look up and notice he already has a coffee cup in his hand. But it's the awful breakroom coffee we are forced to live off when we are here.

I scrunch my nose up in disgust as he points to the coffee he's already holding.

"Not that shit, let's go grab some from the truck outside." I insist. There is a great coffee truck that sits outside the precinct every morning, Brew and Sip. They have a delicious pumpkin spice latte that they keep year-round.

Does that make me a basic bitch? I guess so. But do I care? Nope, not one tiny fuck given.

Seb shrugs and chucks his half-drunk coffee into my trash can, leaving it to spill all over the place. *Thanks for that Seb, that's just delightful...*

After we get our coffee, I pull Seb off to the side to talk about the information we got as well as what our plan is for closing the serial killer case.

I sit down on one of the black iron benches surrounded by beautiful pink hydrangeas nearby and pat the spot next to me for Seb to sit and join me. We haven't really been alone together since the shit show earlier this week. I don't want any of that drama to come in and affect our relationship; especially here at work, so I feel like it needs to be squashed now.

"I'm sorry", Seb apologizes to me. I guess he has been feeling the same way I have about everything...

"I never should have kept mine and Eve's relationship from you, or Hazel. But I swear to you that she is *it* for me, Cali. I can't imagine ever finding anyone else that can make me feel as amazing as she does." The smile on his face is so sweet and genuine.

I slowly blow out a breath, taking in everything he just said. I give him my best 'no bullshit' detective face and ask, "Are you in love with her?"

He doesn't even need a moment to think about it. "Absolutely, I love her", he answers without question. And I can see the love and honesty in his eyes. Which I'm glad because otherwise I might have had to kick his ass.

I nod, then turn back around to people watch. One of my guilty pleasures...but I guess that does make sense considering the career I chose.

Across the street a small Jack Russell terrier just cocked his leg to piss on a bush next to where his owner was sitting; only for half of it to miss the bush and land on the man's work bag. I look away as I begin to laugh.

Sucks to be that guy.

"So, you and Killian are mates?" Seb asks dryly, even though he already knows the answer. I guess he is just looking for something to keep our conversation going.

I laugh and raise my arm up above my head offering him my armpit to sniff, "I think you can answer that for yourself by taking a big whiff, right? With that super smelling Fae nose of yours." Laughing he shoves my arm back down and away from his face, as he pinches his nose and pretends to wave off the smell.

"Yeah, okay. Now please put your pits away. I'm already trying my hardest not to gag over here." he jokes with a huge grin on his face.

"What's your beef with him anyways?"

Seb sighs and shakes his head before finally looking over at me. "I guess I just grew up being pitted against him my whole life. I always had to be stronger and more powerful than the 'Shadow Prince'. It has always been Unseelie vs. Seelie, Light vs. Dark; especially in politics and athletics. When our schools played each other on the field he and I were always vying against each other. And believe me it could get very bloody.

"But I have never interacted with him on a personal level. For all I know he could be a great guy. The Seelie Kingdom just assumes he is as awful as his father, King Erebus." He pauses, then playfully leans over and elbows me in my arm. "But if he makes you happy and treats you like the Queen you are then he and I shouldn't have any problems."

I smile and give him a curt nod of understanding. I'm just glad he didn't say something like 'he killed my dad's entire side of the family', or worse...his dog.

"In all seriousness Cali, congratulations on finding your mate. Most Fae live out their whole lives without ever finding theirs. You two have been blessed by the Gods; never forget that."

I can tell by the look on his face that he is sincere, and this time when I smile, even I can feel how much I really mean it.

"Okay, enough mushy gushy crap. I wanted to talk in private for a reason."

Taking our sweet time finishing our coffee, I fill Seb in on what Scarface disclosed to us yesterday that just isn't sitting right with me. Apparently, he has many reasons to hate the Dark Fae King. The vilest of them all being that the Dark Fae King killed his wife and child after he swore his loyalty to serve him in his army. The king stated his reasoning to be that 'one's spouse and offspring are a distraction that takes away from the undying focus he expects to receive from his soldiers'. Soldiers can't focus entirely upon the king's safety and needs when their thoughts keep straying to their family and home life, especially during times of war.

It literally disgusts me to think about what this tyrant of a king has done to so many Fae throughout his kingdom. Especially if he was sick enough to perform these acts to the Fae who swore their upmost allegiance to him. Killing their loved ones was the thanks they received.

Even with this information being as awful as it is, that's still not what has my nerves on edge today.

Seb takes in everything I tell him with a look mixed with both horror and sadness. "As horrible and disgusting as that is; I hate to say it, but it doesn't surprise me given the reputation King Erebus has made for himself."

I completely understand where he's coming from. With everything I've learned about King Erebus through Cerberus and Killian I shouldn't have been so surprised when I heard about this new level of depravity. The fact that his own son wants to see him dead was my first red flag.

"What really has me worried though is Scarface said that the king has been sending his fellow comrades out on covert missions into the Crimson Pass for years now; only for the soldiers to never return. That just screams bad news. Does it not?"

Scarface explained to me that the Crimson Pass is a perilous path that trails through the center of the Crimson Peak Mountains.

Seb nods in agreement; looking as concerned about this information as I am.

"Do you have any clue what King Erebus could be up to? Or do those mountains hold any meaning to you?" I ask desperately.

Shaking his head, Seb sighs. "Unfortunately, I have no idea what could be drawing his interest to the Crimson Pass. I can try to find out if my father knows anything, but even if he did, I doubt he would share it with me. I am the unappreciative, duty abandoning, sorry excuse of a son after all..."

I purse my lips and slap his arm in response to that ridiculous statement. Seb is the best guy I know, and the amount of honor, bravery, and respect that he has for both his personal and professional life is immeasurable.

As I attempt to change the subject Seb throws out a very significant piece of information. Apparently, the Crimson Pass runs along the northern divide that separates the Unseelie Kingdom from the Bloodlands; more precisely known as the Kingdom of Vampires.

That being said...there is a possibility that maybe the warriors never return from their mission because they are being picked off one by one by the local vampires. Even though that doesn't answer the question as to what the Dark Fae King is trying to accomplish with these secret missions; it does fill me with a little relief that the missing warriors could be due to blood thirsty vampires and not because of some foul play King Erebus has his dark grimy hands in.

CHAPTER 38

CALISTA

"Leave it alone!" I demand, slapping Hazel's hand away from the radio dial.

Hazel is the epitome of what I call 'Grand Theft Audio'.

I swear she cannot listen to a complete song on one radio station before she gets bored and moves on to the next. It is one of my biggest pet peeves and I'm positive it stems from having had to grow up with her as my little sister. We always alternated who got to sit 'shotgun' with Aunt Ellie anytime we left the house, and I always dreaded when it was Hazel's turn. Somehow, we would hear around ten songs on our ten-minute drive to school...well bits and pieces of songs. Never a full song from start to finish...never.

"Please! I don't like this song." Hazel begs while pinning me down with her puppy dog stare. But she is barking up the wrong tree if she thinks that it's going to work on me today.

"That's what you have said about the last five songs!" I aggravatedly remind her.

Looking out of my periphery I can see her hand moving closer to the radio dial. She thinks she is so sneaky.

"Don't. You. Dare!" I threaten her. Preparing myself to strike at her again if she makes a move for the dial. Thank God we mostly use public transportation in DC because it's a miracle we haven't gotten in more car accidents from our radio showdowns during our rare trips outside of the city.

"Will you both just chill!? Besides, look" Eve cuts in, reprimanding us and directing us to look out the window. "We're here already".

She acts like her brain wasn't sitting in the back seat suffering from musical whiplash due to Hazel's song ADHD the last two hours.

But praise be! She is right, we have arrived at Aunt Ellie's, and I can finally get out of this dang car and away from DJ Hazel.

However, now I feel a whole new set of emotions rolling in. Sadness, stress, anger, frustration, confusion...to name a few.

Today is the day I am going to demand some answers from my aunt. It's been almost two weeks now since I learned about my tattoo and I'm finally ready for the truth. I haven't been avoiding the inevitable discussion I need to have with her...I've just been busy with more important things. For instance, training and figuring out a way to set up the two dead Fae assassin bodies so we can 'catch them' and close this serial killer case.

Hazel is knocking on the front door by the time me and Eve finally step onto the porch. I don't know where she gets all her energy from, but I wish she would share some of it with me. Training and work have been leaving me with very little time for rest or 'me time'. I can't even recall the last time I had a nice hot relaxing bubble bath...

"My girls!" Aunt Ellie squeals, gathering us all up in a big group hug. My mind is clearly exhausted, because I find myself locked in a hug before I even noticed the front door had flown open. And even though I am upset with her right now I can't help but return her bright happy smile as she takes us each in.

"Hey Aunt Ellie!" we all say simultaneously. It's so seamless you can tell we have had years of practice.

Seeing Aunt Ellie's face and how happy she is to see us, I decide to wait until after we eat lunch to begin my questioning. There is nothing more awkward than trying to make small talk during a meal after you just had an uncomfortable confrontation.

Besides, she made our favorites, and nothing can brighten my mood like Aunt Ellie's banana pudding.

As I make my way to the kitchen, I can't help but stop and stare at some of my most cherished childhood memories that are captured in pictures hanging all over Aunt Ellie's walls. There is one of the four of us on Christmas Eve morning and we are all huddled together by the stove, covered in flour from head to toe. Aunt Ellie always let us be her little helper elves to bake cookies for Santa. She didn't care about the messes we made trying to help bake, in fact she always said, 'if you don't have flour in every nook and cranny, you're doing something wrong'.

There's the photo of us in front of Cinderella's Castle at Disney World; I begged and begged Aunt Ellie to take us there for my tenth birthday. Being an adult now and knowing how much just one single ticket costs, I realize I was asking for way too much. But dang it if Aunt Ellie didn't save up all year and put in a few extra hours at work to make my birthday wish come true. I will forever be grateful for that gift; the memories we made that day will last a lifetime.

Especially the one of Hazel insisting on riding the teacups right after eating a cinnamon churro; only for her to throw up over the side of the cup mid ride. They had to close the ride down for cast members to show up and clean up the scene.

Eve and I still haven't let her live it down to this day. And we never will.

Then there is the one photo that always gave me the heebie-jee-bies when I was young. It's of Aunt Ellie alongside our mothers and the rest of their coven members. Their High Priestess looks to be in her mid-forties, and she stands in the center of the group. There was always something about her beady little eyes in the photo; it looks like both of her eyes are entirely black but no one else's eyes in the photo appear that way, they all look normal. I assume now there was just an issue with the camera, and she was the unlucky one it showed up on...who knows?

There is no denying she's beautiful; she has long black hair, high cheek bones, and flawless skin without an age line in sight. *It must be Botox.* She also wears this remarkable necklace with a golden pendent in the shape of the sun that holds a red ruby in the center. It was always just those eyes of hers; it's like the photo captured part of her soul and a piece of her is inside the picture staring back at you, watching, and waiting to creep into your room at night and get you while you stare up into those creepy black eyes.

Anyhow, I'm just glad I don't have to see it every day. Now those eyes only get to haunt me when I come visit Aunt Ellie, which I know isn't often enough.

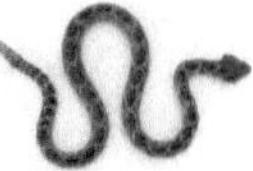

After Aunt Ellie stuffs us full of meatloaf, green beans and banana pudding; we all fix ourselves a cup of nice hot coffee and go into the living room to hang out and catch up.

We catch Aunt Ellie up on everything that has happened; minus the whole 'I have a mate' announcement. From the look on her face, I think it's safe to say she is shell shocked by all the information.

"I'm coming with you!" Aunt Ellie demands, no questions asked.

All three of us tell her there is no way we are letting her go into the Fae Realm with us when it's time to face off with King Erebus. We want to ensure she remains safe, not throw her in the line of danger.

We all argue back and forth with Aunt Ellie until she finally relents to let us clean up this whole mess we have made on our own. I'm sure this is far from the last we will hear about the matter, but I'm anxiously waiting and ready to move this conversation along.

Now is as good as time as any to question her about what her motive was for having me get the rose tattoo behind my ear. I'm not sure where to start so I guess I will just get right to it.

"Aunt El, I need to ask you about something", I say nervously, as I trace my fingers along the ridges of my coffee cup. I can tell by the look on her face that I am worrying her, but she gives a nod and leans forward while taking a sip of her coffee.

"Why...or better yet *how* did you enchant my tattoo you let me get when I turned eighteen? Did you know my dreams I shared with you were real? Why did you want to keep me from dreaming?" I take a deep breath to stop myself from rambling on with more questions. Aunt Ellie raises her brows, and her eyes open wide as I ask her these questions. I think she is surprised that I found out what she did with my tattoo, and maybe even guilty about hiding this from me for all these years. At least I'm hoping she feels a little remorseful for it.

She sounds ashamed when she asks, "I uh—, how did you find out about the tattoo?"

That's a confession if I've ever heard one...

"That doesn't matter right now, answer my questions Aunt El. Why did you hide all this from me?"

Aunt Ellie closes her eyes and takes a deep breath. I can see her coffee cup shaking in her grip and the coffee sloshing around inside the cup. It appears like her nerves from my questioning are getting the better of her.

"Please don't hate me..." she pleads sadly, tears brimming her eyes. "I always thought the imaginative dreams you told us about were just that...dreams. Drifting off in your dreams to a land of darkness and starlight, with crazy looking animals and plants, and your handsome prince charming. But then one night I got this uneasy feeling and started thinking back to what happened with your mothers. I don't know why my mind was taking me back to that awful devastating night, but no matter what I tried to do to distract myself, I could not shake that feeling of unease. I decided I just needed to check on you girls and see for myself that you were safe and snuggled up nice and tight in your beds. Hoping that feeling would go away once I knew everything was alright.

"Hazel and Eve were sleeping peacefully like babies. But when I cracked your bedroom door open Cali, I was not prepared for what I saw..." Aunt Ellie leans back in her chair and runs her hand over her face.

Whatever it was she saw seems to have left a mark on her because she is still hesitant to talk about it with us. Now though she has not only mine but Eve's and Hazel's full attention. The three of us are literally sitting on the edge of our seats waiting for her to continue telling us what happened that night.

"So... what was it? What did you see?", I urge.

Shaking her head in dismay, Aunt Ellie reluctantly continues to tell us what happened. "Cali, you were surrounded by this bright and beautiful white shimmering light. Like starlight itself. But not only that...your body was levitating a few inches above your bed. You were encapsulated by this light, that was both beautiful and terrifying at the same time. Terrifying because I had absolutely no idea what was happening to you." She releases another deep breath to steady herself.

I can't help but stare at her both confused and shocked by this revelation. How could I have no idea this was happening to me?

"Di-Did you wake me up?" I stammer, trying to figure out what the hell had been happening to me.

"I couldn't...and believe me I tried. I yelled your name trying to wake you up, but you didn't so much as flutter your eyelids. And every time I tried to grab onto you the light surrounding you would flare brighter; creating this invisible barrier that my hand could not pass through. It was like the light was shielding your body and keeping it safe while you were asleep and dreaming."

I'm still dumbfounded by what Aunt Ellie is saying to me. This sounds like some alien abduction, Sci-fi shit.

Aunt Ellie comes and sits down next to me, kicking Eve out of her spot. Taking my hands and looking me dead in my eyes, she says to me with complete seriousness, "Cali, it was like your physical body was present, but your soul was not..."

My sisters and I audibly gasp at her words.

Aunt Ellie is looking at me like she is begging me to say something, but I am completely speechless at the moment.

"I freaked out and called around to all my Wiccan contacts to find out if anyone had ever heard of this happening and what it meant. I set up watching you night after night for weeks before one of my contacts in New Orleans got back in touch with me. They said that you must have had some connection to another realm, which was allowing you to astral project."

"To what?", I interrupt.

"Astral projection, it is when a person's soul can separate from their physical body and travel to other dimensions or realms. You may have heard it called 'dream walking'." Aunt Ellie explains.

Hazel begins bouncing excitedly in her seat and points at me. "Cali, it's like that scary movie we watched years ago. What was the name...Oh! *Insidious*. Where the little boy dream walks into a realm with a creepy demon monster and his dad must travel into that realm to try and find him. Remember?!", Hazel looks at me with a huge smile. She is so proud of herself for remembering that movie. But now that she mentions it, I do remember watching that one.

"Oh yeah! That was a good one!", I exclaim trying to match some of her excitement. I just can't believe that is what I was doing all those years ago. I wonder if I can do that now since the spell on the tattoo has been deactivated?

After Aunt Ellie is convinced that I do understand what she is talking about she continues explaining to us what happened next. "There was no way to know for sure where your soul was traveling to, but with your descriptions of your dreams, the Fae Realm was my best guess. Well, my only guess since the Fae Realm is the only other realm we know of that exists besides our own. And if your soul was just wandering around here in our realm then you would not have been surrounded by that magical light, nor would you have recalled such enchanting encounters." Aunt Ellie looks remorseful, as she stares at me. I think she is trying to get a read on how I'm handling this information so far. But I just nod my head to encourage her to keep going.

"The Fae Realm is so dangerous Cali; I couldn't just let your soul keep traveling there every time you dreamed. What if something happened over there and your soul never returned to us." Tears begin to fall from Aunt Ellie's eyes. I can see just by looking at her how fearful she was that something bad was going to happen to me. That she was going to lose me like she lost my mother. And I know she would never have forgiven herself if it had. "I had to find a way to stop it from happening Cali...I couldn't chance the risk of losing you."

"So what? You figured out how to bewitch a tattoo? You played me. That day we spent together was one of my favorite memories, but now when I think of it, I just feel betrayed. You made me believe that getting that tattoo was so special because my mom got her first one on the day of her eighteenth birthday, and you wanted me to have the chance to share that in common with her. But really the whole time you were just scheming and tricking me into getting a tattoo that would cut off my ability to dream... Where was my chance to say 'no' to that?! You took away something so important to me without my knowledge or consent. I always wondered why I stopped dreaming once I turned eighteen..." I scowl at her, hoping she can see how much her actions and secrets have hurt me.

Aunt Ellie looks at me with tear-stained cheeks and remorse. "Please baby girl, don't hate me. I just did what I thought I had to do to keep you safe. I wasn't even sure putting electrolytic iron powder into the ink used for the tattoo would work. But I paid the artist off for him to let me add the iron into the ink, and before he got to work on the tattoo, I put a simple protection spell over the ink.

My contact and I came up with the entire idea. The whole idea was that maybe since iron is the only thing that can cause the Fae harm, that if you had a high purity iron permanently marking your skin it would cut off your connection to the Fae Realm, since the Fae despise iron. Then the protection spell was just an extra measure of precaution to help hide you from any Fae who might try to come into our realm to find you." Before I can stop her, she pulls me into a tight hug, and I can feel her tears dampening my shirt. "I'm so sorry, baby girl. Please forgive me..." she sobs.

I'm so torn right now. Of course I'm going to forgive her, at the end of the day she's our mother, even if we call her our 'aunt'. I know it was all done with my safety in mind, but I'm still going to let her know how much her actions hurt me.

Pulling back from her ridiculously tight embrace I let her see how disappointed I am with her actions. "Well, lucky for you it worked." I stand to put some distance between us. "I spent the rest of my life thinking everything I saw and experienced was all just a dream. That Rose...", I point at the rose tattoo behind my ear, "was all a dream. But guess what Aunt El, he *is* real. And he is my *mate*." I confess to her, releasing the concealment spell I have on my new mating tattoos so she can see them.

She gasps covering her mouth with her hand, "Where did those come from? Are you using magic?!"

"These-", I explain to her, "are my mating marks. They appeared once Rose, or Killian is his actual name, and I sealed our mating bond. So, surprise! I'm technically married now." I announce sarcastically. Reveling in her shocked expression.

"Luckily Killian figured it out and slashed a thin line through the tattoo, enough to separate the lines and break the spell. So, you didn't just keep me from my dreams all these years...you also kept me from my mate! My mate, Aunt El!" I yell scornfully at her.

Eve quickly jumps up and takes my arm, leading me away into the kitchen to calm down. I was admittedly getting too heated towards Aunt Ellie, so stepping away from the situation was a good call on Eve's part.

I guzzle a glass of water from the sink and then head back to the living room where everyone else is sitting around anxiously waiting for me to return. Seeing how torn up Aunt Ellie looks sitting snuggled up against Hazel and Eve breaks something inside of me. Before I can stop myself, I walk over to my family and embrace them all in another group hug; then I wrap Aunt Ellie in my arms where she has a good cry all over my shirt as I promise her that everything is forgiven.

After dropping the bomb shell on Aunt Ellie about me having a mate, I decided I might as well go ahead and tell her I may be the heir to the entire Fae Realm. That went over about as well as I thought it would. She swears she had no clue that my mom was part Fae; she honestly thinks my mother didn't even know that she was part Fae. And I believe her.

We spend the rest of the evening reminiscing, drinking our hot coffee and eating scrumptious banana pudding. Aunt Ellie keeps apologizing to me at random moments even though I have assured her that all is forgiven.

And she insists on meeting Killian as soon as possible. She's even threatening to drive to DC just to meet him if I don't bring him to her house in the next few weeks.

I'm so happy to have all the feelings of betrayal and frustration lifted off my chest. I feel one hundred pounds lighter. Now we can just sit back and enjoy our time with Aunt Ellie today, before we must head back to all the madness that has become our life in DC over these last few weeks.

CHAPTER 39

CALISTA

"Ouch! That doesn't count you're a filthy cheater!" I lunge at Killian as he teleports back and forth all around me.

We came over to the Fae Realm to practice this evening. I tried to get out of it using the excuse that it would be getting dark outside soon but seeing as how it is always dark here in Unseelie anyways, that excuse didn't work out for me.

Killian suddenly appears directly in front of me; he doesn't even appear close to being out of breath from all our sparring. "Just because I'm better than you at fighting doesn't make me a cheater." he claims with a wicked grin. "Maybe if you spent less time being a sore loser you could focus on the fight and keep me from knocking you on your ass every time." Before I get a chance to take the bait he's gone, appearing again about fifty yards out.

I can't stand how easy it is for him to get under my skin...but he's right I need to learn to take the loss and focus on our next round. But if there is one thing I hate more than anything else, it's losing. Especially to an arrogant male. It's one of the few things in life I've just never been good at; and no, I'm not conceited, I'm just confident.

That's why I practiced day in and day out when I first decided to go into law enforcement; I wanted to make sure I could put all those egotistical men flat on their backs when we met on the mats during physical combat training.

Focusing I aim to teleport directly on top of where Killian is standing. As soon as my feet reappear and hit the ground, he is already gone and standing right where I just came from.

Damn he irks me!

Focus Cali! Focus

I concentrate my mind on the exact spot I'm standing in right now. I'm hoping I can pull one over on him. I've never tried teleporting such a miniscule distance; basically, only moving maybe two inches to my right at most, it's like jumping in place so it shouldn't be too difficult...I hope.

What I hope will happen is that as soon as I disappear Killian will take the bait and teleport to the spot I was just at, only I will be reappearing right beside him as soon as he hits the ground. This should catch him off guard long enough for me to land a punch to his stupid chiseled jaw line.

Here goes nothing...

Closing my eyes I focus with everything I've got on my intended destination. Allowing my power to flow freely through my entire being, I let go of the leash that keeps it in check and set it free. I feel my body rapidly evaporate particle by microscopic particle into the air itself. Then...Wham! My body is instantly thrown back together, causing a sharp fast pain to radiate through every cell existing throughout my body.

"Ahhh!" I scream out in pain, as soon as my feet hit the ground. On the bright side I landed exactly where I was aiming for, but on the not so bright side, my scream alerted Killian to my position. By the time he whips around to see me standing directly behind him the pain has gone. But I did not miss the look of complete bewilderment that passed over Killian's face.

I strike out with a strong right hook, aiming directly for his jaw. Right as my fist is about to make contact and I can claim this round as a 'win'; Killian's shadows shoot out and stop my fist. The tiny victory smile that had already started spreading across my face is instantly wiped away.

Now it's his turn to shine that deviously delicious grin of his.

His shadows pull my right fist down and behind my back, followed by my left hand. More shadows join in to wrap across my chest and arms securing them firmly to my sides. It looks like this round is going to him too. *Fae-hole!*

Killian walks to stand right over me; leaning down like he is coming in for a kiss.

"Is this some weird sex fantasy of yours?", I tease. If I'm honest with myself, it is kind of hot. Being tied up by his shadows...my body left completely at his mercy.

Hell, what is wrong with me...

Killian's eyes flare and he chuckles darkly. He leans down further allowing our lips to barely graze then he whispers softly against my lips, "Now it is, *princess*." The purr in his voice when he calls me princess has heat building between my thighs. Normally I hate it when he calls me that, but I'll give him a pass this time.

Giving into desire, I rise onto my toes to close the distance between our lips, but he steps away.

Leaving me feeling like a complete idiot.

Turning his back on me and walking away he looks back over his shoulder and orders, "Get yourself free of my shadows."

There are a thousand different insults I want to throw at him right now, but to keep some of my dignity, I try not to show him how much his actions and words just *'affected'* me.

I bet he can smell... Ah! I hate Fae!

"How am I supposed to free myself? Your shadows will just smother my flames." I ask, tilting my head in question.

Suddenly, ever so slightly, I feel the shadows that are wrapped around my chest and wrists start to squeeze.

My eyes fly open at this realization.

Killian just casually slings his silver bangs out of his face and shrugs his shoulders as he prods at me, "Tapping out already? I guess that seems about right for a little princess. Because a viper would be cunning and harder to take out. So, which is it Cali? Are you a vicious viper or a dainty princess?"

That son-of-a—Focus!

He knows I have never backed down from a challenge, and that is not going to change today.

Okay, think, I know my fire and flames won't work against his shadows, so what else do I have in my arsenal? Fire is the sole power I've worked to harness thus far, but what all is fire comprised of? Raw energy, heat....come on think Calista!

Light! Yes! Duh...fire provides light. And what destroys shadows? Light! Light vs. Dark, Sunlight vs. Shadows. I am a descendant of the moon goddess who's twins with the sun goddess, so technically the blood and power of the sun goddess is also coursing through my veins. Meaning I should be able to produce light which would vanquish Killian's shadows, that are now so tight I can barely take a full breath. But how?! Think of Seb...

Digging deep, I focus on the flames fueling my power from inside. Grabbing hold of the flame with my mind I begin to dissect it, trying to pull the light itself out of the burning flame. Isolating the light component of the flame. It's white and blinding; burning my mind's eyes. It's burning hot, maybe even more so than the flame itself.

Now I just need to figure out how to use it.

Picturing Seb and the way his body glowed from the inside out when he was saving me in my apartment; I try my best to mimic him. I let my power flow into the light; letting the small ball of light grow until it's so large that I can no longer cage it inside. I let go of the leash on my power; and with my mind I show the light what I want it to do, what I pictured happening to Seb when he used his light power.

The ball of light dispersed throughout my body, spreading throughout all my limbs, including my head. The skin on my entire body begins to feel like it's being burned by the intense rays from the sun. A burning sensation starts to build up behind my eyeballs until it is so intense it feels like if I don't open my eyes immediately my eyeballs will be burned from their sockets.

With that fear fresh in my mind, I open my eyes...the only thing I can see is the white blinding light. But I can feel the light along the outside of my skin, encompassing my entire body.

I feel the pressure around my chest release, and I can finally take a full breath. The light leaves my eyes so I can lift my freed hand and take in the light shining out from my body. It looks like I just made myself into a human glow stick. But it worked...the shadows are gone, and I am free.

I win!

As I call my power back inside the light slowly disappears. Leaving me and Killian staring at one another face to face. I must have a look of complete elation and shock on my face. I had no idea I could do that!

Killian's looking at me like that was the most astonishing thing he has ever seen, with his large eyes and somewhat goofy smile.

"Holy shit!", I exclaim, jumping excitedly in place.

"Ho-ly shit!" Killian agrees slowly. I don't think he has even blinked once since he witnessed my new magic trick.

In three large strides he closes the distance between us, bringing us so close together I can feel his warm breath against my cheeks.

"So not only did you inherit your ancestors fire power, but the power of light as well.", he sounds mesmerized as he runs his fingers down the side of my neck. Once his fingers reach the base of my throat, he wraps his large hand around it and pulls my body until it's flush against his. Not letting go he wraps his other hand around my waist and leans down running his nose along mine. Sharing the same breath, as his lips tease mine with a light caress he confesses, "You are extraordinary", then his lips are crashing into mine.

A small moan escapes from my throat as his tongue enters my mouth and begins tangling with mine. He runs his hand through my hair and deepens the kiss. I reach up and run both of my hands through his soft silver hair before grabbing hold of the short strands and pulling him closer.

The growl I can hear rumbling from deep down in his throat has my toes curling.

We haven't been intimate with one another since the day I was attacked. After I overheard him and his friends discussing mine and my sisters' fate. And Gods have I missed this; being tangled up together and the taste of his kiss.

Pulling away to catch my breath, I look up at him as my fingers play with his hair. "Now I just need to awaken the moon goddess powers flowing within my blood. Maybe I'll have shadow powers too. Then my shadows can kick your shadows asses." I smile teasingly.

He lets out a bark of laughter. "I guess we'll have to wait and see, Viper." Then he pulls me in for another kiss.

I guess that's the end of this training session...

CHAPTER 40

CALISTA

Without a word, Killian teleports us directly back to our beautiful villa deep inside the forest. I have been painfully denying the pull of our mating bond for over a week now. Still not one-hundred percent sure if I should put my full trust back into Killian. I'm not sure if I possess enough willpower to resist falling right back under his spell—which will result in me putting my trust in him *again*, only to find out in the end that I was right the first time, and he has, in fact, been playing me like a fool this entire time. Hence why I have been keeping my distance from him lately.

But now that he has me back in his strong arms, there's no chance of extinguishing the flames of desire that are currently scorching through every fiber of my being. Begging me to give in to my cravings. I've been yearning to feel his warm silk skin moving along every inch of my body and hungering for the taste of his tongue as he devours my mouth with his kiss.

We leave a trail of destruction throughout the villa while making our way to the bedroom. It seems like now that we finally have our hands on each other, neither of us is willing to fully break the contact we both have been lusting for. Afraid that if we lose all points of contact between us everything will stop.

I pull my shirt over my head and then wrap my arms around Killian's neck. Grabbing my thighs he picks me up, trailing kisses and teeth down my neck. I wrap my legs around his waist right before he slams my back into the wall across from the burning fireplace.

Killian takes his hand and pulls down my lacey midnight blue bra, leaving my breast bare for him. Leaning down he takes one of my hardened nipples into his warm mouth; licking and sucking as I moan with pleasure. I roll my hips against his crotch and find him hard and ready for me. The groan that elicits from him sends a thrilling shiver down my spine.

Ripping me off the wall he turns and carries me into the bedroom and tosses me onto the bed. Standing, he slowly unbuttons his jeans and lets them slide down his thick toned legs all the way to the ground, leaving him in only his black boxer briefs. He silently turns and walks to the foot of the bed.

He leans against the tall bed post with his arm above his head; looking like the sculpted god he is.

I swear it looks like Michelangelo himself came down and hand carved every line and cut along this man's body.

As he stands there devouring me with his sight alone, I notice the gleam within his dark starlit eyes that promises me a mixture of pain and pleasure.

"Get over here", he commands darkly.

Following his orders, I rise and walk to the foot of the bed, never letting my eyes roam away from his. The tone of his command and that look in his eyes has the hair on the back of my neck rising from the wariness and anticipation coursing through my body.

He closes the distance between us. Twisting his fist in my hair, pulling my head back to deepen our kiss. A small moan escapes my throat as his tongue slides against mine. He growls, stepping forward and pressing my back up against the bed post. This kiss is rough and greedy; fueled by the lust we let build up between us. And right now, in this moment...it's perfect!

I bite his bottom lip so hard that I can taste the coppery tang of his blood. I feel his groan rumbling up from inside his chest, when suddenly my hands are tied up to the bed post high above my head. Whipping my head up I see that my wrists are being restrained by dark smokey shadows. When I look back at Killian, he has a devious grin smeared across his beautiful face.

My heart rate begins increasing. I know we joked about this earlier, but I didn't think it would happen. I'm both terrified and aroused from my vulnerability and lack of control. I am completely at his mercy now...and from the look he has in his eyes I don't think he will be showing me any kind of mercy tonight.

He leans his forehead against mine as he lightly trails his fingers down my right thigh. Sending a light shiver through my body.

Pulling back just enough to look me in the eyes he asks, "Do you trust me?" He must see that I am nervous. I want to take my control back but at the same time I want to see how this plays out.

Studying him from head to toe, I lean my head back against the bed post and breathlessly reply, "No way in Hell".

Laughing darkly, he lifts my right leg and places my foot upon the bed, leaving me spread out for the taking. Running kisses and skimming his teeth along the skin beneath my belly button, he slowly gets on his knees before me. Looking up beneath his long lashes, wearing a wicked smile he replies, "Good, keep it that way."

Before I can think about what exactly he means by that; his tongue is dragging along my slick entrance all the way up to my favorite spot. I throw my head back with a loud moan, completely forgetting what it was I was trying to think about. He groans out as he feasts on my arousal, licking up every drop and gliding it over my sensitive clit. The way he is circling his tongue in long slow strokes is making my eyes roll back in my head. I swear I'm starting to see stars, and I haven't even orgasmed yet.

He continues teasing me with long lavish strokes up and down my entire center causing me to submit and beg him for 'more'. I need more of him or I'm going to lose my mind. I'm clinching my fist together, dying to have them grabbing ahold of his hair so I can take control and ride his face until I find my release. The heat and pressure are twisting around in my core, moving closer and closer to the edge of nirvana that I'm so desperate to reach.

I cry out as he slides a finger inside of me and begins to pump in and out, matching the same rhythm as his tongue. He begins focusing his tongue on my clit, driving me mad with the need to come. Finally, he shows me mercy and shoves in a second finger. Pumping his fingers hard and fast as he continues to feast with his tongue, causing me to scream out his name in ecstasy as I hit my release.

He doesn't stop though, he continues to pump and curl his fingers just right, dragging out my pleasure as he rides out my release.

As my legs begin to shake Killian finally begins to rise, trailing kisses up my body as he goes. Stopping only for a moment to bite on one of my hardened nipples. I'm so breathless from screaming through my release I can't even react to the sharp pain...which thankfully morphs right into pleasure.

He stares down at me with that cocky smile of his, knowing he is damn good at what he does.

Grabbing my hips he twists me around so that my stomach is now pressed against the bed post and my arms are crossed in an 'x' above my head. I look back over my shoulder right as he drops his boxers, freeing his enormous thick cock and revealing a bead of cum on the tip. Before his boxers even hit the floor, he shoves me against the bed post and rams inside me with one long thrust.

My scream becomes a moan as the pain of adjusting to his large size turns into pure heated pleasure. A pleasure unlike anything I have ever experienced before, and I desire to experience it for the rest of my life.

As each thrust of his hips against my ass becomes harder and faster, I can't help but to lose myself in this man. Hell, if this is what being lost feels like then I don't ever want to be found.

Already I feel myself moving towards my second orgasm.

"More, please Killian", I shamelessly beg as I am completely at his mercy. Moaning and whispering his name like both a curse and a plea as he continues to pound inside of me.

In answer to my plea, he grabs hold of my left leg and places my foot up on the bed where my right one had just been. This new angle allows him to thrust deeper and hit just the right spot.

Taking a fist full of my hair he pulls my head back exposing my neck. In the next moment he sinks his sharp canines deep into my neck, causing me to scream out in immense pleasure as his bite sends me shooting off into the sky where I am literally seeing stars.

I am completely out of breath and still coming down from my second climax when Killian releases his shadows and flips me over onto the bed. He crawls onto the bed, covering my body with his as he thrusts himself back inside of me. Picking up right where he left off in chasing his own release. His lips meet mine in a claiming kiss I can feel all the way down to my bones.

Wrapping my legs around his back I run my fingers into his silver hair, pulling him closer and deepening our kiss. As he begins nipping and kissing my neck, I rake my nails down his shoulders. A moan escapes him as he finds pleasure in the pain. I'm sure my nails are drawing blood from how hard I must hold on with his savage pace...a delicious type of savage that is.

My eyes are blissfully closed as I lay there thrusting my hips up, meeting him stroke after stroke. I can already feel another orgasm building up inside. I feel like if I have another one, I'm going to fall over dead from all the endorphins flowing through my veins.

"Killian I can't!", I cry breathlessly. Letting him know I am close to another climax.

Leaning up onto his forearms he looks down at me; sweat is causing his silver hair to stick to his forehead and the rest of it is sticking out all over the place from me running my fingers all throughout it, and yet somehow this disheveled look makes him appear even more sexy. "You can and you will", he growls out. Lifting my hips to allow him a better angle.

My eyes roll shut again, and Killian gently runs one of his hands through my hair, stopping to caress my face.

"Eyes on me", he commands in a husky voice. My eyes fly open, and I feel his cock thicken. He is close to his own release. "I want to look into those beautiful eyes when I make you come again..." he thrusts in deeper eliciting a groan of pleasure from us both, "Come for me baby."

And on command like a good little girl, I scream his name out as another wave of pleasure courses through me, taking me right back over that edge I've become very acquainted with. Killian immediately roars out from the pleasure of his own release as he follows me right over the edge of that same cliff.

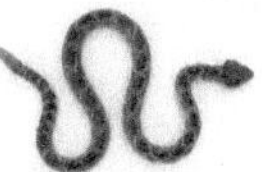

Rolling off me, Killian takes me into his arms and pulls me against his glistening chest. We are both covered in sweat after what just transpired between the two of us.

He places soft sweet kisses to the top of my head while running his hand up and down my spine, and if he doesn't stop, I may fall asleep. "I'm sorry I lost your trust, Cali. But I *need* you to know without any doubt in your mind that I love you with everything I am, body, mind and soul. And that will never change...even if you decide to walk away and never see me again once this is all over." he whispers softly into my hair.

Looking up into his eyes that hold the starry night sky within, I quietly confess, "I am afraid to allow myself to trust you again, fully trust you that is. But no matter how much I wanted to hate you, and believe me I tried to, I just couldn't. I love you Killian, hell, I think I've loved you since the day you saved my life from that jabberwocky." The relaxed smile I've been giving him turns into a worried frown as I look down at his chest and trace my fingers over his mating mark. Looking back up into his concerned gaze I implore of him, "You have stolen my heart Killian. It has already been shattered once from losing you years ago...and I don't think my heart could survive losing you again. So, please—please, don't let it break again." A lonely tear rolls down my cheek, but Killian gently kisses it away.

Killian starts to respond but gets cut off as Nightshade storms into the room and dives right on top of us. Showering us with his sloppy kisses.

But how could we be mad at that cute fuzzy face of his?

We give him some ear scratches and belly rubs until Killian swoops me off the bed. "She's mine", Killian playfully growls at Nightshade as he carries us into the bathroom to clean off. I can't help the smile on my face; being with the two of them just brings back so many happy memories.

I just pray we can make more...and my heart doesn't end up in pieces again after everything's said and done.

Killian drew us a very satisfying hot bubble bath in the massive golden claw foot tub I've been dying to try out ever since I saw it the first time I came in here. I may have 'subtly' mentioned my love of bubble baths several times since we started training together. Especially after an intense training session when my muscles were sore and begging for relief.

It makes my heart flutter to realize that he not only listened to me but also remembered what I had told him.

I feel so at peace right now; leaning back against Killian's chest as we let the water relax our tired muscles. He's so tall that even with me sitting between his legs and laying my back against his chest, I'm still able to relax my head back on his shoulder.

I smile to myself, thinking of this moment and how we must look like we are starring in some romantic chick-flick.

Killian reaches over and grabs a wash rag and soap, lathering up the rag and bringing out the smell of eucalyptus. That is my go-to scent when I need to relax; at home I will light my eucalyptus candle and cover myself with the same scented body cream.

It's divine!

I go to move so he can bathe himself, but he wraps his large arm around my waist, holding me in place. I look back at him confused as he smiles and begins running the wash rag down my arm. Realizing his plan, I relax back into his body and allow him to lather me up.

This small act somehow feels so intimate. I love every stroke of the rag passing over my body; the sensation I get from letting go and allowing him to take care of me feels wonderful. Not only on my body but within my soul itself.

"Lean forward" he whispers against my ear, bringing out goosebumps along my skin. I do as he says, and he starts running the soapy rag down my spine. Setting every nerve ending on fire in the best way.

This moment being shared between us is so special and means more to me than I can put into words. But I know myself, and I will never be able to fully relax until Killian answers some questions that keep running through my brain.

Unfortunately, if I intend to relax, I must break up this magical silence so I can finally clear my head.

Well as much as I'm able to relax with my impending death from fighting the Dark Fae King, that is.

"Kill—, what's going to happen with *us* once everything is over with the king? We are literally from two different realms—"

Killian quickly cuts me off before I can finish. "Shhh. Lean back here." he soothes, pulling me back against his chest and wrapping his arms around me. He nuzzles his face into my neck, using his nose to move my hair away from my ear, then he lays his head against mine and talks quietly into my ear...almost like he's telling me a secret.

"Once the king has been dealt with it will be safe for you to stay here in Unseelie, with me. Here in our home, like we planned together all those long years ago. And Nightshade will be here too."

I giggle at that last part, because let's face it...Nightshade is the biggest selling point for me.

"I would love to stay here with Nightshade...oh and you, of course!" I tease. Leaning further into him I sigh and remind him of the hard truth, "But my entire life is in the Mortal Realm. I have a career and family to think about, plus I could never leave my sisters...and I'm not sure they would go for uprooting their lives and moving here."

"Fuck your job! You were born to be a Queen; you should have people doing all the work for you, you should never have to raise a finger again." he says, playfully biting at my neck to make me laugh. "And your sisters can come stay with us...I'm sure if we get Dante and Callum to swoon them, they will easily come over here."

I burst out laughing. "You have lost your mind. First off, Eve is with Sebastian, and secondly, Hazel can't stand Dante...she will be happy to put a whole world of distance between them."

"Hmm" is the only response I get as he strokes his fingers through my hair, which seems very suspicious. Does he know something I don't?

"I guess my boys have gotten really full of themselves over in the Mortal Realm, because they seem to have a different opinion on the nature of their relationships with your sisters..."

"What!?" I jerk forward so I can twist around enough to look him in the eye. "What the hell are you talking about!? You're just playing with me, right?" He just smiles that wicked little grin of his and shrugs, leaning back against the tub as he finds joy in watching me lose my mind. Fae-*hole*.

I keep begging him a little longer to spill the beans about my sisters and his friends, but his stupidly juicy lips are sealed shut. Apparently, I need to have a long talk with both my sisters when I get back.

"So, I'm guessing you won't consider coming to stay in the Moral Realm with me?" I ask shyly, already knowing what his answer will be.

"I wish it was that easy baby, but I'm needed here. With the king gone, the kingdom is going to be in complete madness for a while as everyone adjusts to having a new king on the throne. Cal, Dante and I are going to have our hands full trying to keep the Umbra Court and the battalion stationed within the castle walls in line with all the changes.

"Besides you are the heir to Stellaris, you belong in the Fae Realm." With all the conviction in his voice I know there is no changing his mind on this matter.

And I have zero desire to become the Queen of Stellaris; I know nothing about how the Fae live or how their realm works.

Unfortunately, this conversation didn't give me the answers I needed. Or maybe it did, and I am just going to keep my head in the sand for as long as I can. Neither one of us wants to abandon our current lives, bringing us to a stalemate.

We either attempt a long, and I mean *long*, distance relationship between realms, or one of us makes the sacrifice to keep us together. Or of course there is always the option of us going our separate ways; maybe meeting up every so often to satiate our mating bond.

Sighing in defeat, I lay my head back against his shoulder. "Just forget I brought this up; we can discuss what comes 'after' when King Erebus is dead and gone. Hell, there may not even be an 'after' for me once King Erebus gets a hold of me..."

Suddenly I am lifted into the air and spun around; landing now facing Killian, with my legs wrapped around his waist and my arms around his neck.

He takes hold of my face with both hands, staring straight into my eyes with a burning intensity that I have yet to see from him. His eyes darken along with his voice as everything about him becomes deadly. "Do you really believe I will sit back and watch you die?" His voice is raspy as if it pains him to even think of such a thing.

Shadows explode out from underneath the tub and climb up the walls, darkening out the world around us. There is just enough light being emitted from a few candles sitting on the shelf next to the tub and the natural moonlight shining through the skylight overhead that I can still see his face. Leaning his forehead to mine, his voice darkens as he whole heartedly vows to me, "I will smother this entire realm and the next in the darkness of my shadows, slowly suffocating the life out of every being within, including myself, if it means keeping you safe."

I stare at him with my lips ajar; speechless. His deadly vow is terrifying yet thrilling. Because I know deep in my soul that he means every single dark word that left his lips. I can *feel* the truth of this vow through his emotions shooting down the bond we share. Passion. Love. Anger. Possessiveness. Obsession. Fear.

This man would burn the world to the ground and douse the embers in rain, all so I could live.

When I still haven't spoken, he lightly runs his thumb along my cheek, searching in my eyes for any sign of comprehension. His voice is low and thick with emotion as he asks, "Do you understand?"

My eyes are brimming with tears, not out of fear but from an overwhelming feeling of love for this mate of mine.

"Y—Yes", is all I manage to say before he is crashing his lips into mine. I moan and he groans possessively as he slides his tongue into my mouth, claiming every part of me. This kiss is crazy, filled with every emotion one can imagine. There is a desperation to it; like he is determined to do whatever it takes to keep his word, screw whatever consequences his actions may bring.

CHAPTER 41

CALISTA

Before I headed back into the Mortal Realm this morning; I had Killian take us to the Tree of Resurrection; the same tree that now is crying golden tears.

Apparently, the golden liquid trailing down its trunk never stopped, even after I left the realm. I can tell because the tree is now surrounded by a pool of golden liquid; like the tree has a two-foot-wide mote circling and protecting it.

Try as I could, I was unable to figure out how to reopen the hole in the trunk of the tree that Selenity's viper Drax went through. I have this feeling that for me to truly reveal myself as the rightful heir to the Fae Realm, I must find a way to reopen the tree. What should I expect to find inside? I have no clue...well other than the viper called Drax.

I do not want to stick my hand blindly into that tree with that 'danger noodle'. If he bites me and I'm not immune to his venom I will die!

Back at the precinct, Seb and I sit anxiously, stealing glances at one another from our desks, awaiting the call that will finally bring this serial killer case to an end.

Seb, Callum, and Dante work surprisingly well as a team. They came up with a masterful plan to not only dispose of the two Fae bodies that were killed in my apartment, but to also close the case. I asked Dante where they had stored the bodies to keep them from decomposing while they came up with this plan, but he just gave me a cocky wink and told me not to worry about it.

Fae-hole!

Killian had texted me about twenty minutes ago that phase one of our plan had been set into motion. So, the anticipation was driving me insane; I just wanted the stupid phone to – *Ring! Ring! Ring!*

Finally!

Seb and I both perk up as soon as we hear the phone ringing in the Lieutenant's office. Quickly putting our heads back down we begin to look as busy and uninterested as possible. If anyone sees us looking too conspicuous that could cause BIG problems for us. We can't let anyone find out we are tied to this in any way, shape, or form.

"Adams, Prince, my office now!", Lieutenant Daniels yells angrily across the room. I'm just hoping his sour mood is due to the call he just received and not anything to do with me and Seb; especially us in relation to the subject matter of the call.

We hurry into his office and Seb shuts the door behind us. "Lieutenant?", I say as both a greeting and a question.

"DCFD Station 25 called in reporting the discovery of two dead bodies while putting out a house fire in Congress Heights." he explains.

"Arson?", Seb questions.

"Appears that way."

"Why do you need us on it? Can't Ortega and Jones handle this one? We still have a serial killer running around out there that we are trying to pin down.", I bravely ask...or stupidly. I clench my jaw as I prepare for the Lieutenant to bite my head off for my insubordination.

He turns to me with a look that could bring even the toughest man to their knees, but I stand strong and hold my chin high calling his bluff.

Here comes the yelling. "I'm sorry *Adams*, is your job too difficult for you?! Should we reassign you to an easier job? One you can handle. Maybe back in booking!?" His face is red, and he is seething.

Dropping my head, faking defeat, I apologize for stepping out of line. "Sorry sir...we will head over there right now."

"Wait!", he yells as I turn to leave. "Just so happens this might involve your serial killer case after all...we think they may have found 'trophies' taken from each of the victims."

Both Seb and I act surprised by this revelation.

"Now get your asses out of my office and don't come back until you solve this damn case!", he commends sharply, as Seb and I hurriedly leave his office.

The sound of the Lieutenant angrily slamming his office door behind us, has us quickening our pace as we head for the exit.

Seb and I eagerly arrive at the scene. The Lieutenant said they called in a 'house fire', but what I'm seeing in front of me is a late model brown and white motorhome parked in the side yard of an old, vacant house that is being taken over by the surrounding plant life.

Which is brilliant!

I'm slightly pissed that they deviated away from our original plan of setting the desolated house on fire, but this motorhome idea makes my life so much easier in terms of closing this case.

If my mind is on the right track, it seems like the guys set up the scene so that the law enforcement officers, CSI team, and the Emergency Service agencies would conclude that these were just two serial killers who stole a motorhome to travel around to God knows where, murdering innocent unsuspecting women.

And once it's been determined that there were no prior murders matching the MO of these serial killers; we can all assume they were starting their horrendous acts here in Washington DC, the capital of the United States.

The Fire Chief allowed us to carefully examine the scene. Both bodies were burned beyond recognition, which to be fair one already was. They determined there was a gas leak in the main cabin and when they turned on their gas stove the spark was enough to cause an explosion. They believe that both men were in the kitchenette area when this occurred. The force from the explosion propelled them back with enough force for them to hit their heads, leaving them unconscious...where they unfortunately were burned alive.

Lucky for them they were already dead...

Now for the most critical part of our plan... "Chief, do you mind explaining why my department was needed here for this incident? It looks pretty cut and dry; these men tragically died in a fire caused by a gas leak fueled explosion in their motorhome." I ask, right as Seb starts walking over to us wearing thick white gloves and holding a small, scorched metal box.

The Chief points to the box Seb is holding. "This fireproof box was one of the few items we salvaged from the fire. When the Captain opened it, we expected to find some form of documentation to identify the two victims. Instead, we found this..." The Chief nods for Seb to open the box.

As Seb lifts the lid and my eyes roam over the contents inside the box, I feign shock. Gasping as I place my hand over my mouth.

Inside the box I stare at the exact items Seb informed me would be in there. Personal items that can be traced back to all three of the victims, Jessa Walkens, Valerie Elkins, and Tilly Townsen.

Dante, Callum, and Killian oversaw selecting the killers' 'trophies'. Since we were taking them long after the victims' murders had occurred, they had to take discreet items that no one close to the victims would notice had disappeared long after their death, but not so discreet that the victims' friends or family wouldn't be able to recognize them and make the connection.

There is a high school class ring belonging to Ms. Walkens; taken from her jewelry box sitting on her vanity.

They had retrieved an ID card for Ms. Elkins that was from participating in a dance competition when she was twelve. It has both her name and a picture of her younger self on it. Apparently that competition must have been important to her if she still had it laying around her room.

And lastly, there was Ms. Townsen... Finding something inconspicuous of hers was a little more difficult. Her family, I'm assuming, had already packed away ninety-five percent of her shop. The guys had to plunder through loads of boxes before they found anything usable. They finally decided on a handmade bracelet that read 'Spice Up Your Life'; since she did own a spice shop.

Even if the 'trophy' selected to represent Ms. Townsen is 'weak evidence'...we can deduce by using the strong connection of our other two victims that this must have belonged to Ms. Townsen. Giving us enough evidence to close this case.

"Holy Shit! Did we just pull that off?" Seb asks excitedly, running his hands over the top of his perfectly styled blonde hair.

I just laugh in response. We showered the Fire Chief with our appreciation at possibly helping us finally solve our serial killer case and insured him we would take the firebox straight to our forensics team at DCMDP.

Still laughing in disbelief I admit, "I never thought this phrase would ever come out of my mouth, but...Damn I love those Fae assholes, or as I call them, Fae-holes. Including you of course." I finish smiling over at Seb. He shoots me one of his charming grins like always.

Back at the office everyone is congratulating us on finally being able to close the case. We can all breathe a sigh of relief knowing that the FBI doesn't have to get involved now. They leave the department in a complete wreck by the time they get the hell out; causing so much discord between agents and officers, and they literally just leave their shit all over the place. It is madness, and I'm so glad we dodged that bullet.

I spend the rest of the workday filling out all the paperwork and case files that goes along with closing this case. I've been keeping up with all the documentation along the way, so I just need to clean everything up and then wrap up the incident report for today.

With the guys setting up the scene so ingeniously, they basically served up everything we needed to close this case on a silver platter. I owe them big time!

I'm not sure if I owe them so much as 'taking on the Dark Fae King', but I guess it's my turn to pay up.

When five o'clock rolls around I am ready to get the hell out of here and celebrate! I will cross all my "T's' and dot my 'I's' tomorrow after I meet with the Captain and Lieutenant for a final briefing regarding the case.

I send out a group text to my sisters including all the guys:

Cali:

Case closed bitches! Time to celebrate! All Souls 9pm! =)

Hazel:

Hell to the Yes! We are getting Cali drunk!

Cali:

I'll be getting myself drunk thank you very much =p

Eve:

Finally! Thank God we can finally take that off our plate.

Dante:

You're welcome...and you can just call me Dante

Hazel:

You wish asshole!

Killian:

Way to go Viper! Have I told you how incredible you are? Love you baby, see you soon!

Hazel:

OMG gross, get a room!

Eve:

I second that!

Callum:

Kill's gone soft!

Dante:

Yeah, RIP Kill

Killian:

Fuck you guys!

Cali:

Holy shit! I look away for ten seconds and come back to all this. Ok, group text privileges revoked. Oh, and I love you more Kill!

GROUP CHAT CLOSED

CHAPTER 42

CALISTA

I am already starting to feel toasty from the two glasses of wine I had in my celebratory bubble bath. The steamy water and tasty wine made my muscles and mind relax in no time at all.

I think I'm still in shock that the guys actually came through for us on their part of our deal. Now I just must focus on coming through with our side of it. But that is an issue for another day, because tonight we throw caution to the wind and celebrate our victory!

I'm not planning on running anywhere tonight so I pulled out my cute black heels that I had thrown in the back of my closet after that first time I met Killian at All Souls. They pair perfectly with my black skinny jeans and sleeveless black blouse. The blouse is backless; connected only along my bra line by a long golden metal snake, making it look as if a snake is slithering across my back.

After everything that has come to light over these past few weeks; I feel like my wardrobe, jewelry, and home decor choices were all trying to point me in that direction. Apparently, Selenity, Goddess of the Moon had a fondness for snakes, vipers in particular.

How I would have ever put two and two together I haven't the slightest clue. I'm glad Killian came along to open my eyes to who and where I'm descended from. Revealing the chance for me to choose a whole different destiny for myself, in a whole different realm.

But I can't just up and leave my life here. I know they say it's my destiny to wear the crown of Stellaris, but that still sounds insane. Like this couldn't possibly be real, and everyone is just pulling this prank on me.

Maybe I would fall in love with life in the Fae Realm?... I could always stay for a while to learn more about my roots and then come back here whenever I decide.

Walking over to my kitchen sink I pour myself a glass of water to drink before I head out the door. If I don't take a minute to hydrate now, I know I will regret it in the morning. My body can't recover as quickly from hangovers as it used to be able to. I miss the days when I could party all night, crawl into bed at three in the morning and wake up five hours later to head in to work, without feeling like death incarnate. Pop myself some ibuprofen and chug a bottle of water and I would be good to go. Now, it takes me a whole weekend to recover from a night of hard drinking.

After finishing up a glass and a half of water, I pull out my phone and text my sisters that I am grabbing my purse then heading over to the bar.

Right as I am about to leave all the water I drank hits me at once and I have to make a detour to relieve myself.

Once finished, I grab my purse to head out again. I check my phone and see that neither of my sisters have seen my message nor responded.

But that's fine, I don't mind entertaining myself at the bar until everyone starts arriving. I'm sure they will be right behind me anyways.

I open my door as I grab my keys off the entry way table. But as soon as I glance up, I startle. A stranger is standing right outside my doorway in the dimly lit hallway, as if they have been waiting for me to open my door this whole time...

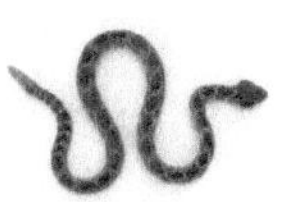

"Uh...Can I help you?", I ask, suspiciously eyeing the stranger. I can't quite put my finger on it, but I have this eerie feeling that I've seen them before.

This woman seems to be in her late thirties and carries herself confidently. It's hard to tell if she's genuinely important or just self-important.

Either way she is very disrespectful and must have some sort of death wish...

She gives me a beautiful smile that is laced with malice as she walks forward, shoving me aside so she can enter my apartment uninvited.

"I'm sorry but just who the hell do you think you are? Am I supposed to know you or something? Because I think you have the wrong apartment lady. Now speak or get the fuck out before I call the police." I demand and threaten as she continues to look around the room with her back to me.

She finally spins around to face me, whipping her long black hair through the air. Her dark red lips pull into a viciously cruel smile that manages to put every nerve in my body on high alert. I can just feel from her aura she's giving off, that this lady is one huge walking red flag.

Her beautiful silver floor length gown that has a slit plum up to her hip on one side, appears to be blowing in a breeze that's nonexistent. Focusing my abilities on her I can tell she isn't Fae, but she is something powerful. Every so often I get a glimpse of an old decrepit face behind the mask she is wearing.

Maybe she is an old witch of some kind? But why is she here?

She examines me from head to toe with her dark ominous eyes. The longer I stare the more I realize it's her eyes that make me believe I've seen her before. They are so dark as if all the light has been drained from them, appearing almost as black as her hair. I'm stuck here trying to piece together where I've met this woman before. It's driving me absolutely bonkers. But before I can demand for her to tell me who she is, she brings all my thoughts to a standstill as she casually calls my bluff.

"Why would you call the police when you are one, Calista?" The way she says my name gives me chills. She's definitely trouble with a capital "T".

Unexpectedly she lets out a maniacal laugh and points her finger at me as she swirls it around in the air. "You must have inherited their spit fire personality. But beware, that attitude of yours can get you in all sorts of trouble where I'm taking you..." she says menacingly.

Who is this person? How do they know me? Does she know who my real parents are?

I'm stunned...and have sooo many questions running through my mind, but one is more important than the others right now.

"I'm sorry", I laugh sarcastically as I approach her, "but you still haven't told me who the hell you are...but more importantly, I'm not going anywhere with you. So, you need to get your creepy psycho bitch ass up out of my home right now!" I shout, no longer willing to put up with whatever bullshit she just steamrolled into my space with.

"I have people waiting on me right now, so I am leaving." I turn to leave, because to Hell with this lady. I would rather leave her standing in my own home than spend another minute in her company. She can steal or break anything she wants but at least I will be safely away from her.

She lets out a low deep laugh before she brings my world to a complete halt. "I wouldn't do that if I were you. Walk out that door and you will never see your sisters again..."

I freeze mid-step, with my back towards her.

Looking down at my phone I see that they still haven't messaged me back, and that is not like them. Hazel would be glued to her phone; all excited about us meeting up at the bar without her having to force us for once.

My blood goes cold at the thought that maybe this lady isn't bluffing and something bad has been done with my sisters.

I slowly turn back around to face the pale skinned bitch. Fantasies of me snapping her thin little neck are starting to come to life in my mind. I will kill for my sisters...no questions asked. The only reason I'm not wrestling this woman down to the ground now is because I need to find out where my sisters are and if they are safe.

Maybe if I don't show up soon the boys will come looking for me and my sisters, if they really are missing.

"You're bluffing", I snarl at her. Walking closer to size her up and show her I am not afraid to fight.

"Do you really want to take that chance? Maybe I am or maybe I'm not. Maybe they are sitting by the bar waiting for their big sis, *or* maybe they are chained up at the foot of King Erebus's throne; praying that their big sister will show up and save them." She narrows her stare, waiting to see if I call her bluff.

She knows that I would never gamble with my sisters' lives.

"Who. Are. You?", I growl bringing flames to the surface of my hands as my vision starts to bleed red.

She takes in my flaming hands and shakes her head; obviously not concerned in the slightest. Slowly she circles me, like a shark circling a bloody shipwreck survivor, sizing up its meal before it goes in for the kill.

"King Erebus has sent me here to collect you for him. Seeing as how his warriors were too incompetent to do so."

Holy-shit this is really happening!

What should I do!?

I start to internally panic; all the time I still hoped to have strengthening my abilities to go up against the king and even stand a chance is now fizzling out right before my eyes. The time has come; and I am nowhere near ready for this. Plus, with my sisters chained up and Killian having no clue as to what's happening, it looks like I am going to be doing this completely on my own.

So much for celebrating tonight...

Surrendering to my fate I lower my hands and extinguish the flames.

"If I go with you, will you make a deal with me to let my sisters go? Only one of us needs to die to break the prophecy, so let them go, please. I'm the strongest out of the three of us, so remove me from the equation and the king will have no threat to his reign." I try to bargain with her.

And I mean everything I said, I will willingly take my chances against King Erebus if she swears to release Eve and Hazel and never go after them again.

"How self-sacrificing you are", she drawls as she runs her finger up my throat, stopping underneath my chin. "That decision is for the King to decide, so you can plead your case with him once we arrive."

"Fine!" I yell out, slapping her hand away from me. "But before I go anywhere with you willingly, I need proof. Proof that you really have my sisters..."

"You will get your proof once we are there... Or you can turn and run out the door now, saving yourself, and leaving your sisters to suffer the king's wrath all on their own..."

Yeah right! How stupid does she think I am? I know she isn't letting me leave this room.

In a split-second decision, I throw my purse, keys, and phone down in a 'show of anger', hoping that she doesn't catch on, and that when the guys come looking for me, assuming they will, they will see my stuff scattered across the floor and know something isn't right.

"You win!" I shout out thrusting my hand out for her to take hold of, "now take me to my sisters!".

"As you wish", she purrs grabbing tightly onto my hand and sinking her long nails into my skin.

She raises her free hand, and a long vertical black slit appears in the air. She must have the ability to slice open the veil between our realms. Just as I'm about to ask how it's supposed to work, she tells me to hold on tight, and then she shoves me into the black line where I begin falling forward surrounded by nothing but darkness.

CHAPTER 43

CALISTA

My landing was rough; if it wasn't for the woman's hold keeping me on my feet, I would have embarrassingly face planted in front of everyone present.

Quickly taking in my surroundings I notice that we are outside in what appears to be a curved shaped courtyard; I would bet if I were to look down at it from above it would appear to be shaped like a crescent moon. I'm positive that the beautiful structure surrounding the courtyard is the Castle of Shadows. Killian has spoken about it many times.

He told me that he enjoys laying under the moon in the middle of the courtyard on quiet nights because this is where the moon shines the brightest. And given what I'm seeing with my own eyes I don't think he was exaggerating. Looking around, the light shining down from the moon above is bright enough to cast light across the entire courtyard.

The light emitting from the moon feels almost rejuvenating as it touches my skin; like I am a solar powered battery that is being recharged by the light of the moon instead of that from the sun.

Not to mention the sheer size of the moon. It puts the harvest moons in the Mortal Realm to shame. It appears to be so much closer within this realm. I feel like if I could grow wings and fly, I could soar right up and touch it.

From here I can't see a lot of the castle but from what I do see it is absolutely stunning. The castle itself is constructed of dark blackish-grey concrete. If the moon along with all the stars in the sky were to go out, the castle itself would disappear into its surroundings like that of a shadow. There are also three tall turrets marking sections of the castle; two seem to mark the furthest ends to the right and left of the castle, leaving the largest standing tall and proud in the center...I'm sure that's where the king's quarters are located.

The castle is surprisingly made up of large floor to ceiling windows outlining the perimeter of the courtyard. Maybe to allow in as much light from the moon and stars as possible...or just for the incredible view itself.

I wonder if the windows line the front of the castle too?

The part of me that loves history, and the architecture of old buildings is dying to see the inside of the castle, but the logical part of me knows I have more important things to focus on now...like not actually dying.

What really caught me off guard here is the number of Unseelie Fae gathered all throughout the courtyard. The males slightly outnumber the females. Both males and females alike are all stunningly beautiful. Wearing anything from gorgeous shimmering ballgowns in shades of silver and black, to see through lingerie that leaves hardly anything to the imagination.

Most don't even seem to notice us arrive, they are too busy drinking, dancing, and taking part in what I would call indecent public displays.

I'm almost positive that group of Fae off to my far left are in the middle of having an orgy, open for anyone to join or watch. Then some Fae are laying around stark naked just soaking in the moonlight, which appears to be one of the tamest activities happening here.

I've always been told the Fae Realm is full of mischief and debauchery and judging by this party or whatever it is, I certainly agree.

Pulling me along behind her, the lady leads me to the far back center of the courtyard. Two gorgeous stained-glass doors mark the entrance into the castle from the courtyard. Before I can take in any more detail as to what is depicted within the stained-glass, my eyes fall upon a dais and a large onyx black throne stationed front and center. And perched upon that large throne with a vile grin pulling at the corners of his mouth, must be the one and only, King Erebus.

I swallow, taking in this tyrant I have heard so much about. One look upon his slimy, arrogant face, and I can see the black sludge that coats his very soul rolling off his body... On his exterior his beauty rivals that of every Fae in this courtyard, but underneath his flawless moonlit skin, this Fae harbors nothing but pure evil in his heart.

He is handsome in every sense of the word. His broad shoulders almost match the entire width of the huge throne, not to mention his sheer height even when he is sitting down. His body stature puts me in mind of Killian's, I bet if they stood next to one another the only difference would be that Killian may stand an inch or two higher than the king.

A black three-piece suit sits upon his large frame, and that is surrounded by a black shimmering cape that looks like literal stars were taken from the sky and sewed into the material. Setting off his entire regal look though, is the intimidating black onyx crown encircled with deadly sharp four-inch-long black spikes. His crown alone is a deadly weapon; those spikes could easily pierce through a man's heart.

The 'crown of death' sits upon his very light grey hair with a single onyx black stripe running along each side of his head.

For me, I think it's the stark contrast between his dark crown and light hair that is reinforcing the 'villain' vibes he's giving off.

As much as I hate to take my eyes off him as we continue to move closer, I know I have to. I need to locate my sisters and make sure they are unharmed.

I look all around...left, right, behind, and hell even up, but my sisters are nowhere to be seen. That must mean—

This bitch tricked me...

Worse I fell for it...

Fuck I'm fucked...

On the bright side, hopefully that means my sisters are safe and sound waiting for me to arrive at the bar.

Not only are they safe, but soon when I don't show up someone is going to go looking for me... And maybe Killian will think about checking here. I guess here's to hoping...

"Who is this lovely creature you've brought for your King?"

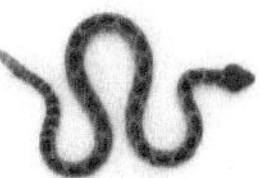

I can't keep myself from cringing in response to King Erebus's question he asks of the beautiful, dangerous, stranger still tightly grasping my hand and arm. The way his question rolled off his tongue like a purr, and the dark intent laced behind it made my insides turn.

Maybe he thinks I'm just another 'mortal' plaything being gifted to him for his own personal entertainment?

Hell No!

"Your Majesty, I have brought you a most glorious gift!", my captor practically squeals out with excitement after taking a deep bow.

King Erebus lifts his brow and tilts his head, intrigued by this declaration. "OH? Go on then...what is so special about this new pet you bring me?" he asks curiously as he waves his hand towards me.

"I'm not a damn pet", I snap. The king's eyes flare open revealing both anger at the disrespect I showed, and unfortunately for me, even more interest as to who or *what* I am.

"I'm so sorry Your Majesty, this one is feisty as you can tell.", the lady apologizes, tightening her grip on my arm. At this point if she squeezes any harder those long nails of hers are going to puncture straight through my skin.

"You are wasting my time, Hera!", the King yells angrily. "Get to the point or you will be the next target on the Wheel of Daggers."

She flinches and looks off at something for a split second. Following her stare I see a huge wooden board, spinning rapidly, with someone strapped into the center, arms and legs spread wide. Daggers are flying at them as they scream in terror. It is a scene I've seen a million times in scary movies or cartoons, but never in real life. Never!

Hera? Why is that so familiar?

How am I just now noticing the blood curdling screams?

I am most definitely going to die tonight...

Focus Cali!...

"Your Majesty, I went myself into the Mortal Realm and secured for you one of the witches the prophecy speaks of." the lady, or I guess 'Hera' announces proudly. She is breathing so fast it sounds like she just ran a marathon. Can she get any more excited about this?

Someone give this lady a trophy to shut her up!

As soon as those words are out of her mouth a wave of shadows erupts from the king. The entire courtyard is engulfed in darkness as the king's shadows block out the light of the moon, getting everyone's attention.

Especially mine!

The shadows disappear just as fast as they appeared, except for the snare of shadows that's now tightly wrapped around my throat.

The king prowls closer to inspect his prey, but not too close I notice. He is powerful and conceited but deep within his dark eyes I can see a tiny speck of fear...it's small but it is there. And I somehow must use that to my advantage.

"Where are the other two?!" the king roars out. Ungrateful bastard that he is. He can't be satisfied with just one he has to catch us all...what are we, Pokémon?

He storms over to Hera who has finally removed her claws from my skin. Leaving red half-moon indents in my skin.

He is so close in her face that I can see her hair blowing back and forth from his raging breaths. But I'll hand it to her, she stands her ground and doesn't back down or show fear.

"Your Majesty, all three witches are needed to fulfill the prophecy. Eliminating one will nullify it. The witch before you is the strongest, with abilities exceeding the others. Killing her will render the remaining witches powerless and harmless. Think of it as cutting off the head of the snake." Hera explains sweetly as she runs her hand up and over his shoulder, gently turning him in my direction so I now have his full focus.

"Well, if I only need to kill her that would make my life easier... are you certain that the prophecy will be nullified?" he asks as he places his hand underneath his chin, considering his options.

"Positive, Your Majesty. I will swear my life on it if that puts you at ease."

"That won't be necessary, besides your life already belongs to me." he laughs darkly. I don't miss the slight flinch Hera has to his statement.

Strange, she must have made a deal with him that somehow put her life in his hands? I hope the deal was worth it...

Finally sick and tired of hearing the two of them talk about me like I'm not standing five feet away, I step forward. Moving closer in the king's direction. I'll be damned if I show this worthless piece of shit a sliver of fear. Even if his shadows that are currently wrapped around my neck can most likely kill me with just a quick snap of his fingers.

Since arriving in this courtyard, I've already made peace with the fact that I'm not going to make it out of here alive, so if I'm going to die anyways, I'm going to go out swinging. I'm not going to make it easy for this chump.

"Or..." I wave and point to myself as they give me their full attention, "yep, I'm still here, Hi." I say it sarcastically. "You could just let me go back into the Mortal Realm, alive, and leave me and the other two alone. Forever!"

Both King Erebus and Hera erupt with laughter. Looking at me like I'm now sporting a second head on my shoulders.

No wonder Cerberus and Killian want my help with killing the king; he is undeniably awful. I don't think I could find that he has a single redeeming quality if I dug through his mind with a spade head shovel.

"We do *NOT* want your stupid crown! Hell, we didn't even know you existed until you sent those assassins after us. Oh, they are dead, by the way." I pause to give him a triumphant grin. His eyes go wide, and his cheeks start to redden as his temper rises to the surface. I'm sure he isn't upset by the fact that they are dead but more so because they were no match for me and my sisters.

No need to tell him I got help from the Seelie Prince...

"So let me go, keep your crown, and leave me and my sisters the fuck alone!" I yell angrily. Realizing too late that I let a very important detail slip.

And I can tell he caught on to it from the way his anger suddenly disappears and is replaced with a wicked smile.

"Sisters...no wonder you speak to me like you have no regard for your life. You would willingly sacrifice yourself to keep them safe, wouldn't you?" he questions, as he stomps towards me. He releases another shadow rope that now pins my arms to my sides so I cannot use my hands to cast my powers.

Before I can answer he begins yelling at me. His voice carrying across the courtyard for all to hear, his face turning blood red with anger. "You should be dead by now from the way you speak to me like I am any other mortal in your pathetic realm. *I AM THE KING!* And you will mind your tongue and address me as such."

I stand my ground and do not cower as he towers over me yelling. Spitting his venom all over my face. This Fae is no king though, he is just a power-hungry coward; afraid of three little witches. And being the stubborn woman I am, I will never show this man even an ounce of respect...no matter how many death threats—promises, he aims at me.

Glaring up into his dark sinister eyes, I pull out my irresistible puppy dog eyes along with my sweet innocent smile. Then in the kindest voice I can muster up I sarcastically reply, "Oh no! My apologies Your Majesty...I am but a mere mortal and have never been in the presence of such greatness, let alone interacted with it. Here let me try again...Your Majesty, thank you for bringing me here against my will and attempting to murder my sisters and me. Now please, if it's not too much trouble Your Majesty...Go. Fuck. Yourself!"

To top it off, I lean forward and spit on the ground before his feet.

I stand tall, chin held high and shoulders back, as I brace myself for the consequences.

One, two, three seconds pass and he still hasn't made the slightest move or even breathed as far as I can tell. Slowly I raise my head to look up at the king as he continues to just stand there towering over me with his eyes locked on me.

A shiver crawls down my spine as he continues to stand there not reacting at all. I thought he would go off screaming, punching, or finishing me off with his shadow necklace I'm still wearing snuggly around my neck.

But no... he's quiet...too quiet.

The king suddenly steps back away from me...laughing. This unexpected reaction makes me jump...and I internally scold myself for it. I hope no one noticed.

He points to me, and his laughter abruptly stops. "You, insolent girl." he growls out through clenched teeth. "You remind me of my son. The only problem with that though, is that I *detest* my worthless excuse of a son."

BAM

My skull is throbbing as I try to blink through the pain from the closed fist punch the king just laid me out with. I didn't even see it coming until the pain was already radiating across my face.

I can vaguely hear laughter from King Erebus, Hera, and the other Fae gathered throughout the courtyard. I am so embarrassed I didn't see this coming...I should have known he would take the cheap shot.

Spitting blood, I clumsily rise to my feet. It's hard to move when your arms are bound to your side by a rope made of shadows. The look of surprise on the king's face when I stand is priceless, and totally worth looking like a newborn fawn learning to walk in front of this entire audience.

He walks to stand before me again. "Look, it wants some more!", he announces loudly, exciting everyone who has gathered around to cheer on their king.

Yeah, he is soo *brave and strong, beating up a defenseless girl.*

But if training with Killian has taught me anything it's that I am not defenseless...

Focusing on every ounce of energy I have; I dig deep to awaken my powers. Lucky for me, I think the king underestimates me, so he is most likely not wasting the full strength of his powers on the shadows he has ahold of me with.

I stand completely still and stare straight ahead, forcing the fire within me to relinquish its light into my control.

I can make out some of what the king is spitting out to his followers. He is currently bragging about how he has turned me into a statue that's 'frozen' with fear.

But little does he know...I'm not a 'frozen' statue, I'm an undetectable iceberg and he's the Titanic. I'm his ruin that he won't see coming until it's too late.

The king steps directly in front of me with his chest barely an inch from mine. I lift my head up to look him in the eyes, not moving too quickly because I don't want to lose my grip on my power.

"Ready for more, pet?" the king goads.

I release the leash on my power and let it erupt from within. Light flares out from my skin, annihilating the shadows holding me captive around my arms and neck, setting myself free.

Shock crosses the king's face, giving me that one second, I need to make my move. Revving up, as hard as I can I jump up and headbutt the shit out of 'His Majesty'. Resulting in blood flying through the air as his nose cracks and gushes blood.

Damn that's satisfying!

I only get a moment to revel at the sight of the king grasping his bleeding nose and shooting me a wary glance before two large Fae males grab me from behind. They must be part of the king's Royal Guard seeing as how they are decked out in armor. This event doesn't put me in mind of one that would list 'armor' as optional attire.

Each Fae takes an arm and then precedes to kick the backs of my knees, causing my legs to buckle out from under me.

Coward can't even fight his own battle.

Marching forward, his nose already healed by magic, he slams his large black boot right into the center of my abdomen, forcing every molecule of air out of my lungs.

I struggle, silently gasping as I try to take in a fresh breath of air. But my lungs painfully feel like they have been kicked all the way up into my throat.

Finally, after what feels like hours my lungs slowly expand, and I take in a large breath of air. However, I don't have time to rejoice as the king prowls forward ready to attack his prey again...and by prey, I mean me.

My eyes follow his fist as he pulls back to land another blow to my face. I try to mentally prepare myself for another hard hit. But before he releases his fist upon my face, shadows encase his hand, giving him even more power for the impact he's preparing to make.

I'm powerless to defend myself with these two beastly Fae holding me in place as the king's personal punching bag. All I can do is brace myself for the unavoidable pain to come.

As soon as I close my eyes, there is an indescribable amount of pain that fills up the entire left side of my face.

The sound of bones crunching is undeniable.

I think the bastard shattered my cheek bone...again.

My head whips to the right so quickly and forcefully that I hear a loud pop coming from my neck. Thankfully, I can still feel all my limbs and move my head...slowly, so nothing was snapped or severed.

I'm slightly glad he aimed more towards my jaw, because if he had hit me in the side of my head, I have zero doubt that the impact from his shadow powered fist would have cracked my skull open.

Looking down I can see droplets of my own blood splattering against the dark grass. Licking my lip, the tang of blood covers my tongue. Not only do I have a busted nose, but he also gave me a huge, busted lip. It feels deep enough to require stitches, but I don't figure that will be happening.

I can only imagine what I look like, because it feels like my face is currently a bruised up bloody mess.

I need to get loose before he comes back for another attack... Spitting my blood towards the king I focus with all the strength I have left and release my power. I feel my fire burning and blazing with light; almost like starlight itself is waiting to be released. And I am more than happy to oblige.

The fire spills from my pores, flowing along every inch of my skin. My victims are none the wiser, as my invisible fire hunts along my body for its intended targets. I can feel when it finds what it's been searching for. It feels as if my power itself latches onto the victim, creating an invisible link between us so I can feel as it rushes into the other being. It feels exhilarating...like burning the very life force out of them is in turn refueling my own strength and power.

Screams fill the air as the two Fae holding me captive begin to burn alive from the inside out.

The king seems dazed as he stares on trying to figure out what is happening to his guards.

I don't miss the small step he takes backwards, retreating out of my reach.

The screams come to an abrupt stop as the Fae fall dead at my sides. Appearing completely unharmed on the outside.

The entire crowd gasps in bewilderment. Unable to figure out what has just happened.

I remain on my knees trying to use this moment of the king's wariness to regain some strength and control through all the pain that is currently shooting through my body from his merciless assault.

But my recovery is short lived as the king steps forward and pulls out his sword that until now has been sheathed on his hip.

I raise my chin high, showing no fear as he moves forward with the blade of his sword aiming directly for my throat. I refuse to cower for this sorry excuse of a man. He didn't even have the balls to fight me on his own.

"What did you do to my men?", he shouts in demand.

I narrow my eyes on him with a vicious grin and reply wickedly, "The same thing I'm going to do to you, *Your Majesty*."

He pulls his lips back in a snarl revealing his sharp canines and presses the tip of his blade into the flesh of my throat. I can't even swallow without the tip piercing my skin and causing a drop of blood to roll down my neck.

Before he gets a chance to finish the job and ram his sword right through my throat, the crowd gasps and turn their attention to something else.

With a sword pressed to my vulnerable throat, I don't have a way to turn around and see what has suddenly grabbed their attention. What could be more exciting than this?

It must be very important because even the king has taken interest; releasing the tip of his blade from my throat as he moves aside to get a better look.

I fall forward onto my hands, taking this moment to regain my control and strategize. I need to think of what I can do next to try and get myself away from here.

That's when I hear it...a voice I would recognize anywhere.

He came for me...

"What poor soul has the honor of being tortured by your hands tonight, Your Majesty?" he asks the king, confidence radiating from his voice along with a pinch of arrogance.

Standing there looking as if he just jumped out of a fairytale is my very own prince, Killian. The 'charming' part is still up for debate.

He's wearing all black, from his black trousers tucked into his black riding boots that rise to just below his knees, all the way up to his black shirt and leather jacket. Oh, and I can't leave out the scabbard strapped around his chest that holds the badass sword that's sticking out from behind his back.

And here I thought it wasn't physically possible for him to be any sexier...I am happily mistaken.

A feeling of relief and hope washes over me. I prayed my mate would find me and here he is. With Killian here maybe now I stand a real chance of making it out alive.

He stops approaching when he reaches my side. I look up to him with thankful eyes, hiding a small smile that only he can see. But all I get from him is nothing...nada...zilch. Not even a quick wink or a second glance. He looks completely uncaring about the situation.

I must say he is doing a fantastic job acting like he has no idea who I am, which is exactly what we need the king to believe until we attack.

Judging by the look on the king's face he is not happy with Killian's arrival. He has been gone for weeks now, but he has already prepared a cover story about where he and the others have been all this time away.

A malicious grin pulls at the king's lips as he finally addresses Killian's presence.

The king snarls at Killian, "It seems you have returned just in time to join in on the fun, *son*."

CHAPTER 44
CALISTA

"Are you going to introduce me to your new pet, father?" Killian tilts his head to the side while keeping his eyes completely glued on me. I can feel him assessing all my injuries with his eyes, and I can feel the fury and anger boiling up through the bond with every new injury he discovers. *"Are you okay? I'm sorry I wasn't here sooner. I came as soon as we realized you were missing. I failed you..."* Killian's voice is filled with sadness and remorse as he speaks into my mind.

"I'm better now that you're here.", I tell him, sending my love down the bond as to reassure him none of this is his fault and I do not hold him responsible for his father's actions. *"Do you have a plan?"*

Killian is pulled away from our conversation as the king addresses him. "You would know who this horrible creature is if you weren't out gallivanting around all of Stellaris with your two stooges." the king remarks in anger. "And you will address me as Your Majesty when you speak to me, *boy*." he scolds, intentionally demeaning his son before the entire crowd of Fae.

Now I can see why Killian is on board with his father's death.

"Apologies, Your Majesty." Killian states as he clenches his jaw to hold his tongue. We don't need him to rile up his father any more than I already have.

"This..." the king purrs as he walks behind me and runs his finger along my jawline, "is one of the wretched creatures the prophecy foretells will dare to come for my crown." he explains to Killian, his voice dripping with disgust.

The king yanks my head back by my hair and yells out for everyone to hear, "The Gods of old insult me. Do they truly believe that a king as powerful as I could fall at the hands of this pathetic witch?" Laughing, he throws my head forward as he releases my hair.

Laughter echoes out around the courtyard as the guests emulate their king; almost as if it's expected of them.

I can feel the rage building within the bond as Killian watches his father manhandle me, but he still doesn't act. He continues his performance, maintaining his calm, uncaring appearance for everyone to see.

Once King Erebus takes a seat back on his throne, Killian moves forward and grabs me by the chin, moving my face from side to side as if he too is unimpressed by what he sees. All the while, he is stealthily releasing his magic beneath my skin, healing my busted lip, nose, and shattered cheek.

He doesn't heal my lip completely...that would be too obvious for the king to notice. But at least now it's a simple busted lip I've received many of times on the training mats at the precinct, and not one that requires stitches.

Killian shrugs, as he releases my chin and steps away. "Maybe the old Gods were mistaken, or the prophecy was falsely created with the malicious intent to plague your mind, Your Majesty."

Nervous laughter grabs my attention as Hera re-enters my field of vision, stepping up behind the king, and running her hand over his shoulder as he sits upon his throne. "Your Majesty, I assure you my oracle is nothing if not completely loyal to you and your reign. What the prince suggests is ludicrous." she insists, although the slight quiver in her voice and her nervous laughter has me suspicious.

So, it's her oracle who 'received' this prophecy and passed it along to the king? Interesting...

"Silence!", King Erebus scowls at Hera. "It is because of *your* oracle that I'm in this mess to begin with...if she was as remarkable as you say, she should have seen that the witches we eliminated all those years ago had daughters of their own. My men could have eradicated their entire lineage in one sweep."

My mind is reeling as I begin to put the pieces all together. Mine, Hazel's, and Eve's mothers all believed their coven's High Priestess was in cahoots with the Dark Fae King. Trafficking humans over into the Fae Realm for youth and vitality in return.

But when our mothers couldn't tie the priestess to anything they removed themselves from their coven. They hadn't been in contact with their old coven for years before they were murdered.

But...

What if our mothers were still looking into the High Priestess and her possible involvement with all the missing girls? Maybe they were getting close to discovering something important that would have incriminated the priestess, possibly leading to her arrest. If the priestess found this out, she could have asked the king, King Erebus in this case, to help her handle getting rid of our mothers.

However, law enforcement does not cross over between realms. Even if King Erebus was found guilty alongside the priestess it would be out of law enforcements hands in the Mortal Realm. So only she would go down for their crimes. Knowing this, the king probably didn't want to dirty his hands just to aid the priestess. He seems to be the 'what's in it for me?' type of person, so he most likely decided that losing that priestess and what she had to offer wasn't worth wasting his time and energy to kill our mothers.

Just like most people, when backed into a corner we can find ourselves willing to do drastic things to survive and thrive. Making up a 'false' prophecy that directly affects the king and his rule is brilliant.

King Erebus is a self-righteous arrogant asshole who would do anything to assure there was no threat to his throne and crown. So, tell him your oracle 'prophesized' three specific witches that would result in his downfall, and there is no way in hell he would let them live.

Holy-shit!... The whole thing is made up! The prophecy is bullshit! Made up by the priestess herself to save her own ass and keep her hands clean in doing so.

"Calista!" Killian calls out into my mind.

I blink and shake my head, refocusing on the situation at hand. I guess he could tell my mind had taken me somewhere else.

Luckily, it seems like King Erebus was distracted arguing with Hera the whole time I was zoned out. It couldn't have been but a minute, but I still wouldn't want him to catch me in such an unguarded state of mind.

I didn't notice it before, but Hera is toying with a chain around her neck; it must be a habit of hers when she is nervous. Something about her still pulls me in... her familiarity, her looks, and the way she interacts with the king. Or better yet, the way the king acted towards her when she first arrived with me in hand...

No way...

He asked her what new toy she had brought for him tonight... As if her showing up and gifting him humans is a normal occurrence. Like maybe she traffics him humans and her young appearance is a mask...maybe she's an old hag inhabiting a thirty-something year old body?

You've got to be—

It feels like a slap to the face, a wake-up call directly from Hell.

There beneath her fidgeting hand is a large golden sun shaped pendant, housing a deep red ruby directly in the center. It's a necklace I would recognize anywhere.

How could I not? I saw it day in and day out, hanging around the neck of the lady who gives me the creeps, in the picture hanging on the wall of my childhood home, Aunt Eleanor's wall.

The lady who 'kidnapped' me here, is none other than the lady responsible for our mothers' deaths. Hera is none other than the High Priestess of their old coven.

This Bitch!

The pure rage that is taking over every cell in my body is unlike anything I have ever experienced. After twenty-four years of having my mother brutally taken from me, I am finally standing face to face with the woman responsible.

Yes, the king's men did the dirty work, but Hera set the event into action with her cowardice and false prophecies.

My eyes lock on Hera as I slowly rise to my feet. The king watches me closely with a furrowed brow, but it is the evil witch beside of him I cannot take my eyes from. There is fear in her eyes as she takes me in; she has known this entire time who I am, and from the look of pure hatred I have locked on her now, I think she realizes that I have finally figured out exactly who she is as well.

The woman who instigated our mothers' murders...

I swear, even if it results in me taking my last dying breath...I will see to it that this witch who killed our mothers will die by my hand.

I release a low deep maniacal laugh that surprises Killian and puts the king on edge.

"Seize her!", the king quickly commands Killian. I guess he was hoping I would just stay down and accept my fate at his hands.

Sorry asshole, not in this lifetime...

Killian unsheathes his sword and brings the blade before my face as he takes hold of my upper arm.

"Sorry about this, I'm just waiting for Cal and Dante to get into place before we make a stand." he informs me as he subtly strokes my arm with his thumb, sending a feeling of comfort down the bond.

"Where are my sisters? Are they safe?" I eagerly ask him. I've been dying to know ever since he showed up, but we haven't had the chance to talk given the shitshow he walked into.

"Yes, they are safe, the guys are watching over them." he tries to assure me.

"What!? You brought them here?! Why would you do that? Oh my god...", I scold as I begin freaking out. Why on earth would he bring them here?! What was he thinking?!

I rapidly look around the audience of Fae that has gathered around us in the courtyard, searching for two familiar faces. I can't spot them anywhere though, and I can't take my time looking around or the king will get suspicious. And the last thing I want is for him to know he has all three of us within his reach.

I do a double take though when my vision comes across a large, hooded figure with a pair of exotic captivating eyes that are locked directly on me. Not the king, nor the prince, or anyone else surrounding us for that matter...it appears that I am the sole focus of their attention and curiosity.

However, the intensity in which the stranger is staring me down is not what caught my attention. It is the unusual color of their eyes...

Deep golden amber, like that of a wolf's eyes, has locked me in their sight and captured my attention. Before I can get a good look at the hooded Fae these rare and mysterious eyes belong to, they disappear. Literally there one second and gone the next; somehow disappearing in the span of a single blink of an eye.

"Have you met your sisters? They were very insistent. It reminds me of someone else...", Killian chances a glance down at me as he jokes, trying to ease my stress that I know he can feel flowing through our bond.

But shit, I know he's right. I would never have stayed back in the Mortal Realm if the situation was reversed. I must stay focused though. My sisters are powerful enough to look after themselves when things go south, and they have the guys with them to help keep them safe.

However, before I confront the king's right-hand bitch...I mean witch, I need one more thing from Killian...

"Killian, promise me…if something happens to me get them to safety. Please!" I stare up at the side of his face, I know he can't turn and look at me, but I hope he can feel my eyes on him…pleading with him.

Before he can promise me anything, the king raises his voice so all gathered can hear. He has been quietly studying me for some time since I stood, I'm sure he was trying to decide on what he's going to do with me. And I guess he has finally come to a decision.

King Erebus narrows his dark eyes at me as a malicious grin pulls at his lips. I know what he is about to say before he even voices it. You don't even need to have years of experience working as a detective to read this evil man.

I can see Killian's body tense up next to me out of my peripheral. He too is well aware of what's about to happen.

Pulling his lips back into a snarl the king looks to Killian and sounds out the command for all to hear, "Kill the witch!"

CHAPTER 45
CALISTA

It's Show Time!

"Wait!" I demand, yelling at the top of my lungs. "The prince was correct! The prophecy you have let plague your mind with fear all these years is nothing, but a ruse devised by Hera herself to manipulate you into doing her dirty work for her..."

"How *dare* you slander my name! Your Majesty, you must not believe the lies this witch spills from her tongue. Please give me the honor of ending her life myself." she begs, moving closer as she waits for permission to strike me dead.

I step closer and Killian moves along with me, keeping his blade in place and his hold on my arm. I want to be staring this witch in the eyes when I call her out on her bullshit. I want to see the fear ripple over her skin as I expose her to her 'precious' king. I channel all the hatred shared between me and my sisters as I look into her bleak lifeless eyes. It's like she doesn't have a soul left underneath her fake skin to bring any light into her dark eyes.

"Just like you killed my mother and her two friends? Oh wait... that's right, you tricked the king into killing them for you so you wouldn't have to get any blood on your hands." I viciously state as I accuse her in front of everyone.

Hera's eyes fly open and for a second, I swear I can see Hellfire flaming from deep within them. She knows the gig is up and that I know exactly who she is and her dirty little secret she's kept hidden from the king for all these years.

Checkmate Bitch!

Before she can utter another sound from her disgusting mouth the king grabs her by the throat. "If she lies then why is the smell of your fear assaulting my senses?! Did you play me like a fool?" He shakes her ferociously and snarls, "Not only bringing me a false prophecy depicting my doom years ago, but also allowing my distress to drown my mind these past weeks, believing the prophecy could still come to pass?"

Hera's face is turning a darker shade of red as the king's grip tightens on her throat. Scrambling, she desperately pulls and scrapes her nails down the king's arm and the hand that's strangling her. She finally manages to make a sound that lets the king know she is unable to answer him if he doesn't allow her some air. Loosening his hold, but not entirely releasing her, Hera pathetically pleads for mercy as her voice trembles. "Y—Your Majesty, I was des-desperately in need of your help. Th—they were so close to uncovering our secrets...th—they would have destroyed me. I couldn't allow them to lock me away, left to slowly wither and rot for the rest of my life. I refused."

She sucks in another long breath of air and continues feeding us her excuses, while also damning herself in the process. That part I enjoy.

Oh hell, let's be honest I'm enjoying this entire groveling session. "Y—you were my only hope, Your M—Majesty...but you turned me away when I came to you for help. So, I created a false prophecy that linked the three witches I needed eliminated to your demise. I apologize Your Majesty for lying to force your hand, but you were never in any real danger, so I didn't see the harm in it."

Now it is King Erebus's turn to turn a bright red. From his tense muscles and the deadly daggers he is staring Hera down with right now, I feel like it wouldn't surprise me to be able to see his blood boiling underneath his skin if I got close enough.

Maybe I'll even get lucky, and this revelation will cause him to become so angry he keels over from a heart attack...or simply explodes into thin air.

Can Fae explode? Nah...?

Seeing the reaction the king is having to her confession, Hera continues trying to explain herself, but instead she's just digging herself into a deeper hole.

"When you recently contacted me thinking the prophecy was still in play; I quickly realized what you had felt was the link of the shared powers passed down from the mothers to their daughters. Their powers are born of the same blood...that is why you recognize the feel of their magic. But I swear to you, Your Majesty, I did *not* know back when you had the three witches slain, that they had heirs of their own. That was a complete surprise to me as well.

"The only reason I didn't reveal the truth to you when you contacted me weeks ago, was because I figured eliminating their daughters would be nothing but beneficial on our part. In case they too ever decided to start sticking their noses in places they don't belong, like their mothers did. Then after the daughters were disposed of you could be certain that the prophecy was void. There was really no harm intended.

"So, see I've always had your best interests in mind. Everything I did was to keep you and our business safe. Please, Your Majesty, forgive my foolishness...this will never happen again." Hera's bottom lip trembles as her begging comes to an end. Just like I'm certain her miserable life is about to.

"I l—love you, Erebus. Don't throw our life together away because of that conniving witch.", she whispers softly to the king before slinging an accusatory finger at me.

The king stares at her a moment longer, allowing a speck of hope to come to life in Hera's darkened eyes.

Then out of nowhere, roaring at the top of his lungs, the king throws Hera across the courtyard.

Her body slams into the side of the castle at full force before falling limply towards the ground. The gathered Fae turn to stare at Hera's broken body that now lays spread out on the ground, her limbs distorted in all different directions.

The king's rage is palpable as he approaches Hera's shattered form. "You dare deceive me and think your feeble excuses would save you?" His voice booms, echoing through the courtyard. The Fae, transfixed by the unfolding drama, watch in silence.

I haven't even wrapped my mind around the fact that the woman who implemented our mothers' murders, may just have been murdered herself, when the king turns his anger back on me. I'm not upset she's dead...just that I didn't get to kill her myself. That was a justice owed to me and my sisters, not this murder crazy king.

Even as the sound of the king's heavy footfalls move closer, I keep my eyes locked onto Hera's unmoving, supposedly dead, body. I won't believe it until I get an up close and personal look at her. Knowing my luck, she is like a cockroach and has like a thousand lives; she's just taking a second to recover before she rolls back over and scurries off.

My eyes finally fall upon the king as he stands before me and his son, he is seething with anger and betrayal. The air itself is thick with tension, as the Fae murmur among themselves, shocked by the revelation of Hera's deceit.

Pressing my luck I remind the king, "See, the other two witches and myself are of no threat to you, it was all a lie. You're welcome, by the way, for revealing Hera's evil scheme to you. Now, as thanks, if you could let Killian take me back to the Mortal Realm that would be awesome." Motioning between the king and myself I add like the smart ass I am, "We can call it even."

Some would say I must have a death wish. But I know no matter what changed between the king and Hera, he still isn't letting me leave here alive. So, I am going out being my stubborn sarcastic self.

Or maybe not?...

The King raises his brows like I just said something that piqued his interest...so maybe he is going to consider letting me go home?

The King moves closer to me, glancing over at Killian as he darkly inquires, "You want *Killian* to take you back to your Mortal Realm, you say?"

I scrunch my brow, not understanding why he is reiterating my request back to me. He doesn't seem angered he just seems smug and almost satisfied...like a spider who finally caught a fly in their sticky well placed web.

Taking in my confusion the King goes on to explain, "It just seems rather odd to me that you specifically requested Killian, because if I remember correctly, and I do, I never told you my son's name."

Oh Shit! Oh Shit! Oh Shit!

Did I really slip up?

This is bad...very bad.

The time for me to pull something out of my ass is now or never. "I heard some of your guests speaking his name when he arrived earlier, I just put two and two together..." I lie, holding the king's stare the entire time so hopefully he thinks I'm speaking the truth.

"Uh-huh" he mutters skeptically. "Well in that case my son or as you call him 'Killian' won't hesitate when I do this." He steps over placing himself toe to toe with his son. Furrowing his brow and raising his voice in command to Killian he demands, "Kill her!"

Doing exactly what the king expected him to do...

Killian hesitates...

A tense silence fills the air, the kind that precedes a looming storm. Killian and I stand tall, our resolve unyielding, our eyes locked on the King who has caused so much suffering throughout this entire kingdom. Not to mention, he is also responsible for the murder of mine and my sisters' mothers.

I can feel Killian's determination through our bond; it matches that of mine.

This day has come sooner than we had planned but tonight will be the night King Erebus meets his end.

I shriek, grabbing my head from a sharp pain that vanished as quickly as it arrived. Killian's voice unexpectedly slammed into my skull with such force it was physically painful.

"RUN!" Killian screams out before the king's shadows burst from his hands and slams directly into his chest, sending him flying backwards releasing a grunt of pain.

As soon as Killian's back hits the ground, Callum and Dante appear standing by his side, their swords gleaming in the dim light. Ready to fight.

Briefly distracted over Killian's wellbeing, the king takes this opportunity to strike, grabbing my arms, legs, and neck in whips of shadows, forcing me to bow on the ground before him.

Even in my precarious situation I smile smugly and goad the king on, hoping to give Killian a chance to recover and rejoin the fight. "If I remember correctly, and I do, this didn't work out so well for you the last time you tried this." His left eye ticks as his anger grows, and his shadows tighten.

King Erebus laughs dark and low, "Yes, but they weren't here to witness it before." He nods in the direction of the guys, but when I follow his stare, standing there now with worry drowning their features are Eve and Hazel. They still look pretty badass with swords strapped to their backs, armed and ready for battle. The damn bastard was baiting them out from the crowd. "Just as I thought, where you find one witch there will always be more... Better to show up late than not to show at all, isn't that right pets?" he mocks, raising his voice for my sisters to hear.

Killian rises and joins the other four. They march forward until they are standing directly behind me within arm's reach.

The King, with his usual arrogance, is uncaring, as he surveys the scene before him with a smug smile, unaware that his reign is about to crumble. His shadows continue to dance ominously around him, acting as a testament to his dark power.

I go to reach for my power to free myself from the king's shadows, but to my pleasant surprise, my powers are still freely flowing throughout my body. I no longer need time to dig deep and retrieve them, pulling them into action. They are already there and waiting for me. Ready to take action.

With a simple thought my powers shoot into action; light flares down each whip of shadows that is holding me captive. The king releases a hiss as the light eviscerates his shadows, almost like my light forced itself all the way into the internal source of the king's powers. As if, I didn't only destroy the shadows being created by his power, but his actual power in and of itself. The core functioning center that stores all of his power until it's needed. Once free, I rise to my feet and rejoin the others. Hugging my sisters tight and whispering in their ears, "If we make it out of here alive, I'm going to kill you for coming here." which puts a small smile on their faces.

For the first time I've seen tonight, doubt flickers in his eyes as he faces the combined might of the six of us who stand against him.

I step forward, ensuring my voice is resolute and clear. "This ends tonight," I declare, my words echoing throughout the courtyard. "For our mothers!" I step forward in solidarity with Eve and Hazel. This is a justice we have been thirsting for since we were young girls. And finally, after twenty-four years, our mothers will be avenged, and our thirsts will be quenched.

Following suit, Killian steps forward as he enthusiastically speaks on behalf of the Unseelie Kingdom. "King Erebus...*father*.", his words are filled with resentment. "For too long, you have brought nothing but pain and suffering to our kingdom. A once glorious kingdom revered by all, is now nothing but a kingdom filled with fear and disgrace. Tonight, we reclaim our freedom and bring the Unseelie Kingdom back to its former glory!" Killian thrust his fist high into the air in declaration, with Callum and Dante stepping up behind him, raising their fists in solidarity.

The courtyard becomes divided as some cheer and raise their fists along with their prince, while others stand there with their heads buried in the sand and their tails tucked between their legs. I'm willing to bet they are cheering silently on the inside, but too cowardly to risk ending up on the king's bad side on the chance that he comes out being the victor of this fight.

Which makes no sense because I'm pretty sure King Erebus only has a bad side...

The King laughs, a cold, hollow sound. Bringing the entire courtyard into complete silence. "You think you can defeat me?" he sneers. "I am immortal. I am invincible!"

"No!" I shake my head and flash him a mischievous grin. "You may be a bitch to kill, but I saw you bleed earlier. And if you can bleed—you can die..."

CHAPTER 46

CALISTA

The king pulls his lips back, baring his sharp fangs as he growls. The tendrils of shadows flowing around him darken and pulse with malevolent energy.

I swallow hard and gather my resolve. The final battle has come... the key to freeing us from our deals we made with both Cerberus and Killian. Yes, I would have loved more time to train and hone my powers, but this is the hand I've been dealt. And I'll be damned if I'm not going to put on my iron clad poker face and hit this tyrant with everything I have in my arsenal.

"Calista!" Callum calls, grabbing my attention as he tosses me my own sword.

I send out a battle cry as I summon the light and fire churning within me. My flames flare to life, sending a comforting blanket of warmth over my entire body.

Using both hands I throw two large balls of pure fire towards the king, but his shadows bat them away as if they were nothing more than pesky mosquitoes.

Well fire is a bust, but I know for certain darkness hates light. My light has defeated his shadows twice now, so fingers crossed for a third.

Killian steps in on my right, fighting his father with both shadows and steel. The sound of their swords clashing sends a shiver through me each time the metal meets. I must remind myself that my mate can take care of himself, and I need to focus on getting myself out of this situation alive and in one piece.

Plus, I feel the bond, and as long as I can feel that then I can remind myself he is still okay.

The king's guards join the battle, wielding their swords and powers. As I face off against one of the guards, I glance around for a split second to ensure my sisters are safe. Well, as safe as they can be amidst a battle.

That moment was all he needed to bring his sword down on my left shoulder, ripping through the thin fabric and creating a long gash that spans halfway down my arm. This isn't as bad as it could have been though...if I hadn't jumped back at the last second my head would be hanging off from my right shoulder.

I land a hard right kick to his left knee sending him leaning forward as I knock his sword off to the side with my own. Giving me the opportunity I need to reach forward and place my hand to his forehead. The poor soul looks at me with confusion until my powers seep in through his skin, setting him on fire internally in a matter of seconds. As I turn my attention back to the king the guard's body hits the ground, now as nothing more than a skin suit filled with goo.

I use my powers of light to counter the king's dark energy, illuminating the surroundings with a brilliant glow that pierces through the shadows. The king recoils, his fangs glinting menacingly as he hisses in defiance. With a determined step forward, I focus my energy, turning my usual sphere shape into a large beam. I'm hoping that I can use the beam to target the internal core of the king's darkness.

I take aim and send the beam slicing through the air, its radiant force clashes against the malevolent shadows that ripple around King Erebus. Upon impact the courtyard becomes bathed in light, and for a moment, it feels as though hope itself has taken physical form.

However, King Erebus is relentless. And we are exerting too much energy trying to hold off his guards long enough for us to focus our attacks on him.

He gathers the shadows around him, forming a dense cloak of impenetrable darkness. My beam falters, struggling to push through the thickening gloom. I grit my teeth, channeling every ounce of strength I possess into the light, refusing to let it diminish.

Around me, I can hear the cries of determination coming from my friends as they give their all to this battle. With a quick sweep of my head I take in the destruction that surrounds us. The courtyard has become a battlefield of wills, a clash of light and darkness.

I suddenly hear a cry of pain and instinctively glance over to see Eve clutching her thigh, blood has begun to seep through her fingers. My heart ceases to beat. The fact that I can't run to her and help shatters me...all I can do is pray that it didn't hit her femoral artery.

I begin repeating a new mantra in my mind:

My sisters will make it off this battlefield alive...

The king's growl deepens, grabbing my attention. It's a guttural sound that reverberates through the stone walls. He steps forward, his fangs gleaming like daggers in the flickering light.

It feels like all my powers are doing is agitating him; not causing him any real harm.

I prepare for another strike but am caught by surprise as Killian's shadows come from behind and wrap tightly around the king's throat. His eyes fly open, panic flashing within them, even if just for a second. Teaming up, I send out another beam of light, striking the king directly over his wicked black heart.

But before I can force my light any deeper a guard takes me by surprise, knocking my feet out from behind me, causing me to fall flat on my back.

Forced to focus on my new opponent, I raise my sword before my face just in time to block the sharp blood coated blade that is aiming straight for my head. But this guy is strong, and his filthy blade of death keeps getting closer to my face one millimeter at a time each passing second.

I hear a loud grunt as Dante appears, ramming his shoulder into the guard sending him falling several feet away. He reaches down to offer me a hand up and I gratefully accept.

"Thanks for saving my ass", I say breathlessly. Raking my gaze over his ripped shirt that is covered in blood. Whether it is his or our enemies I'm unsure, but the large gash running along the left side of his face is all his.

A sour pit builds up in my gut even when I think of this annoying Fae-hole getting fatally wounded during this battle.

Before I can ask him if he is alright, he pats me on the shoulder and runs off to his next target. He yells back at me encouragingly, "Keep at it, little witch!"

I would have never dreamed in a million years that Dante would be the one to give me my second wind, but here we are.

"Cerberus", I yell hoping he can lend us some aid. But after I finish getting another busted lip from a now deceased guard, I get the feeling he is not coming to help.

Coward!

Taking another unnecessary risk, I glance around in hopes of finding my sisters still holding their own and kicking ass.

I find them almost immediately and thank God they are safe and together. They also seem to have teamed up, working together in a tactic that is working rather well. Hazel seems to be demobilizing the guards using two methods; by getting into their minds, causing them to lose focus or grasp their heads in pain, or on some it seems she is using her telekinesis to lock on to their armor and hold them in place. Then Eve comes up and uses her powers to form long vines that curl around the soldiers completely immobilizing them.

Right as I go to look away Hazel's movement catches my eye, she too, has sustained an injury that is causing her to limp. But just like Eve, her face is etched with the determination to keep fighting despite the injury.

A feeling of pride fills my soul.

Wow! That's my girls!

The sight of my sisters wounded fuels my fury, and I push forward with renewed vigor.

Killian, Callum, and Dante are still locked in combat, their faces grim but resolute. Though they bear injuries of their own, they refuse to relent, their swords and powers striking with unwavering precision. Each clash of metal sends sparks flying, a testament to their relentless battle against the king's darkness.

A sense of satisfaction runs through me as I look over and find the king's injured; his blood is bathing the battlefield right along with ours. Bright red blood flows down his arm from a deep wound on his right bicep; I'm a little surprised his blood doesn't match the color of his soul...black. A trail of blood also runs down his chin from a slice along his cheek.

I charge him with my sword held high, the clash of my blade against his sending vibrations down all the way to my toes. It may have taken me ten years to put it to use, but I am so thankful to Killian for making me a solid badass with a sword when he trained me, and we fought together all those years ago. Maybe he knew a day like this would come?

The king's shadows form a fist in the air and punch the side of my head, causing me to lose my balance and fall backwards. I keep my footing and release a fireball directly at the hovering fist to buy me time to get creative. Focusing I bend my powers to imitate what I've created using my imagination...a sword...made of pure light. It's going to take more than steel to mortally wound this Fae and if it's the last thing I do on this field, I will snuff out his darkness with my light.

The king's gaze follows mine as I take in the mesmerizing sword I now hold in my hand. The light is so pure it's almost blinding to behold. The hilt appears like my tattoo; a viper is twining upward around it, but it doesn't stop at the pommel. No, the viper created from blinding light continues up, wrapping itself around my wrist and part way up my forearm. Making it appear as if the sword itself is an extension of my own arm.

I reengage, meeting the king blow for blow. Every shadow he sends my way I send out my fire to block the attack. He's better than me with a sword that's for sure, but I am managing to hold my own.

Until...

Midway through my strike the king vanishes before my eyes... This catches me off guard, giving the king the extra second he needs to reappear directly behind me with his sword already swinging down towards my neck. I spin around just in time to see his blade heading right for me. I attempt to jump back out of reach of the blade, but I'm not quick enough.

I scream out as his insanely sharp blade easily slices through my skin like it's slicing through butter. The blade caught my left side, sliding across my skin in a diagonal, gliding right below my left breast and stopping right above my belly button.

If I had hesitated to turn around one more second, I would be holding my intestines up with my hands right now...in other words, dead.

I drop down on one knee, placing my left hand over my wound. I can feel the warm blood flowing between my fingers. I am going to need stitches, but I should be fine...I have to be.

The king brings his blade that now drips with my own blood, down right for my head. That blade is so deadly it could and will split a skull right in two. I yell out, lifting my blade to block his attack. This movement sends blinding pain shooting down my left side.

Blocking his strike, I use all my strength to knock his sword off to the side, giving me the chance to even the playing field. I slam my own fist created by my flames directly into his gut, causing him to double over just like I hoped he would. Taking my sword of light I lunge forward off my knee and drive the magnificent blade through his right shoulder, causing him to release a pain filled scream that is music to my ears.

I don't even get a moment to cherish the pain I caused him. He whips out a wave of pulsing black shadows that slams into the center of my chest and sends me flying off across the courtyard.

My head hits the ground hard when I land, allowing darkness to seep into my vision as I lose consciousness.

I'm not sure how long I was out for when my eyes finally reopen, landing on Killian's battle worn face leaning over me.

"Cali! Thank the Gods...there you are. Hey, are you okay? Can you hear me baby?" He sighs in relief as he scoops me up into his arms. I groan in pain as I rub at the sore spot on my chest where his father's shadows hit me.

"Yeah...How long—"

"Not long, maybe five minutes. Cal and Dante are keeping my father busy. Your sisters are fine too...holding their own rather impressively." he assures me.

I nod, looking around. Losing hope with each passing second as I take in the scene. We are outnumbered and outmatched. The king is stronger than all of us...maybe if we could work together, but with all the guards stepping in our way that's impossible.

As soon as that thought leaves my head I look up; my eyes landing on a face I am ecstatic to see...Scarface!

"Raidus!" I shout, looking at him with a renewed sense of hope.

He must be here to help us, right?

Killian follows my gaze right as Raidus emerges from the crowd of onlookers. Fae are just standing around watching this shit show like that's exactly what all this is...just a show! Not even willing to lend us a hand to win this battle that we are fighting on behalf of their freedom.

Those Fae are tossed to the side as many more soldiers follow behind Raidus, ready to join him on the battlefield.

I just hope they are on our *side...*

The king takes notice of his soldiers' arrival, turning to them and commanding, "Kill them! Defend your king!"

Raidus lifts his blade as he roars out loud to get everyone's attention, bringing the fighting to a sudden halt, "You are not my king! Attack!" At his command Raidus and his fellow soldiers charge onto the field, clashing swords with their fellow Fae. He managed to bring around twenty men with him, and that is plenty to turn the tide on this small but critical battle.

CHAPTER 47

CALISTA

Raidus and his men have given us the relief we need to be able to focus our attacks onto the king.

Killian and I advance towards the king as the others peel away from their current opponents to join us. I wipe the right side of my head as I feel a tickling sensation, only to find blood smeared on my hand when I pull it away.

I thought it was sweat trickling down my face, but I guess I landed hard enough to cause a small cut in my hairline. Oh well...just add it to the list of my injuries sustained today.

As the six of us approach the king's laughter fills the air, mocking our efforts. He thinks he can break us, but he underestimates the strength of our bond.

I tighten my grip on my sword, channeling my light into a concentrated force. With a roar, I use my sword as a conduit to channel and release a beam of light, aiming straight for the heart of the shadows that thrives within the king.

This is it. The final showdown. As the king and I face off, it feels like the world itself is holding its breath, waiting for the moment when light will finally overcome the darkness that has haunted this kingdom for far too long.

My light is met by the king's darkness, barely stopping my attack from hitting its intended mark, the core where his darkness breeds and grows with every passing minute. It's not his heart...it's not an organ or inanimate object at all...it's more of a black hole that is a part of his soul itself. It's the area within ourselves where our powers lie dormant...the core that stores our powers. And earlier my powers of light felt it when they encountered his core center of darkness...even if just for a second.

That is what I am aiming for...

Looking to my right, I find Killian standing there staring in awe of me. On second glance, it's not just him but Callum, Dante, and my sisters are also looking at me like I'm the most extraordinary thing they have ever witnessed.

It's kind of unsettling because I'm not special. Plus, I would much rather them pick their jaws off the floor and get to helping me take down this royal asshole.

Taking charge, I yell out to Killian, "Don't hit him with your shadows, it will just feed into his, which will only benefit him. Use them to help restrain him."

Nodding in understanding, Killian sends ropes of his shadows slithering and eating up the distance between him and his father. They latch on to his hands and feet, pinning him in place. He tries to add one around his throat to help coerce him onto his knees, but the king keeps using his own shadows to tear at Killian's, ripping them away and freeing himself.

Callum and Dante are no match for the king's shadows as they try to get close enough to ram their blades through his chest. He sends out a leash of shadows that wraps around their ankles causing them to fall on their asses. Where they stay, desperately trying to get free from his shadows.

Even with all the distractions, the king's dark beam of shadows that is pressing back against my beam of bright shining light, pulses with even greater intensity. Threatening to overwhelm my efforts at sustaining a strong beam of light. But I stand firm in my defiance against this tyrant and his encroaching darkness.

Callum and Dante break free of their shadow restraints and despite their wounds, they push forward. Their determination and loyalty are unwavering.

Killian continues to fight and restrain his father using his own shadows. The hate and rage he feels towards his father is written all over his face. It's like every strike of his shadows carries the anger and pain that he felt each time his father wronged him and his kingdom.

My arms are starting to feel weak as they feed my power into my sword.

In my exhaustion I lean my head back to release some of the pressure building up in my neck...that's when I see it. Just barely.

A glimmer of steel from a spinning dagger catches my eye. A dagger that is heading directly for Killian who is completely unaware...given his attention is focused elsewhere at the moment.

I could scream out in warning, but it still wouldn't be quick enough to get him out of its deadly path, as it's aimed directly at his heart.

I panic at the thought of my mate being in danger and the possibility of losing him. Emotions flood my system...I honestly can't even think straight. All I know is I cannot let harm come to my mate, but I also cannot release my weakening hold on the beam of light, which may be our only salvation.

As the dagger crosses the invisible threshold of no return my mind suddenly clicks off...instinct taking over.

I let out an ear-piercing scream, "NO!", my voice carrying over the entire courtyard. At that same moment, I release my left hand from the hilt of my sword and swing it towards Killian. I feel a slight chill runs down my arm all the way to my fingertips, and that's when it happens...

A wall of shimmering shadows forms directly in front of Killian right as the dagger hits it and falls to the ground. Killian whips his head around and looks at me in shock. I guess my shadow powers, presumably from the moon goddess, finally decided to make their debut.

I stare back at him for a moment, just as shocked as him before I turn my attention back to my light and the king. Maybe it's just exhaustion but I think the king is looking concerned now that he knows I have the powers of fire, light, and shadows.

The king releases a loud growl that turns into a snarl, his frustration is evident now that he has witnessed the powers I possess. He gathers the shadows tighter and presses harder against my light. I gasp out loud, before I take a deep breath and push my own power harder.

Right when doubt starts to creep into my mind, I feel not one but two smooth hands, one on each of my arms. Glancing around I see Eve and Hazel have come to my aid, joining together just like the *fake* prophecy predicted, to take this king down.

Maybe it wasn't completely made up after all? Or the universe is just helping us to manifest this event?

"This may hurt a bit..." Eve whispers in my ear, dragging a small knife along my forearm before I even have the chance to ask her what she means by that. It stings only for a moment. She then takes the knife and makes a small cut on her palm. Passing the knife over to Hazel she does the same thing, placing a small cut on my arm and then her own palm.

Before I can ask them what they are planning on doing they place their blood-filled palms against the cuts on my arms that are now raining droplets of blood onto the ground.

As soon as their blood touches mine I feel a rush of power enter my body. That power begins swirling around and combining to form an incredibly strong and dangerous storm.

I gasp aloud along with Eve and Hazel...they must be feeling our powers combining as well. I can't help the smile that graces my lips as I think to myself how incredible and brave my sisters are. Here they are injured as well, and yet they still step up and lend me their powers to join me in my efforts to eliminate the king.

His shadows tremble, wavering under the assault of our combined efforts. Eve and I send our powers down through our connection, giving Hazel the edge she needs to break through the king's mental shields. Once she does, she grabs hold of his mind with hers and squeezes; like she is trying to squash a grape.

The king begins screaming out in what sounds like unimaginable pain. His shadows falter more as he struggles to focus through the agony.

Next up, Hazel and I pass our powers to Eve. I hear her take in a sudden breath as our power reaches her. She was ready to strike as soon as our powers linked together with hers. Vines rapidly grow as if from thin air and shoot up from the ground, wrapping tightly around the king's ankles and wrists, anchoring deep underground securing the king in place.

With Hazel wreaking destruction on his mind, the king appears to be losing full control over the darkness that resides inside of him. His shadows try to break apart Eve's vines that are keeping him captive, but he is unable to give them the strength they need to do so, while also holding back my beam of light.

This is it. This is our moment, our chance to bring an end to King Erebus's reign of terror and avenge our mothers, and our childhood... all the love and experiences this man stole from us when he selfishly removed them from our lives.

With one final, desperate push, we unleash everything we have left inside of ourselves. My sisters' powers flood into my system, giving me the strength, power, and support I need to end this fight. The feeling of this storm I have brewing inside that's created from all three of our powers uniting is euphoric.

When I release the storm, it strikes as fast as lightning, shooting away from my body, and racing through my extended arms and into my sword of light. Leaving a burning sensation in its trail.

As the power merges into my sword the beam of light explodes, becoming larger, brighter, and more powerful than ever before.

Everyone around drops their blades and stops what they are doing to place their hands up to shield their eyes from the dazzling light. It doesn't affect me nor my sisters since it is my own power and our powers are linked at this moment.

We watch on as the beam of light presses the beam of shadows back, until there is so little space between our light and the king's hand, I can see smoke rising from the burning skin of his palm. Not only is this light bright, but it is also scorching hot.

In a desperate move the king creates a wall of cloudy shadows that surrounds him; they aren't even as dark anymore...I think they are finally losing their strength.

His wall of shadows doesn't stand a chance against my light as we watch it pierce through the darkness of his cloudy shadows, shattering them into fragments that dissipate into the air itself.

Shutting my eyes I give my light one final boost, sending it deep within the king's body. Focusing on allowing my light to search out that core of darkness that's harbored within the king himself. Once my light makes contact, I can feel the darkness pressing back in defiance.

The king roars out in pain as my light devours every ounce of darkness residing under his flesh, deep within his very soul. The king's roar turns into a cry of anguish as he staggers back, his power diminishing right before his very eyes.

As his shadows finally flicker out, he collapses to the ground, cursing out in anger and pain. He knows that not only has he been defeated, but with my light devouring his powers he is now practically human.

Mortal and easily killed.

My body goes slack as I fall to the ground, my sisters on either side of me taking hold under each arm and lifting me back up. I'm fine, I just need a quick breather after exerting all that energy and power.

Energy and power I could have never scrounged up all on my own. If it wasn't for Eve and Hazel stepping in to combine and share powers, I don't know what would have become of us. I will have to ask them how they came up with the idea, and if they even knew it would actually work.

Letting me use them as a crutch, we follow behind Killian and the boys as we slowly approach the king.

Looking down at his father in anger, pity, and disgust Killian drives home the metaphorical knife, "You lose asshole. This —"

Killian is cut off by the king's maniacal laugh. The insinuation within the king's laugh has us all taking pause and sharing concerned glances.

The king sneers up at Killian, his voice dripping with self-righteousness and loathing as he proclaims, "You can't kill me *boy*! If I die, Stellaris will soon befall the same fate. Dooming all of those living within the realm to succumb to a most gruesome demise."

This information seems to give Killian pause which does not go unnoticed by the king. His lips pull back into a devious smile, "You don't want to have your traitorous hands stained with the blood of an entire realm...do you now, *son*?"

The way the king continues to speak towards Killian, his own son, sets my anger ablaze. And the fact that Killian is still standing there before his father, letting him continue to draw breath as he contemplates the validity of his words, isn't doing anything to calm my rising temper.

The longer he hesitates to eliminate the king, the king's appearance becomes smug and self-satisfied. He knows he is extorting his son's empathy and love he has for not only this kingdom but all Stellaris. All in hopes that Killian will show him mercy and thus save himself from death, and having his soul sent into The Flaming Hollows to suffer for all of eternity.

I, for one though, have heard enough of his bullshit. Especially with how he is so demeaning to Killian.

Not waiting a second longer, I make my way to Killian's side. Taking hold of Dante's sword and pulling it free from its scabbard where it hangs from his hip along the way.

Killian's eyes meet mine, going wide with surprise as he sees me approach. However, with my mind made up I lock eyes with my target and continue forward to carry out my mission. Which if successful will also break my sisters and I free from our bargains with both Cerberus and Killian.

King Erebus glares at me in contempt as I continue towards him. Shooting quick glances up at his son in hopes that he will put a stop to my advancing. Thankfully, Killian does no such thing.

Once I'm standing at Killian's side looking down upon his tyrant of a king and father, the king begins to yell. King Erebus's face turns red as he fumes and shouts at me angrily, spittle flying from his lips. "You stupid girl! You kill me and you damn the entire realm!", he screams out at the top of his lungs.

Staring down at him I show him no more concern than I would for a disgusting cockroach. In one smooth motion I step forward and thrust the sword through the center of his chest, and hopefully through his empty black heart.

Leaning down with a cocky smile, I look him directly in his dying eyes and state matter-of-factly, "We'll take our chances".

His eyes fly open with shock and fear, as I stand there and watch as the life drains from his eyes. A small smile graces my lips at the thought of his soul never finding peace in the afterlife. Instead, his soul will be burned and shredded apart again and again in The Flaming Hollows.

That is the justice our mothers deserve.

CHAPTER 48

KILLIAN

I'll be damned. She pulled it off...she really did it.

I never thought this day would come. Let alone, that three untrained half-witch/half-Fae...or whatever they're called, would be the reason this day was even possible.

Thanks to the three of them and their bravery and love for one another, the prayers of the Unseelie Kingdom have now been answered.

I was uncertain of how I would feel once my father met his demise. I often wondered if I would feel any type of remorse or regret, but as I watched the light go out in his eyes and listened as he took his last breath, I felt...free. Relieved, happy, and free! It was like a leash had been released from around my throat and I could finally take in a full breath of fresh air.

With King Erebus out of the way, I can now rise to the throne and bring peace to this kingdom. Take charge and lead our lands and people back to the prosperous and respectable ways of the past.

My reign will be the beginning of a new era for the Unseelie Kingdom. I will work to assure that my father's nightmarish reign is a thing of the past, leading my kingdom into a more benevolent future that will always be remembered.

And myself and my kingdom owe it all to the three small, yet fierce, women standing before me. One, with her dark shimmering hair and her emerald green and golden flecked eyes, that have a way of staring at me as if they can see into my very soul.

CHAPTER 49

CALISTA

My feet leave the ground as Callum and Dante take turns spinning me around in celebration. Eve and Hazel are hysterically punching at them to let me go so they can have their turn celebrating with me.

The joyous, stress-free laughter coming from my own mouth seems almost foreign to me after all these weeks of not knowing if my sisters and I would ever make it out of our deals with Cerberus and Killian alive. But now the evil king is dead, and we are finally free!

Even in our celebration I look over to steal glances of Killian who seems to be watching us with a look of awe and contentment on his face. I'm happy to see that, because a part of me was worried that in the end after it was done, he would come to resent me for killing his father. Even if he was an evil bastard.

When my sisters follow Callum and Dante to share in the celebration and give thanks to all the soldiers who stepped in to help us, I'm left standing there staring over at my other half...my mate.

Killian walks towards me wearing a schoolboy grin that sends my heart fluttering. Even bruised and bleeding from battle he still looks impossibly handsome. The grin is just like the cherry on top.

"You did it, Viper." Killian proudly congratulates as he steps up to me. Standing so close that I am forced to lift my head back just to be able to look him in those dark star-filled eyes.

"*We* did it, Rose." I correct as I stare up at him with a foolish schoolgirl smile slapped across my face.

He raises an eyebrow, surprised, and teases, "Are you really sharing your glory with me? Where is the stubborn, confident, but undeniably beautiful woman I fell in love with?"

Taken back by his playful remark I place my hands against his chest and try to push him away. But he's fast and has his arm wrapping around my waist and pulling me flush against him, causing me to release an excited gasp. He places his free hand along my cheek and gently strokes the bruise that has already appeared on my skin. I'm sure my face looks worse for wear given his look of concern and sadness I'm seeing.

Slowly I feel a tingling sensation flowing through me, targeting the injuries I've sustained from this fight.

He's healing me.

Gently he lifts my chin up to look me in the eyes. The conflicting look he's giving me is breaking my heart. I'm sure he is blaming himself for each and every injury his magic finds and heals, but none of this was his fault. We knew this day was coming...we just hoped we had more time to prepare. But all in all, everything worked out in the end.

Maybe I can have my Happily-Ever-After, after all.

"I love you, Calista", Killian declares lovingly as he leans down and gently places his lips on mine.

This kiss is soft and sweet. Filled with love, passion, and desire. It speaks all the words of affirmation we long to say to one another in this moment.

I want to bottle this feeling inside my heart to keep it with me forever.

When he finally pulls away, he leaves his forehead pressed against mine. Closing his eyes he whispers in a tone I can't quite make out, "I'm sorry...so fucking sorry, Cali."

I begin shaking my head but right before I can tell him none of this was his fault I hear Eve cry out, "She's gone!"

Both mine and Killian's head snap up in search of what Eve is freaking out about. When my gaze follows hers and lands on the spot where Hera's lifeless body had been laying before the battle began, my stomach drops.

Blinking and glancing around to make sure what I'm seeing is correct, dread begins to fill me up as I realize that Hera's body is in fact gone.

No....

Is she still alive?!

There is no way she just got up and walked it off.

Damn Cockroach!

My mind is spinning and the only thing keeping me anchored to reality is the feel of Killian's strong arms wrapped around me.

Until suddenly, they're not and he's pulling away from me.

I look over to see what has grabbed his attention.

When I do an uncomfortable chill runs down my spine as I notice his eyes are still glued on me. His attention is focused solely on me...

The ground itself buckles beneath my feet and sends me plunging headfirst into the abyss when Killian looks to the guards and gives his first order as the new king, "Guards! Seize the three witches!"

I'm rendered speechless momentarily as I just stand there staring at Killian with betrayal.

How could he do this to me? To his own mate?!

I can't believe this is happening. And what's worse is that I let it happen! I heard him and the guys talking about betraying us, and yet I still feel for his bullshit 'promise' that he would never hurt me or my sisters.

This is entirely my own stupid fault. I can't believe I trusted him!

Several of the guards corral me and my sisters into a circle before their soon to be *new king*. Swords facing us and at the ready to skew us alive without question if we try to escape.

If stares could kill, Killian would be dead right now. My voice sounds broken as I hold his gaze and demand to know, "Why?! Why are you doing this?! You promised me..." My last words come out more like a whisper as my voice breaks, but I know he can hear it with his ridiculous Fae hearing.

I try to keep calm as I wait for him to answer me by relishing in the distress that's plaguing his features. This decision he has made seems to be hurting him as well, but it's not even close to how deep my pain runs.

I notice Callum, Dante, Raidus, and most of the guards that fought alongside us in the battle are looking at Killian confused. I guess he didn't tell them this part of the plan.

Then it hits me...he wasn't concerned or blaming himself for my injuries. No, he was distraught because he had made the decision to betray me. And he knew that once he did, he would lose me forever.

The kiss we shared was not a Happily-Ever-After kiss; it was a farewell. This is the second time our story has ended before it even began, with no chance of a happy ending. Only heartbreak.

"I've been waiting and preparing my whole life to take my father's place upon the throne. I can't let you get in the way of that. I don't expect you to understand this decision, but maybe over time you will, and maybe one day you will even come to forgive me..." Killian responds loudly, so he can be heard throughout the courtyard. Already sounding like a king.

"Take them to the dungeons to be delt with later." he commands his guards. His eyes are drowning with remorse, but I can tell by his straight posture and clinched jaw, that he is going to stand by his decision.

I thrash and pull, trying to free myself from the guards holding each of my arms. Like he said earlier, I'm stubborn and I do not plan on making this easy for them.

It's almost laughable at how there are eight guards trying to wrangle my sisters and me. I guess they aren't taking any chances after seeing the powers we can possess and wield. If only they knew that we are completely exhausted and tapped out. I don't think I could even light a candle if my life depended on it.

Digging my feet into the grass, I fight with all my might to pull away from my captors. I cry out to Killian as I whip my head back to look at him, "I don't want your throne! Just let us go back home. We held up our end of the bargain now let us go, *please* Killian."

I can see the hurt flash through his eyes; I'm sure my eyes are reflecting the very same thing.

He looks away shaking his head. He's not even going to address my pleas. *Asshole*. I can't believe the Gods chose this man to be my mate.

Since he refuses to acknowledge the option of sending us back home, I'm going to try another route to gain his attention.

"I am the Queen of Stellaris!" I shout with determination. "The lost heir that has finally returned home! So, I demand that you show me the respect I deserve!" My voice echoes through the courtyard, causing a ripple of murmurs amongst the spectators.

Killian's expression hardens, but a flicker of concern flashes across his face. "Enough!" he barks, his frustration quickly turning to anger. "You are no queen here. Take them away!"

As the guards drag us towards the dungeons, I feel the weight of our failure pressing down on me. Yet, amidst the despair, a spark of defiance ignites within. The prophecy about the heir and the tree with golden leaves begins to haunt my thoughts, giving me one last angle to try here.

"The tree!" I shout, looking around in hopes that my outburst has gathered everyone's attention. "The tree with the golden leaves. 'Crying tears of gold when the true heir returns home.' It did! When I placed my hand against the tree, golden liquid began to run down its trunk. If you don't believe me, go look for yourselves. There is a mote of golden liquid circling the base of the tree at this very moment".

By the time I finish speaking I am short of breath from struggling against my guards.

Killian steps forward to silence everyone's racing thoughts and fast-moving lips that are questioning if I could really be the lost heir of Stellaris.

"Quiet!" Killian roars out to silence the crowd. "Even if the tree is crying gold like you say, how do we know it was really you who caused it to happen? What proof do you have?" he asks as he prowls closer to me, making sure I alone am able to see the devious smirk on his face.

He knows he has me backed into a corner with no way out. He was the only one with me when it happened, and of course he isn't going to admit to witnessing it.

Even knowing I've already lost, I sternly accuse him of being there with me when it happened. His denial comes as no surprise and his court is having themselves a good laugh over my crazy accusation.

Reluctantly I accept defeat. I hang my head and unroot my feet from the ground so the guards can carry me away. But not before I look back at him one last time and shake my head disappointedly; trying to project the pain and sadness I feel onto him from my stare alone.

However, the mask he now wears is one of complete uncaring. It's like I'm staring at a stranger. Not someone I gave my heart and soul to...not my mate.

CHAPTER 50

KILLIAN

As I watch her and her sisters being led away towards the dungeons, my knees threaten to buckle from the stabbing pain destroying my heart. But I can't let them see me crack, I'm to be their new king, and I must stand strongly behind my decision even if it destroys a part of myself, I feel I may never get back.

Hell, I honestly hadn't planned on betraying her...them. But watching everyone celebrating the king's death, and the way everyone seemed to be drawn towards her, praising and accepting her into their ranks forced my hand.

I foolishly let myself fall in love with the stubborn little witch. Unfortunately, she ended up being so much more than just a witch, and that is why I can't keep her around. If my people discover the truth of her lineage there could be a rebellion. And I will not allow anything to threaten my claim to the throne. Even her...even love.

I hear Dante and Callum approaching as I stand there watching her being led away with her head hanging low. I hate that I'm the reason she has lost that fire inside of her...that fight I know she has.

"Are you sure about this?" Callum asks hesitantly.

"You could just send them back? That's what they want anyways." Dante offers as he too watches them leave.

It appears that these three little witches have left big impacts on all three of us.

Removing my gaze from her sends another pain shooting through my chest as I face the guys. Hoping my voice doesn't reveal how unsure I'm feeling on the inside I nod and slowly say, "I'm sure. Their stay in the dungeons will only be temporary, but for now I need Calista out of the way while also knowing where she is at all times. The truth about her cannot come out. Am I clear?"

Both nod in agreement even as I catch a glimpse of regret in their eyes.

Great, all I need is to turn the guys against me during this crucial time at the start of my reign.

Even though the death of the king, my father, would normally be cause for a celebration, I don't think I have it in me tonight. We can celebrate it at my coronation, which I plan on happening in the next couple of days. There will be no mourning period for the former king...only celebration.

"Inform the guards to clear out the courtyard. The show's over and we need to discuss next—", I'm cut off from the sudden commotion coming from the direction the guards were taking the girls.

Looking over I find the guards that were overseeing the girls laid out on the ground unconscious. However, my concern is locked onto the cause of this commotion. Three large, hooded male figures, stand before me blocking my view of Calista...and her sisters.

Drawing my sword, I advance on the intruders with Callum and Dante following suit on either side of me. The males are wearing hoods over their heads, making it hard for me to determine exactly who they are, and the possible reasoning behind their unexpected and uninvited presence.

The fur lining the top of their boots and the neckline of their jackets, along with the thick gloves they wear, insinuates they come from somewhere with a much colder climate. This observation alone, not to mention their physical attributes, has the hair on the back of my neck rising in warning of the imminent danger these strangers pose.

There is only one place in Stellaris that stays cold enough to wear fur at this time of year. A place withheld from the clutches of both the moon and sun. A place suspended between the darkness of night and the light of day. A place birthed in death and blood.

I pray to all the Gods that may still be out there taking mercy upon our realm that I'm mistaken, but if I'm not then this could only be messengers of King Gideon...fearful ruler of the Bloodlands.

CHAPTER 51

CALISTA

It all happened so fast.

One moment I'm being restrained and led away to rot in the castle dungeons, when suddenly a gust of wind blows through my hair. Then the next thing I know, I am on the ground kneeling alongside my sisters staring up at the backsides of three large intimidating figures standing before us.

Looking around I find that all the guards who were manhandling us and leading us to our doom only seconds ago, are now lying upon the ground around the three of us, unconscious.

At least I don't think they're dead...

My sisters and I stay on our knees, huddling together closely behind our saviors that seem to be purposefully placing themselves between us and Killian.

Shit, at least I hope these men are heroes...we were three damsels in distress, and they rescued us from our captors.

With that thought fresh in my mind my gut suddenly begins to sour, and nausea builds up at the base of my throat. Maybe it's just a coincidence...I was forced to eat lunch earlier at one of those weird tofu places with Seb and Ortega, thanks to Seb's insufferable insistence that I join them, of course.

Peeking out from behind one of the hooded figures, I see Killian advancing in our direction. And damn he looks pissed...I wouldn't want to be on the receiving side of that stare.

Just when I think he is about to raise his sword and swing it at our protectors' neck he comes to a sudden stop.

He just stops dead in his tracks. Almost like he ran into an invisible barrier about three yards out from us.

And I'll be damned...

Did I just see fear written across his face for a quick second? There's no way...Killian wouldn't back down from a confrontation.

Unless there really is reason to be fearful of the three hooded strangers we thought had maybe come to rescue us from being locked inside the dungeon. If Killian's body language is any inclination, then maybe we should reconsider staying here and taking our chances in the dungeons.

I'm sure with my sisters by my side, our dungeon cell will transform into a 'homey' feeling before we know it.

"You're lucky I'm not the 'kill first, ask questions later' type of king. State your name and the reason behind this unwelcomed intrusion." Killian snarls out in demand as he stands before the hooded figures.

Even though I would rather sell my soul to the devil than count on him to keep me and my sisters safe, I keep my eyes locked on him. Watching for any tells of his that might provide me with some insight into what exactly is going on, and if my sisters and I are still in danger...now even more so than before.

While doing so I can't help but notice that his gaze keeps falling on me. It keeps giving me this nagging feeling that a part of him may care about me and my safety, but I now know for certain that is absolute bullshit.

The stranger standing directly in front of me takes a step forward before stating his introduction loud enough for the entire courtyard to hear. "We have been sent on behalf of His Majesty, King Gideon, all mighty ruler of the Bloodlands. We have come to collect something of *immense* importance to His Majesty." He drawls out intimidatingly, showing zero fear of Killian or his surrounding court.

Killian meets my gaze as he starts to speak. "Pray tell, what is it exactly that King Gideon believes he has a rightful claim to here within *my* kingdom?" Killian demands aggressively. "I can't imagine anything, seeing as how your *kind* has been banned from stepping foot in Unseelie lands for centuries."

"Your kind?", I address this question directly into Killian's mind using the bond that still unites us as one, even after his unforgivable betrayal.

"These creatures are deadly Cali and not to be trusted." he quickly responds.

"Oh, so you mean they are exactly like you...powerful and full of shit. Great!" I retort sarcastically, not missing the opportunity to throw out a verbal jab even given the seriousness of the situation at hand.

Killian flinches at my words, *"Cali, I—"*

The hooded male cuts Killian off unknowingly before he can finish whatever he was about to say to me. He nods behind himself where I am now kneeling on the ground with my sisters. The three of us quickly whip our heads around in search of someone or something of importance behind us, but all we see are a bunch of Fae standing around. Still getting their kicks by watching the free shit show taking place right before their eyes.

Confusion, fear, and realization hit me all at once, before the words have even left the stranger's mouth. "The woman."

Son-of-a—

Why would another king be interested in us? Is there another fake prophecy floating around about us?

Hold on a second...he didn't say 'women' he said 'woman', as in singular.

The hooded stranger slightly turns around to face us, but only long enough to lock eyes with me and wink. He winked at me...

I guess that answers the question as to which 'woman' he was referring to.

Shit!

"No chance in Hell! Tell your king he's going to have to find himself a different woman to suck dry." Killian's sudden outburst startles me, causing me to jump out of my skin. He must have come to the same conclusion about which 'woman' the king has his sight on.

Suck. Dry?!

"*Killian...?*" I implore shamelessly. I wishfully pray that he will give me some clarity as to what the hell is going on.

Killian releases a dark, slow, threatening growl as he proclaims for all to hear, "She's *mine!*"

Just the sound of his voice and the possessiveness of it has my stupid heart shivering with every single beat. I may hate him, but it appears my body has not received the memo yet.

The hooded male barks out a laugh, dismissing Killian's threat as nothing more than a mere suggestion. Reaching into the pocket of his jacket, he pulls out a piece of parchment that has been rolled up tightly and held together by a ribbon. He quickly tosses the rolled-up paper to Killian, who seamlessly catches it.

As Killian's eyes roam over the words written on the piece of paper his brow furrows deeper and his jaw ticks in anger. Red is even beginning to tint his cheeks the further down he reads.

Finally, with shaking hands he crumbles the paper in his fist and throws it to the ground. Stomping and grinding it into the earth for good measure.

"This is complete lunacy! He cannot have her!", he roars out, losing the facade of his calm demeanor. Killian is seething with rage from whatever was written on that piece of paper.

"*What's happening, Killian?*" I ask impatiently, not even attempting to mask the fear in my voice.

But he doesn't get a chance to answer before the stranger whips around and lifts me up by my arm. I can't help but wince in pain from the strength of his hold.

My sisters jump up to come to my aid, but they are swiftly restrained by the other two strangers.

"Now that you have read over the agreement, you can plainly see the binding signatures of both His Majesty, King Gideon and the woman's father. She now belongs to the king and will be returning with us to the Bloodlands."

I begin struggling to break his hold on my arm, but my effort is futile because he is way too strong. "Pardon me asshole, but I don't belong to anyone!", I drive my point home by stomping on his foot as hard as I possibly can. But it's to no avail, he just laughs at my pathetic attempt to free myself.

Still laughing, he turns to joke with his two companions. "I think the king is going to like this one...she's feisty."

Why does it seem like all men are attracted to a woman who fights back and doesn't take their shit?

I pull my lips back and snarl as I continue to fight against his hold.

Killian attempts to come to my aid, but Callum and Dante restrain him from helping me.

"He cannot have her! She is mine! My mate! Get your hands off her!" Killian goes berserk, yelling and fighting against the guys' hold on him, even as my savior turned captor lifts me up and tosses me over his shoulder to walk away.

"Killian, let her go! There's nothing you can do for now. Killing them or keeping her will incite a war." Callum tries his best to make him see reason, but he still fights relentlessly against their hold on him.

His powers must be tapped out too, otherwise he could easily break free from their hold.

"Listen to him, Kill! Cal's right, we can't do anything right now. We will figure out a way to get her back but for now it's over. She is no longer yours to keep." Dante's words seem to break through to him. He looks so broken as he falls to his knees, the guys are keeping him in a restraining hold just to be safe.

As I'm carried away his eyes stay locked onto mine. Blinking be damned.

My captor tosses one last threat over his shoulder before he shoots us off with super speed, way faster than the Fae I have come to know these last few weeks. "Remember *Your Majesty*, she belongs to him now. Any defiance on your part will be considered a call to war."

As all the blood begins to rush into my skull, Killian's voice is the last thing I hear before blackness creeps into my vision, and I allow myself to slip into the darkness.

"I'll fix this Cali...I'll fucking fix this!"

CHAPTER 52

CALISTA

My eyes slowly blink open as I am roughly shaken awake by strong hands. My mind quickly begins replaying everything that has happened over the last couple of hours.

Shivers race over my body from the freezing air surrounding me. I glance down and see that someone has placed a blanket over me to fight against the cold air. The cold air that I am now realizing is coming from the snow filled forest I find myself in.

Where the hell did all this snow come from?

Then it clicks, everything comes rushing back into my brain.

I'm no longer in the Unseelie Kingdom...I'm being taken against my will to some other tyrant king who thinks they can just take anything they want without any repercussions.

Well tough shit, because I plan on making this man's life a living hell for thinking he can just suddenly 'own' me.

And seeing as how I'm now surrounded by a Winter Wonderland I think it's safe to assume that I have been asleep for way longer than a couple of hours.

How long was I out for?

Just as I gather my thoughts, my captor abruptly interrupts my mental peace.

"Time to wake up, pretty princess...welcome to your new home." he taunts, knowing damn well I do not want to be here.

But whoa!

A humongous archaic castle stands ahead of us, standing tall above the wintery landscape that surrounds it. I count five circular spires accenting each wing that extends out from the castle and then one taller one in the very center. The architecture of this castle is stunning. It's like something straight out of a fairytale...except a villain resides inside, not a sweet animal loving princess.

As we come to a stop at the entrance to the castle, my breath catches in my throat. My mouth suddenly feels like I haven't had anything to drink in days, so dry it feels almost impossible to open my mouth to speak. My heart is rapidly pounding inside my chest, making it even harder for me to breathe.

There must be a logical way out of this predicament. Something I can offer the king in return for my freedom; another bargain I will most likely regret making in the long haul. But right now, I will agree to almost anything if it allows my sisters and me to return to our normal lives in the Mortal Realm.

Almost anything...

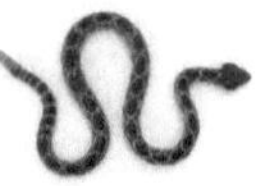

The intricate designs covering almost every inch of the enormous doors I'm standing before are unbelievable. I could spend an entire day just taking in the beauty of the carvings in the wood, tracing my fingers along the dips and swirls of every line.

But for now, that must wait...because behind these doors my future will be revealed in the shape of a man, a king. He will either show mercy and agree to let me and my sisters go free, or I will remain trapped here for whatever reason he saw fit to sign a binding agreement with my *father* to give him 'ownership' over me.

Who in the hell is my father? And in what realm does he have any say over anything concerning my life. The life he has never cared to involve himself in until now! *How convenient...*

Well on a positive note maybe behind these double doors is the answer to who my father is.

And if I do find out who he is...who dared to sell me off to some arrogant king...I will hunt him down if it's the last thing I ever do, and stare into his eyes as he bleeds out all over the floor, realizing the child he never cared about is the cause of his demise...

After what feels like an eternity the doors swing open, revealing a masculine yet gorgeous throne room.

A huge breath-taking throne, constructed from some type of black shimmering stone sits dead center at the end of the aisle. The arms of the throne end in sharp claws that curve down the front.

This detailed accent makes the entire throne 'scream' predator, which is fitting giving the predator sitting upon it.

I gasp at my first sight of him...at those eyes. They are like two golden pools of honey boring a hole directly into my very being.

Those eyes...

I feel like those eyes have haunted me in my dreams...watching me...waiting...

He was there today, before the battle broke out. I could recognize those eyes out of any lineup. They locked onto mine for the briefest of seconds as I stood before King Erebus today. But he didn't fight in the battle...no, I would have spotted those eyes.

Why didn't he just wait until the battle was over and claim me himself if I was still alive?

I steel my spine and hold my head high as I walk into my own personal purgatory. As much as I would love to fight against my captors' hold, there is one on each of my arms, I refrain. I fear their grip on me is the only thing keeping me up right now, because my knees are quivering like they're experiencing their own personal earthquakes.

My captors bring me to a stop once we reach the base of the dais the throne sits upon. At first, a trinkle of dread creeps down my spine at the thought of having to walk up the steps to where the king now sits upon his throne. Staring down at me as if I'm nothing more than the scum beneath his feet.

King Gideon, ruler of the Bloodlands...blah, blah, blah. He is insanely gorgeous. He has an ethereal beauty about him that rivals Killian. But handsome or not, he will not look at me with such disrespect.

No matter the fact that it seems physically impossible for me to pull my roaming gaze away from his amber eyes. They lured me in and now I find myself stuck in the golden honey. His dark brown hair is the richest, deepest color of brown I've ever seen. It magnifies the draw into his golden eyes, making them 'pop'. The contrast between the light and dark is stunning.

His face is a picture of perfection; carved straight from a statue of Hercules himself. And he has the muscular build and definition that goes right along with it. I can tell from the way his thin forest green shirt and tight black pants cling to every curve and outline of his muscles. Straight nose, high cheekbones, strong jawline, and olive skin tone...he is delectable to behold.

But the only 'beholding' I'm going to be doing is with my eyes. I'll be damned if I fall for another handsome, arrogant, untrustworthy man ever again. Human or Fae.

After I finish wasting time ogling over the king, I tear my arms free of my captors. Thankfully they willingly release me this time.

Facing the man responsible for bringing me here I forcefully demand, "Who the fuck do you think you are? You think just because you signed a piece of paper with my *father*, whom I've never met or have any clue as to who the hell they are, by the way, that suddenly makes me *yours*?

"Fuck that and fuck you!" I point up at him while angrily continuing my rant. "Because I'm no one's property! Is that clear? Oh, and please excuse the yelling, I just want to make sure you can hear me all the way up there on your 'scary' little throne."

Wow so much for keeping my cool and gaining his favor to bargain with me for my freedom... I've now scolded and taunted this very powerful, very intimidating king.

I brace myself for his wrath, but it doesn't come. Instead, I look up and see a devilish smile creeping across his face.

The guy on my right starts to laugh, "You're going to have your hands full with this one, boss" he teases.

This joke is instantly followed up by the guy on my left as he bounces back and forth on his feet like he can't contain his excitement, or he just did a line of coke in the bathroom. "Yeah boss! If you're lucky she might even bite back!", he jokes as he lunges forward and snaps at me with his large canines.

Except those aren't just abnormally large canines...NO, those are fangs!

That's what Killian had meant by 'your kind' and 'suck dry'...these aren't just any 'Fae'...

They're Vampires!

My blood goes cold at the sudden realization.

My life is now at the mercy of not just any king, but the King of Vampires! Suddenly the only bargain I care to make now is one to keep him from sinking his fangs into my throat.

I quickly try to regain my composure before the king can notice my fear and surprise, but no such luck...

A low, dark, nefarious chuckle captures my attention as the king's grin widens just enough to give me a clear look at his deadly fangs.

My eyes lock on his and I'm again hypnotized by their amber glow.

They give me a strange sense of familiarity...

A shiver of terror courses down my spine as he finally speaks. Allowing his deep husky voice, that could make even the hardest woman swoon, to entirely upend and demolish my entire reality with just two simple words...

"Hello, *Wife*."

EPILOGUE

KILLIAN

Two weeks have passed since King Gideon trespassed into *my* kingdom and claimed *my* mate for himself. Two weeks of sleepless nights laying restless in my bed, trying to determine a plan of action that will succeed in freeing Calista from his clutches, without starting a war between the Unseelie Kingdom and the Bloodlands.

I fail time and time again to understand why her father promised her hand in marriage to the King of Vampires. Did he really see that as a better alternative than serving as my captive in the dungeons for a short time?

If she had stayed here, I would have released her and her sisters by now. I would never have been able to stay away from her for long. He should have known that! But now the Gods only know what King Gideon is putting her through...if he hasn't already drained her of every drop of blood she has in her veins.

To make matters worse; the kingdom has been in a state of disarray after my father's death and me rising up to claim the throne. I spend the better part of my days, signing off on new decrees to aid the kingdom, as well as nullifying the majority of the ones my father had put into place.

Callum is currently out with a small brigade searching for his and Dante's fathers. As soon as they received word about my father's death, they seemed to have vanished. Under any other circumstances I wouldn't waste the manpower to hunt them down and retrieve them, but an unforeseen situation is on the verge of becoming dire.

Eight days ago, a body was found on the outskirts of the kingdom. The body itself was slack like everything on the inside had been drained out, leaving only a skin covered skeleton. It was one of the strangest things I have ever seen. As the days continued, an increasing number of bodies were discovered in the very same state. And with each passing day, bodies are being discovered closer to the more centralized part of Unseelie. Where the majority of our people reside.

As these bodies continue to turn up, I can't get my father's last words out of my head. He warned that if we killed him, darkness would follow, and the entire realm would be doomed. I thought they were empty threats, spoken in the hope that we would cower at his words and spare his life.

Now I fear there was truth behind his words. I'm not certain if his death was the catalyst for these events; I pray it is just coincidence. However, if anyone would know it would be his two closest companions; General Olethros and the Duke of Verigast, so it is essential they are found and questioned immediately.

Up until now, I've only seen a body turn up in this condition once, when I was a young boy, and I had hoped that would be the one and only time. For only one vile creature kills in this manner, and they were thought to be extinct or damn well near it.

My priority still lies with getting Cali back by my side. She may hate me now, but I will win her back over time...or die trying.

Once she is back, she and I can turn our focus towards unraveling my father's secrets. Determining if his death really has anything to do with these murders and if so, how? And how do we put a stop to them?

Cali may be the answer; if the prophecy is true and Cali is the Queen of Stellaris, she is destined to save our realm.

And if there ever was anything that our realm would need saving from, it would be the horrible life-draining army I fear my father has created to reign havoc in the event of his downfall.

The Volge...

ACKNOWLEDGEMENTS

Thank you so much for joining me on this wild new journey I have embarked upon. Getting to use my imagination and creativity to captivate readers and take them on an unforgettable adventure has been an absolute honor. I hope this story was able to capture your heart and provide a magical escape for your mind from the stressors of everyday life. These characters have become so special to me, and I can't wait to continue their story in *Rise of the Viper Queen*.

To Ami and Whitney, without the two of you this story wouldn't even exist. Your support and brainstorming sessions over our favorite pickle pizza is so valued. Thank you for always making me laugh and brightening up my days. Who would have guessed that our monthly girl's night out over never-ending pasta dishes at Olive Garden would lead us on this grand adventure in the enchanting realm of Stellaris.

To my amazing husband, thank you for always believing in me and supporting me in following my dreams. You have provided me and the pups with the most fantastic life. Your unconditional love means everything to me, and I want you to know how much I appreciate everything you do for me. We really do make the perfect team, and I love you with everything I am.

To my wonderful mom, thank you for being as beautiful on the inside as you are on the outside. You have always been in my corner and cheering me on, encouraging me to accomplish anything I set my mind to. I love you more than words can express...and I should know I have written a lot of them.

To my incredible stepdad, thank you for loving me as your very own daughter from the very beginning. Your love and encouragement broadened my small world and helped guide me into the blessed life I have today. Blood or not, you are my dad, and I love you to the moon and back.

To my questionably insane dad— who would like to be referred to as 'Batman'— thank you for showing me so much love and spoiling me rotten. You helped shape me into who I am today; a proud-stubborn woman who is as tough as any man. I love you with all my heart and I will always be your little Rat.

To my dogs, Loki and Tucker. Thank you for all the tail wags, smoochy kisses, and happy wiggles you fill our lives with each and every day. You bring so much joy and happiness into our lives, and we love you more than anything in this world. I promise to give you extra chicken nuggies and ice-cream to make up for not being able to give you my full attention every minute of the day while writing this book.

To my family, thank you for continuing to believe in me and surrounding me with your love and support. It means more to me than you will ever know.

To you, my readers. I am so incredibly grateful for each and every one of you. Thank you for taking a chance on me and coming along with me on this magical journey. Without you my story is just a bunch of words in a book, it's when you come along and open your heart and expand your mind that you breathe life into my story. Here's to you! Until the next time we meet again in Stellaris, happy reading!

ABOUT THE AUTHOR

J.D. Semmes earned a Master of Science in Public Health (MSPH) from Campbell University. Shortly into her career as a preparedness coordinator, she fell ill and was diagnosed with Lyme Disease. Forced to leave her career to focus on her health, J.D. passed the time by letting her mind wander off on enchanting adventures found inside books. She is now a stay-at-home wife and mom to two adorable pups. When she is not reading or writing her own adventures, you can find her curled up with her pups watching horror movies, planning her next Disney trip, and wishfully hoping that this will be the year she finishes her TBR list.